The first romance stories Stephanie Laurens read were set against the backdrop of Regency England, and these continue to exert a special attraction for her. As an escape from the dry world of professional science, Stephanie started writing Regency romances.

Stephanie's last twelve titles have been *New York Times*, *USA Today* and *Publishers Weekly* bestsellers. Stephanie lives in a leafy suburb of Melbourne, Australia, with her husband and two daughters, along with two cats, Shakespeare and Marlowe.

Learn more about Stephanie's books from her website at www.stephanielaurens.com

A Rake's Vow

Stephanie Laurens

PIATKUS

Copyright © 1998 by Savdek Management Proprietory Ltd.

First published in Great Britain in 2007 by
Piatkus Books Ltd.,
5 Windmill Street, London W1T 2JA
email: info@piatkus.co.uk

This edition published 2007

First published in the United States in 1998 by
Avon Books, an imprint of HarperCollins Publishers USA

The moral right of the author has been asserted

A catalogue record for this book is available from the British Library

ISBN 0 7499 3717 3

Data manipulation by Phoenix Photosetting, Chatham, Kent
www.phoenixphotosetting.co.uk
Printed and bound in Great Britain by
Clays Ltd, Bungay, Suffolk

A Rake's Vow

The Bar Cynster Family Tree

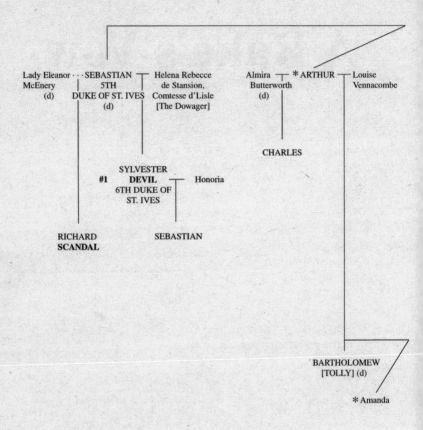

Lady Eleanor · · · SEBASTIAN ┬ Helena Rebecce
McEnery   5TH   de Stansion,
(d)   DUKE OF ST. IVES   Comtesse d'Lisle
      (d)   [The Dowager]

Almira ┬ * ARTHUR ┬ Louise
Butterworth   Vennacombe
(d)

CHARLES

#1   SYLVESTER
    DEVIL ┬ Honoria
   6TH DUKE OF
    ST. IVES

RICHARD   SEBASTIAN
SCANDAL

BARTHOLOMEW
[TOLLY] (d)

* Amanda

THE BAR CYNSTER SERIES
#1 Devil's Bride
#2 A Rake's Vow

MALE CYNSTERS named in capitals.   * denotes twins

* GEORGE — Horatia Rotherwell   Augusta—Herbert Marquess of Huntly   MARTIN — Lady Celia Hammond

#2 SPENCER **VANE**

HARRY **DEMON**

RUPERT **GABRIEL**

ALASDAIR **LUCIFER**

* Amelia   SIMON   Henrietta   Mary

Heather   Elizabeth   Angelica

Chapter 1

October 1819
Northamptonshire

"**Y**ou want to get a move on. Looks like the Hounds of Hell are on our heels."

"What?" Jerked from uneasy contemplation, Vane Cynster lifted his gaze from his leader's ears and glanced around, bringing Duggan, his groom, into view—along with the bank of lowering thunderheads sweeping down on them from behind. "Blast!" Vane looked forward and flicked the reins. The pair of matched greys harnessed to his curricle stepped out powerfully. He glanced over his shoulder. "Think we can outrun it?"

Considering the storm clouds, Duggan shook his head. "We got three miles on it, maybe five. Not enough to turn back to Kettering, nor yet to make Northampton."

Vane swore. It wasn't the thought of a drenching that exercised his mind. Desperation dug in its spurs; his eyes on the road as the greys swept on, he searched for some option, some route of escape.

Only minutes before, he'd been thinking of Devil, Duke of St. Ives, his cousin, boyhood companion, and closest friend—and of the wife fate had handed him. Honoria, now Duchess of St. Ives. She who had ordered Vane and the other four as-yet-unmarried members of the Bar Cynster not only to pay for but attend the dedication service for the roof of the church in Somersham village, close by the ducal

1

seat. Admittedly, the money she'd decreed they surrender had been ill-gotten gains, their winnings from a wager of which neither she nor their mothers had approved. The age-old adage that the only women Cynster males need be wary of were Cynster wives still held true for this generation as it had for those past. The reason why was not something any male Cynster liked to dwell on.

Which was why he felt such a driving need to get out of the path of the storm. Fate, in the guise of a storm, had arranged for Honoria and Devil to meet, in circumstances that had all but ensured their subsequent marriage. Vane wasn't about to take unnecessary chances.

"Bellamy Hall." He clung to the idea like a drowning man. "Minnie will give us shelter."

"That's a thought." Duggan sounded more hopeful. "The turnoff should be close."

It was around the next bend; Vane took the turn at speed, then cursed and slowed his cattle. The narrow lane was not as well surfaced as the road they'd left. Too fond of his high-stepping horses to risk injuring them, he concentrated, easing them along as fast as he dared, grimly conscious of the deepening gloom of an unnatural, too-early twilight and the rising whine of the wind.

He'd left Somersham Place, Devil's principal residence, soon after luncheon, having spent the morning at church, at the dedication service for the roof he and his cousins had paid for. Intending to visit friends near Leamington, he'd left Devil to enjoy his wife and son and headed west. He'd expected to reach Northampton and the comfort of the Blue Angel with ease. Instead, thanks to fate, he would be spending the night with Minnie and her inmates.

At least he would be safe.

Through the hedges to their left, Vane glimpsed distant water, leaden grey beneath the darkening sky. The River Nene, which meant Bellamy Hall was close; it stood on a long, sloping rise looking down on the river.

It had been years since he'd visited—he couldn't offhand remember how many, but of his welcome he had not a doubt. Araminta, Lady Bellamy, eccentric relict of a wealthy man, was his godmother. Unblessed with children,

Minnie had never treated him as a child; over the years, she'd become a good friend. A sometimes too-shrewd friend uninhibited in her lectures, but a friend nonetheless.

Daughter of a viscount, Minnie had been born to a place in the *ton*. After her husband, Sir Humphrey Bellamy, died, she'd retired from socializing, preferring to remain at Bellamy Hall, presiding over a varying household of impecunious relatives and worthy charity cases.

Once, when he'd asked why she surrounded herself with such hangers-on, Minnie had replied that, at her age, human nature was her main source of entertainment. Sir Humphrey had left her wealthy enough to stand the nonsense, and Bellamy Hall, grotesquely gargantuan, was large enough to house her odd *ménage*. As a sop to sanity, she and her companion, Mrs. Timms, indulged in the occasional bolt to the capital, leaving the rest of the household in Northamptonshire. Vane always called on Minnie whenever she was in town.

Gothic turrets rose out of the trees ahead, then brick gateposts appeared, the heavy wrought-iron gates left ajar. With a grimly satisfied smile, Vane turned his horses through; they'd beaten the storm—fate had not caught him napping. He set the greys trotting down the straight drive. Huge bushes crowded close, shivering in the wind; ancient trees shrouded the gravel in shifting shadows.

Dark and somber, its multitude of windows, dull in the encroaching gloom, watching like so many flat eyes, Bellamy Hall filled the end of the tunnel-like drive. A sprawling Gothic monstrosity, with countless architectural elements added cheek by jowl, all recently embellished with Georgian lavishness, it ought to have looked hideous, yet, in the overgrown park with the circular courtyard before it, the Hall managed to escape outright ugliness.

It was, Vane thought, as he swept about the courtyard and headed for the stables, a suitably esoteric dwelling for an eccentric old woman and her odd household. As he rounded the side of the house, he saw no sign of life.

There was, however, activity in the stables, grooms hurriedly settling horses in preparation for the storm. Leaving Duggan and Minnie's stableman, Grisham, to deal with the greys, Vane strode to the house, taking the path through the shrubbery. Although overgrown, it was navigable; the path debouched onto a stretch of poorly tended lawn which continued around the corner of one wing. Around that corner, Vane knew, stood the side door, facing a wide sweep of lawn hosting a small army of huge stones, remnants of the abbey upon which the Hall was partly built. The ruins stretched for some distance; the Hall itself had grown about the guesthall of the abbey, otherwise ransacked during the Dissolution.

As he neared the corner, the blocks of weathered sandstone came into view, scattered crazily over a thick green carpet. In the middle distance, a single arch, all that remained of the abbey's nave, rose against the darkening sky. Vane smiled; all was exactly as he remembered. Nothing about Bellamy Hall had changed in twenty years.

He rounded the corner—and discovered he was wrong.

He halted, then blinked. For a full minute, he stood stock-still, gaze riveted, his mind entirely focused. Then, gaze still transfixed, his mind fully occupied by the vision before him, he strolled forward, his footsteps muffled by the thick lawn. He halted opposite a large bow window, two paces from the semicircular flower bed before it.

Directly behind the lady, clothed in fine, wind-driven sprigged muslin, bent over, fossicking in the flowers.

"You could help." Patience Debbington blew aside the curls tangling with her eyelashes and frowned at Myst, her cat, sitting neatly in the weeds, an enigmatic expression on her inscrutable face. "It's got to be here somewhere."

Myst merely blinked her large blue eyes. With a sigh, Patience leaned as far forward as she dared and poked among the weeds and perennials. Bent over at the waist, reaching into the flower bed, gripping its soft edge with the toes of her soft-soled shoes, was hardly the most elegant, let alone stable, position.

Not that she need worry over anyone seeing her—everyone else was dressing for dinner. Which was precisely what she should be doing—would have been doing—if she hadn't noticed that the small silver vase which had adorned her windowsill had vanished. As she'd left the window open, and Myst often used that route to come and go, she'd reasoned that Myst must have toppled the vase in passing and it had rolled out, over the flat sill, and fallen into the flower bed below.

The fact that she had never known Myst unintentionally to knock over anything she'd pushed aside; it was better believing that Myst had been clumsy than that their mysterious thief had struck again.

"It's not here," Patience concluded. "At least, I can't see it." Still bent over, she looked at Myst. "Can you?"

Myst blinked again, and looked past her. Then the sleek grey cat rose and elegantly padded out of the flower bed.

"Wait!" Patience half turned, but immediately swung back, struggling to regain her awkward balance. "There's a storm coming—this is *not* the time to go mousing."

So saying, she managed to straighten—which left her facing the house, looking directly at the blank bow windows of the downstairs parlor. With the storm darkening the skies, the windows were reflective. They reflected the image of a man standing directly behind her.

With a gasp, Patience whirled. Her gaze collided with the man's—his eyes were hard, crystalline grey, pale in the weak light. They were focused, intently, on her, their expression one she couldn't fathom. He stood no more than three feet away, large, elegant and oddly forbidding. In the instant her brain registered those facts, Patience felt her heels sink, and sink—into the soft soil of the flower bed.

The edge crumbled beneath her feet.

Her eyes flew wide—her lips formed a helpless "Oh." Arms flailing, she started to topple back—

The man reacted so swiftly his movement was a blur—he gripped her upper arms and hauled her forward.

She landed against him, breast to chest, hips to hard thighs. The breath was knocked out of her, leaving her gasping, mentally as well as physically. Hard hands held her upright, long fingers iron shackles about her arms. His chest was a wall of rock against her breasts; the rest of his body, the long thighs that held them braced, felt as resilient as tensile steel.

She was helpless. Utterly, completely, and absolutely helpless.

Patience looked up and met the stranger's hooded gaze. As she watched, his grey eyes darkened. The expression they contained—intensely concentrated—sent a most peculiar thrill through her.

She blinked; her gaze fell—to the man's lips. Long, thin yet beautifully proportioned, they'd been sculpted with a view to fascination. They certainly fascinated her; she couldn't drag her gaze away. The mesmerizing contours shifted, almost imperceptibly softening; her own lips tingled. She swallowed, and dragged in a desperately needed breath.

Her breasts rose, shifting against the stranger's coat, pressing more definitely against his chest. Sensation streaked through her, from unexpectedly tight nipples all the way to her toes. She caught another breath and tensed—but couldn't stop the quiver that raced through her.

The stranger's lips thinned; the austere planes of his face hardened. His fingers tightened about her arms. To Patience's stunned amazement, he lifted her—easily—and carefully set her down two feet away.

Then he stepped back and swept her a negligent bow.

"Vane Cynster." One brown brow arched; his eyes remained on hers. "I'm here to see Lady Bellamy."

Patience blinked. "Ah . . . yes." She hadn't known men could move like that—particularly not men like him. He was so tall, large, lean but well muscled, yet his coordination had been faultless, the smooth grace investing the languid courtesy rendering it compelling in some ill-defined way. His words, uttered in a voice so deep she could have mistaken it for the rumble of the storm, eventually impinged on her consciousness; struggling to harness her thoughts, she gestured to the door at her right. "The first gong's gone."

Vane met her wide gaze, and managed not to smile wolfishly—no need to frighten the prey. The view he now had—of delectable curves filling a gown of ivory sprigged muslin in a manner he fully approved—was every bit as enticing as the view that had first held him—the gorgeous curves of her derriere clearly delineated beneath taut fabric. When she'd shifted, so had those curves. He couldn't remember when a sight had so transfixed him, had so tantalized his rake's senses.

She was of average height, her forehead level with his throat. Her hair, rich brown, lustrously sheening, was confined in a sleek knot, bright tendrils escaping to wreathe about her ears and nape. Delicate brown brows framed large eyes of hazel brown, their expression difficult to discern in the gloom. Her nose was straight; her complexion creamy. Her pink lips simply begged to be kissed. He'd come within a whisker of kissing them, but tasting an unknown lady before the requisite introductions was simply not good form.

His silence had allowed her to steady her wits; he sensed her growing resistance, sensed the frown gathering in her eyes. Vane let his lips curve. He knew precisely what he wanted to do—to her, with her; the only questions remaining were where and when. "And you are . . . ?"

Her eyes narrowed fractionally. She drew herself up, clasping her hands before her. "Patience Debbington."

The shock hit him, heavy as a cannonball, and left him winded. Vane stared at her; a chill bloomed in his chest. It quickly spread, locking muscle after muscle in reactive denial. Then disbelief welled. He glanced at her left hand. No band of any sort decorated her third finger.

She *couldn't* be unmarried—she was in her mid-twenties; no younger woman possessed curves as mature as hers. Of that, he was sure—he'd spent half his life studying feminine curves; in that sphere he was an expert. Perhaps she was a widow—potentially even better. She was studying him covertly, her gaze sliding over him.

Vane felt the touch of her gaze, felt the hunter within him rise in response to that artless glance; his wariness returned. "*Miss* Debbington?"

Looking up, she nodded—Vane almost groaned. Last chance—a spinster, impecunious, and without connections. He could set her up as his mistress.

She must have read his mind; before he could formulate the question, she answered it. "I'm Lady Bellamy's niece."

A crack of thunder all but drowned out her words; under cover of the noise, Vane swore beneath his breath, only just resisting the impulse to direct his ire heavenward.

Fate looked at him through clear hazel eyes.

Disapproving hazel eyes.

"If you'll come this way"—with a wave, she indicated the nearby door, then haughtily led the way—"I'll have Masters inform my aunt of your arrival."

Having assimmilated the style, and thus the standing, of Minnie's unexpected caller, Patience made no attempt to hide her opinion; dismissive contempt colored her tone. "Is my aunt expecting you?"

"No—but she'll be pleased to see me."

Was that subtle reproof she detected in his far-too-suave tones? Swallowing a hoity humph, Patience swept on. She felt his presence, large and intensely masculine, prowling in her wake. Her senses skittered; she clamped a firm hold on them and lifted her chin. "If you'll wait in the parlor— it's the first door on your right—Masters will fetch you when my aunt is ready to receive you. As I mentioned, the household is presently dressing for dinner."

"Indeed."

The word, uttered softly, reached her as she halted before the side door; Patience felt a cool tingle slither down her spine. And felt the touch of his grey gaze on her cheek, on the sensitive skin of her throat. She stiffened, resisting the urge to wriggle. She looked down, determined not to turn and meet his eyes. Jaw firming, she reached for the door handle; he beat her to it.

Patience froze. He'd stopped directly behind her, and reached around her to grasp the handle; she watched his long fingers slowly close about it. And stop.

She could feel him behind her, mere inches away, could sense his strength surrounding her. For one definable instant, she felt trapped.

Then the long fingers twisted; with a flick, he set the door swinging wide.

Heart racing, Patience sucked in a breath and sailed into the dim passage. Without slowing her pace, she inclined her head in regal, over-the-shoulder dismissal. "I'll speak to Masters directly—I'm sure my aunt won't keep you long.'' With that, she swept on, down the passage and into the dark hallway beyond.

Poised on the threshold, Vane watched her retreat through narrowed eyes. He'd sensed the awareness that had flared at his touch, the quiver of consciousness she hadn't been able to hide. For gentlemen such as he, that was proof enough of what might be.

His gaze fell on the small grey cat which had hugged Patience Debbington's skirts; it now sat on the runner, considering him. As he watched, it rose, turned, and, tail high, started up the corridor—then stopped. Turning its head, it looked back at him. ''*Meeow!*''

From its imperious tone, Vane deduced it was female.

Behind him, lightning flashed. He looked back at the darkened day. Thunder rolled—a second later, the heavens opened. Rain pelted down, sheets of heavy drops obliterating the landscape.

Fate's message couldn't have been clearer: escape was impossible.

His features grim, Vane closed the door—and followed the cat.

''Nothing could be more fortuitous!'' Araminta, Lady Bellamy, beamed delightedly at Vane. ''Of course you must stay. But the second gong will go any minute, so cut line. How is everyone?''

Propping his shoulders against the mantelpiece, Vane smiled. Wrapped in expensive shawls, her rotund figure encased in silk and lace, a frilled widow's cap atop sprightly white curls, Minnie watched him through eyes bright with intelligence, set in a soft, lined face. She sat enthroned in her chair before the fire in her bedchamber; in its mate sat Timms, a gentlewoman of indeterminate years, Minnie's devoted companion. ''Everyone,'' Vane knew, meant the Cynsters. ''The youngsters are thriving—Simon's starring at Eton. Amelia and Amanda are cutting a swath through the *ton*, scattering hearts right and left. The elders are all well and busy in town, but Devil and Honoria are still at the Place.''

"Too taken with admiring his heir, I'll wager. Daresay that wife of his will keep him in line." Minnie grinned, then sobered. "Still no word of Charles?"

Vane's face hardened. "No. His disappearance remains a mystery."

Minnie shook her head. "Poor Arthur."

"Indeed."

Minnie sighed, then slanted an assessing glance at Vane. "And what about you and those cousins of yours? Still keeping the *ton*'s ladies on their toes?"

Her tone was all innocence; head bowed over her knitting, Timms snorted. "More like on their backs."

Vane smiled, suavely charming. "We do our poor best." Minnie's eyes twinkled. Still smiling, Vane looked down and smoothed his sleeve. "I'd better go and change, but tell me—who do you have staying at present?"

"A whole parcel of odds and ends," Timms offered.

Minnie chuckled and drew her hands free of her shawl. "Let's see." She counted on her fingers. "There's Edith Swithins—she's a distant Bellamy connection. Utterly vague, but quite harmless. Just don't express any interest in her tatting unless you've an hour to spare. Then there's Agatha Chadwick—she was married to that unfortunate character who insisted he could cross the Irish Sea in a coracle. He couldn't, of course. So Agatha and her son and daughter are with us."

"Daughter?"

Minnie's gaze lifted to Vane's face. "Angela. She's sixteen and already a confirmed wilter. She'll swoon away in your arms if you give her half a chance."

Vane grimaced. "Thank you for the warning."

"Henry Chadwick must be about your age," Minnie mused, "but not at all in the same mold." Her gaze ran appreciatively over Vane's elegant figure, long muscular legs displayed to advantage in tight buckskins and top boots, his superbly tailored coat of Bath superfine doing justice to his broad shoulders. "Just setting eyes on you should do him some good."

Vane merely raised his brows.

"Now, who else?" Minnie frowned at her fingers. "Edmond Montrose is our resident poet and dramatist. Needless to say, he fancies himself the next Byron. Then there's the General and Edgar, who you must remember."

Vane nodded. The General, a brusque, ex–military man, had lived at Bellamy Hall for years; his title was not a formal one, but a nickname earned by his emphatically regimental air. Edgar Polinbrooke, too, had been Minnie's pensioner for years—Vane placed Edgar in his fifties, a mild tippler who fancied himself a gamester, but who was, in reality, a simple and harmless soul.

"Don't forget Whitticombe," Timms put in.

"How could I forget Whitticombe?" Minnie sighed. "Or Alice."

Vane raised a questioning brow.

"Mr. Whitticombe Colby and his sister, Alice," Minnie supplied. "They're distant cousins of Humphrey's. Whitticombe trained as a deacon and has conceived the notion of compiling the *History of Coldchurch Abbey*." Coldchurch was the abbey on whose ruins the Hall stood.

"As for Alice—well, she's just Alice." Minnie grimaced. "She must be over forty and, though I hate to say it of one of my own sex, a colder, more intolerant, judgmental being it has never been my misfortune to meet."

Vane's brows rose high. "I suspect it would be wise if I steered clear of her."

"Do." Minnie nodded feelingly. "Get too close, and she'll probably have the vapors." She glanced at Vane. "Then again, she might just have hysterics anyway, the instant she sets eyes on you."

Vane cast her a jaundiced look.

"I think that's it. Oh, no—I forgot Patience and Gerrard." Minnie looked up. "My niece and nephew."

Studying Minnie's radiant face, Vane didn't need to ask if she was fond of her young relatives. "Patience and Gerrard?" He kept the question mild.

"My younger sister's children. They're orphans now. Gerrard's seventeen—he inherited the Grange, a nice little property in Derbyshire, from his father, Sir Reginald Debbington." Minnie frowned at Vane. "You might be too young to remember him. Reggie died eleven years ago."

Vane sifted through his memories. "Was he the one who broke his neck while out with the Cottesmore?"

Minnie nodded. "That's the one. Constance, m'sister, died two years ago. Patience has been holding the fort for Gerrard pretty much since Reggie died." Minnie smiled. "Patience is my project for the coming year."

Vane studied that smile. "Oh?"

"Thinks she's on the shelf and couldn't care less. Says she'll think about marrying after Gerrard's settled."

Timms snorted. "Too single-minded for her own good."

Minnie folded her hands in her lap. "I've decided to take Patience and Gerrard to London for the Season next year. She thinks we're going to give Gerrard a little town bronze."

Vane raised a cynical brow. "While in reality, you plan to play matchmaker."

"Precisely." Minnie beamed at him. "Patience has a tidy fortune invested in the Funds. As for the rest, you must give me your opinion once you've seen her. Tell me how high you think she can reach."

Vane inclined his head noncommittally.

A gong boomed in the distance.

"Damn!" Minnie clutched her slipping shawls. "They'll be waiting in the drawing room, wondering what on earth's going on." She waved Vane away. "Go pretty yourself up. You don't stop by that often. Now you're here, I want the full benefit of your company."

"Your wish is my command." Vane swept her an elegant bow; straightening, he slanted her an arrogantly rakish smile. "Cynsters never leave ladies unsatisfied."

Timms snorted so hard she choked.

Vane left the room to chortles, chuckles, and gleeful, anticipatory whispers.

Chapter 2

Something odd was afoot. Vane knew it within minutes of entering the drawing room. The household was gathered in groups about the large room; the instant he appeared, all heads swung his way.

The expressions displayed ranged from Minnie's and Timms's benevolent welcomes, through Edgar's approving appraisal and a similar response from a young sprig, who Vane assumed was Gerrard, to wary calculation to outright chilly disapproval—this last from three—a gentleman Vane tagged as Whitticombe Colby, a pinch-faced, poker-rigid spinster, presumably Alice Colby, and, of course, Patience Debbington.

Vane understood the Colbys' reaction. He did, however, wonder what he'd done to deserve Patience Debbington's censure. Hers wasn't the response he was accustomed to eliciting from gently bred ladies. Smiling urbanely, he strolled across the wide room, simultaneously letting his gaze touch hers. She returned his look frostily, then turned and addressed some remark to her companion, a lean, dramatically dark gentleman, undoubtedly the budding poet. Vane's smile deepened; he turned it on Minnie.

"You may give me your arm," Minnie declared the instant he'd made his bow. "I'll introduce you, then we really must go in, or Cook will be in the boughs."

Before they reached even the first of Minnie's "guests," Vane's social antennae, exquisitely honed, detected the undercurrents surging between the groups.

13

What broth was Minnie concocting here? And what, Vane wondered, was brewing?

"It's a pleasure to meet you, Mr. Cynster." Agatha Chadwick gave him her hand. A firm-faced matron with greying blond hair half-hidden by a widow's cap, she gestured to the pretty, fair-haired girl beside her. "My daughter, Angela."

Round-eyed, Angela curtsied; Vane returned a noncommittal murmur.

"And this is my son, Henry."

"Cynster." Heavily built and plainly dressed, Henry Chadwick shook Vane's hand. "You must be glad to be able to break your journey." He nodded at the long windows through which the rain could be heard, drumming on the terrace flags.

"Indeed." Vane smiled. "A fortuitous chance." He glanced at Patience Debbington, still engrossed with the poet.

The General and Edgar were both pleased that he remembered them. Edith Swithins was vague and flustered; in her case, Vane surmised that wasn't due to him. The Colbys were as frigidly disapproving as only those of their ilk could be; Vane suspected Alice Colby's face would crack if she smiled. Indeed, it occurred to him that she might never have learned how.

Which left, last but very definitely not least, the poet, Patience Debbington, and her brother Gerrard. As Vane approached, Minnie on his arm, both men looked up, their expressions eager and open. Patience did not even register his existence.

"Gerrard Debbington." Brown eyes glowing beneath a shock of brown hair, Gerrard thrust out his hand, then colored; Vane grasped it before he could tie himself in knots.

"Vane Cynster," he murmured. "Minnie tells me you're for town next Season."

"Oh, yes. But I wanted to ask—" Gerrard's eyes were alight, fixed on Vane's face. His age showed in the length of his lanky frame, his youth in his eager exuberance. "I came past the stables just before the storm broke—there's a bang-up pair of greys stabled there. Are they yours?"

Vane grinned. "Half-Welsh. High-steppers with excellent endurance. My brother, Harry, owns a stud; he supplies all my cattle."

Gerrard glowed. "I *thought* they looked prime-uns."

"Edmond Montrose." The poet leaned across and shook Vane's hand. "Have you come up from town?"

"Via Cambridgeshire. I had to attend a special church service near the ducal seat." Vane glanced at Patience Debbington, mute and tight-lipped on the other side of Minnie. The information that he was permitted to enter a church did not melt her ice one jot.

"And this is Patience Debbington, my niece," Minnie put in, before Gerrard and Edmond could monopolize him further.

Vane bowed elegantly in response to Patience's abbreviated bob. "I know," he drawled, his gaze on her stubbornly averted eyes. "We've met."

"You have?" Minnie blinked at him, then looked at Patience, now staring, dagger-eyed, at Vane.

Patience glanced, somewhat evasively, at Minnie. "I was in the garden when Mr. Cynster arrived." The glance she flicked Vane was exceedingly careful. "With Myst."

"Ah." Minnie nodded and scanned the room. "Right then—now everyone's been introduced, Vane, you may lead me in."

He dutifully did so, the others filing in in their wake. As he conducted Minnie to the foot of the long table, Vane wondered why Patience did not want it known she'd been searching for something in the flower bed. As he settled Minnie in her chair, he noticed a place had been set directly opposite, at the table's head.

"Daresay you'd like to chat with your godson." Whitticombe Colby stopped beside Minnie's chair. He smiled unctuously. "I would be happy to surrender my place—"

"No need for that, Whitticombe," Minnie cut in. "What would I do without your erudite company?" She looked up at Vane, on her other side. "You take the chair at the head, dear boy." She held his gaze; Vane raised a brow, then bowed—Minnie tugged and he leaned closer. "I need a man I can trust sitting there."

Minnie's whisper reached only him; Vane inclined his head slightly and straightened. As he strolled down the room, he studied the seating arrangements—Patience had already claimed the chair to the left of his alloted place, with Henry Chadwick beside her. Edith was settling in opposite Patience while Edgar was making for the next seat along. Nothing in the arrangement suggested a reason for Minnie's comment; Vane couldn't imagine that Minnie, with wits like quicksilver, thought her niece, presently armored in cold steel, could possibly need protection from the likes of Colby.

Which meant Minnie's utterance had some deeper meaning; Vane inwardly sighed, and made a mental note to ferret it out. Before he escaped from Bellamy Hall.

The first course was served the instant they all sat. Minnie's cook was excellent; Vane applied himself to the meal with unfeigned appreciation.

Edgar started the conversational ball rolling. "Heard that the Whippet's odds on for the Guineas."

Vane shrugged. "There's been a lot of blunt laid on Blackamoor's Boy and Huntsman's well fancied, too."

"Is it true," Henry Chadwick asked, "that the Jockey Club's thinking of changing their rules?"

The ensuing discussion even drew a tittering comment from Edith Swithins: "Such fanciful names you gentlemen give the horses. Never anything like Goldie, or Muffins, or Blacky."

Neither Vane, Edgar, or Henry felt qualified to take that point further.

"I had heard," Vane drawled, "that the Prince Regent's battling debtors again."

"Again?" Henry shook his head. "A spendthrift through and through."

Under Vane's subtle direction, the talk turned to Prinny's latest eccentricities, on which Henry, Edgar, and Edith all entertained firm opinions.

On Vane's left, however, perfect silence reigned.

A fact which only increased his determination to do something about it, about Patience Debbington's adamant disapproval. The itch to tweak her nose, to prick her into response, waxed strong. Vane kept the lid on his temper; they were not alone—yet.

The few minutes he'd spent changing, slipping into a familiar routine, had settled his mind, cleared his vision. Just because fate had succeeded in trapping him here, under the same roof as Patience Debbington, was no reason to consider the battle lost. He would stay the night, catch up with Minnie and Timms, deal with whatever was making Minnie uneasy, and then be on his way. The storm would probably blow itself out overnight; at the worst, he'd be held up only a day or so.

Just because fate had shown him the water, didn't mean he had to drink.

Of course, before he shook the gravel of the Bellamy Hall drive from his boots, he'd deal with Patience Debbington, too. A salutary jolt or three should do it—just enough to let her know that he knew that her icy disapproval was, to him, a transparent facade.

He was, of course, too wise to take things further.

Glancing at his prey, Vane noted her clear complexion, soft, delicate, tinged with gentle color. As he watched, she swallowed a mouthful of trifle, then sent her tongue gliding over her lower lip, leaving the soft pink sheening.

Abruptly, Vane looked down—into the big blue eyes of the small grey cat—the cat known as Myst. She came and went as she pleased, generally hugging Patience's skirts; she was presently seated beside Patience's chair, staring unblinkingly up at him.

Arrogantly, Vane lifted a brow.

With a silent mew, Myst stood, stretched, then padded forward to twine about his leg. Vane reached down and rubbed his fingers over the sleek head, then ran his nails down her spine. Myst arched, tail stiffening; the rumble of her purr reached Vane.

It also reached Patience; she glanced down. "Myst!" she hissed. "Stop bothering Mr. Cynster."

"She's not bothering me." Capturing Patience's gaze, Vane added: "I enjoy making females purr."

Patience stared at him, then blinked. Then, frowning

slightly, she turned back to her plate. "Well, as long as she doesn't bother you."

It took a moment before Vane could get his lips back to straight, then he turned to Edith Swithins.

Not long after, they all rose; Minnie, with Timms beside her, led the ladies to the drawing room. Her gaze on Gerrard, Patience hesitated, her expression alternating between consternation and uncertainty. Gerrard didn't notice. Vane watched Patience's lips set; she almost glanced his way, then realized he was watching—waiting. She stiffened and kept her lids lowered. Reaching out, Vane drew her chair farther back. With a brief, excessively haughty inclination of her head, Patience turned and followed in Minnie's wake.

Her pace wouldn't have won the Guineas.

Dropping back into his chair at the head of the table, Vane smiled at Gerrard. With a lazy wave, he indicated the vacant chair to his right. "Why don't you move up?"

Gerrard's grin was radiant; eagerly, he left his place for the one between Edgar and Vane.

"Good idea. Then we can talk without shouting." Edmond moved closer, taking Patience's chair. With a genial grunt, the General moved up the table. Vane suspected Whitticombe would have kept his distance, but the insult would have been too obvious. His expression coldly severe, he moved to Edgar's other side.

Reaching for the decanter Masters had placed before him, Vane looked up—directly at Patience, still lingering, half-in and half-out of the door. Obviously torn. Vane's eyes touched hers; coolly arrogant, he raised his brows.

Patience's expression blanked. She stiffened, then slipped out of the door. A footman closed it behind her.

Vane smiled to himself; lifting the decanter, he poured himself a large glass.

By the time the decanter had circulated once, they'd settled on the best tip for the Guineas. Edgar sighed. "We really don't see much excitement here at the Hall." He smiled self-consciously. "I spend most of my days in the library. Reading biographies, y'know."

Whitticombe sniffed contemptuously. "Dilettante."

His gaze on Vane, Edgar colored but gave no other sign of having heard the jibe. "The library's quite extensive—it includes a number of journals and diaries of the family. Quite fascinating, in their way." The gentle emphasis he placed on the last three words left him looking much more the gentleman than Whitticombe.

As if sensing it, Whitticombe set his glass down and, in superior accents, addressed Vane. "As I daresay Lady Bellamy informed you, I am engaged on an extensive study of Coldchurch Abbey. Once my investigations are complete, I flatter myself the abbey will once again be appreciated as the important ecclesiastical center it once was."

"Oh, yes." Edmond grinned ingenuously at Whitticombe. "But all that's the dead past. The ruins are perfectly fascinating in their own right. They stir my muse to remarkable effect."

Glancing from Edmond to Whitticombe, Vane got the impression this was an oft-trod argument. That impression deepened when Edmond turned to him, and Vane saw the twinkle in his expressive eyes.

"I'm scripting a play, inspired by the ruins and set amongst them."

"Sacrilege!" Whitticombe stiffened. "The abbey is God's house, not a playhouse."

"Ah, but it's not an abbey any longer, just a heap of old stones." Edmond grinned, unrepentant. "And it's such an *atmospheric* spot."

Whitticombe's disgusted snort was echoed by the General. "Atmospheric, indeed! It's damp and cold and unhealthful—and if you plan to drag us out to be your audience, perched on cold stone, then you can think again. My old bones won't stand for it."

"But it *is* a very beautiful place," Gerrard put in. "Some of the vistas are excellent, either framed by the ruins or with the ruins as a focal point."

Vane saw the glow in Gerrard's eyes, heard the youthful fervor in his voice.

Gerrard glanced his way, then colored. "I sketch, you see."

Vane's brows rose. He was about to express interest, polite but unfeigned, when Whitticombe snorted again.

"Sketches? Mere childish likenesses—you make too much of yourself, m'boy." Whitticombe's eyes were hard; headmaster-like, he frowned at Gerrard. "You should be out and about, exercising that weak chest of yours, rather than sitting in the damp ruins for hours on end. Yes, and you should be studying, too, not frittering away your time."

The glow vanished from Gerrard's face; beneath the youthful softness, the planes of his face set hard. "I am studying, but I've already been accepted into Trinity for the autumn term next year. Patience and Minnie want me to go to London, so I will—and I don't need to study for that."

"No indeed," Vane smoothly cut in. "This port is excellent." He helped himself to another glass, then passed the decanter to Edmond. "I suspect we should offer due thanks for the late Sir Humphrey's well-qualified palate." He settled his shoulders more comfortably; over the rim of his glass, he met Henry's eye. "But tell me, how has the gamekeeper managed with Sir Humphrey's coverts?"

Henry accepted the decanter. "The wood over Walgrave way is worth a visit."

The General grunted. "Always plenty of rabbits about by the river. Took a piece out yesterday—bagged three."

Everyone else had some contribution to make—all except Whitticombe. He held himself aloof, cloaked in chilly disapproval.

When the talk of shooting threatened to flag, Vane set down his glass. "I think it's time we rejoined the ladies."

In the drawing room, Patience waited impatiently, and tried not to stare at the door. They'd been passing the port for more than half an hour; God only knew what undesirable views Gerrard was absorbing. She'd already uttered innumerable prayers that the rain would blow over and the following morning dawn fine. Then Mr. Vane Cynster would be on his way, taking his "gentlemanly elegance" with him.

Beside her, Mrs. Chadwick was instructing Angela: "There are six of them—or were. St. Ives married last year.

But there's no question on the matter—Cynsters are so well bred, so very much the epitome of what one wishes to see in a gentleman.''

Angela's eyes, already round as saucers, widened even more. "Are they *all* as well set-up as this Mr. Cynster?''

Mrs. Chadwick shot Angela a reproving glance. "They are all very elegant, of course, but I've heard it said Vane Cynster is the most elegant of them all.''

Patience swallowed a disgusted humph. Just her luck— if she and Gerrard had to meet a Cynster, why did it have to be the most elegant one? Fate was playing games with her. She'd accepted Minnie's invitation to join her household for the autumn and winter and then to go to London for the Season, sure that fate was smiling benevolently, intervening to smooth her path. There was no doubt she'd needed help.

She was no fool. She'd seen months ago that, although she'd been nursemaid, surrogate mother, and guardian to Gerrard all his life, she could not provide the final direction he needed to cross the last threshold into adulthood.

She couldn't be his mentor.

Nowhere in his life had there been a suitable gentleman on whose behaviour and standards Gerrard could base his own. The chances of discovering such a gentleman in deepest Derbyshire were slight. When Minnie's invitation had arrived, informing her that there were gentlemen staying at Bellamy Hall, it had seemed like fate's hand at work. She'd accepted the invitation with alacrity, organized for the Grange to run without her, and headed south with Gerrard.

She'd spent the journey formulating a description of the man she would accept as Gerrard's mentor—the one she would trust with her brother's tender youth. By the time they reached Bellamy Hall, she had her criteria firmly fixed.

By the end of their first evening, she'd concluded that none of the gentlemen present met her stringent requirements. While each possessed qualities of which she approved, none was free of traits of which she disapproved. Most especially, none commanded her respect, complete and absolute, which criterion she'd flagged as the most crucial.

Philosophically, she'd shrugged and accepted fate's decree, and set her sights on London. Potential aspirants to the position of Gerrard's mentor would clearly be more numerous there. Comfortable and secure, she and Gerrard had settled into Minnie's household.

Now comfort and security were things of the past—and would remain so until Vane Cynster left.

At that instant, the drawing-room door opened; together with Mrs. Chadwick and Angela, Patience turned to watch the gentlemen stroll in. They were led by Whitticombe Colby, looking insufferably superior as usual; he made for the *chaise* on which Minnie and Timms sat, with Alice in a chair beside them. Edgar and the General followed Whitticombe through the door; by mutual consent, they headed for the fireplace, beside which Edith Swithins, vaguely smiling, sat tatting industriously.

Her gaze glued to the door, Patience waited—and saw Edmond and Henry amble in. Beneath her breath, she swore, then coughed to disguise the indiscretion. *Damn Vane Cynster.*

On the thought, he strolled in, Gerrard by his side.

Patience's mental imprecations reached new heights. Mrs. Chadwick had not lied—Vane Cynster was the very epitome of an elegant gentleman. His hair, burnished chestnut several shades darker than her own, glowed softly in the candlelight, wave upon elegant wave sitting perfectly about his head. Even across the room, the strength of his features registered; clear-cut, hard-edged, forehead, nose, jaw, and cheeks appeared sculpted out of rock. Only his lips, long and thin with just a hint of humor to relieve their austerity, and the innate intelligence and, yes, wickedness, that lit his grey eyes, gave any hint of mere mortal personality—all else, including, Patience grudgingly acknowledged, his long, lean body, belonged to a god.

She didn't want to see how well his grey coat of Bath superfine hugged his broad shoulders, how its excellent cut emphasized his broad chest and much narrower hips. She didn't want to notice how precise, how wondrously elegant his white cravat, tied in a simple "Ballroom," appeared.

And as for his legs, long muscles flexing as he moved, she definitely didn't need to notice them.

He paused just inside the door; Gerrard stopped beside him. As she watched, Vane made some smiling comment, illustrating with a gesture so graceful it set her teeth on edge. Gerrard, face alight, eyes glowing, laughed and responded eagerly.

Vane turned his head; across the room, his eyes met hers.

Patience could have sworn someone had punched her in the stomach; she simply couldn't breathe. Holding her gaze, Vane lifted one brow—challenge flashed between them, subtle yet deliberate, quite impossible to mistake.

Patience stiffened. She dragged in a desperate breath and turned. And plastered a brittle smile on her lips as Edmond and Henry reached them.

"Isn't Mr. Cynster going to join us?" Angela, oblivious of her mother's sharp frown, leaned around to stare past Henry to where Vane and Gerrard still stood talking by the door. "I'm sure he'd be much more entertained talking to us than to Gerrard."

Patience bit her lip; she did not agree with Angela, but she fervently hoped Angela would get her wish. For an instant, it seemed she might; Vane's lips curved as he made some comment to Gerrard, then he turned—and strolled to Minnie's side.

It was Gerrard who joined them.

Hiding her relief, Patience welcomed him with a serene smile—and kept her gaze well away from the *chaise*. Gerrard and Edmond immediately fell to plotting the next scene in Edmond's melodrama—a common diversion for them. Henry, one eye on Patience, made a too-obvious effort to indulgently encourage them; his attitude, and the too-warm look in his eye, irked Patience, as it always did.

Angela, of course, pouted, not an especially pretty sight. Mrs. Chadwick, inured to her daughter's witlessness, sighed and surrendered; she and Angela, now beaming with delight, crossed to join the group about the *chaise*.

Patience was content to remain where she was, even if that meant withstanding Henry's ardent gaze.

Fifteen minutes later, the tea trolley arrived. Minnie

poured, chatting all the while. From the corner of her eye, Patience noted Vane Cynster discoursing amiably with Mrs. Chadwick; Angela, largely ignored, was threatening to pout again. Timms looked up and offered some comment which made everyone laugh; Patience saw her aunt's wise companion smile affectionately up at Vane. Of all the ladies about the *chaise*, only Alice Colby appeared unimpressed— not, however, unaffected. To Patience's eyes, Alice was even more tense than usual, as if holding back her disapproval by sheer force of will. The object of her ire, however, seemed to find her invisible.

Inwardly humphing, Patience tuned her ears to her brother's conversation, currently revolving about the "light" in the ruins. Undoubtedly a safer topic than whatever glib sally caused the next wave of laughter from the group about the *chaise*.

"Henry!"

Mrs. Chadwick's call had Henry turning, then he smiled and nodded to Patience. "If you'll excuse me, my dear, I'll return in a moment." He glanced at Gerrard. "Don't want to miss any of these scintillating plans."

Knowing full well Henry had no real interest in Gerrard or in Edmond's drama, Patience simply smiled back.

"I'd actually favor doing that scene with the arch in the background." Gerrard frowned, clearly picturing it. "The proportions are better."

"No, no," Edmond returned. "It *has* to be in the cloister." Looking up, he grinned—at a point past Patience. "Hello—are we summoned?"

"Indeed."

The single word, uttered in a voice so deep it literally rumbled, rang in Patience's ears like a knell. She swung around.

A teacup in each hand, Vane, his gaze on Edmond and Gerrard, nodded toward the tea trolley. "Your presence is requested."

"Right-ho!" With a cheery smile, Edmond took himself off; without hesitation, Gerrard followed.

Leaving Patience alone, stranded on an island of privacy in the corner of the drawing room with the one gentleman in the entire company she heartily wished at the devil.

"Thank you." With a stiff inclination of her head, she accepted the cup Vane offered her. With rigid calm, she sipped. And tried not to notice how easily he had isolated her—cut her out from her protective herd. She'd recognized him immediately as a wolf; apparently, he was an accomplished one. A fact she would henceforth bear in mind. Along with all the rest.

She could feel his gaze on her face; resolutely, she lifted her head and met his eyes. "Minnie mentioned you were on your way to Leamington, Mr. Cynster. I daresay you'll be eager to see the rain cease."

His fascinating lips lifted fractionally. "Eager enough, Miss Debbington."

Patience wished his voice was not so very deep; it made her nerves vibrate.

"However," he said, his gaze holding hers, his words a languid rumble, "you shouldn't sell the present company short. There are a number of distractions I've already noted which will, I'm convinced, make my unplanned stay worthwhile."

She was not going to be intimidated. Patience opened her eyes wide. "You intrigue me, sir. I wouldn't have imagined there was anything at Bellamy Hall of sufficient note to claim the attention of a gentleman of your . . . inclinations. Do, pray, enlighten me."

Vane met her challenging look, and considered doing just that. He raised his teacup and sipped, holding her gaze all the while. Then, looking down as he set his cup on its saucer, he stepped closer, to her side, so they stood shoulder to shoulder, he with his back to the room. He looked at her along his shoulder, and raised a brow. "I could be a rabid fan of amateur theatricals."

Despite her patently rigid resolve, her lips twitched. "And pigs might fly," she returned. Looking away, she sipped her tea.

Vane's brow quirked; he continued his languid prowl, slowly circling her, his gaze caressing the sweep of her throat and nape. "And then there's your brother." Instantly, she stiffened, as poker-rigid as Alice Colby; behind her, Vane raised both brows. "Tell me," he murmured, before she could bolt, "what's he done to get not only Whitticombe and the General, but Edgar and Henry, too, casting disapproving glances his way?"

The answer came, swift, decisive, and in distinctly bitter tones. "Nothing." After a second's pause, during which the defensive tension in her shoulders eased slightly, she added: "They've simply got totally inaccurate views of how youths of Gerrard's age might behave."

"Hmm." The explanation, Vane noted, shed very little light. Finishing his stroll, he halted by her side. "In that case, you owe me a vote of thanks." Surprised, she looked up; he met her eyes and smiled. "I stepped into the breach and stopped Gerrard responding to one of Whitticombe's set-downs with rather too much heat."

She searched his eyes, then looked away. "You only did so because you didn't want to listen to a deal of pointless wrangling."

Watching as she sipped, Vane haughtily raised his brows; she was, as it happened, half-right. "You also," he said, lowering his voice, "haven't yet thanked me for saving you from sitting in the flower bed."

She didn't even look up. "It was entirely your fault that I nearly did. If you hadn't sneaked up on me, I wouldn't have been in any danger of landing in the weeds." She glanced briefly at him, a touch of color in her cheeks. "A gentleman would have coughed or something."

Vane trapped her gaze, and smiled—a slow, Cynster smile. "Ah," he murmured, his voice very low. He shifted fractionally closer. "But, you see, I'm not a gentleman. I'm a Cynster." As if letting her into some secret, he gently informed her: "We're conquerors—not gentlemen."

Patience looked into his eyes, into his face, and felt a most peculiar shiver slither down her spine. She'd just finished her tea, but her mouth felt dry. She blinked, then blinked again, and decided to ignore his last comment. She narrowed her eyes at him. "You're not, by any chance, attempting to make me feel grateful—so that I'll imagine myself in your debt?"

His brows quirked; his mesmerizing lips curved. His

eyes, grey, intent, and oddly challenging, held hers. "It seemed the natural place to start to undermine your defenses."

Patience felt her nerves vibrate to the deep tenor of his voice, felt her senses quake as she registered his words. Her eyes, locked on his, widened; her lungs seized. In a mental scramble, she struggled to marshal her wits, to lay her tongue on some sharp retort with which to break his spell.

His eyes searched hers; one brow lifted arrogantly, along with the ends of his long lips. "I didn't cough because I was entirely distracted, which was entirely *your* fault." He seemed very close, totally commanding her vision, her senses. Again his eyes scanned hers, again one brow quirked. "Incidentally," he murmured, his voice velvety dark, "what were you searching for in the flower bed?"

"*There* you are!"

Breathless, Patience turned—and beheld Minnie, descending like a galleon in full sail. The entire British fleet wouldn't have been more welcome.

"You'll have to excuse an old woman, Patience dear, but I really must speak with Vane privately." Minnie beamed impartially on them both, then laid her hand on Vane's sleeve.

He immediately covered it with his. "I'm yours to command."

Despite his words, Patience sensed his irritation, his annoyance that Minnie had spiked the gun he'd turned on her. There was an instant's hiatus, then he smiled charmingly down at Minnie. "Your rooms?"

"Please—so sorry to drag you away."

"Not at all—you're the reason I'm here."

Minnie beamed at his flattery. Vane raised his head and met Patience's eyes. His smile still in place, he inclined his head. "Miss Debbington."

Patience returned his nod and quelled another shiver. He might have surrendered gracefully, but she had the distinct impression he hadn't given up.

She watched him cross the room, Minnie on his arm, chattering animatedly; he walked with head bent, his attention fixed on Minnie. Patience frowned. From the instant she'd recognized his style, she'd equated Vane Cynster with her father, another smooth-tongued, suavely elegant gentleman. All she knew about the species she'd learned from him, her restless, handsome sire. And what she'd learned she'd learned well—there was no chance she'd succumb to a well-set pair of shoulders and a devilish smile.

Her mother had loved her father—dearly, deeply, entirely too well. Unfortunately, men such as he were not the loving kind—not the kind wise women loved, for they did not value love, and would not accept it, nor return it. Worse, at least in Patience's eyes, such men had no sense of family life, no love in their soul to tie them to their hearth, their children. From all she had seen from her earliest years, elegant gentlemen avoided deep feelings. Avoided commitment, avoided love.

To them, marriage was a matter of estate, not a matter of the heart. Woe betide any woman who failed to understand that.

All that being so, Vane Cynster was high on her list of gentlemen she would definitely *not* wish Gerrard to have as his mentor. The very last thing she would allow was for Gerrard to turn out like his father. That he had that propensity none could deny, but she would fight to the last gasp to prevent him going that road.

Straightening her shoulders, Patience glanced around the room, noting the others, before the fireplace and about the *chaise*. With Vane and Minnie gone, the room seemed quieter, less colorful, less alive. As she watched, Gerrard threw a brief, watchful glance at the door.

Draining her teacup, Patience inwardly humphed. She would need to protect Gerrard from Vane Cynster's corrupting influence—nothing could be clearer.

A niggle of doubt slid into her mind, along with the image of Vane behaving so attentively—and, yes, affectionately—toward Minnie. Patience frowned. Possibly corrupting. She shouldn't, she supposed, judge him by his wolf's clothing, yet that characteristic, in all her twenty-six years, had never proved wrong.

Then again, neither her father, nor his elegant friends,

nor the others of that ilk she had met, had possessed a sense of humor. At least, not the sort of sparring, fencing humor Vane Cynster deployed. It was very hard to resist the challenge of striking back—of joining in the game.

Patience's frown deepened. Then she blinked, stiffened, and swept across the room to return her empty teacup to the trolley.

Vane Cynster was *definitely* corrupting.

Chapter 3

Vane helped Minnie up the stairs and down the gloomy corridors. After Sir Humphrey's death, she'd removed to a large suite at the end of one wing; Timms occupied the room next door.

Minnie paused outside her door. "A stroke of fate you should stop by just now."

I know. Vane suppressed the words. "How so?" He set the door wide.

"There's something strange going on." Leaning heavily on her cane now she was no longer "in public," Minnie crossed to the armchair by the hearth. Closing the door, Vane followed. "I'm not at all sure what it is"—Minnie settled in the chair, arranging her shawls—"but I do know I don't like it."

Vane propped his shoulder against the mantelpiece. "Tell me."

Minnie's brow furrowed. "I can't recall when it actually started, but it was sometime after Patience and Gerrard arrived." She looked up at Vane. "That's not to say I think they have anything to do with it—their arrival is merely a convenient gauge of time."

Vane inclined his head. "What did you notice?"

"The thefts started first. Little things—small items of jewelry, snuff boxes, trinkets, knickknacks. Anything small and portable—things that could fit in a pocket."

Vane's face hardened. "How many thefts have there been?"

"I don't know. None of us do. Often, things have been gone for days, even weeks, before they're noticed as missing. They're those sort of things."

Things that might fall into a flower bed. Vane frowned. "You said the thefts came first—what followed?"

"Odd happenings." Minnie's sigh overflowed with exasperation. "They're calling it 'the Spectre.' "

"A ghost?" Vane blinked. "There are no ghosts here."

"Because you and Devil would have found them if there had been?" Minnie chuckled. "Quite right." Then she sobered. "Which is why I know it's the work of someone alive. Someone in my household."

"No new servants—new helpers in the gardens?"

Minnie shook her head. "Everyone's been with me for years. Masters is as mystified as I."

"Hmm." Vane straightened. The disapproval aimed at Gerrard Debbington started to make sense. "What does this Spectre do?"

"It makes noises, for a start." Minnie's eyes flashed. "Always starts up just after I've fallen asleep." She gestured to the windows. "I'm a light sleeper, and these rooms look out over the ruins."

"What sort of noises?"

"Moans and clunks—and a grating noise, as if stones are grinding against each other."

Vane nodded. He and Devil had shifted enough stones in the ruins for him to remember the sound vividly.

"And then there's lights darting about the ruins. You know what it's like here—even in summer, we get a ground fog at night, rolling up from the river."

"Has anyone attempted to catch this Spectre?"

Chins setting, Minnie shook her head. "I refused to countenance it—I insisted they all give me their word they won't venture it. You know what the ruins are like, how dangerous it can be, even in broad daylight. Chasing a will-o'-the-wisp at night through the fog is insanity. Broken limbs, broken heads—no! I won't hear of it."

"And have they all held to their promise?"

"As far as I know." Minnie grimaced. "But you know this house—there's doors and windows aplenty they could get in or out. And I *know* one of them is the Spectre."

"Which means if he's getting out and in without being detected, others could." Vane folded his arms. "Go through the household—who has any interest in the ruins?"

Minnie held up her fingers. "Whitticombe, of course. I told you of his studies?" Vane nodded. Minnie went on: "Then there's Edgar—he's read all the biographies of the abbots and those of the early Bellamys. He has quite an interest there. And I should include the General—the ruins have been his favorite walk for years." She progressed to her last finger. "And Edmond with his play—and Gerrard, of course. Both spend time in the ruins—Edmond communing with his muse, Gerrard sketching." She frowned at her hand, having run out of fingers. "And lastly, there's Patience, but her interest is simply abiding curiosity. She likes to poke about on her walks."

Vane could imagine. "None of the other women or Henry Chadwick has any particular interest?"

Minnie shook her head.

"That's quite a cast of characters—five men all told."

"Exactly." Minnie stared at the fire. "I don't know what worries me more, the Spectre or the thief." She heaved a sigh, then looked up at Vane. "I wanted to ask, dear boy, if you would stay and sort it out."

Vane looked down, into Minnie's face, at the soft cheeks he'd kissed innumerable times, at the bright eyes that had scolded and teased and loved him so well. For one instant, the image of another face interposed, that of Patience Debbington. Similar bone structure, similar eyes. Fate, once again, stared him in the face.

But he couldn't refuse, couldn't walk away—every particle of his Cynster character refused to consider it. Cynsters never accepted defeat, although they often courted danger. Minnie was family—to be defended to the death.

Vane refocused on Minnie's face, her own once again; he opened his lips—

A shrill scream split the stillness, rending the night.

Vane hauled open Minnie's door before the first echo faded. Less intense screeches guided him through the maze of the Hall, through the ill-lit corridors, up and down stairways joining the uneven levels. He tracked the screams to the corridor in the wing opposite Minnie's, one floor up.

The source of the screams was Mrs. Chadwick.

When he reached her she was near swooning, propped against a side table, one hand pressed to her ample breast.

"A man!" She clutched Vane's sleeve and pointed down the corridor. "In a long cloak—I saw him standing there, just in front of my door."

The door in question was shrouded in gloom. Only one sconce holding a single candle lit the corridor, casting a weak glow by the intersection behind them. Footsteps came hurrying, pounding on the polished floors. Vane put Mrs. Chadwick from him. "Wait here."

Boldly, he strode down the corridor.

There was no one lurking in the shadows. He strode to the end, to where stairs led up and down. There was no sound of retreating footsteps. Vane retraced his steps. The household was gathering about Mrs. Chadwick—Patience and Gerrard were there; so, too, was Edgar. Reaching Mrs. Chadwick's door, Vane set it wide, then entered.

There was no one in the room, either.

By the time he returned to Mrs. Chadwick, she was bathed in light cast by a candelabrum Patience held high and sipping water from a glass. Her color had improved.

"I'd just come from Angela's room." She glanced fleetingly at Vane; he could have sworn her color deepened. "We were having a little chat." She took another sip, then continued, her voice strengthening, "I was going to my room when I saw him." She pointed down the corridor. "Right there."

"Standing before your door?"

Mrs. Chadwick nodded. "With his hand on the latch."

Just going in. Considering the time it had taken him to traverse half the house, the thief—if that's who it had been—would have had ample time to disappear. Vane frowned. "You said something about a cloak."

Mrs. Chadwick nodded. "A long cloak."

Or the skirts of a woman's dress. Vane looked back down the corridor. Even with the additional light thrown by the candelabrum, it would be hard to be sure if a figure was male or female. And a thief could be either.

"Just *think*! We could be murdered in our beds!"

All heads, and it was indeed all—Minnie's household had assembled in its entirety—swung Angela's way.

Eyes huge, she stared back. "It must be some madman!"

"Why?"

Vane had opened his mouth to voice the question; Patience beat him to it. "Why on earth would someone come all the way out here," she continued, "struggle into this particular house, go to your mother's door—and then vanish as soon as she screamed? If it was a madman intent on murder, he had plenty of time to do the deed."

Both Mrs. Chadwick and Angela stared at her, stunned by her ruthless common sense.

Vane forced his lips straight. "There's no need for melodrama—whoever it was is long gone." But possibly not far away.

The same thought had occurred to Whitticombe. "Is everybody here?" He looked about, as did the others, confirming that indeed, everyone was present, even Masters, who stood at the back of the crowd. "Well, then," Whitticombe said, scanning the faces, "where *was* everyone? Gerrard?"

Vane was quite sure it wasn't chance that had brought that name first to Whitticombe's lips.

Gerrard was standing behind Patience. "I was in the billiard room."

"Alone?" Whitticombe's insinuation was transparent.

Gerrard's jaw set. "Yes, alone."

The General grunted. "Why on earth would someone spend time in the billiard room alone?"

Color crept into Gerrard's cheeks. He flicked a glance at Vane. "I was just knocking a few balls around."

That swift glance was enough for Vane; Gerrard had been practicing shots, waiting for him to come down. The billiard room was precisely the sort of place a gentleman such as he might be expected to choose to spend an hour or so before retiring. Indeed, if events had not taken the course they had, he would have gone there himself.

Vane didn't like the accusing stares that were being

aimed at Gerrard. Neither did Patience, Minnie, or Timms. He spoke before they could. "That's you accounted for. Where was everyone else?"

He made each one state their last location. Bar himself and Minnie, Angela, Mrs. Chadwick, Patience, and Timms, not one had been in sight of anyone else. Whitticombe had returned to the library; Edgar had gone in to retrieve a tome, then retreated to the back parlor. Edmond, oblivious to all once his muse had taken hold, as apparently it had, had remained in the drawing room. The General, irritated by Edmond's spontaneous spoutings, had slipped back to the dining room. From his deepened color, Vane suspected the brandy decanter had been his goal. Henry Chadwick had retired to his room.

When Vane asked for her whereabouts, Alice Colby glared at him. "I was in my room, one floor below this."

Vane merely nodded. "Very well. I suggest that now the thief is long gone, we should all retire."

In the face of that dampeningly dull suggestion, most of the party, muttering and grumbling, did so. Gerrard hung back, but when Patience noticed and gave him a push, he shot an apologetic glance at Vane and went. Predictably, Patience, Minnie, and Timms stood their ground.

Vane eyed their set faces, then sighed and waved them back. "In Minnie's room." He took Minnie's arm, concerned when he felt how heavily she leaned on him. He was tempted to carry her, but knew her pride of old. So he matched his pace to hers. By the time they reached her rooms, Timms had the fire blazing and Patience had plumped the cushions in Minnie's chair. Vane helped her to it and she sank down with a weary sigh.

"It wasn't Gerrard."

The trenchant statement came from Timms. "I can't abide how they all cast suspicion his way. They're making him a scapegoat."

Minnie nodded. Patience simply met Vane's eyes. She stood by Minnie's chair, head up, hands clasped too tightly before her, daring him to accuse her brother.

Vane's lips twisted wryly. "He was waiting for me." Strolling forward, he took up his customary position, shoulders propped against the mantelpiece. "Which, the last time I checked, wasn't a crime."

Timms sniffed. "Exactly so. That much was obvious."

"If we're agreed on that, then I suggest we forget the incident. There's no way I can see to link it to anyone."

"Masters couldn't fault any of the other alibis." Patience lifted her chin when Vane looked her way. "I asked him."

Vane regarded her for a moment, then nodded. "So tonight has revealed nothing—there's nothing more to do but head for bed."

He kept his eyes on Patience's face; after a moment, she inclined her head. "As you say." She bent down to Minnie. "If you don't need me, ma'am?"

Minnie forced a tired smile. "No, my love." She clasped Patience's hand. "Timms will take care of me."

Patience kissed Minnie's cheek. Straightening, she exchanged a conspiratorial look with Timms, then glided to the door. Vane fell in in her wake, reaching around her as she halted before the door to open it. Their positions were the same as they'd been that afternoon, when he'd deliberately discomposed her. This time it was she who hesitated, then glanced up, into his face. "You don't believe it was Gerrard."

Half question, half statement. Vane held her gaze, then shook his head. "I know it wasn't Gerrard. Your brother couldn't lie to save himself—and he didn't try."

Briefly, she searched his eyes, then inclined her head. Vane opened the door, closed it behind her, then headed back to the fire.

"Well," Minnie sighed. "Will you take on my commission?"

Vane looked down at her and let his Cynster smile show. "After that little interlude, how could I refuse?" How indeed.

"Thank heavens!" Timms declared. "Lord knows we need a little sound sense around here."

Vane stored that comment up in case of later need—he suspected Patience Debbington thought she had the sound sense market cornered. "I'll start nosing around tomorrow.

Until then—'' He looked at Minnie. "As I said, it would be best to forget about tonight.''

Minnie smiled. "Knowing you'll be staying will be enough to ease my mind.''

"Good.'' With a nod, Vane straightened and turned.

"Oh—ah, Vane . . . ?''

He glanced back, one brow rising, but didn't halt in his progress to the door. "I know—but don't ask me for a promise I won't keep.''

Minnie frowned. "Just take care of yourself—I wouldn't want to have to face your mother if you break a leg, or, worse yet, your head.''

"Rest assured—I don't intend to break either.'' Vane glanced back from the door, one brow arrogantly high. "As you've no doubt heard, we Cynsters are invincible.''

With a rakish grin, he left; Minnie watched the door close. Reluctantly smiling, she tugged at her slipping shawls. "Invincible? Huh!''

Timms came to help. "Given all seven of the present generation returned from Waterloo, unscathed and with nary a scratch, I'd say they have some claim to the title.''

Minnie made a distinctly rude sound. "I've known Vane and Devil from the cradle—and the others almost as well.'' She poked Timms's arm affectionately. With her help, she struggled to her feet. "They're very much mortal men, as hot-blooded and bold as they come.'' Her words gave her pause, then she chuckled. "They may not be invincible, but be damned if they're not the next best thing.''

"Precisely.'' Timms smiled. "So we can leave our problems on Vane's shoulders—Lord knows, they're broad enough.''

Minnie grinned. "Very true. Well, then—let's get me to bed.''

Vane made sure he was early down to breakfast. When he entered the breakfast parlor, only Henry was present, working his way through a plate of sausages. Exchanging an amiable nod, Vane headed for the sideboard.

He was heaping a plate with slices of ham when Masters appeared, bearing another platter. He set it down on the sideboard. Raising a brow, Vane caught his eye. "No sign of any break-in?"

"No, sir." Masters had been Minnie's butler for twenty and more years. He knew Vane well. "I did my rounds early. The ground floor had already been secured before the . . . incident. I checked again afterward—there was no door or window left open."

Which was no more nor less than Vane had expected. He nodded noncommittally and Masters left.

Strolling to the table, Vane drew out the chair at its end.

Henry, in the next chair along, looked up as he sat. "Dashed odd business, last night. The mater's still shaken. Hate to say it, but I really do feel young Gerrard's gone far enough with this 'Spectre' nonsense."

Vane raised his brows. "Actually—"

A snort from the door cut him off; Whitticombe entered. "The young bounder should be thrashed—scaring gently bred females like that. Needs a firm hand applied to his reins—he's been left in the care of women too long."

Inwardly, Vane stiffened; outwardly, not a ripple marred his habitually urbane expression. He swallowed an impulse to defend Patience, and Minnie, too. Instead, he manufactured an expression of boredom only mildly piqued. "Why are you so sure it was Gerrard last night?"

At the sideboard, Whitticombe turned, but was beaten to speech by the General. "Stands to reason," he wheezed, stumping in. "Who else could it have been, heh?"

Again, Vane's brows rose. "Almost anyone, as far as I could see."

"Nonsense!" the General huffed, leaning his stick against the sideboard.

"Other than myself, Minnie, Timms, Miss Debbington, Angela, and Mrs. Chadwick," Vane reiterated, "any one of you could have been the culprit."

Turning, the General glared at him from under overhanging brows. "You've shaken a screw loose with too much racketing about. Why the devil would any of *us* want to put the wind up Agatha Chadwick?"

Gerrard, bright-eyed, swung through the door—and

came to a dead halt. His face, initially filled with boyish anticipation, drained of expression.

Vane trapped Gerrard's gaze, then, with his eyes, indicated the sideboard. "Indeed," he drawled as Gerrard, now stiff and tense, moved to serve himself, "but, using precisely the same reasoning, why would Gerrard?"

The General scowled and shot a glance at Gerrard's back. Carrying a plate piled high with kedgeree, the General pulled out a chair farther along the table. Whitticombe, tight-lipped, censoriously silent, took a place opposite.

Frowning, Henry shifted in his seat. He, too, looked at Gerrard, busy at the sideboard, then studied his now-empty plate. "I don't know—but I suppose boys will be boys."

"As one who used that excuse to extremes, I feel compelled to point out that Gerrard is several years past the stage where that explanation applies." Vane met Gerrard's eyes as he turned from the sideboard, a full plate in his hands. Gerrard's face was lightly flushed, his gaze watchful. Vane smiled easily and waved to the chair beside his. "But perhaps he can suggest something? What say you, Gerrard—can you give us a reason why someone might want to scare Mrs. Chadwick?"

To his credit, Gerrard didn't rush into speech; he frowned as he set his plate down, then shook his head slowly as he sat. "I can't think of any reason why anyone would want to make Mrs. Chadwick screech." He grimaced at the memory. "But"—he flicked a grateful glance at Vane—"I did wonder if the fright was incidental and the person at the door was really the thief."

The suggestion made all at the table think—after a moment, Henry nodded. "Could be—indeed, why not?"

"Regardless," Whitticombe put in, "I can't conceive who this thief could be either." His tone made it clear he still suspected Gerrard.

Vane directed a mildly questioning glance at Gerrard.

Encouraged, Gerrard shrugged. "I can't see what any of us would want with all the knickknacks and fripperies that have disappeared."

The General gave one of his distinguishing snorts. "Perhaps because they're fripperies? Just the sort of things to woo a flighty maid with, heh?'' His penetrating stare again fixed on Gerrard.

Ready color rose to Gerrard's cheeks.

"Not guilty! On my honor, I swear it!"

The words came in ringing tones from the doorway. They all looked around—on the threshold, Edmond stood poised in the attitude of a supplicant pleading for justice from the bench. He broke from his pose; grinning, he bowed, then straightened and loped to the sideboard. "Sorry to disappoint you, but I feel obliged to puncture that fantasy. None of the maids here would accept such tokens of esteem—the staff have all been alerted to the thefts. And as for the surrounding villages"—he paused dramatically and rolled an anguished eye at Vane—"*believe me*, there's not a likely miss within a day's ride!"

Vane hid his grin behind his coffee cup; over the rim, he met Gerrard's laughing eyes.

The sound of briskly swishing skirts drew all eyes to the door. Patience appeared in the doorway. Chairs scraped as they all made to rise. She waved them back. Pausing on the threshold, she swiftly scanned the room, her gaze fixing at the last on Gerrard. And his affectionate smile.

Vane noticed the way Patience's breasts rose and fell, noticed the light blush in her cheeks. She'd been scurrying.

She blinked, then, with a general nod, headed for the sideboard.

Vane redirected the conversation to matters less fraught.

"The Northants Hunt is the nearest," Henry replied to his question.

At the sideboard, Patience forced herself to breathe deeply while absentmindedly filling her plate. She'd intended to wake early and be here in time to protect Gerrard. Instead, she'd slept in, drained by escalating worry, followed by unsettling dreams. The other ladies generally took breakfast on trays in their chambers, a habit to which she'd never subscribed. Ears tuned to the rumble of conversation behind her, she heard Vane's lazy drawl and felt her skin prickle. She frowned.

She knew the male members of the household too well—there was no possiblity they'd omitted to mention last night's contretemps, nor that they hadn't, in one way or another, accused Gerrard of it. But he was clearly unperturbed, which could mean only one thing. For whatever reason, Vane Cynster had taken up the cudgels in her stead and deflected the household's unreasoning suspicions of Gerrard. Her frown deepened as she heard Gerrard's voice, youthful enthusiasm ringing as he described a nearby ride.

Eyes widening, Patience picked up her plate and whirled. She advanced on the table, to the chair beside Gerrard. Masters drew it out and held it while she sat.

Gerrard turned to her. "I was just telling Vane that Minnie kept the best of Sir Humphrey's hunters. And the rides hereabouts are quite reasonable."

His eyes glowed with a light Patience hadn't seen in them before. Smiling, he turned back to Vane. Her heart sinking, Patience looked to the head of the table, too. Vane sat relaxed, wide shoulders encased in a grey hacking jacket settled comfortably against the chair back, one hand resting on the chair's arm, the other stretched on the table, long fingers crooked about the handle of a coffee cup.

In daylight, his features were as hard-edged as she'd thought them, his face every bit as strong. His heavy lids hid his eyes as, with lazy interest, he listened to Gerrard extol the equestrian virtues of the locality.

To her right, the General snorted, then pushed back his chair. Whitticombe rose, too. One after the other, they left the room. Frowning, Patience applied herself to her breakfast and tried to think of another subject with which to capture the conversation.

Vane saw her frown. The devil in him stirred and stretched, then settled to contemplate this latest challenge. She would, he felt sure, avoid him. Shifting his hooded gaze, he studied Gerrard. Vane smiled. Lazily. He waited until Patience took a bite of her toast.

"Actually," he drawled, "I was thinking of filling in the morning with a ride. Anyone interested?"

Gerrard's eager response was instantaneous; Patience's response, though far less eager, was no less rapid. Vane stifled a grin at the sight of her stunned expression as, with her mouth inhibitingly full, she heard Gerrard accept his invitation with undisguised delight.

Patience looked out through the long parlor windows. The day was fine, a brisk breeze drying the puddles. She swallowed, and looked at Vane. "I thought you would be leaving."

He smiled, a slow, devilish, fascinating smile. "I've decided to stay for a few days."

Damn! Patience bit back the word and looked across the table at Edmond.

Who shook his head. "Not for me. The muse calls—I must do her bidding."

Patience inwardly cursed, and switched her gaze to Henry. He considered, then grimaced. "A good idea, but I should check on Mama first. I'll catch up if I can."

Vane inclined his head, and slanted a smiling glance at Gerrard. "Looks like it's just the two of us, then."

"No!" Patience coughed to disguise the abruptness of her answer; then took a sip of tea and looked up. "If you'll wait while I change, I'll come, too."

She met Vane's eyes, and saw the grey glint wickedly. But he smoothly, graciously, inclined his head, accepting her company, which was all she cared about. Setting down her teacup, she rose. "I'll meet you at the stables."

Rising with his customary grace, Vane watched as she left, then sank back, elegantly asprawl. He lifted his coffee cup, thus hiding his victorious smile. Gerrard, after all, wasn't blind. "Ten minutes, do you think?" He lifted a brow at Gerrard.

"Oh, at least." Gerrard grinned and reached for the coffeepot.

Chapter 4

By the time she gained the stable yard, Patience had the bit firmly between her teeth. Vane Cynster was not a suitable mentor for Gerrard, but, given the evidence of her eyes, Gerrard was already well on the way to an unhealthy respect, which could all too easily lead to adulation. Hero worship. Dangerous emulation.

It was all very clear in her mind.

The train of her lavender-velvet riding habit over her arm, she strode into the yard, heels ringing on the cobbles. Her reading of the situation was instantly confirmed.

Vane sat a massive grey hunter with elegant ease, effortlessly controlling the restive beast. Beside him, on a chestnut gelding, Gerrard blithely chatted. He looked happier, more relaxed, than he had since they'd arrived. Patience noted it, but, halting in the shadows of the stable arch, her attention remained riveted on Vane Cynster.

Her mother had often remarked that "true gentlemen" looked uncommonly dashing on horseback. Quelling an inward sniff—her normal reaction to that observation, which had invariably alluded to her father—Patience reluctantly conceded she could now see her mother's point: There was something about the harnessed power of the man, dominating and harnessing the power of the beast, that made her stomach tighten. The clop of hooves had drowned out her approach; she stared for a minute longer, then gave herself a mental shake, and walked forward.

Grisham had the brown mare she favored saddled and

43

waiting; Patience ascended the mounting block, then climbed into the saddle. She settled her skirts and picked up the reins.

"Ready?"

The question came from Vane. Patience nodded.

Naturally, *he* led the way out.

The morning greeted them, crisp and clear. Pale grey clouds dotted the washed-out sky; the smell of damp greenery was all-pervasive. Their first stop was a knoll, three miles from the Hall. Vane had ridden the fidgets from his mount in a series of short gallops that Patience had tried hard not to watch. After that, the grey had cantered beside her mare. Gerrard had ridden on her other side. None of them had spoken, content to look about and let the cool air refresh them.

Reining in beside Vane on the top of the knoll, Patience looked around. Beside her, Gerrard scanned the horizon, gauging the view. Twisting in his saddle, he eyed the steep mound beyond Vane, covering one end of the knoll.

"Here." Thrusting his reins into her hands, Gerrard dismounted. "I'm going to check the view."

Patience glanced at Vane, sitting his grey with deceptive ease, hands crossed on the saddlebow. He smiled lazily at Gerrard but made no move to follow. They watched as Gerrard scrambled up the steep sloping side of the mound. Gaining the top, he waved, then looked about. After a moment, he sank down, his gaze fixed in the distance.

Patience grinned and transferred her gaze to Vane's face. "I'm afraid he might be hours. He's very much taken with landscapes at present."

To her surprise, the grey eyes watching her showed no sign of alarm at that news. Instead, Vane's long lips curved. "I know," he said. "He mentioned his current obsession, so I told him about the old burial mound."

He paused, then added, his eyes still on hers, his smile deepening, "The views are quite spectacular." His eyes glinted. "Guaranteed to hold a budding artist's attention for a considerable space of time."

Patience, her gaze locked in the grey of his, felt a tingling sensation run over her skin. She blinked, then frowned.

"How kind of you." She turned to study the views herself. And again felt that odd sensation, a ripple of awareness sliding over her nerves, leaving them sensitized. It was most peculiar. She would have put it down to the touch of the breeze, but the wind wasn't that cold.

Beside her, Vane raised his brows, his predator's smile still in evidence. Her lavender habit was not new, hardly fashionable, yet it hugged her contours, emphasizing their softness, leaving him with an urgent longing to fill his arms with their warmth. The grey shifted; Vane steadied him. "Minnie mentioned you and your brother hail from Derbyshire. Do you ride much while there?"

"As much as I can." Patience glanced his way. "I enjoy the exercise, but the rides in the vicinity of the Grange are rather restricted. Are you familiar with the area around Chesterfield?"

"Not specifically." Vane grinned. "That's a bit farther north than my usual hunting grounds."

For foxes—or females? Patience stifled a humph. "From your knowledge of the locality"—she glanced at the mound beside them—"I take it you've visited here before?"

"Often as a child. My cousin and I spent a few weeks here most summers."

Patience humphed. "I'm surprised Minnie survived."

"On the contrary—she thrived on our visits. She always delighted in our exploits and adventures."

When she returned no further comment, Vane softly said, "Incidentally, Minnie mentioned the odd thefts that have occurred at the Hall." Patience looked up; he trapped her gaze. "Is that what you were looking for in the flower bed? Something that disappeared?"

Patience hesitated, searching his eyes, then nodded. "I told myself Myst must have knocked it out of the window, but I hunted high and low, in the room and in the flower bed. I couldn't find it anywhere."

"What was 'it'?"

"A small silver vase." She sketched the shape of a bud vase. "About four inches high. I've had it for years—I don't suppose it's particularly valuable, but . . ."

"You'd rather have it than not. Why were you so keen not to mention it last night?"

Her face setting, Patience met Vane's eyes. "You aren't going to tell me the *gentlemen* of the household didn't happen to mention over the breakfast table this morning that they think Gerrard is behind all these odd occurrences—the Spectre, as they call it, and the thefts as well?"

"They did, as it happens, but we—Gerrard, myself, and, surprisingly enough, Edmond—pointed out that that notion has no real foundation."

The unladylike sound Patience made was eloquent—of irritation, frustration, and overstretched tolerance.

"Indeed," Vane concurred, "so you have yet another reason to feel grateful to me." As Patience swung his way, he frowned. "And Edmond, unfortunately."

Despite herself, Patience's lips quirked. "Edmond would gainsay the elders simply for a joke—he doesn't take anything seriously, other than his muse."

"I'll take your word for it."

Instead of being distracted, Patience continued to study his face. Vane raised one brow. "I did tell you," he murmured, holding her gaze, "that I'm determined to put you in my debt. You needn't concern yourself over the gentlemen's attitude to Gerrard while I'm about." He didn't think her pride would allow her to accept an outright offer of a broad shoulder to deflect the slings and arrows of the present Hall society; presenting his aid in the guise of a rake's machinations, would, he hoped, permit her to let the matter go with a shrug and a tart comment.

What he got was a frown. "Well, I do thank you if you tried to set them straight." Patience glanced up to where Gerrard was still communing with the horizon. "But you can see why I didn't want to make a fuss over my vase—they'd only blame Gerrard."

Vane raised his brows noncommittally. "Whatever. If anything more disappears, tell me, or Minnie, or Timms."

Patience looked at him and frowned. "What—"

"Who's this?" Vane nodded at a horseman cantering toward them.

Patience looked, then sighed. "Hartley Penwick." Although her expression remained bland, her tone grimaced. "He's the son of one of Minnie's neighbors."

"Well met, my dear Miss Debbington!" Penwick, a well-set gentleman attired in tweed jacket and corduroy breeches, and astride a heavy roan, swept Patience a bow more wide than it was elegant. "I trust I find you well?"

"Indeed, sir." Patience gestured to Vane. "Allow me to make you known to Lady Bellamy's godson." Briefly, she introduced Vane, adding the information that he had stopped to take shelter from last night's storm.

"Ah." Penwick shook Vane's hand. "So your visit's in the nature of a forced halt. Daresay you'll be on your way soon. The sun's drying the roads nicely, and there's nothing in this backwater to compare with *ton*nish pursuits."

If Penwick had declared that he wanted him gone, he could not have been more explicit. Vane smiled, a gesture full of teeth. "Oh, I'm in no especial hurry."

Penwick's brows rose; his eyes, watchful from the instant he had beheld Vane, grew harder. "Ah—on a repairing lease, I take it?"

"No." Vane's gaze grew chilly, his diction more precise. "I'm merely in the way of pleasing myself."

That information did not please Penwick. Patience was about to step into the breach, to protect Penwick from likely annihilation, when Penwick, searching for the person to match the third horse, glanced up.

"Great heavens! *Get down* from there, you scallywag!"

Vane blinked and glanced up. Eyes glued to the horizon, the scallywag feigned deafness. Turning back, Vane heard Patience haughtily state: "It's perfectly all right, sir. He's looking at the views."

"Views!" Penwick snorted. "The sides of that mound are steep and slippery—what if he should fall?" He looked at Vane. "I'm surprised, Cynster, that you permitted young Debbington to embark on a mad scheme guaranteed to overturn his sister's sensiblities."

Patience, suddenly no longer sure of Gerrard's safety, looked at Vane.

His gaze on Penwick, Vane slowly raised his brows. Then he turned his head and met Patience's potentially worried gaze. "I thought Gerrard was seventeen?"

She blinked. "He is."

"Well, then." Vane sat back, shoulders relaxing. "Seventeen is more than old enough to be responsible for his own safety. If he breaks a leg on his way down, it will be entirely his own fault."

Patience stared at him—and wondered why her lips insisted on twitching upward. Vane's eyes met hers; the calm, rocklike confidence she saw in the grey steadied her—and steadied her confidence in Gerrard.

The unsuccessfully muffled laugh that drifted over their heads forced her to straighten her lips and turn to Penwick. "I'm sure Gerrard is more than capable of managing."

Penwick came close to scowling.

"Here's Edmond." Patience looked past Penwick as Edmond urged his mount up the rise. "I thought you were trapped by your muse?"

"Fought free of it," Edmond informed her with a grin. He nodded at Penwick, then turned back to Patience. "Thought you might be glad of more company."

While Edmond's expression remained ingenuous, Patience was left with little doubt as to his thinking. She fought an urge to glance at Vane, to see if he, too, had picked up the implication; she was quite sure he would have—the man was certainly not slow.

That last was borne out by the purring murmur that slid past her right ear. "We've just been admiring the views."

On the instant, before she'd even turned to him, that tingling sensation washed over her again, more intense, more wickedly evocative than before. Patience caught her breath and refused to meet his eyes. She allowed her gaze to rise only as far as his lips. They quirked, then eased into a teasing smile.

"And here's Chadwick."

Patience swallowed a groan. She turned and confirmed that Henry was, indeed, trotting up to join them. Her lips set; she'd only come on the ride because none of them had been interested in riding—and now here they all were, with even Penwick thrown in, riding to her rescue!

She didn't need rescuing! Or protecting! She wasn't in

the slightest danger of succumbing to any "elegant gentleman's" rakish lures. Not, she had to concede, that Vane had thrown any her way. He might be considering it, but his subtlety left the others looking like floundering puppies, yapping in their earnest haste.

"Such a fine day—couldn't resist the thought of a brisk ride." Henry beamed engagingly at her; the image of a panting puppy, tongue lolling in a hopeful canine grin, impinged forcefully on Patience's mind.

"Now we're all gathered," Vane drawled, "perhaps we should ride on?"

"Indeed," Patience agreed. Anything to cut short this farcical gathering.

"Gerrard, come down—your horse has forgotten why it's out here." Vane's command, delivered in world-weary tones, elicited nothing more than a chuckle from Gerrard.

He stood, stretched, nodded to Patience, then disappeared around the other side of the mound. Within minutes, he reappeared at ground level, dusting his hands. He grinned at Vane, nodded to Edmond and Henry, and ignored Penwick. Accepting his reins, he flashed Patience a smile, then swung up to the saddle. "Shall we?"

A lift of one brow and a brief wave accompanied the question. Patience stiffened—she stared. She knew precisely where Gerrard had picked up both those little mannerisms.

"How were the views?" Edmond paired his horse with Gerrard's. They led the way down the rise, Gerrard responding readily, describing various vistas and expounding on the interplay of light, cloud, and haze.

Her gaze fixed on Gerrard, Patience set her horse to follow his. Consternation ensued. With Vane holding steady on her right, Penwick and Henry jostled for the position on her left. By dint of defter management, Penwick secured the prize, leaving Henry sulking in the rear. Inwardly, Patience sighed, and made a mental note to be kind to Henry later.

Within three minutes, she would gladly have strangled Penwick.

"I flatter myself, Miss Debbington, that you are clear-sighted enough to comprehend that I have your best interests at heart.'' That was Penwick's beginning. From there he progressed to: ''I cannot but be convinced it does your sisterly sensitivities, those softer emotions with which gentlewomen are so well endowed, no good at all to be constantly abraded by the youthful but sadly inconsiderate exploits of your brother.''

Patience kept her gaze on the fields and let Penwick's dissertation pass her by. She knew he wouldn't notice her abstraction. Other men always brought out the worst in Penwick—in his case, the worst was an unassailable belief in his own judgment, combined with an unshakable certainty that she not only shared his views, but was well on the way to being Mrs. Penwick. How he'd arrived at such a conclusion Patience was at a loss to understand; she'd never given him the slightest encouragement.

His portentous pronouncements flowed past her as they ambled on. Henry fidgeted, then coughed, then butted in with: ''Do you think we'll get more rain?''

Patience fell on the witless question with relief and used it to distract Penwick, whose other obsession, beyond the sound of his own voice, was his fields. By dint of a few artless inquiries, she set Henry and Penwick to arguing over the effect of the recent rain on the crops.

Throughout, Vane said nothing. He didn't have to. Patience was quite sure of his thoughts—as cynical as her own. His silence was more eloquent, more powerful, more successful in impinging on her senses, than Penwick's pedantic statements or Henry's garrulous chatter.

To her right lay a sense of security, a front she did not, for the moment, need to defend. His silent presence gave her that; Patience inwardly sniffed. Yet another thing, she supposed, for which she should be grateful to him. He was proving adept at that cool, arrogant, subtle yet unrelenting maneuvering she associated with ''elegant gentlemen.'' She was not surprised. From the first, she'd identified him as an expert practitioner.

Focusing on Gerrard, Patience heard him laugh. Over his shoulder, Edmond threw her a smiling glance, then reapplied himself to Gerrard. Then Gerrard made some comment, underscoring his point with the same indolent wave he'd used before.

Patience set her teeth. There was nothing wrong, *per se*, with the gesture, although Vane did it better. At seventeen, Gerrard's artist's hands, although well made, had yet to gain the strength and mature form Vane Cynster's hands possessed. When he performed that gesture, it reeked of a masculine power Gerrard had yet to attain.

But copying gestures was one thing—Patience worried that Gerrard's emulation would not stop there. Still, she reasoned, glancing swiftly at Vane riding quietly beside her, it was only a mannerism or two. Despite Penwick's beliefs, she was not a female overburdened with nonsensical sensivities. She was, perhaps, more acutely conscious of Vane Cynster and his propensities, more watchful than she would be with other men. But there seemed no real reason to intervene. Yet.

With a laugh, Gerrard broke away from Edmond; wheeling his horse, he brought his chestnut alongside Vane's grey. "I've been meaning to ask"—Gerrard's eyes shone with enthusiasm as he looked into Vane's face—"about those greys of yours."

A disturbance on her other side forced Patience to glance that way, so she missed Vane's answer. His voice was so deep that, when he was facing away from her, she couldn't discern his words.

The disturbance proved to be Edmond, taking advantage of Penwick's distraction with Henry to insinuate his horse between Penwick's and Patience's. "There!" Edmond blithely ignored Penwick's outraged glare. "I've been waiting to ask your opinion of my latest verse. It's for the scene where the abbot addresses the wandering brothers."

He proceeded to declaim the recent fruits of his brain.

Patience gritted her teeth; she felt literally torn. Edmond would expect her to comment intelligently on his work, which he took with all the seriousness he failed to devote to more worldly matters. On the other hand, she desperately wanted to know what Vane was saying to Gerrard. While one part of her mind followed Edmond's rhymes, she strained her ears to pick up Gerrard's words.

"So their chests are important?" he asked.

Rumble, rumble, rumble.

"Oh." Gerrard paused. "Actually, I thought weight would give a fair indication."

A long series of rumbles answered that.

"I see. So if they do have good stamina . . ."

Patience glanced to her right—Gerrard was now closer to Vane. She couldn't even hear his half of the conversation.

"So!" Edmond drew in a breath. "What do you think?"

Head snapping back, Patience met his eyes. "It didn't hold my interest—perhaps it needs more polish?"

"Oh." Edmond was deflated, but not cast down. He frowned. "Actually, I think you might be right."

Patience ignored him, edging her mare nearer Vane's grey. Vane glanced her way; both eyes and lips appeared gently amused. Patience ignored that, too, and concentrated on his words.

"Assuming they're up to the weight, the next most important criterion is their knees."

Knees? Patience blinked.

"High-steppers?" Gerrard suggested.

Patience stiffened.

"Not necessarily," Vane replied. "A good action, certainly, but there must be power behind the stride."

They were still talking about carriage horses; Patience almost sighed with relief. She continued to listen, but heard nothing more sinister. Just horses. Not even wagering or the racecourses.

Inwardly frowning, she settled back in her saddle. Her suspicions of Vane were well-founded, weren't they? Or was she overreacting?

"I'll take my leave of you here." Penwick's acid declaration cut across Patience's musing.

"Indeed, sir." She gave him her hand. "So kind of you to drop by. I'll mention to my aunt that we saw you."

Penwick blinked. "Oh, yes—that is, I trust you'll convey my regards to Lady Bellamy."

Patience smiled, coolly regal, and inclined her head. The gentlemen nodded; Vane's nod held an element of menace—how he managed it, Patience couldn't have said.

Penwick wheeled his horse and cantered off.

"Right then!" Free of Penwick's trenchantly disapproving presence, Gerrard grinned. "How about a race back to the stables?"

"You're on." Edmond gathered his reins. The lane to the stables lay on the other side of an open field. It was a straight run, with no fences or ditches to cause difficulty.

Henry chuckled indulgently and flicked Patience a smile. "I suppose I'll be in on it, too."

Gerrard looked at Vane.

Who smiled. "I'll give you a handicap—lead off."

Gerrard waited for no more. With a "Whoop!" he sprang his horse.

Edmond made to give chase, as did Henry, but, as Patience tapped her heels to her mare's sides, they moved off with her. Letting her mare have her head, Patience followed in her brother's wake; Gerrard was forging ahead, unchallenged. The three other men held their horses back, matching the mare's shorter strides.

Ridiculous! What possible benefit could any of them gain by keeping to her side over one short field? Patience fought to keep a straight face, to keep from grinning and shaking her head at the sheer silliness of men. As they neared the lane, she couldn't resist a brief glance at Vane.

Keeping station on her right, the grey held easily in check, he met her gaze—and raised one brow in weary self-deprecation.

Patience laughed—an answering gleam lit Vane's eyes. The lane drew near; he glanced forward. When he looked back, the light in his eyes had hardened, sharpened.

He edged his grey closer, crowding her mare. The mare reacted by lengthening her stride. Henry and Edmond fell behind, forced to hold back as the grey and the mare swept into the lane, only wide enough for two horses abreast.

Then they were clattering under the arch and into the yard. Pulling up, Patience dragged in a breath and looked back; Edmond and Henry were some way behind.

Gerrard, having won the race, laughed and set his chestnut prancing. Grisham and the grooms came running.

Patience looked at Vane and saw him dismount—by bringing his leg over the saddlebow and sliding to the ground, landing on his feet. She blinked, and he was by her side.

His hands closed about her waist.

She almost gasped when he lifted her from the saddle as if she weighed no more than a child. He didn't swing her down, but slowly lowered her to earth, setting her on her feet beside the mare. Less than a foot from him. He held her between his hands; she felt the long fingers flex about her, fingertips on either side of her spine, thumbs against her sensitive midriff. She felt . . . captured. Vulnerable. His face was a hard mask, his expression intent. Her eyes locked on his, Patience felt the cobbles beneath her feet, but her world continued to spin.

It *was* he—the source of those peculiar sensations. She'd thought it must be, but she'd never felt such sensations before—and those streaking through her now were far stronger than those she'd felt earlier. It was his touch that did it—the touch of his eyes, the touch of his hands. He didn't even need to contact bare skin to make every square inch she possessed react.

Patience dragged in a breath. A flicker at the edge of her vision made her shift her focus. To Gerrard. She saw him dismount, exactly as Vane had done. Grinning, brimming with prideful good humor, Gerrard crossed the cobbles toward them.

Vane turned, smoothly releasing her.

Patience dragged in another breath and fought to steady her giddy head. She plastered a bright smile on her lips for Gerrard's benefit—and continued to breathe deeply.

"A wily move, Cynster." Edmond, grinning good-naturedly, dismounted in the customary way. Patience noted it was a great deal slower than the way Vane had achieved the same end.

Henry also dismounted; Patience got the impression he hadn't liked seeing Vane lift her down. But he directed one of his hearty smiles at Gerrard. "Congratulations, my boy. You beat us fairly and squarely."

Which was laying it on a great deal too thick. Patience

glanced swiftly at Gerrard, expecting some less than gracious response. Instead, her brother, standing beside Vane, merely raised one brow—and smiled cynically.

Patience gritted her teeth; her jaw set. Of one thing she was quite sure—she wasn't overreacting.

Vane Cynster was going too far, far too fast—at least with respect to Gerrard. As for the rest—his teasing of her senses—she suspected he was merely amusing himself without any serious intent. As she was not susceptible to seduction, there seemed no reason to call him to account for that.

Over Gerrard, however . . .

She mulled over the situation as the horses were led away. For a few moments, all four men stood together in the center of the yard; a little to one side, she studied them—and acknowledged she could hardly blame Gerrard for choosing Vane to emulate. He was the dominant male.

As if sensing her regard, he turned. One brow quirked, then, inherently graceful, he offered her his arm. Patience steeled herself and took it. As a group, they walked to the house; Edmond left them at the side door. They climbed the main stairs, then Gerrard and Henry turned aside, heading for their rooms. Still on Vane's arm, Patience strolled into the gallery. Her room was down the same corridor as Minnie's. Vane's was on the floor below.

There wasn't any point voicing her disapproval unless there was a real need. Patience paused in the archway leading from the gallery, from where they would go their separate ways. Drawing her hand from Vane's arm, she looked up, into his face. "Are you planning a long stay?"

He looked down at her. "That," he stated, his voice very low, "depends largely on you."

Patience looked into his grey eyes—and froze. Every muscle was paralyzed, all the way to her toes. The idea that he was amusing himself, without any real intent, died— slain by the look in his eyes.

The *intent* in his eyes.

It couldn't have been clearer had he put it into words.

Bravely, drawing on an inner reserve she hadn't known she possessed, she lifted her chin. And forced her lips to curve, just enough for a cool smile. "I think you'll find you're mistaken."

She uttered the words softly, and saw his jaw lock. A premonition of intense danger swept her; she didn't dare say anything more. With her smile still in place, she haughtily inclined her head. Sweeping about, she passed through the arch and into the safety of the corridor beyond.

Narrow-eyed, Vane watched her go, watched her hips sway as she glided along. He remained in the archway until she reached her door. He heard it shut behind her.

Slowly, very slowly, his features eased, then a Cynster smile tugged at his lips. If he couldn't escape fate, then, *ipso facto*, neither could she. Which meant she would be his. The prospect grew more alluring by the minute.

Chapter 5

It was time to act.

Later that evening, waiting in the drawing room for the gentlemen to reappear, Patience found it increasingly difficult to live up to her name; inside, she mentally paced. Beside her, Angela and Mrs. Chadwick, occupying a settee, were discussing the best trim for Angela's new morning gown. Nodding vaguely, Patience didn't even hear them. She had weightier matters on her mind.

A dull ache throbbed behind her temples; she hadn't slept well. Worries had consumed her—worry over the increasingly pointed accusations aimed at Gerrard, worry over Vane Cynster's influence on her impressionable brother.

Added to that, she now had to cope with the distraction occasioned by her odd reaction to Vane Cynster, "elegant gentleman." He'd affected her from the first; when she'd finally succumbed to sleep, he'd even followed her into her dreams.

Patience narrowed her eyes against the ache behind them.

"I think the cerise braid would be *much* more dashing." Angela threatened a pout. "Don't you think so, Patience?"

The gown they were discussing was palest yellow. "I think," Patience said, summoning up what she could of that virtue, "that the aquamarine ribbon your mother suggested would be much more the thing."

Angela's pout materialized; Mrs. Chadwick promptly warned her daughter of the unwisdom of courting wrinkles. The pout magically vanished.

Drumming her fingers on the arm of her chair, Patience frowned at the door and returned to her preoccupation—to rehearsing her warning to Vane Cynster. It was the first time she'd had to warn any male off—she would much rather she didn't have to start now, but she couldn't let things go on as they were. Quite aside from her promise to her mother, tendered on her deathbed, that she would always keep Gerrard safe, she simply couldn't countenance Gerrard getting hurt in such a way—by being used as a pawn to win her smiles.

Of course, they all did it to some degree. Penwick treated Gerrard as a child, playing to her protectiveness. Edmond used his art as a link to Gerrard, to demonstrate his affinity with her brother. Henry pretended an avuncular interest patently lacking in real emotion. Vane, however, went one better—he actually did things. Actively protected Gerrard, actively engaged her brother's interest, actively interacted— all with the avowed intention of making her grateful, of placing her in his debt.

She didn't like it. They were all using Gerrard, but the only one from whom Gerrard stood in danger of taking any hurt was Vane. Because the only one Gerrard liked, admired, potentially worshiped, was Vane.

Patience surreptitiously massaged her left temple. If they didn't finish with the port soon, she would have a raging migraine. She would probably have one anyway—after her disturbed night, followed by the surprises of the breakfast table, capped by the revelations of their ride, she'd spent most of the afternoon thinking of Vane. Which was enough to warp the strongest mind.

He distracted her on so many levels she'd given up trying to untangle her thoughts. There was, she felt sure, only one way to deal with him. Directly and decisively.

Her eyes felt gravelly, from staring unblinking at nothing for too long. She felt like she hadn't slept in days. And she certainly wouldn't sleep until she'd taken charge of the situation, until she'd put a stop to the relationship developing between Gerrard and Vane. True, all she'd seen and heard between them thus far had been innocent enough—but no one—*no one*—could call Vane innocent.

He wasn't innocent—but Gerrard was.

Which was precisely her point.

At least, she thought it was. Patience winced as pain shafted from one temple to the other.

The door opened; Patience sat up. She scanned the gentlemen as they wandered in—Vane was the last. He strolled in, which was of itself enough to assure her that her tortuous reasoning was right. All that prowling, arrogant masculinity set her teeth on edge.

"Mr. Cynster!" Without a blush, Angela beckoned. Patience could have kissed her.

Vane heard Angela and saw her wave; his gaze flicked to Patience, then, with a smile she unhesitatingly classed as untrustworthy, he prowled in their direction.

As a group, the three of them—Mrs. Chadwick, Angela, and Patience—rose to greet him, none wishing to risk a crick in the neck.

"I wanted to ask particularly," Angela said, before anyone else could essay a word, "whether it's true that cerise is currently the most *fashionable* color for trimming for young ladies."

"It's certainly much favored," Vane replied.

"But not on pale yellow," Patience said.

Vane looked at her. "I devoutly hope not."

"Indeed." Patience took his arm. "If you'll excuse us, Angela, ma'am"—she nodded to Mrs. Chadwick—"I have something I really must ask Mr. Cynster." So saying, she steered Vane toward the far end of the room—and thanked the deity he consented to move.

She felt his gaze, slightly surprised, distinctly amused, on her face. "My dear Miss Debbington." Beneath her hand, his arm twisted—and then he was steering her. "You need only say the word."

Patience flashed him a narrow-eyed glance. The purring tones in his voice sent shivers down her spine—delicious shivers. "I'm very glad to hear you say that, for that's precisely what I intend to do."

His brows rose. He searched her face, then raised a hand and gently rubbed one fingertip between her brows.

Patience stilled, shocked, then drew her head back.

"Don't do that!" A warm glow suffused the area he'd touched.

"You were frowning—you look like you have a headache."

Patience frowned harder. They'd reached the end of the room; halting, she swung to face him. And plunged into the attack. "I take it you're not leaving tomorrow?"

He looked down at her. After a moment, he replied, "I can't see myself departing in the foreseeable future. Can you?"

She had to be sure. Patience met his gaze directly. "Why are you staying?"

Vane studied her face, her eyes—and wondered what was bothering her. The feminine tension gripping her rippled about him; he translated it as "bee in her bonnet," but, from long association with strong-willed women, his mother and aunts, let alone Devil's new duchess, Honoria, he had learned the wisdom of caution. Uncertain of her tack, he temporized. "Why do you imagine?" He raised one brow. "What, after all, could possibly exercise sufficient interest to hold a gentleman like me, here?"

He knew the answer, of course. Last night, he'd seen how the land lay. There were situations where justice, blindfolded as she was, could easily be misled—the situation here was one such. The undercurrents were considerable, running unexpectedly, inexplicably, deep.

He was staying to help Minnie, to defend Gerrard—and to aid Patience, preferably without letting on he was aiding her. Pride was something he understood; he was sensitive to hers. Unlike the other gentlemen, he saw no reason to suggest that she'd failed in any way with Gerrard. As far as he could tell, she hadn't. So it could be said he was acting as her protector, too. The role felt very right.

He'd capped his question with a charming smile; to his surprise, it made Patience stiffen.

She drew herself up, clasped her hands before her, and fixed him with a censorious look. "In that case, I'm afraid I must insist that you refrain from encouraging Gerrard."

Inwardly, Vane stilled. He looked down, into her disapproving eyes. "What, exactly, do you mean by that?"

Her chin rose. "You know very well what I mean."

"Spell it out for me."

Her eyes, like clear agates, searched his, then her lips compressed. "I would rather you spent as little time as possible with Gerrard. You're only showing an interest in him to win points with me."

Vane arched one brow. "You take a lot to yourself, my dear."

Patience held his gaze. "Can you deny it?"

Vane felt his face set, his jaw lock. He couldn't refute her accusation; it was in large part true. "What I don't understand," he murmured, his eyes narrowing on hers, "is why my interaction with your brother should occasion the slightest concern. I would have thought you would be glad to have someone extend his horizons."

"I would be," Patience snapped. Her head was pounding. "But you're the very last person I would want to guide him."

"Why the devil not?"

The steel sliding beneath Vane's deep voice was a warning. Patience heard it. She was heading for thin ice, but, having come thus far, she was determined not to retreat. She set her teeth. "I don't want you guiding Gerrard, filling his head with ideas, because of the sort of gentleman you are."

"And what sort of gentleman am I—in your eyes?"

Rather than rising, his tone was becoming softer, more lethal. Patience quelled a shiver, and returned his edged glance with one equally sharp. "In this instance, your reputation is the opposite of a recommendation."

"How would you know of my reputation? You've been buried in Derbyshire all your life."

"It precedes you," Patience retorted, stung by his patronizing tone. "You only need walk into a room, and it rolls out like a red carpet before you."

Her sweeping gesture elicited a grunt. "You don't know what you're talking about."

Patience lost her temper. "What I'm talking about is your propensities with respect to wine, women, and wagering. And, believe me, they're obvious to the meanest intelligence! You may as well have a banner carried before you." With her hands, she sketched one in the air. "Gentleman rake!"

Vane shifted; he was suddenly closer. "I believe I warned you I was no gentleman."

Looking into his face, Patience swallowed, and wondered how she could possibly have forgotten. There was nothing remotely gentlemanly in the presence before her—his face was hard, his eyes pure steel. Even his austerely elegant attire now seemed more like armor. And his voice no longer purred. At all. Clenching her fists, she drew a tight breath. "I don't want Gerrard turning out like you. I don't want you to—" Despite her best efforts, innate caution took hold—it froze her tongue.

Almost shaking with the effort of restraining his temper, Vane heard himself suggest, his tone sibilantly smooth, "Corrupt him?"

Patience stiffened. She lifted her chin, her lids veiling her eyes. "I didn't say that."

"Don't fence with me, Miss Debbington, or you're liable to get pinked." Vane spoke slowly, softly, only just managing to get the words past his teeth. "Let's be sure I have this correctly. You believe I've stayed at Bellamy Hall *purely* to dally with you, that I've befriended your brother *for no other reason* than to further my cause with you, and that my character is such that you consider me unsuitable company for a minor. Have I forgotten anything?"

Poker-straight, Patience met his eyes. "I don't think so."

Vane felt his control quake, felt his reins slither from his grasp. He clenched his jaw, and both fists. Every muscle in his body locked, every mental sinew strained with the effort of holding on to his temper.

All Cynsters had one—a temper that normally lazed like a well-fed cat but could, if pricked, change to a snarling predator. For one instant, his vision clouded, then the beast responded to the rein and drew back, hissing. As his fury subsided, he blinked dazedly.

Hauling in a deep breath, he swung halfway around and, dragging his gaze from Patience, forced himself to scan the room. Slowly, he exhaled. "If you were a man, my dear, you wouldn't still be upright."

There was an instant's pause, then she said, "Not even you would strike a lady."

Her "not even" nearly set him off again. Jaw clenched, Vane slowly turned his head, caught her wide hazel gaze—and raised his brows. His hand itched to make contact with her bottom. Positively burned. For one instant, he teetered on the brink—her widening gaze, as, frozen like prey, she read the intent in his eyes, was small comfort. But the thought of Minnie made him fight down the nearly over-powering compulsion to bring Miss Patience Debbington to an abrupt understanding of her temerity. Minnie, sup-portive though she was, was unlikely to prove *that* forgiv-ing. Vane narrowed his eyes, and spoke very softly. "I have only one thing to say to you, Patience Debbington. You're *wrong*—on every count."

He turned on his heel and stalked off.

Patience watched him go, watched him stride directly across the room, looking neither left nor right. There was nothing languid in his stride, no vestige of his usual lazy grace; his every movement, the rigid set of his shoulders, shrieked of reined power, of temper, of fury barely leashed. He opened the door and, without even a nod to Minnie, left; the door clicked shut behind him.

Patience frowned. Her head throbbed remorselessly; she felt empty and—yes—cold inside. As if she'd just done something terribly wrong. As if she'd just made a big mis-take. But she hadn't, had she?

She woke the next morning to a grey and dripping world. Through one eye, Patience stared at the unrelenting gloom beyond her window, then groaned and buried her head be-neath the covers. She felt the dipping of the mattress as Myst jumped up, then padded closer. Settling against the curve of her stomach, Myst purred.

Patience sank her head deeper into her pillow. This was clearly a morning to avoid.

She dragged her limbs from the comfort of her bed an hour later. Shivering in the chilly air, she hurriedly dressed, then reluctantly headed downstairs. She had to eat, and cowardice was not, in her book, sufficient reason to put the staff to the unexpected trouble of making up a tray for her. She noted the time as she passed the clock on the stairs—nearly ten o'clock. Everyone else should have finished and departed; she should be safe.

She walked into the breakfast parlor—and discovered her error. *All* the gentlemen were present. As they rose to greet her most nodded benignly—Henry and Edmond even conjured smiles. Vane, at the head of the table, didn't smile at all. His grey gaze settled on her, coldly brooding. Not a muscle in his face flickered.

Gerrard, of course, beamed a welcome. Patience summoned a weak smile. Steps dragging, she headed for the sideboard.

She took her time filling her plate, then slipped into the chair beside Gerrard, wishing he was somewhat larger. Large enough to shield her from Vane's darkling gaze. Unfortunately, Gerrard had finished all but his coffee; he lay sprawled comfortably back in his chair.

Leaving her exposed. Patience bit her tongue against the impulse to tell Gerrard to sit straight; he was still too coltish to bring off that lounging pose. Unlike the gentleman he was copying, who brought it off all too well. Patience kept her eyes on her plate and her mind on eating. Other than the brooding presence at the head of the table, there was precious little other distraction.

As Masters cleared their plates, the gentlemen fell to discussing the day's possibilities. Henry looked at Patience. "Perhaps, Miss Debbington, if the skies clear, you might be interested in a short walk?"

Patience glanced very briefly at the sky beyond the windows. "Too muddy," she pronounced.

Edmond's eyes gleamed. "How about charades?"

Patience's lips thinned. "Perhaps later." She was in a waspish mood; if they weren't careful, she'd sting.

"There's a pack of cards in the library," Edgar volunteered.

The General, predictably, snorted. "Chess," he stated. "Game of kings. That's what I shall do. Any takers?"

There were no volunteers. The General subsided into vague mutterings.

Gerrard turned to Vane. "How about a round of billiards?"

One of Vane's brows rose; his gaze remained on Gerrard's face, yet, watching him from beneath her lashes, Patience knew his attention was on her. Then he looked directly at her. "A capital idea," he purred, then both voice and face hardened. "But perhaps your sister has other plans for you."

His words were soft, distinct, and clearly loaded with some greater significance. Patience ground her teeth. She was avoiding his eye; he was focusing every eye on her. Not content with that, he was making no attempt to mask the coolness between them. It colored his words, his expression; it positively shrieked in the absence of his suavely charming smile. He sat very still, his gaze unwaveringly fixed on her. His grey eyes were coldly challenging.

It was Gerrard, the only one of the company apparently insensitive to the powerful undercurrent, who broke the increasingly awkward silence. "Oh, Patience won't want me about, under her feet." He flicked a confident grin her way, then turned back to Vane.

Vane's gaze didn't shift. "I rather think that's for your sister to say."

Setting down her teacup, Patience lifted one shoulder. "I can't see any reason you shouldn't play billiards." She made the comment to Gerrard, steadfastly ignoring Vane. Then she pushed back her chair. "And now, if you'll excuse me, I must look in on Minnie."

They all rose as she stood; Patience walked to the door, conscious of one particular gaze on her back, focused right between her shoulder blades.

There was nothing wrong with playing billiards.

Patience kept telling herself that, but didn't believe it. It wasn't the billiards that worried her. It was the chatting, the easy camaraderie that the exercise promoted—the very sort of interaction she did not wish Gerrard to engage in with *any* elegant gentleman.

Just the knowledge that he and Vane were busily potting

balls and exchanging God knew what observations on life reduced her to nervous distraction.

Which was why, half an hour after she'd seen Gerrard and Vane head for the billiard room, she slipped into the adjacent conservatory. One section of the irregularly shaped garden room overlooked one end of the billiard room. Screened by an assortment of palms, Patience peered between the fringed leaves.

She could see half the table. Gerrard stood leaning on his cue beyond it. He was talking; he paused, then laughed. Patience gritted her teeth.

Then Vane came into view. His back to her, he moved around the table, studying the disposition of the balls. He'd taken off his coat; in form-fitting waistcoat and soft white shirt, he looked, if anything, even larger, more physically powerful, than before.

He halted at the corner of the table. Leaning over, he lined up his shot. Muscles shifted beneath his tight waistcoat; Patience stared, then blinked.

Her mouth was dry. Licking her lips, she refocused. Vane took his shot, then, watching the ball, slowly straightened. Patience frowned, and licked her lips again.

With a satisfied smile, Vane circled the table and stopped by Gerrard's side. He made some comment; Gerrard grinned.

Patience squirmed. She wasn't even eavesdropping, yet she felt guilty—guilty of not having faith in Gerrard. She should leave. Her gaze went again to Vane, taking in his lean, undeniably elegant form; her feet remained glued to the conservatory tiles.

Then someone else came into view, pacing about the table. Edmond. He looked back up the table and spoke to someone out of her sight.

Patience waited. Eventually, Henry came into view. Patience sighed. Then she turned and left the conservatory.

The afternoon continued damp and dreary. Grey clouds lowered, shutting them in the house. After luncheon, Patience, with Minnie and Timms, retired to the back parlor to set stitches by candlelight. Gerrard had decided to sketch settings for Edmond's drama; together with Edmond, he climbed to the old nurseries for an unrestricted view of the ruins.

Vane had disappeared, only God knew where.

Satisfied Gerrard was safe, Patience embroidered meadow grasses on a new set of cloths for the drawing room. Minnie sat dozing in an armchair by the fire; Timms, ensconced in its mate, busily plied her needle. The mantelpiece clock ticked on, marking the slow passage of the afternoon.

"Ah, me," Minnie eventually sighed. She stretched her legs, then fluffed up her shawls and glanced at the darkening sky. "I must say, it's a huge relief that Vane agreed to stay."

Patience's hand stopped in midair. After a moment, she lowered the needle to the linen. "Agreed?" Head down, she carefully set her stitch.

"Hmm—he was on his way to Wrexford's, that's why he was passing so close when the storm struck." Minnie snorted. "I can just imagine what devilry that crew had planned, but, of course, once I asked, Vane immediately agreed to stay." She sighed fondly. "No matter what else one might say of the Cynsters, they're always reliable."

Patience frowned at her stitches. "Reliable?"

Timms exchanged a grin with Minnie. "In some ways, they're remarkably predictable—you can always rely on help if needed. Sometimes, even if you don't ask for it."

"Indeed." Minnie chuckled. "They can be quite terrifyingly protective. Naturally, as soon as I mentioned the Spectre and the thief, Vane wasn't going anywhere."

"He'll clear up this nonsense." Timms's confidence was transparent.

Patience stared at her creation—and saw a hard-edged face with grey, accusing eyes. The lump of cold iron that had settled in her stomach the previous night grew colder. Weightier.

Her head throbbed. She closed her eyes, then snapped them open as a truly sickening thought occurred. It couldn't be, wouldn't be, true—but the dreadful premonition wouldn't go away. "Ah..." She tugged her last stitch tight. "Who are the Cynsters, exactly?"

"The family holds the dukedom of St. Ives." Minnie settled herself comfortably. "The principal seat is Somersham Place, in Cambridgeshire. That's where Vane was coming from. Devil's the sixth duke; Vane's his first cousin. They've been close from the cradle, born a mere four months apart. But the family's quite large."

"Mrs. Chadwick mentioned six cousins," Patience prompted.

"Oh, there's more than that, but she would have been referring to the Bar Cynster."

"The Bar Cynster?" Patience looked up.

Timms grinned. "That's the nickname the *ton*'s gentlemen use to refer to the six eldest cousins. They're all male." Her grin widened. "In every way."

"Indeed." Minnie's eyes twinkled. "The six of them all together are a veritable sight to behold. Known to make weak females swoon."

Looking down at her stitching, Patience swallowed an acid retort. Elegant gentlemen, all, it seemed. The lead weight in her stomach lightened; she felt better. "Mrs. Chadwick said that . . . Devil had recently married."

"Last year," Minnie corroborated. "His heir was christened about three weeks ago."

Frowning, Patience looked at Minnie. "Is that his real name—Devil?"

Minnie grinned. "Sylvester Sebastian—but better, and, to my mind, more accurately known as Devil."

Patience's frown grew. "Is 'Vane' Vane's real name?"

Minnie chuckled evilly. "Spencer Archibald—and if you dare call him that to his face, you'll be braver than any other in the *ton*. Only his mother can still do so with impunity. He's been known as Vane since before he went to Eton. Devil named him—said he always knew which way the wind was blowing and what was in the breeze." Minnie raised her brows. "Oddly far-sighted of Devil, actually, for there's no doubt that's true. Instinctively intuitive, Vane, when all's said and done."

Minnie fell pensive; after two minutes, Patience shook

out her cloth. "I suppose the Cynsters—at least, the Bar Cynster—are . . ." Vaguely, she gestured. "Well, the usual gentlemen about town."

Timms snorted. "It would be more accurate to say that they're the pattern card for 'gentlemen about town.' "

"All within the accepted limits, of course." Minnie folded her hands across her ample stomach. "The Cynsters are one of the oldest families in the *ton*. I doubt any of them could be bad *ton*, not even if they tried—quite out of character for them. They might be outrageous, they might be the *ton*'s most reckless hedonists, they might sail within a whisker of that invisible line—but you can guarantee they'll never cross it." Again, she chuckled. "And if any of them sailed too close to the wind, they'd hear about it— from their mothers, their aunts—and the new duchess. Honoria's certainly no insipid cypher."

Timms grinned. "It's said the only one capable of taming a Cynster male is a Cynster woman—by which they mean a Cynster wife. Strange to tell, that's proved true, generation after generation. And if Honoria's any guide, then the Bar Cynster are not going to escape that fate."

Patience frowned. Her previously neat, coherent mental image of Vane as a typical, if not the archetype, "elegant gentleman" had started to blur. A reliable protector, amenable if not positively subject to the opinions of the women in his family—none of that sounded the least like her father. Or the others—the officers from the regiments based about Chesterfield who had so tried to impress her, the London friends of neighbors who, hearing of her fortune, had called, thinking to beguile her with their practiced smiles. In many respects, Vane fitted the bill to perfection, yet the Cynster attitudes Minnie had expounded were quite contrary to her expectations.

Grimacing, Patience started on a new sheaf of grasses. "Vane said something about being in Cambridgeshire to attend a church service."

"Yes, indeed."

Detecting amusement in Minnie's tone, Patience looked up, and saw Minnie exchange a laughing glance with Timms. Then Minnie looked at her. "Vane's mother wrote to me about it. Seems the five unmarried members of the Bar Cynster got ideas above their station. They ran a wagers book on the date of conception of Devil's heir. Honoria heard of it at the christening—she promptly confiscated all their winnings for the new church roof and decreed they all attend the dedication service." A smile wreathing her face, Minnie nodded. "They did, too."

Patience blinked and lowered her work to her lap. "You mean," she said, "that just because the duchess said they had to, they did?"

Minnie grinned. "If you'd met Honoria, you wouldn't be so surprised."

"But . . ." Brow furrowing, Patience tried to imagine it—tried to imagine a woman ordering Vane to do something he didn't wish to do. "The duke can't be very assertive."

Timms snorted, choked, then succumbed to gales of laughter; Minnie was similarly stricken. Patience watched them double up with mirth—adopting a long-suffering expression, she waited with feigned patience.

Eventually, Minnie choked her way to a stop and mopped her streaming eyes. "Oh, dear—that's the most ridiculously funny—ridiculously *wrong*—statement I've ever heard."

"Devil," Timms said, in between hiccups, "is the most outrageously arrogant dictator you're ever likely to meet."

"If you think Vane is bad, just remember it was Devil who was born to be a duke." Minnie shook her head. "Oh, my—just the thought of a nonassertive Devil . . ." Mirth threatened to overwhelm her again.

"Well," Patience said, frowning still, "he doesn't sound particularly strong, allowing his duchess to dictate to his cousins over what is held to be a male prerogative."

"Ah, but Devil's no fool—he could hardly gainsay Honoria on such a matter. And, of course, the reason Cynster men always indulge their wives was very much to the fore."

"The reason?" Patience asked.

"Family," Timms replied. "They were all gathered for the christening."

"Very family-focused, the Cynsters." Minnie nodded.

"Even the Bar Cynster—they're always so good with children. Entirely trustworthy and utterly reliable. Probably comes from being such a large brood—they always were a *prolific* lot. The older ones are used to having younger brothers and sisters to watch out for."

Cold, heavy, the weight of dismay started to coalesce in Patience's stomach.

"Actually," Minnie said, chins wobbling as she resettled her shawls, "I'm very glad Vane will be staying for a while. He'll give Gerrard a few hints on how to go on— just the thing to prepare him for London."

Minnie looked up; Patience looked down. The lump of cold iron swelled enormously; it sank straight through her stomach and settled in her gut.

In her head, she replayed her words to Vane, the thinly veiled insults she'd leveled at him in the drawing room the previous night.

Her gut clenched hard about the lump of cold iron. She felt positively ill.

Chapter 6

The next morning, Patience descended the stairs, a brittlely bright smile on her face. She swept into the breakfast parlor and nodded with determined cheerfulness to the gentlemen sitting at the table. Her smile froze, just for an instant, when she saw, wonder of wonders, Angela Chadwick, chatting loquaciously, greatly animated, in the chair to Vane's left.

He sat at the table's head as usual; Patience allowed her smile to flow over him, but didn't meet his eyes. Despite Angela's outpourings, from the moment she'd appeared, Vane's attention had fixed on her. She helped herself to kedgeree and kippers, then, with a smile for Masters as he held her chair, took her place beside Gerrard.

Angela immediately appealed to her. "I was just saying to Mr. Cynster that it would be *such* a welcome diversion if we could get up a party to go to Northampton. Just *think* of all the shops!" Eyes bright, she looked earnestly at Patience. "Don't you think that's a *wonderful* idea?"

For one instant, Patience was sorely tempted to agree. Anything—even a day shopping with Angela—was preferable to facing what had to be faced. Then the idea of sending Vane shopping with Angela occurred. The vision that rose in her mind, of him in some milliner's establishment, teeth gritted as he coped with Angela's witlessness, was priceless. She couldn't stop herself glancing up the table . . . her priceless image evaporated. Vane wasn't interested in Angela's wardrobe. His grey gaze was fixed on her face; his expression was impassive, but there was a frown in his eyes. He narrowed them slightly, as if he could see through her facade.

Patience immediately looked at Angela and increased the intensity of her smile. "I think it's a little far to do much shopping in a day. Perhaps you should ask Henry to escort you and your mother down for a few days?"

Angela looked much struck; she leaned forward to consult Henry, farther down the table.

"It looks like it'll stay fine." Gerrard glanced at Patience. "I think I'll take my easel out and make a start on the scenes Edmond and I decided on yesterday."

Patience nodded.

"Actually"—Vane lowered his voice so its rumble ran beneath Angela's excited chatter—"I wondered if you'd show me the areas you've been sketching."

Patience looked up; Vane trapped her gaze.

"If"—his voice turned steely—"your sister approves?"

Patience inclined her head graciously. "I think that's an excellent idea."

A frown flashed through Vane's eyes; Patience looked down at her plate.

"But what can we do today?" Angela looked about, clearly expecting an answer.

Patience held her breath, but Vane remained silent.

"I'm going sketching," Gerrard declared, "and I won't want to be disturbed. Why don't you go for a walk?"

"Don't be silly," Angela returned scornfully. "It's far too wet to go strolling."

Patience inwardly grimaced and forked up her last mouthful of kedgeree.

"Well then," Gerrard retorted, "you'll just have to amuse yourself doing whatever it is that young ladies do."

"I will," Angela declared. "I'll read to Mama in the front parlor." So saying, she stood. As the gentlemen rose, Patience blotted her lips with her napkin and grasped the moment to make her exit, too.

She needed to hunt out her most waterproof walking shoes.

An hour later, she stood at the side door and surveyed

the expanse of sodden grass between her and the ruins. Between her and the apology she had to make. A brisk breeze was blowing, carrying the scent of rain; there seemed little likelihood the grass would dry soon. Patience grimaced and glanced down at Myst, sitting neatly beside her. "I suppose it's part of my penance."

Myst looked up, enigmatic as ever, and twitched her tail.

Patience determinedly stepped out. In one hand, she twirled her furled parasol; there was just enough weak sunshine to excuse it, but she'd really picked it up simply to have something in her hands. Something to fiddle with, something defensive—something to glance at if things got truly bothersome.

Ten yards from the door, and the hem of her lilac walking dress was wet. Patience gritted her teeth and glanced around for Myst—and realized the cat wasn't there. Looking back, she saw Myst, sitting primly on the stone stoop of the side door. Patience pulled a face at her. "Fine-weather friend," she muttered, and resumed her stroll.

Her hem got wetter and wetter; gradually, water found its way through the seams of her kid boots. Patience doggedly slogged on. Wet feet might be part of her penance, but she was sure it would be the lesser part. Vane, she was certain, would provide the greater.

Abruptly, she pushed that thought aside—it was not a thought she need dwell on. What was to come would not be easy, but if she allowed herself to think too much, her courage would desert her.

Quite how she had come to be so wrong she really couldn't fathom. To have been wrong on one point would have been bad enough, but to find herself so comprehensively off target was incomprehensible.

As she detoured around the first of the fallen stones, her jaw set. It wasn't fair. He *looked* like an elegant gentleman. He *moved* like an elegant gentleman. In many ways, he *behaved* like an elegant gentleman! How could she have known that in nonphysical ways he was so different?

She clung to the thought, trying it on for comfort, seeing if it would bolster her courage—then relucantly shrugged it aside. She couldn't duck the fact that she was very much at fault. She'd judged Vane entirely by his wolf's clothing. Although he was, indeed, a wolf, he was, apparently, a *caring* wolf.

There was no way out but to apologize. Her self-respect wouldn't accept anything less; she didn't think he would either.

Reaching the ruins proper, she looked about. Her eyes ached; she'd got even less sleep last night than she had the night before. "Where are they?" she muttered. If she could get this over with, and free her mind of its most vexing problem, perhaps she could nap this afternoon.

But first, she had to give the wolf his due. She was here to apologize. She wanted to do it quickly—before she lost her nerve.

"Really? I didn't know that."

Gerrard's voice led her to the old cloisters. His easel before him, he was sketching the arches along one side. Stepping into the open courtyard, Patience searched—and spotted Vane lounging in the shadows of a half-shattered cloister arch some paces behind Gerrard.

Vane had already spotted her.

Gerrard glanced up as her boots scraped on the flags. "Hello. Vane's just been telling me that sketching's considered quite the thing among the *ton* at present. Apparently, the Royal Academy holds an exhibition every year." Charcoal in hand, he turned back to his sketch.

"Oh?" Her gaze on Vane, Patience wished she could see his eyes. His expression was unreadable. Shoulders propped against the stone arch, arms folded across his chest, he watched her like a hawk. A brooding, potentially menacing hawk. Or a wolf anticipating a meal.

Giving herself a mental shake, she stepped up to Gerrard's shoulder. "Perhaps we can visit the Academy when we go up to town."

"Hmm," Gerrard said, entirely absorbed with his work.

Patience studied Gerrard's sketch.

Vane studied her. He'd seen her the instant she'd appeared, framed by a break in the old wall. He'd known she was near an instant before that, warned by some sixth sense, by a faint ripple in the atmosphere. She drew his senses like a lodestone. Which, at present, was not helpful.

Gritting his teeth, he fought to block his memories of the previous night from crystallizing in his mind. Every time they did, his temper took flight, which, given she was near, within easy reach, was the opposite of wise. His temper was very like a sword—once unsheathed, it was all cold steel. And it took real effort to resheathe it. Something he hadn't yet accomplished.

If Miss Patience Debbington was wise, she would keep her distance until he had.

If he was wise, he'd do the same.

His gaze, dwelling, entirely without his permission, on her curves, on the play of her skirts about her legs, dropped to inspect her ankles. She was wearing kid half boots—and her skirts were distinctly wet.

Inwardly, Vane frowned. He stared at her wet hems. She *had* changed tack—he'd thought she had over breakfast, then dismissed the idea as hopeful fancy. He couldn't see why she would have changed her mind. He'd already convinced himself there was nothing he could say to refute her accusations—they all held a grain of truth, and, if he was honest, he'd set himself up with his attempts at masterful manipulation. He'd concluded there was only one way to correct her misguided notions—he would *prove* them wrong, not by word, but by deed. And then he would be able to savor her confusion, and her apologies.

Straightening, pushing away from the stone arch, Vane realized that, somehow or other, her apologies were coming early. He wasn't about to place extra hurdles in her path. Slowly, he strolled forward.

Patience was instantly aware of him. She glanced swiftly his way, then looked back at Gerrard's sketch. "Will you be much longer?"

"Hours," Gerrard replied.

"Well . . ." Patience lifted her head and boldly met Vane's eyes. "I wonder, Mr. Cynster, if I could prevail on you to lend me your arm back to the house. It's more slippery than I'd thought. Some of the stones are quite treacherous."

Vane raised one brow. "Indeed?" Smoothly, he offered

her his arm. "I know a route back that has a number of advantages."

Patience shot him a suspicious look, but she placed her fingers on his sleeve and allowed him to turn her toward the old church. Gerrard absentmindedly acknowledged their good-byes, and Patience's sisterly admonition to return to the house in time for lunch.

Giving her no time to think of anything further to tell Gerrard, Vane led her into the nave. The single remaining arch soared above them; within minutes they were out of Gerrard's sight and hearing, strolling side by side down the long central aisle.

"Thank you." Patience made to lift her hand from his sleeve; Vane covered it with his.

He felt her fingers jerk, then still, sensed the ripple of awareness that streaked through her. Her head came up, chin tilting, lips firming. He caught her gaze. "Your hems are wet."

Hazel eyes flashed. "So are my feet."

"Which suggests you came on this expedition for a purpose."

She looked forward. Vane watched, with interest, as her breasts swelled, straining the bodice of her dress.

"Indeed. I came to aplogize."

The words were bitten off, uttered through clenched teeth.

"Oh? Why?"

Abruptly, she stopped and, eyes narrowing, faced him. "Because I believe I owe you an apology."

Vane smiled, directly into her eyes. He didn't try to hide his steel. "You do."

Lips compressed, Patience met his gaze, then nodded. "So I apprehend." She drew herself up, clasping her hands on the top of her parasol, tilting her chin determinedly. "I apologize."

"For what, exactly?"

One long look into his grey eyes told Patience she was not going to escape lightly. She narrowed her eyes anew. "For casting unjustified aspersions on your character."

She could see him considering, matching that against her

unwise words. Rapidly, she did the same. "And your motives," she grudgingly added. Then she thought again. And frowned. "At least, some of them."

His lips twitched. "Definitely only some of them."

His voice had regained its purr; a shivery sensation slid down Patience's spine.

"Just to be clear, I take it you rescind absolutely all your *unjustified* claims?"

He was teasing her; the light in his eyes was definitely untrustworthy. "Unreservedly," Patience snapped. "There! Now what more can you want?"

"A kiss."

The answer came back so fast, so definitely, Patience's head whirled. "A kiss?"

He merely raised one arrogant brow, as if the suggestion barely rated a blink. None-too-subtle challenge lit his eyes. Patience frowned and bit her lip. They stood in the open central aisle, nothing within yards of them. Totally unscreened, totally exposed. Hardly a site that lent itself to impropriety. "Oh, very well."

Swiftly, she stretched on her toes; putting one hand on his shoulder for balance, she placed a quick peck on his cheek.

His eyes opened wide, then filled with laughter—more laughter than she could stand.

"Oh, no." He shook his head. "*Not* that sort of kiss."

She didn't need to ask what sort of kiss he wanted. Patience focused on his lips—long, lean, hard. Fascinating. They were not going to get any less fascinating. Indeed, the longer she contemplated them . . .

Hauling in a quick breath, she held it, stretched upward, shut her eyes, and fleetingly touched her lips to his. They were as hard as she'd imagined, very like sculpted marble. Sensation flared at the brief contact; her lips tingled, then throbbed.

Patience blinked her eyes wide as she lowered her heels to earth. And refocused on his lips. She saw the ends curve upward, heard his low, wickedly teasing laugh.

"Still not right. Here—let me show you."

His hands came up to frame her face, her jaw, tilting her

lips up as his descended. Of their own volition, her lids fell, then his lips touched hers. Patience couldn't have quelled the shudder that passed through her had her life depended on it.

Stunned, poised to resist, she mentally paused. Strong, sure, his lips covered hers, moving slowly, langorously, as if savoring her taste, her texture. There was nothing threatening in the unhurried caress. Indeed, it was beguiling, luring her senses, focusing them on the practiced slide and glide of cool lips which seemed to instinctively know how to soothe the heat rising in hers. Hers throbbed; his pressed, caressed, as if drinking in her heat, stealing it from her.

Patience felt her lips soften; his firmed in response.

No, no, noo. . . . Some small part of her mind tried to warn her, but she was long past listening. This was new, novel—she'd never felt such sensations before. Never known such simple delight existed.

Her head was whirling, but not unpleasantly. His lips still seemed hard, cool—Patience couldn't resist the temptation to return the pressure, to see if his lips would soften to hers.

They didn't, they only became harder. The next instant, she felt a searing heat sweep over her lips. She stilled; the questing heat returned—with the tip of his tongue, he traced her lower lip. The contact lingered, an unspoken question.

Patience wanted more. She parted her lips.

His tongue slid between, slowly, with his customary assured arrogance, quite certain of his welcome, confident in his expertise.

Vane held the reins of his desire in a grip of iron and refused to let his demons loose. Deep, primal instincts urged him on; experience held him back.

She'd never yielded her mouth to any man, never shared her lips willingly. He knew that absolutely, sensed the truth in her untutored response, read it in her lack of guile. But she was rising to him, her passion, her desire, answering his call, sweet as the dew on a crisp spring morning, virginal as snow on an inaccessible peak.

He could reach her—she would be his. But there was no

need for any hurry. She was untouched, unused to the demands of a man's hands, a man's lips, much less a man's body; if he pressed too fast, she'd turn skittish and balk. And he'd have to work harder to bring her to his bed.

Angling his head over hers, he kept every caress slow, every plundering stroke deliberate. Passion lay heavy, languid, almost somnolent between them; as he claimed every sweet inch of the softness she offered him, he laced the heady sensation into every caress, and let it sink into her senses.

It would lie there, dormant, until next time he touched her, until he called it forth. He would let it rise by degrees, feed it, nurture it until it became the inescapable compulsion that would, in the end, bring her to him.

He would savor her slowly, savor her slow surrender—all the more sweet because the end was never in doubt.

Distant voices reached him; inwardly, he sighed, and reluctantly brought the kiss to an end.

He raised his head. Patience's eyes slowly opened, then she blinked, and stared straight at him. For one instant, the look on her face, in her eyes, had him puzzled—then he recognized it. Curious—she wasn't shocked, stunned, or thrown into a maidenly fluster. She was curious.

Vane couldn't stop his rakish grin. Nor could he resist the temptation to brush his lips overs hers one last time.

"What are you doing?" Patience whispered as his head bent to hers. Even at close quarters, she could still see his smile.

"It's called 'kiss and make up.' " The curve of his lips deepened. "It's what lovers do when they fall out."

A vise locked about Patience's heart; panic—it had to be that—streaked through her. "We aren't lovers."

"Yet."

His lips touched hers and she shivered. "We never will be." She might be giddy, but she was quite sure of that.

He stilled, but his confident smile didn't waver. "Don't wager your fortune on it." Again, his lips brushed hers.

Patience's head reeled. To her relief, he straightened and drew back, looking over her head. "Here they come."

She blinked. "They who?"

He looked down at her. "Your harem."

"My *what*?"

His brows rose in unlikely innocence. "Isn't that the correct term for a group of slaves of the opposite sex?"

Patience dragged in a deep breath—she straightened, flicked him a warning glance, then turned. To meet Penwick, Henry, and Edmond, all striding up the aisle. Beneath her breath, Patience groaned.

"My dear Miss Debbington." Penwick took the lead. "I rode over expressly to ask if you would care to essay a ride?"

Patience gave him her hand. "I thank you for your kindness, sir, but I fear I've had a surfeit of fresh air this morning." The breeze was rising, whipping stray tendrils of hair across her forehead, teasing more strands free. Penwick directed a suspicious glance at the large presence looming by her shoulder. Half-turning, Patience saw Vane return Penwick's brief nod with one a great deal more supercilious. "Actually," she stated, "I was about to return indoors."

"Capital!" Henry pressed closer. "I wondered where you'd got to. Thought you must have come out for a walk. Be a pleasure to escort you back."

"I'll come, too." Edmond beamed an understanding smile at Patience. "I came to see how Gerrard's doing, but he gave me my *congé*. So I may as well go in."

There would, Patience felt sure, have been a fight for the position on her right, to be the one whose arm she took, except that the position was already filled. "It seems we're quite a party," Vane drawled. He flicked a glance at Penwick. "Coming, Penwick? We can go by way of the stables."

Patience drew in a deep breath, placed her hand on Vane's arm—and pinched him.

He looked down at her, brows rising innocently. "I was only trying to be helpful." He turned her. The others jostled behind them as he led her up the nave.

The route he took was expressly designed to try her temper. More specifically, to have the others try her temper; Vane wisely kept quiet and let them make the running. With her wet feet now positively frozen from standing too long on cold stone, Patience discovered her stock of forebearance had dipped dangerously low.

By the time they reached the stables, and she gave Penwick her hand in farewell, it was all she could do to fabricate a smile and a polite good-bye.

Penwick squeezed her fingers. "If the rain holds off, no doubt you'll wish to ride tomorrow. I'll call by in the morning."

As if he was in charge of her rides! Patience bit her tongue on a tart rejoinder. Withdrawing her hand, she raised her brows, then haughtily turned away, refusing to fall into the trap of giving Penwick a nod—which could be construed as acceptance. One glance at Vane's face, at the expression in his eyes, was enough to confirm he'd read the exchange clearly.

Luckily, Henry and Edmond drifted off without pushing once they entered the house. As she and Vane climbed the stairs, Patience inwardly frowned. It was almost as if both Henry and Edmond thought they had to protect her from Vane, and Penwick, too, but, once she was in the house, they considered her safe. Even from Vane.

She could imagine why they thought that—this was, after all, Vane's godmother's house. Even rakes, she understood, had lines they would not cross. But she'd already learned she couldn't predict Vane's rakishness—and she wasn't at all sure where *his* lines lay.

They reached the end of the gallery; the corridor to her room stretched ahead. Halting, she drew her hand from Vane's arm and turned to face him.

His expression mild, his eyes gently amused, he met her gaze. He read her eyes, then raised a brow, inviting her question.

"Why did you stay?"

He stilled; again, Patience felt the net draw tight, felt paralysis set in as his predator's senses focused on her. It was as if the world stopped spinning, as if some impenetrable shield closed about them, so that there was nothing but her and him—and whatever it was that held them.

She searched his eyes, but couldn't read his thoughts beyond the fact that he was considering her, considering what to tell her. Then he lifted one hand. Patience caught her breath as he slid one finger beneath her chin; the sensitive skin came alive to his touch. He tipped her face up so that her eyes locked on his.

He studied her, her eyes, her face, for one instant longer. "I stayed to help Minnie, to help Gerrard . . . and to get something I want."

He uttered the words clearly, deliberately, without any affectation. His heavy lids lifted. Patience read the truth in his eyes. The force that held them beat in on her senses. A conqueror watched her through cool grey eyes.

Giddy, she fought for enough strength to lift her chin from his finger. Breathless, she turned and walked away to her door.

Chapter 7

━━━⟶⟀⟵━━━

Late that night, Patience paced before the fire in her bedchamber. About her, the house was silent, all the occupants retired to their rest. She couldn't rest; she hadn't even bothered to undress. There wasn't any point—she wouldn't fall asleep. She was getting very tired of missing out on her sleep, but . . .

She couldn't get her mind off Vane Cynster. He commanded her attention; he filled her thoughts, to the exclusion of everything else. She'd forgotten to eat her soup. Later, she'd tried to drink tea from an empty cup.

"It's all his fault," she informed Myst, sitting, sphinx-like, on the armchair. "How am I supposed to behave sensibly when he makes declarations like that?"

Declared they would be lovers—that he wanted her in that way. Patience slowed. "Lovers, he said—not protector and mistress." She frowned at Myst. "Is there any pertinent distinction?"

Myst looked steadily back.

Patience grimaced. "Probably not." She shrugged and resumed her pacing.

After all Vane had said and done, every precept she'd ever learned stated categorically that she avoid him. Cut him dead if need be. However . . . She halted, and stared at the flames.

The truth was, she was safe. She would be the very last lady to throw her cap over the windmill for a gentleman like Vane Cynster. He might be caring in some ways, he might be so powerfully attractive she couldn't focus on anything else while he was by, but she could never forget what he was. His appearance, his movements, his attitudes, that dangerous purr in his voice—all were constant reminders. No—she was safe. He wouldn't succeed in seducing her. Her deep-seated antipathy to elegant gentlemen would protect her from him.

Which meant she could, with impunity, satisfy her curiosity. Over those odd sensations he evoked, sometimes knowingly, at other times apparently unconsciously. She'd never felt the like before.

She needed to know what they meant. She wanted to know if there was more.

Brow furrowing, she paced on, formulating her arguments. Her experience of the physical was severely limited—she herself had ensured that was so. She'd never before felt the slightest inclination to so much as kiss any gentleman. Or to allow any gentleman to kiss her. But the one, amazingly thorough, astonishingly lengthy kiss she'd shared with Vane had demonstrated beyond doubt that he was a master in that sphere. From his reputation, she'd expected nothing less. Who better to learn from?

Why shouldn't she take advantage of the situation and learn a little more—all within the bounds of the possible, of course. She might not know where his lines lay, but she knew where hers were drawn.

She was safe, she knew what she wanted, and she knew how far she could go.

With Vane Cynster.

The prospect had consumed her thoughts for most of the afternoon and all of the evening. It had been exceedingly difficult to keep her eyes from him, from his large, lean frame, those strong, long-fingered hands, and his increasingly fascinating lips.

Patience frowned and continued to pace.

She looked up as she neared the end of her well-worn route—her curtains were still undrawn. Crossing to the window, she reached a hand to each drape to twitch them shut—in the gloom below, a light gleamed.

Patience froze and stared down. The light was quite

clear, a ball glowing through the fog shrouding the ruins. It bobbed, then moved. Patience didn't wait to see more. Whirling, she hauled open her wardrobe, grabbed her cloak, and ran for the door.

Her soft-soled slippers made no sound on the runners or stair carpet. A single candle left burning in the front hall threw her shadow back up to the gallery. Patience didn't pause. She flew down the dark corridor to the side door.

It was bolted. She wrestled with the heavy bolts, dragging them back, then pulled open the door. Myst shot out. Patience stepped quickly outside, and shut the door. Then she whirled and started out—into thick fog.

Five impulsive steps from the door, she stopped. Shivering, she swung her cloak over her shoulders, quickly tying the cords at the collar. She glanced back. Only by straining her eyes could she make out the wall of the house, the blank eyes of the downstairs windows, and the darker patch that was the side door.

She looked toward the ruins. There was no sign of the light, but the Spectre, whoever he was, could not have reached the house, even using the light to guide him, not before she'd reached the side door.

In all likelihood, the Spectre was still out there.

Setting her back to the house, Patience took a few cautious steps. The fog grew denser, colder.

Tugging her cloak more tightly about her, she set her teeth and forged on. She tried to imagine she was walking in bright sunshine, tried to see in her mind's eye where she was. Then the first of the tumbled stones dotting the lawn loomed out of the fog, a reassuringly familiar sight.

Dragging in a more confident breath, she continued on, carefully picking her way between the toppled stones.

The fog was densest over the lawn; as she neared the ruins, it thinned, enough for her to make out the major structures, from which she could judge her position.

Cold, damp streamers of thick fog wound their way in and out of the shattered arches. A drifting mist obscured, then revealed, then obscured again. There was no real wind, yet a fine thread of sound seemed to whisper through the ruins, like a distant keening from ages past.

As she stepped onto the lichen-covered flags of the outer ward, Patience felt the eerieness close about her. A denser drift of fog wafted about her; one hand outstretched, she felt her way along a short wall, part of the monks' dorter. It ended abruptly; beyond was a large gap giving onto the flagged corridor leading to the remains of the refectory.

She stepped toward the gap; one slipper slid on crumbling masonry. Stifling a gasp, Patience leapt forward onto the corridor flags.

And collided with a man.

She opened her mouth to scream—a hard hand clamped over her lips. An arm like steel locked about her waist, trapping her against a long, hard frame. Patience relaxed; her panic flowed out of her. There was only one body within ten miles like the one she was pressed against.

Reaching up, she pulled Vane's hand from her lips. She drew breath to speak, opened her lips—

He kissed her.

When he eventually consented to stop, he only lifted his lips a bare fraction from hers. And breathed: "Quiet—sound travels very well in fog."

Patience gathered her wits. And breathed back: "I saw the Spectre—there was a light bobbing about."

"I think it's a lantern, but it's gone or shielded now."

His lips touched hers again, then settled, not cool but warm against hers. The rest of him was warm, too, an oasis of heat in the chilly night. Her hands trapped against his chest, Patience fought an urge to snuggle closer.

When he next lifted his head, she forced herself to ask, her words still no more than a whispered breath: "Do you think he'll come back?"

"Who knows? I thought I'd wait for a while."

He followed up the tantalizing brush of his breath against her lips with a much more satisfying caress.

Patience's head spun. "Maybe I'll wait, too."

"Hmmm."

Some unknown minutes later, while taking a necessary pause for breath, Vane commented: "Did you know your cat's here?"

She hadn't known if Myst had followed her or not. "Where?" Patience looked about.

"On the stone to your left. She can probably see better than us, even in the fog. Keep an eye on her—she'll probably disappear if the Spectre returns."

Keep an eye on her. That was difficult while he was kissing her.

Patience snuggled closer to the warm wall of his chest. He adjusted his hold; his hands slid about her waist, beneath her cloak. He drew her more firmly against him, shifting so she was trapped—very comfortably—between him and the old wall. One arm and shoulder protected her from the stones; the rest of him protected her from the night. His arms tightened; Patience felt the strength of him down her length, felt the press of his chest against her breasts, the weight of his hips against her stomach, the solid columns of his thighs hard against her softer limbs.

His lips found hers again; his hands spread over her back, molding her to him. Patience felt heat rise—from her, from him, between them. They were in no danger of taking a chill.

Myst hissed.

Vane raised his head, instantly alert.

A light flashed through the ruins. The fog had grown denser, making it difficult to tell where the lantern was. Reflections bounced off the cut faces of broken stones, setting up distracting glows. It took a moment to locate the strongest source of light.

It shone from beyond the cloisters.

"Stay here." With that whispered command, Vane set her from him, leaving her in the lee of the wall. In the next instant, he disappeared, merging into the fog like a wraith.

Patience swallowed her protest. She looked around—just in time to see Myst slip away in Vane's wake.

Leaving her totally alone.

Stunned, Patience stared after them. Somewhere ahead, the Spectre's lantern still glowed.

"You have to be joking!" With that muttered statement, she hurried after Vane.

She saw him once, as he crossed the courtyard within

the cloisters. The light bobbed some way before him—not near the church but on the other side of the cloister, heading toward the remnants of other abbey buildings. Patience hurried on, glimpsing Myst as she leapt over the stones of the ruined wall of the cloister. As she followed, Patience tried to remember what lay beyond that wall.

A hole, as it happened—she tumbled headlong into it.

Patience valiantly smothered her instinctive shriek, nearly choking in the process. Luckily, it wasn't stone she fell on, but a grassed incline; the impact knocked the air from her lungs and left her gasping.

Twenty yards ahead, Vane heard her muffled shriek. He stopped and looked back, scanning the fog-shrouded stones. A yard behind him, Myst came to a quivering halt atop a stone, ears pricked as she looked back. Then the sleek cat leapt down and streaked back through the fog.

Silently, Vane cursed. He looked ahead.

The light had vanished.

Drawing a deep breath, he let it out, then turned and stalked back.

He found Patience lying where she'd fallen; she was struggling to push herself upright.

"Wait." Vane jumped down by her feet. Leaning over her, he slid his hands under her arms and lifted her. He set her on her feet beside him.

With a smothered cry, Patience crumpled. Vane caught her, lifting her, supporting her against him. "What is it?"

Patience leaned into him. "My knee." She bit her lip, then weakly added, "And my ankle."

Vane cursed. "Left or right?"

"Left."

He shifted to her left, then swung her into his arms, her left leg cradled between them. "Hang on."

Patience did. Holding her against his chest, Vane climbed the short slope. Lifting her high, he set her down on the edge of the hole, then clambered out. Then he bent and lifted her into his arms again.

He carried her into the cloisters, to where a large stone offered a convenient seat. Carefully, he set her down, letting her legs down gently.

Dead grass and damp leaves clung to her bodice. Vane brushed at them. Patience immediately brushed, too, not at all certain what she was brushing away—the detritus, or his hands. Despite the sharp pain in her knee and the duller ache in her ankle, the swift sweep of his fingers across her bodice had made the tips of her breasts crinkle tight.

The sensation left her breathless.

Vane shifted, half behind her. The next instant, she felt his hands slide about her from behind, fingers firming and feeling her ribs. Before she could gather her wits, his fingers slid upward.

"*What are you doing?*" She was so short of breath she sounded hoarse.

"Checking for broken or bruised ribs."

"Nothing hurts there." This time, her voice sounded strangled—the best she could do with his fingers pressed hard beneath her breasts.

A grunt was his answer, but at least he let her go. Patience dragged in a much-needed breath, then blinked as he knelt before her.

He flicked up her skirts.

"*What*—!" Patience desperately tried to push the soft folds back down.

"Stop fussing!"

His tone—clipped and angry—made her do just that. Then she felt his hands close about her sore ankle. His fingers searched, probed gently, then, very carefully, he moved her foot about. "No sharp pain?"

Patience shook her head. His fingers firmed, gently massaging; swallowing a sigh, she closed her eyes. His touch felt so good. The heat of his hands reduced the ache; when he finally released her ankle, it felt much better.

His hands slid upward, following the swell of her calf to her knee.

Patience kept her eyes shut, and tried not to think about how sheer her evening stockings were. Luckily, she wore her garters high, so when his hands closed about her knee, he wasn't touching bare skin.

He might as well have been.

Every nerve in her legs came alive, focused on his touch.

He probed, and pain flashed; Patience jerked—but welcomed the distraction. He was very careful after that. Twice more, she hissed in pain as he tested the joint. Eventually, his hands left her.

Patience opened her eyes and quickly flicked down her skirts. She could feel her blush heating her cheeks. Luckily, in the poor light, she doubted he could see it.

Vane stood and looked down at her. "Wrenched knee, slightly sprained ankle."

Patience shot him a glance. "You're an expert?"

"Of a sort." With that, he picked her up.

Patience clung to his shoulders. "If you would give me your arm, I'm sure I could manage."

"Really?" came the less than encouraging reply. He looked down at her. In the gloom, she couldn't make out his expression. "Luckily, you won't be called upon to put that to the test." His tones remained clipped, excessively precise. The undercurrent of irritation gained in intensity as he continued, "Why the devil didn't you stay where I left you? And didn't Minnie make you promise not to chase the Spectre in the dark?"

Patience ignored his first question, for which she had no good answer. Not that her answer to his second question was particularly good either. "I forgot about my promise— I just saw the Spectre and came rushing out. But what are *you* doing here if it's too dangerous to chase the Spectre?"

"*I* have special dispensation."

Patience felt perfectly justified in humphing. "Where's Myst?"

"Ahead of us."

Patience looked but couldn't see anything. Obviously, Vane could see better than she could. His stride didn't falter as he wound his way through the tumbled blocks; her arms locked about his neck, she was inwardly very glad she didn't have to hobble up that particular stretch of lawn.

Then the side door loomed out of the murk. Myst stood waiting on the stoop. Patience waited to be put down. Instead, Vane juggled her in his arms and managed to open the door. Once across the threshold, he kicked the door shut, then leaned his shoulders back against it.

"Set the bolts."

She did as he said, reaching about him. When the last bolt slid home, he straightened and headed on.

"You can put me down now," Patience hissed as he strode into the front hall.

"I'll put you down in your room"

In the light from the hall candle, Patience saw what she hadn't been able to see before—his face. It was set. In uncompromisingly grim lines.

To her surprise, he headed for the back of the hall, and shouldered open the green baize door. "Masters!"

Masters popped out from the butler's pantry. "Yes, sir?—oh my!"

"Indeed," Vane replied. "Summon Mrs. Henderson and one of the maids. Miss Debbington went wandering in the ruins and has turned her ankle and wrenched her knee."

That, of course, did for her. Very thoroughly. Patience had to put up with Masters, Mrs. Henderson, and Minnie's old dresser, Ada, fussing nonstop about her. Vane led the bleating procession up the stairs—as he'd said, he set her down in her room, not before.

He set her, very gently, on the end of her bed. Frowning, he stood back. Hands on hips, he watched as Mrs. Henderson and Ada fussed with a mustard bath for her ankle and the makings of a poultice for her knee.

Apparently satisfied, Vane turned and trapped Patience's gaze. His eyes were hard. "For God's sake, do as you're told." With that, he strode for the door.

Utterly dumbfounded, Patience stared after him. She couldn't think of anything halfway suitable to hurl at him before he disappeared. The door clicked shut. She snapped her mouth shut, let herself fall back on the bed, and relieved her feelings with a teeth-gritted groan.

Ada fluttered over. "It'll be all right, dear." She patted Patience's hand. "We'll make it all better in a moment."

Patience set her teeth—and glared at the ceiling.

Mrs. Henderson came to wake her the next morning. Patience, lying on her back in the middle of her bed, was surprised to see the motherly housekeeper; she'd expected one of the maids.

Mrs. Henderson smiled as she drew the curtains wide. "I'll need to remove that poultice and bind up your knee."

Patience grimaced. She'd hoped to escape a bandage. She glanced idly at her clock, then stared. "It's only seven o'clock."

"Aye. We doubted you'd sleep all that well, what with the awkwardness."

"I couldn't turn over." Patience struggled to sit up.

"It won't be so bad tonight. Just a bandage should be enough from now on."

With the housekeeper's help, Patience got up. She sat patiently while Mrs. Henderson removed the poultice, clucked over her knee, then bound it up in a fresh bandage.

"I can't walk," Patience protested, the instant Mrs. Henderson helped her to her feet.

"Of course not. You must stay off your feet for a few days if that knee's to heal."

Patience closed her eyes and stifled a groan.

Mrs. Henderson helped her to wash and dress, then let her prop against the bed. "Now, would you like a tray up here, or would you rather go downstairs?"

To *think* of spending the entire day closeted in her room was bad enough; to be forced to do so would be torture. And if she was to go down the stairs, it had best be now, before anyone else was about. "Downstairs," Patience replied decisively.

"Right then."

To her amazement, Mrs. Henderson left her and headed for the door. Opening it, she put her head out, said something, then stood back, holding the door wide.

Vane walked in.

Patience stared.

"Good morning." His expression impassive, he crossed the room. Before she could formulate her thoughts, let alone the words to express them, he stooped and scooped her into his arms.

Patience swallowed her gasp. Just like last night—with one highly pertinent alteration.

Last night, she'd been wearing her cloak; its thick folds had muted his touch sufficiently to render it undisturbing. Now, clad in a morning gown of fine twill, even through her petticoats she could feel every one of his fingers, one set gripping her lower thigh, the others firm beneath her arm, close by the swell of her breast.

As he angled her through the door, then straightened and headed for the gallery, Patience tried to steady her breathing, and prayed her blush wasn't as vivid as it felt. Vane's gaze touched her face, then he looked ahead and started down the stairs.

Patience risked a glance at his face—the hard planes were still set, locked and stony, as they had been last night. His fascinating lips were a straight line.

She narrowed her eyes. "I'm not actually incapacitated, you know."

The glance he sent her was unreadable. He studied her eyes for an instant, then looked ahead once more. "Mrs. Henderson says you must keep off your feet. If I find you on them, I'll tie you to a daybed."

Patience's jaw dropped. She stared at him, but, reaching the bottom of the stairs, he didn't look her way. His boots rang on the hall tiles. Patience drew a deep breath, intending to make her views on his high-handedness plain, only to have to swallow her words; Vane swept into the breakfast parlor—Masters was there. He hurried to pull out the chair next to Vane's, angling it so it faced the head of the table. Gently, Vane deposited her in it. Masters rolled an ottoman into position; Vane set her injured ankle upon it.

"Would you like a cushion, miss?" Masters inquired.

What could she do? Patience conjured a grateful smile. "No, thank you, Masters." Her gaze shifted to Vane, standing in front of her. "You've been more than kind."

"Not at all, miss. Now, what would you like for breakfast?"

Between them, Vane and Masters saw her supplied with suitable nourishment—then watched over her as she ate. Patience bore with their male version of fussing as stocially as she could. And waited.

Vane's shoulders were coated with fine droplets of mist.

His hair was darker than usual, an occasional droplet glittering amid the thick locks. He also broke his fast, working steadily through a plate piled with various meats. Patience inwardly sniffed—he was obviously a carnivore.

Eventually, Masters returned to the kitchen, to fetch chafing dishes to keep the fare warm.

As his footsteps faded, Patience pounced. "You've been out investigating."

Vane looked up, then nodded and reached for his coffee cup.

"Well?" Patience prompted, when he simply sipped.

Lips compressing, he studied her face, then grudgingly informed her: "I thought there might be a footprint or two—a track I could follow." He grimaced. "The ground was wet enough, but the ruins are all either flags, rocks, or matted grass. Nothing to hold any impression."

"Hmm." Patience frowned.

Masters returned. He set down his tray, then crossed to Vane's side. "Grisham and Duggan are waiting in the kitchen, sir."

Vane nodded and drained his coffee cup. He set it down and pushed back his chair.

Patience caught his eye and held it. She clung to the contact; her unspoken question hung in the air.

Vane's face hardened. His lips thinned.

Patience narrowed her eyes. "If you don't tell me, I'll go to the ruins myself."

Vane narrowed his eyes back. He flicked a glance at Masters, then, somewhat grimly, looked back at Patience. "We're going to check for any sign that the Spectre came from outside. Hoofprints, anything to suggest he didn't come from the Hall itself."

Her expression relaxing, Patience nodded. "It's been so wet, you should find something."

"Precisely." Vane stood. "If there's anything to find."

Masters left the parlor, on a return trip to the kitchens. From the direction of the stairs came an airy voice, "Good morning, Masters. Is anyone about yet?"

Angela. They heard Masters's low-voiced answer; Vane looked down and met Patience's wide eyes.

"That's obviously my cue to depart."

Patience grinned. "Coward," she whispered, as he passed her chair.

A heartbeat later, he'd swung about and bent over her, his breath feathering the side of her neck. His strength flowed around her, surrounded her.

"Incidentally," he murmured, in his deepest purr, "I meant what I said about the daybed." He paused. "So, if you have the slightest inkling of self-preservation, you won't move from this chair." Cool, hard lips brushed her ear, then slid lower, to lightly caress, with just the barest touch, the sensitive skin beneath her jaw. Patience lost the fight and shivered; her lids lowered.

Vane tipped her chin up; his lips touched hers in a fleeting, achingly incomplete kiss. "I'll be back before breakfast is over."

Angela's footsteps sounded in the hall.

Patience opened her eyes to see Vane striding out of the parlor. She heard Angela's delighted greeting, then Vane's answering rumble, dying away as he continued striding. A second later, Angela appeared. She was pouting.

Feeling infinitely older, infinitiely wiser, Patience smiled. "Come and have some breakfast. The eggs are particularly good."

The rest of the breakfast crowd gradually wandered in. To Patience's dismay, they, one and all, had already heard of her injury, courtesy of the household grapevine. Luckily, neither she nor Vane had seen fit to inform anyone of the reason for her nighttime excursion, so no one knew how she'd come by her hurts.

Everyone was suitably shocked by her "accident"; all were quick to proffer their sympathy.

"Distressing business," Edgar offered with one of his meek smiles.

"Twisted m'knee once, when I was in India." The General directed a curious glance up the table. "Horse threw me. Native wallahs wrapped it up in evil-smelling leaves. Knee, not the horse. Came good in no time."

Patience nodded and sipped her tea.

Gerrard, beside her, occupying the chair she usually

used, asked softly, "Are you sure you're all right?"

Ignoring the ache in her knee, Patience smiled and squeezed his hand lightly. "I'm hardly a weak creature. I promise you I'm not about to swoon from the pain."

Gerrard grinned, but his expression remained watchful, concerned.

With her pleasant smile firmly in place, Patience allowed her gaze to roam. Until, across the table, she met Henry's frown.

"You know," he said, "I don't quite understand how you came to wrench your knee." His inflection made the statement a question.

Patience kept smiling. "I couldn't sleep, so I went for a stroll."

"Outside?" Edmond's surprise faded to consideration. "Well, yes, I suppose you'd have to stroll outside—strolling *inside* this mausoleum at night would give anyone nightmares." His swift grin dawned. "And presumably you wouldn't have wanted them."

Smiling over clenched teeth was not easy; Patience managed it, just. "I did go outside, as it happened." Silence would have been wiser, but they were all hanging on her words, as avidly curious as only those leading humdrum lives could be.

"But . . ." Edgar's brow folded itself into pin tucks. "The fog . . ." He looked at Patience. "It was a pea-souper last night. I looked out before I blew out my candle."

"It was rather dense." Patience looked at Edmond. "You would have appreciated the eerieness."

"I had heard," Whitticombe diffidently commented, "that Mr. Cynster carried you in."

His words, quietly spoken, hung over the breakfast table, raising questions in every mind. A sudden stillness ensued, fraught with surprise and shocked calculation. Calmly, her smile no longer in evidence, Patience turned and, her expression distant, regarded Whitticombe.

Her mind raced, considering alternatives, but there was only one answer she could give. "Yes, Mr. Cynster did help me back to the house—it was lucky he found me.

We'd both seen a light in the ruins and gone to investigate.''

"The Spectre!" The exclamation came from both Angela and Edmond. Their eyes glowed, their faces lit with excitement.

Patience tried to dampen their imminent transports. "I was following the light when I fell down a hole.''

"I had thought," Henry said sternly, and all heads swung his way, "that we all promised Minnie we wouldn't go chasing the Spectre in the dark." The tenor of his voice and the expression on his face were quite surprising in their intensity. Patience felt a blush touch her cheeks.

"I'm afraid I forgot my promise," she admitted.

"In the chill of the moment, so to speak." Edmond leaned across the table. "Did your spine tingle?"

Patience opened her mouth, eager to grasp Edmond's distraction, but Henry spoke first.

"I think, young man, that this nonsense of yours has gone quite far enough!"

The words were wrath-filled. Startled, everyone looked at Henry—his face was set, skin slightly mottled. His eyes were fixed on Gerrard.

Who stiffened. He met Henry's gaze, then slowly put down his fork. "What do you mean?"

"I mean," Henry replied, biting off the words, "that given the pain and suffering you've caused your sister, I'm shocked to discover you such an unfeeling whelp that you can sit there, beside her, and pretend to innocence."

"Oh, come on," Edmond said. Patience nearly sighed with relief. A second later she stiffened and stared as Edmond continued, his tone the very essence of reasonableness, "How could he know Patience would break her word to Minnie and come out after him?" Edmond shrugged and turned a winning smile on both Patience and Gerrard. "Hardly his fault she did."

With supporters like that . . . Patience swallowed a groan and charged into the breach. "It wasn't Gerrard."

"Oh?" Edgar looked at her hopefully. "You saw the Spectre then?"

Patience bit her lip. "No, I didn't. But—"

"Even if you had, you would still defend your brother, wouldn't you, my dear?" Whitticombe's smooth tones floated up the table. He directed a smile of paternalistic superiority at Patience. "Quite commendable devotion, my dear, but in this case, I fear"—his gaze switched to Gerrard; his features hardened, and he shook his head—"sadly misplaced."

"It wasn't I." Pale, Gerrard made the statement evenly. Beside him, Patience sensed the battle he waged to hold his temper in check. Silently, she sent him support. Under the table, she gripped his thigh briefly.

Abruptly, he turned to her. "I'm not the Spectre."

Patience held his furious gaze levelly. "I know." She filled those two words with complete and utter conviction, and felt some of his heat leave him.

Turning, he flung a challenging stare around the table.

The General snorted. "Touching, but there's no ducking the truth. Boy's tricks, that's what this Spectre is. And you, boy—you're the only boy about."

Patience felt the blow strike, a direct hit to the core of Gerrard's emerging adulthood. He stilled, his face deathly pale, his expression bleak. Her heart wept for him; she longed to throw her arms about him, to shield and comfort him—but knew she could not.

Slowly, Gerrard pushed back his chair and stood. He cast a burning glance around the table, excusing only Patience from its scorn. "If none of you has any more insults to hurl my way . . ." He paused, then continued, his voice threatening to break, "I'll bid you a good morning."

Brusquely, he nodded. With a swift, blank glance for Patience, he swung on his heel and left the room.

Patience would have given her entire fortune to be able to rise and, with haughty scorn, sweep out in his wake. Instead, she was trapped—condemned by her injury to have to keep her own soaring temper within bounds and deal with her aunt's witless household. Despite her threat to Vane, she could not stand, let alone hobble.

Lips compressed, she swept a glance around the table. "Gerrard is not the Spectre."

Henry smiled wearily. "My dear Miss Debbington, I'm afraid you really must face facts."

"Facts?" Patience snapped. "What facts?"

With weighty condescension, Henry proceeded to tell her.

Vane was strolling up from the stables when he saw Gerrard, jaw grimly set, striding toward him.

"What's happened?" he demanded.

Stony-faced, eyes burning, Gerrard halted before him, drew a deep breath, met his gaze briefly, then abruptly shook his head. "Don't ask." With that, he flung past, and continued to the stables.

Vane watched him go. Gerrard's clenched fists and rigid back spoke volumes. Vane hesitated, then his face hardened. Abruptly, he turned and strode for the house.

He reached the breakfast parlor in record time. One glance, and all expression left his face. Patience still sat where he'd left her, but instead of the bright sparkle he'd left in her large eyes, the light flush that had tinted her cheeks, her hazel eyes were now narrowed, flashing with temper, while flags of color flew high on her cheekbones.

Beyond that, she was pale, almost vibrating with suppressed fury. She didn't see him immediately; Henry Chadwick was the current focus of her ire.

"There you are, Cynster! Come and add your voice to ours." The General, swiveling in his chair, appealed to him. "We've been trying to tell Miss Debbington here that she has to see sense. No point bucking the truth, don't you see? That ramshackle brother of hers needs a firmer hand on his reins. A good whipping will bring him into line and stop all this Spectre tommyrot."

Vane looked at Patience. Her eyes, positively blazing, had fixed on the General. Her breasts swelled as she drew breath. If looks could kill, the General was dead. From her expression, she was ready to throttle Henry, too, with Edmond thrown in for good measure.

Smoothly, Vane strolled forward. His movement caught Patience's attention; she looked up, and blinked. Vane trapped her gaze in his. He didn't halt until he stood beside her chair. Then he held out his hand. Commandingly. Without hesitation, Patience laid her fingers in his palm.

Vane closed his hand strongly about hers; with a shudder, Patience felt warmth and strength flow into her. Her temper, almost at the breaking point, fell back from the brink. She drew in another breath and looked again at those about the table.

Vane did the same, his cool grey gaze scanning their faces. "I do hope," he mumured, his languid drawl low but clearly audible, "that, after your ordeal of last night, no one has been insensitive enough to discompose you in any way?"

The quiet words, and the cold steel behind his eyes, were enough to make everyone else at the table still.

"Naturally," he continued, in the same smooth tones, "events such as those of last night lend themselves to speculation. But, of course"—he smiled at them all—"it is just speculation."

"Ah—" Edgar broke in to ask, "You found no evidence—no clue—to the Spectre's identity?"

Vane's smile deepened fractionally. "None. So any thoughts on the identity of the Spectre are, as I said, pure fancy." He caught Edgar's eye. "Based on rather less substance than a tip for the Guineas."

Edgar smiled briefly.

"But," interrupted the General, "stands to reason it's got to be *someone*."

"Oh, indeed," Vane replied, at his languid best. "But ascribing the blame to any particular individual without reasonable *proof* seems to me to smack of . . ." He paused and met the General's eye. "Quite unnecessary slander."

"Humph!" The General sank lower in his chair.

"And, of course"—Vane's gaze swung to Henry— "there's always the thought of how foolish one will look if one's overly enthusiastic assertions prove wrong."

Henry frowned. His gaze dropped to the tablecloth.

Vane looked down at Patience. "Are you ready to go upstairs?"

Patience looked up at him and nodded. Vane bent and scooped her into his arms. Having got used to the sensation of being lifted so easily, Patience made herself comfortable, draping her arms about Vane's neck. The men at the table all came to their feet; Patience glanced across the table—and almost smiled. The look on Henry's and Edmond's faces was priceless.

Vane turned and headed for the door. Edmond and Henry came rushing around the table, almost tripping in their haste.

"Oh, I say—here, let me help." Henry rushed to hold back the already open door.

"Perhaps if we form a chair with our arms?" Edmond suggested.

Vane paused as Edmond moved to intercept them. Patience froze Edmond with an icy glare. "Mr. Cynster is more than capable of managing on his own." She allowed the chill in her voice to strike home, before adding, in precisely the same tone, "I am going to retire—I do not wish to be disturbed. Not by any further speculation, nor unwarranted slander. And least of all"—she shifted her sights to Henry—"by any overly enthusiastic assertions."

She paused, then smiled, and looked at Vane. Utterly unmoved, he raised a brow at her. "Upstairs?"

Patience nodded. "Indeed."

Without further ado, and no further hindrance, Vane carried her from the room.

Chapter 8

"Why," Vane asked, as he steadily climbed the main stairs, "are they so convinced it's Gerrard?"

"Because," Patience waspishly stated, "they can't imagine anything else. It's a *boy's* trick; ergo it must be Gerrard." As Vane gained the top of the stairs, she continued, her tone vitriolic. "Henry has no imagination; neither has the General. They're blockheads. Edmond has imagination to spare, but doesn't care enough to engage it. He's so irresponsible, he considers it all a lark. Edgar is cautious over jumping to conclusions, but his very timidity leaves him permanently astride the fence. And as for Whitticombe"—she paused, breasts swelling, eyes narrowing— "*he's* a self-righteous killjoy who positively delights in calling attention to others' supposed misdemeanors, all with a sickeningly superior air."

Vane shot her a sidelong glance. "Clearly breakfast didn't agree with you."

Patience humphed. Looking ahead, she focused on their surroundings. She didn't recognize them. "Where are you taking me?"

"Mrs. Henderson has set up one of the old parlors for you—so you won't be bothered with the others unless you choose to summon them."

"Which will be after hell freezes." After a moment, Patience glanced up at Vane. In a very different tone, she asked: "You don't think it's Gerrard, do you?"

103

Vane looked down at her. "I *know* it isn't Gerrard."

Patience's eyes widened. "You saw who it was?"

"Yes and no. I only caught a glimpse as he went through a thinner patch of fog. He clambered over a rock, holding his light high, and I saw him outlined by the light. A grown man from his build. Height's difficult to judge at a distance, but build is harder to mistake. He was wearing a heavy coat, something like frieze, although my impression was it wasn't that cheap."

"But you're sure it wasn't Gerrard?"

Vane glanced down at Patience riding comfortably in his arms. "Gerrard's still too lightweight to be mistaken for a fully grown man. I'm quite certain it wasn't he."

"Hmm." Patience frowned. "What about Edmond— he's rather thin. Is he eliminated, too?"

"I don't think so. His shoulders are broad enough to carry a coat well, and with his height, if he was hunched, either against the cold or because he was playing the role of 'the Spectre,' then he could have been the man I saw."

"Well, whatever else," Patience said, brightening, "you can put an end to this scurrilous talk of Gerrard being the Spectre." Her brightness lasted all of ten yards, then she frowned. "Why didn't you clear Gerrard's name just now, in the breakfast parlor?"

"Because," Vane said, ignoring the sudden chill in her voice, "it's patently obvious that someone—someone about the breakfast table—is quite content to cast Gerrard as the Spectre. Someone wants Gerrard as scapegoat, to distract attention from himself. Given the mental aptitudes you so accurately described, the gentlemen are, by and large, easily led. Present the matter right, and they'll happily believe it. Unfortunately, as none of them is *un*intelligent, it's difficult to tell just who's doing the leading."

He stopped before a door; frowning, Patience absentmindedly leaned forward and opened it. Vane shouldered the door wide and carried her in.

As he had said, it was a parlor, but not one usually in use. It lay at the end of the wing housing Patience's bedchamber, one floor down. The windows were long, reaching almost to the floor. Maids had obviously been in, throwing back dust covers, dusting ferociously, and refurbishing the huge cast-iron Empire daybed that faced the long windows. Their curtains tied back, the windows looked over the shrubbery and a section of wilderness—most of the Hall's gardens were wilderness—to the golden brown canopies of the woods beyond. It was as pleasant a prospect as could be found in the present season. Farther to the right lay the ruins; in the distance, the grey ribbon of the Nene wound its way through lush meadows. Patience could recline on the daybed and contemplate the scenery. As the room was on the first floor, her privacy was assured.

Vane carried her to the daybed and carefully lowered her onto it. He plumped the pillows, arranging them supportively about her.

Patience lay back, watching as he settled a tapestry-covered cushion under her sore ankle. "Just what are your intentions over the Spectre?"

Vane met her gaze, then, raising one brow, strolled back to the door—and turned the key in the lock. Returning with the same long-strided prowl, he sat on the bed, beside her hip, bracing one hand on the daybed's iron back. "The Spectre now knows that he was followed last night—that, but for your untimely accident, he might well have been caught."

Patience had the grace to blush.

"All the household," Vane continued, his eyes locking on hers, "the Spectre included, are coming to the realization that I know the Hall well, possibly better than they do. I'm a real threat to the Spectre—I think he'll lie low and wait for me to depart before making another appearance."

Patience made an effort to live up to her name; she pressed her lips tightly together.

Vane smiled understandingly. "Consequently, if we're to lure the Spectre to reveal himself, I suspect it would be wise to let it appear that I'm still willing to entertain the notion that Gerrard—the obvious candidate—is to blame."

Patience frowned. She studied the cool grey of his eyes, then opened her lips.

"I would suggest," Vane said, before she could speak, "that it's not going to hurt Gerrard to let the household think what they like, at least for the immediate future.''

Patience's frown deepened. ''You didn't hear what they said.'' She crossed her arms beneath her breasts. ''The General called him a boy.''

Vane's brows rose. ''Highly insensitive, I agree—but I think you're underestimating Gerrard. Once he knows all the people he cares about *know* he's innocent, he won't worry over what the others think. I suspect he'll view it as an exciting game—a conspiracy to catch the Spectre.''

Patience narrowed her eyes. ''You mean that's how you'll present it to him.''

Vane grinned. ''I'll suggest he responds to any aspersions cast his way with scornful boredom.'' He raised his brows. ''Perhaps he can cultivate a superior sneer?''

Patience tried to eye him with disapproval. She was sure that, as Gerrard's guardian, she shouldn't approve of such plans. Yet she did; she could see Vane's plan was the fastest way to resuscitate Gerrard's confidence, and that, above all, was her primary concern. ''You're rather good at this, aren't you?'' And she didn't just mean his reading of Gerrard.

Vane's grin converted to a rakish smile. ''I'm rather good at lots of things.''

His voice had lowered to a rumbling purr. He leaned closer.

Patience tried, very hard, to ignore the vise slowly closing about her chest. She kept her eyes on his, drawing ever nearer, determined that she wouldn't—absolutely would not—allow her gaze to drop to his lips. As her heartbeat deepened, she raised one brow challengingly. ''Such as?''

Kissing—he was very, very good at kissing.

By the time Patience reached that conclusion, she was utterly breathless—and utterly enthralled by the heady feelings slowly spiraling through her. Vane's confident possession of her lips, her mouth, left her giddy—pleasurably so. His hard lips moved on hers, and she softened, not just her lips, but every muscle, every limb. Slow heat washed through her, a tide of simple delight that seemed to have no greater meaning, no deeper import. It was all pleasure, simple pleasure.

With a mental sigh, she lifted her arms and draped them over his shoulders. He shifted closer. Patience thrilled to the slow surge of his tongue against hers. Boldly, she returned the caress; the muscles beneath her hands tensed. Emboldened, she let her lips firm against his, and reveled in his immediate response. Hard transmuted to harder; lips, muscles, all became more definite, more sharply defined.

It was fascinating—she became softer—he became harder.

And behind his hardness came heat—a heat they both shared. It rose like a fever, turning the swirling pleasure hot. Beyond the caress of his lips, he hadn't touched her, yet every nerve in her body was heating, simmering with sensation. The warm tide spread, swelled; the temperature increased.

And she was flushed, restless—wanting.

The slide of hard fingers over her breasts made her gasp—not in panic but pure shock. Shock at the shaft of sheer delight that speared through her, the sharp tingling that spread over her skin. The fingers firmed, possessively cupping her soft, oddly swollen flesh—which immediately swelled more. His hand closed, fingers kneading; her heated flesh firmed, tingling and tight.

The hot tangling of their tongues and the heat of his hand proved utterly distracting. When he stroked the peak of her breast, Patience gasped again. With something akin to amazement, her senses acutely focused on his fingertips, she marveled at her response to his touch, at the flaring heat that seared her, at the tight ruching of her nipples.

She'd never imagined such sensations existed; she could barely believe they were real. Yet the caresses continued, thrilling her, heating her—she had to wonder what else she didn't know.

What else she had yet to experience.

With every ounce of expertise at his command, Vane deliberately drew her deeper. Her total lack of resistance would have made him wonder, if he hadn't earlier seen the curiosity, the calm calculated intention in her eyes. She was willing, even eager—the knowledge stirred his passions powerfully. He held them in check, aware that she was no wanton, that she'd never been down this road be-fore—and that, despite her guileless confidence, her open-ness—her implicit trust was a fragile thing which could all too easily be shattered by overly aggressive loving.

She was naive, innocent—she needed to be loved ten-derly, coaxed to passion gently, savored slowly.

As he was savoring her now, the softness of her mouth his to enjoy, her breast firm under his fondling hand. Her innocence was refreshing—heady, addictive, entrancing.

Angling his head, Vane deepened the kiss for an instant, then drew back, releasing her lips. But not her breast.

He waited, fingers stroking the swollen mounds, first one, then the other, waiting . . . until he saw her eyes glint be-neath her lashes. He caught her gaze, then slowly, delib-erately, lifted his fingers to the top button of her bodice.

Patience's eyes widened under her heavy lids; her breasts swelled as she drew in a shocked breath. The sudden re-lease of the top button was almost a relief. Her senses reeled as his fingers moved down—to the next button; she felt every slow beat of her heart, pulsing under her skin, as, one after another, the tiny pearl rounds slipped their moorings.

And her bodice slowly opened.

For one fraught instant, she wasn't sure what she wanted—whether she even wanted to know what came next. The hesitation lasted only a second—the second it took for Vane to slowly brush aside the soft fabric of her bodice, for his fingers to slide knowingly in.

One gentle tug, and her chemise slid down. Then came the first tantalizing touch of his fingertips on her skin; Patience's senses whirled. Aghast, agape, utterly enthralled, her every nerve tingled to his touch, to the caress of his palm, to those long, hard fingers as they closed about her breast.

Vane watched her reaction from under heavy lids, watched flaring passion light her eyes. Sparks of pure gold flashed in the hazel depths as he gently kneaded, then sent his fingers gliding over her silken skin. He knew he should kiss her, distract her, from what came next—but the com-pulsion to witness, to know her reaction as she learned what he would do, as he filled his senses with her, waxed strong.

Deliberately, he shifted his hand; his fingers closed confidently about one tightly budded nipple.

Patience gasped—the sweet sound filled the room. Instinctively, she arched, pressing her breast more firmly into the hard palm surrounding it, seeking relief from the sharp sensation that speared her—again and again as his fingers firmed.

Vane bent his head and his lips found hers.

Patience clung to his kiss, held to it like an anchor in her suddenly whirling world. Pure streams of heat arced through her, waves of hot pleasure sank to her bones, pooled in her loins. She clutched Vane's shoulders, and kissed him back, suddenly desperate to know, to feel, to appease the desire throbbing in her veins.

Abruptly, he broke their kiss. He shifted, and his lips touched her throat. No longer cool, they seared like a brand as he traced the long sweep of her throat. Patience pressed her head back into the pillows and fought to catch her breath.

Only to lose it entirely a bare second later.

His lips closed about one tightly furled nipple—Patience thought she would die. Gasping desperately, she clenched her hands on his shoulders, fingers sinking deep. His lips firmed, he suckled gently—Patience felt the earth quake. The heat of his mouth shocked her—the wet sweep of his tongue scalded her. She gave a strangled cry.

That sound, keenly feminine, acutely evocative, caught and focused Vane's attention. Focused every hunter's instinct. Desire heightened, need escalated. His demons turned frenzied—her siren's song lured them on. Urged him on. Compulsion swelled—tense, turbulent, powerful. Desire seethed hotly. He drew a ragged breath—

And remembered—all he'd nearly forgotten, all her wild responses had driven from his mind. This was one seduction he had to, needed to, manage perfectly—this time, there was meaning beyond the act. Seducing Patience Debbington was too important to rush—conquering her senses, her body, was only the first step. He didn't want her just once—he wanted her for a lifetime.

Dragging in a shuddering breath, Vane caught hold of

his reins and hauled his impulses up short. Something in him wailed with frustration. He shut his mind to the relentless pounding of his arousal.

And set himself to soothe hers.

He knew how. There were planes of warm desire on which women could float, neither driven, nor quiescent, but simply buoyed on a sea of pleasure. With hands and lips, mouth and tongue, he soothed her fevered flesh, took the sting from her aches, the edge from her passion, and eased her into that pleasured sea.

Patience was beyond understanding—all she knew was the peace, the calm, the profound pleasure that welled and washed through her. Content, she flowed with the tide, letting her senses stretch. The whirling that had disorientated her slowed; her mind steadied.

Full consciousness, when it came, was no shock; the continuing touch of Vane's hands, the artful caress of his lips, his tongue, were familiar—no threat.

Then she remembered where they were.

She tried to open her eyes, but her lids were too heavy. Finding breath enough to whisper was just possible. "What if someone comes in?"

Her words ended on a sigh as Vane lifted his head, lifted his lips from her breast. His voice rumbled softly through her. "The door's locked—remember?"

Remember? With his lips brushing hers, with his fingers caressing her breast, Patience was hard-pressed to remember her own name. The peace holding her stretched, her senses slowly sank. Every muscle gradually relaxed.

Vane had noticed the dark rings under her large eyes. He wasn't surprised to find her drifting close to sleep. Gradually, he slowed his caresses, then stopped. Carefully, he drew back, and smiled—at the soft smile that curved her kiss-bruised lips, the soft glow that lit her face.

He left her sleeping.

Patience wasn't sure when she realized he was gone— she sleepily cracked open her lids—and saw the windows rather than him. The warm peace that pervaded her was too deep to leave; she smiled and closed her eyes again.

When she finally awoke, the morning had gone. Blinking her eyes wide, she wriggled higher on the pillows. And frowned.

Someone had left her embroidery on the table beside the daybed; dredging through her foggy memories, she vaguely recalled Timms dropping by, remembered a hand gently stroking her hair.

Remembered a hand gently stroking her breasts. Patience blinked. Other memories, other sensations, crowded into her mind. Her eyes widened. "No—that *must* have been a dream." Frowning, she shook her head—but couldn't dull the sharpness of the sensual images, rising one after another in her mind. To dispel the nagging uncertainty, she glanced down—uncertainty crystallized to fact.

Her bodice was undone.

Horrified, Patience muttered an imprecation, and rapidly did it up. "Rakes!" Frowning direfully, she glanced about. Her gaze collided with Myst's. The small grey cat was settled comfortably on a side table, sitting on her brisket, front paws neatly tucked in.

"Have you been there all this time?"

Myst blinked her wide blue eyes—and stared steadily back.

Patience felt color rise in her cheeks—and wondered if it was possible to feel shy of a cat. Because of what a cat might have seen.

Before she could make up her mind, the door opened—Vane strolled in. The smile on his face, curving those fascinating lips, was more than enough to make Patience inwardly swear that she would not, not for anything, give him the pleasure of knowing how flustered she felt. "What's the time?" Nonchalance laced her tones.

"Lunchtime," replied the wolf.

Feeling very like Red Riding Hood, Patience smothered a feigned yawn, then held up her arms and waved him closer. "You may carry me down then."

Vane's smile deepened. With elegant ease, he lifted her into his arms.

Their entry into the dining room was noted by all. The rest of the household was already assembled about the table, with one notable exception. Gerrard's chair was empty.

Minnie and Timms both smiled benignly as Vane settled Patience into her chair. Mrs. Chadwick inquired after her injury with matronly politeness. Patience responded to the ladies with smiles and gentle words—and totally ignored all the men.

Except Vane—she couldn't ignore him. Even if her senses would have allowed it, he didn't—he insisted on instituting a general conversation on mild and unprovocative topics. When, encouraged by the prevailing sense of calm, Henry, under the pretext of helping her to more ham, tried to engage her with a smile and a gentle query about her knee, Patience froze him with a reply couched in sheet ice, and felt, beneath the table, Vane's knee jog hers. She turned and fixed him with an innocent look—he met her gaze, his eyes a flat grey, then ruthlessly drew her into the conversation.

When he lifted her into his arms at the end of the meal, Patience was in no very good mood. Not only had the undercurrents at the table abraded her nerves, but Gerrard had not appeared.

Vane carried her up to her private parlor and settled her back on the daybed.

"Thank you." Patience wriggled and prodded at her pillows, then sank back and reached for her embroidery. She threw Vane a quick, somewhat darkling glance, then shook out the linen cloth.

Stepping back, Vane watched her pull colored silks from her bag, then turned and strolled to the window. The day had started clear, but now clouds were rolling in, greying the sky.

Glancing back, he studied Patience. She sat amid the pillows and cushions, her work in her hands, bright silks strewn about her. But her hands were still; an absentminded frown had settled on her face.

Vane hesitated, then his lips firmed. He swung to face her. "If you like, I'll go and look for him."

He made the offer nonchalantly, leaving her the option of declining without embarrassment.

She looked up, her expression difficult to read. Then

color seeped into her cheeks—and Vane knew she was recalling all she'd accused him of only two days before. But she did not look down, did not shift her gaze from his. After a further moment of consideration, she nodded. "If you would, I would be . . ."

Patience stopped, and blinked—but couldn't stop the word that rose to her lips. "Grateful." Her lips quirked; she looked down.

The next instant, Vane was beside her. Fingers sliding beneath her chin, he tipped her face up. He looked down at her for a long moment, his expression unreadable, then he stooped and touched his lips to hers. "Don't worry— I'll find him."

Instinctively, she returned the kiss. Gripping his wrist, she held him back, searching his face, then squeezed and let him go.

When the door closed behind him, Patience drew a deep, very deep breath.

She'd just placed her trust in an elegant gentleman. More than that, she'd trusted him with the one thing on earth she held most dear. Had he addled her wits? Or had she simply lost them?

For a full minute, she gazed unseeing at the window, then frowned, shook her head, shook her shoulders, and picked up her embroidery. There was no point wrestling with facts. She knew Gerrard was safe with Vane—safer than with any other gentleman within Bellamy Hall, safer than with any other gentleman she'd ever met.

And, she thought, pulling her needle free, while she was on the subject of startling admissions, she might as well admit that she felt relieved as well—relieved that Vane was there, that she wasn't, any longer, Gerrard's sole protector.

As startling admissions went, *that* took the prize.

"Here, you must be hungry by now." Vane dropped the sack he'd brought onto the grass beside Gerrard, who jumped like a scalded cat.

Gerrard looked around, then stared as Vane lowered himself to the grassy top of the old burial mound. "How did you know I'd be here?"

His gaze on the horizon, Vane shrugged. "Just a guess." A lilting smile touched his lips. "You hid your horse well enough, but you left tracks aplenty."

Gerrard humphed. His gaze fell on the sack. He pulled it closer and opened it.

While Gerrard munched on cold chicken and bread, Vane idly studied the views. After a while, he felt Gerrard's gaze on his face.

"I'm not the Spectre, you know."

Vane raised his brows arrogantly. "I do, as it happens."

"You do?"

"Hmm. I saw him last night—not well enough to recognize but enough to know it definitely wasn't you."

"Oh." After a moment, Gerrard went on, "All that talk of me being the Spectre—well, it always was just so much rot. I mean, as if I'd be silly enough to do such a thing anywhere near Patience." He snorted derisively. "Of *course* she'd go to look. Why—she's worse than I am." A second later, he asked, "She is all right, isn't she? I mean, her knee?"

Vane's expression hardened. "Her knee's as well as can be expected—she has to stay off it for at least a few days, which, as you can imagine, is not improving her temper. At the moment, however, she's worrying—about you."

Gerrard colored. Looking down, he swallowed. "I lost my temper. I suppose I'd better go back." He started to pack up the sack.

Vane halted him. "Yes, we'd better get back and put a stop to her worrying, but you haven't asked about our plan."

Gerrard looked up. "Plan?"

Vane filled him in. "So, you see, we need you to continue to behave"—he gestured widely—"exactly as you have been—like a sapskull with his nose put out of joint."

Gerrard chuckled. "All right, but I am allowed to sneer dismissively, aren't I?"

"As much as you like, just don't forget your role."

"Minnie knows? And Timms?"

Vane nodded and got to his feet. "And Masters and Mrs. Henderson. I told Minnie and Timms this morning. As the staff are all reliable, there seemed little point keeping them in the dark, and we can use all the eyes we can get.''

"So," Gerrard said, untangling his legs and rising, ''we let it appear that I'm still chief suspect, all but convicted, and wait for the Spectre—''

"*Or* the thief—don't forget you're prime suspect there, too.''

Gerrard nodded. ''So we wait and we watch for their next move.''

"Right." Vane started down the mound. "That, at the moment, is all we can do.''

Chapter 9

Two days later, Patience sat in her private parlor and applied herself to her embroidery. The cloths for the drawing room were almost finished; she'd be glad to see the last of them. She was still confined to the daybed, her knee still bound, her foot propped on a cushion. Her suggestion, made earlier that morning, that she could probably hobble perfectly well using a stick, had made Mrs. Henderson purse her lips, shake her head, and pronounce that four days' complete rest would be wiser. *Four days!* Before she could voice her utter antipathy to the idea, Vane, in whose arms she'd been at the time, had weighed in, backing Mrs. Henderson.

When, after breakfast, Vane had carried her here and laid her on the daybed, he'd reminded her of his earlier threat to tie her to it should he discover her on her feet. The reminder had been couched in sufficiently intimidating terms to keep her reclining, attending to the household linens with apparent equanimity.

Minnie and Timms had come to bear her company; Timms was busy knotting a fringe while Minnie watched, lending a finger whenever an extra was needed. They were all used to spending hours in quiet endeavors; none saw any reason to fill the peace with chatter.

Which was just as well; Patience's mind was fully occupied elsewhere—mulling over what had ensued the first time Vane had carried her to this room. What with hiding her reaction, and her worries over Gerrard and the accusations hurled his way, it had been that night before she'd had time to fully examine the event.

Ever since, she had, at one level or another, thought of little else.

She should, of course, feel scandalized, or at the very least, shocked. Yet whenever she allowed herself to recall all that had happened, sweet pleasure washed through her, leaving her skin tingling and her breasts deliciously warm. Her "shock" was exciting, thrilling, an enticing reaction, not one of revulsion. She should feel guilty, yet whatever guilt she possessed was swamped beneath a compulsion to know, to experience, and an intense recollection of how much she'd enjoyed that particular experience.

Lips firming, she set a stitch. Curiosity—it was her curse, her bane, the cross she had to bear. She knew it. Unfortunately, knowing didn't quell the impulse. This time, curiosity was prompting her to waltz with a wolf—a dangerous enterprise. For the last two days, she'd watched him, waiting for the pounce she'd convinced herself would come, but he'd behaved like a lamb—a ridiculously strong, impossibly arrogant, not to say masterful lamb, but with a guileless newborn innocence, as if a halo had settled over his burnished locks.

Squinting at her work, Patience swallowed a disbelieving humph. He was playing some deep game. Unfortunately, due to lack of experience, she had no idea what.

"Actually"—Minnie settled back in her chair as Timms shook out the shawl they'd been working on—"this thief is worrying me. Vane might have scared the Spectre off, but the thief seems made of sterner stuff."

Patience glanced at Timms. "Your bracelet's still missing?"

Timms grimaced. "Ada turned my room upside down, and Minnie's, too. Masters and the maids have hunted high and low." She sighed. "It's gone."

"You said it was silver?"

Timms nodded. "But I wouldn't have thought it of any great value. It was engraved with vine leaves—you know the sort of thing." She sighed again. "It was my mother's and I'm really quite . . ."—she looked down, fiddling with the fringe she'd just knotted—"*bothered* that I've lost it."

Patience frowned absentmindedly and set another stitch.

Minnie sighed gustily. "And now here's Agatha similarly afflicted."

Patience looked up; so did Timms. "Oh?"

"She came to me this morning." Minnie frowned worriedly. "She was quite upset. Poor woman—what with all she's had to cope with, I wouldn't have had this happen for the world."

"What?" Patience prompted.

"Her earrings." Her expression as grim as it ever got, Minnie shook her head. "The last small piece she had left, poor dear. Oval drop garnets surrounded by white sapphires. You must have seen her wearing them."

"When last did she see them?" Patience remembered the earrings well. While handsome enough, they couldn't have been overly valuable.

"She wore them to dinner two nights ago," Timms put in.

"Indeed," Minnie nodded. "That was the last she saw of them—when she took them out that night and placed them in her box on her dressing table. When she went to get them last night, they were gone."

Patience frowned. "I thought she seemed a bit distracted last night."

"Agitated." Timms nodded grimly.

"She searched everywhere later," Minnie said, "but she's now quite sure they've vanished."

"Not vanished," Patience corrected. "They're with the thief. We'll find them when we catch him."

The door opened at that moment; Vane, followed by Gerrard, strolled in.

"Good morning, ladies." Vane nodded to Minnie and Timms, then turned his smile on Patience. His eyes, teasing grey, met hers; the quality of his smile, the expression at the back of his eyes, altered. Patience felt the warmth of his gaze as it slid lazily over her, over her cheeks, her throat, the swell of her upper breasts revealed by the scooped neckline of her morning gown. Her skin tingled; her nipples tightened.

She suppressed a warning scowl. "Did you enjoy your

ride?'' Her tone was as guilelessly innocent as his; both yesterday and today had been gloriously fine—while she'd been stuck inside, metaphorically tied to the daybed, he and Gerrard had enjoyed themselves on horseback, cantering about the county.

"Actually," Vane drawled, gracefully settling in a chair facing the daybed, "I've been introducing Gerrard to all the hedge-taverns within reach."

Patience's head jerked up; aghast, she stared at him.

"We've been checking if any of the others have been there," Gerrard eagerly explained. "Perhaps selling small things to tinkers or travelers."

From beneath her lashes, Patience threw Vane a darkling glance. He smiled, far too sweetly. His halo continued to glow. Patience sniffed and looked down at her work.

"And?" Minnie prompted.

"Nothing," Vane replied. "No one from the Hall—not even one of the grooms—has visited any of the local dives recently. No one's heard any whispers of anyone selling small items to tinkers and the like. So we still have no clue as to why the thief is stealing things, nor what he's doing with his ill-gotten gains."

"Speaking of which." Briefly, Minnie described the loss of Timms's bracelet and Mrs. Chadwick's earrings.

"So," Vane said, his expression hardening, "whoever it is has not been dissuaded by our pursuit of the Spectre."

"So what now?" Timms asked.

"We'll need to check Kettering and Northampton. It's possible the thief has a connection there."

The mantel clock chimed the half hour—twelve-thirty. Minnie gathered her shawls. "I'm due to see Mrs. Henderson about the menus."

"I'll leave the rest of this 'til later." Timms folded the shawl they'd been fringing.

Vane rose and offered Minnie his arm, but she waved him away. "No, I'm all right. You stay and keep Patience company." Minnie grinned at Patience. "Such a trying thing—to be tied to a daybed."

Suppressing her reaction to those innocent words, Patience smiled graciously, accepting Minnie's "gift"; once

Minnie had passed on her way to the door, Patience lifted her embroidery, fixed her gaze upon it, and grasped the needle firmly.

Gerrard held the door open for Minnie and Timms. They passed through; he looked back at Vane. And grinned engagingly. ''Duggan mentioned he'd be exercising your greys about now. I might just nip down and see if I can catch him.''

Patience whipped her head around, just in time to catch Gerrard's brotherly wave as he went out of the door. It shut behind him. In disbelief, she stared at the polished panels.

What were they all thinking of—leaving her alone with a wolf? She might be twenty-six—but she was an inexperienced twenty-six. Worse, she had a strong notion Vane viewed her age, let alone her inexperience, more as a positive than a negative.

Looking back at her work, she recalled his earlier jibe. Her temper rose, a helpful shield. Lifting her head, she studied him, standing before the daybed some four feet away. Her gaze was coolly measuring. ''I do hope you don't intend to drag Gerrard into every inn—every '*dive*'—in Kettering and Northampton.''

His gaze, already fixed on her, didn't waver; a slow, untrustworthy smile curved his lips. ''No inns or taverns—not even dives.'' His smile deepened. ''In the towns, we'll need to visit the jewelers, and the moneylenders. They often advance cash against goods.'' He paused, then grimaced. ''My one problem is that I can't see what anyone at the Hall would want with extra cash. There's nowhere about to wager or game.''

Lowering her embroidery to her lap, Patience frowned. ''Perhaps they need the money for something else.''

''I can't see the General or Edgar—much less Whitticombe—paying upkeep for some village maid and her brat.''

Patience shook her head. ''Henry would be shocked at the notion—he's stolidly conservative.''

''Indeed—and, somehow, the notion doesn't ring true for Edmond.'' Vane paused. Patience looked up—he trapped her gaze. ''As far as I can see,'' he said, his voice lowering to a purr, "Edmond seems more inclined to planning, rather than performance."

The implication, so strong Patience couldn't doubt she'd read it aright, was that *he* placed more emphasis on the latter. Ignoring the vise slowly choking off her breathing, she raised a haughty brow. "Indeed? I would have thought planning was always to be recommended." Greatly daring, she added, "In any enterprise."

Vane's slow smile curved his lips. Two prowling strides brought him to the daybed's side. "You misunderstand me—good planning's essential to any successful campaign." Trapping Patience's gaze, he reached for the embroidery lying forgotten in her lap.

Patience blinked free of his hold as the linen slipped from her lax grasp. "I daresay." She frowned—just what were they talking about? She followed the embroidery as Vane lifted it—and met his eyes over the top of the hoop.

He smiled—all wolf—and tossed her work—linen, hoop and needle—into the basket beside the daybed. Leaving her without protection.

Patience felt her eyes grow round. Vane's smile deepened—a dangerous glint gleamed in his grey eyes. Languidly, he lifted a hand and, long fingers sliding beneath her chin, gripped it gently. Deliberately, he brushed his thumb—gently—over her lips.

They throbbed; Patience wished she had the strength to pull free of his light hold, to wrench free of his gaze.

"What I meant," he said, his voice very deep, "was that planning without the subsequent performance is worthless."

He meant she should have hung on to her embroidery. Too late, Patience caught his drift. He'd seen through her plan to use her work as a shield. Breath bated, she waited for her temper to come to her aid, to rise in response to being read so effortlessly, to being affected so readily.

Nothing happened. No searing fury erupted.

The only thought in her head as she studied his grey eyes was what *he* was planning to do next.

Because she was watching, was so deep in the grey, she caught the change, the subtle shift, the flash of what looked suspiciously like satisfaction that glowed, briefly, in his eyes. His hand fell; lids lowering, he turned away.

"Tell me what you know of the Chadwicks."

Patience stared at him—at his back as he returned to his chair. By the time he sat and faced her, she'd managed to school her features, although they felt curiously blank.

"Well"—she moistened her lips—"Mr. Chadwick died about two years ago—missing at sea."

With the help of Vane's prompts, she recounted, stiltedly, all she knew of the Chadwicks. As she reached the end of her knowledge, the gong sounded.

His rake's smile returning, Vane stood and strolled toward her. "Speaking of performance, would you like me to carry you to lunch?"

She wouldn't—narrowing her eyes at him, Patience would have given half her fortune to avoid the sensation of being scooped so easily into his arms, and carried away so effortlessly. His touch was unnerving, distracting; it made her think of things she really should not. And as for the sensation of being helpless in his arms, trapped, at his mercy, a pawn to his whim—that was even worse.

Unfortunately, she had no choice. Coolly, inwardly girding her loins, she inclined her head. "If you would."

He grinned—and did.

The next day—the fourth and, Patience vowed, the very last day of her incarceration—she once more found herself committed to the daybed in her quiet parlor. After their usual early breakfast, Vane had carried her upstairs—he and Gerrard were to spend the day checking Northampton for any sign of items stolen from the Hall. The day was fine. The idea of a long drive, the wind whipping her hair as she sat on his box seat, behind the greys she'd already heard far too much about, had seemed like heaven. She'd been sorely tempted to ask that they put off the excursion—just for a day or so—until her knee improved sufficiently to allow her to sit in a carriage for a few hours, but, in the end, she'd held her tongue. They needed to discover who the thief was as soon as possible, and the weather, while fine today, could not be guaranteed.

Minnie and Timms had sat with her through the morning; as she couldn't go downstairs, they'd taken lunch on trays. Then Minnie had retired for her nap. Timms had helped Minnie to her room, but hadn't returned.

She'd finished the cloths for the drawing room. Idly examining designs, Patience wondered what project she should attempt next. Perhaps a delicate tray-piece for Minnie's dresser?

A knock on the door had her looking up in surprise. Neither Minnie nor Timms usually knocked.

"Come in."

The door opened tentatively; Henry's head appeared around its edge. "Am I disturbing you?"

Patience inwardly sighed, and waved to a chair. "By all means." She was, after all, bored.

Henry's puppy grin split his face. Straightening his shoulders, he entered, one hand held rather obviously behind his back. He advanced on the daybed, then halted—and, like a magician, produced his gift—a collection of late roses and autumn border blooms, greenery provided by Queen Anne's lace.

Primed, Patience widened her eyes in feigned surprise and delight. The delight waned as she focused on the ragged stems and the dangling remnants of roots. He'd ripped the flowers from the bushes and borders, not caring of the damage he did. "How—" She forced a smile to her lips. "How lovely." She took the poor flowers from him. "Why don't you ring for a maid so I can ask for a vase?"

Smiling proudly, Henry crossed to the bellpull and yanked it vigorously. Then, clasping his hands behind his back, he rocked on his toes. "Wonderful day outside."

"Is it?" Patience tried not to sound wistful.

The maid arrived and returned quickly with a vase and a pair of garden shears. While Henry prattled on about the weather, Patience tended the flowers, loping off the ragged ends and roots and setting them in the vase. Finished, she set the shears aside and turned the small side table she'd worked on toward Henry. "There." With a gracious wave, she sat back. "I do thank you for your kindness."

Henry beamed. He opened his lips—a knock cut off his words.

Brows rising, Patience turned to the door. "Come in."

As she'd half expected, it was Edmond. He'd brought his latest stanza. He beamed an ingenuous grin at both Patience and Henry. "Tell me what you think."

It wasn't just one stanza—to Patience, trying to follow the intricacies of his phrasing, it seemed more like half a canto.

Henry shifted and shuffled, his earlier brightness fading into petulance. Patience fought to stifle a yawn. Edmond prosed on.

And on.

When the next knock sounded, Patience turned eagerly, hoping for Masters or even a maid.

It was Penwick.

Patience gritted her teeth—and forced her lips to curve over them. Resigned, she held out her hand. "Good morning, sir. I trust you are well?"

"Indeed, my dear." Penwick bowed low—too low, he nearly hit his head on the side of the daybed. Pulling back just in time, he frowned—then banished the expression to smile, far too intently, into Patience's eyes. "I've been waiting to fill you in on the latest developments—the figures on production after we instituted the new rotation scheme. I know," he said, smiling fondly down at her, "how interested you are in 'our little patch.' "

"Ah—yes." What could she say? She'd always used agriculture, and having run the Grange for so long she had a more than passing knowledge of the subject, to distract Penwick. "Perhaps—?" She glanced hopefully at Henry. Tight-lipped, his gaze was fixed, not amiably, on Penwick. "Henry was just telling me how fine the weather's been these last few days."

Henry obligingly followed her lead. "Should stay fine for the foreseeable future. I was talking to Grisham only this morning—"

Unfortunately, despite considerable effort, Patience could not get Henry to switch to the effect of the weather on the crops, nor could she get Penwick to, as he usually did, distract Henry and himself with such matters.

To crown all, Edmond kept taking snippets from both Henry's and Penwick's words and fashioning them into verse, then, across whoever was speaking, trying to engage her in a discussion of how such verses might fit with the development of his drama.

Within five minutes, the conversation descended into a three-way tug-of-war for her attention—Patience was ready to throttle whichever foolish servant it was who'd divulged her up-until-then-secret location.

At the end of ten minutes, she was ready to throttle Henry, Edmond and Penwick as well. Henry held his position and pontificated on the elements; Edmond, nothing loath, was now talking of including mythological gods as commentators on his main characters' actions. Penwick, losing out to the chorus, puffed out his chest and portentously asked: "Where's Debbington? Surprised he isn't here, bearing you company."

"Oh, he tagged along with Cynster," Henry offhandedly informed him. "They escorted Angela and Mama to Northampton."

Finding Patience's gaze riveted on his face, Henry beamed at her. "Deal of sunshine, today—shouldn't wonder if Angela doesn't claim a turn in Cynster's curricle."

Patience's brows rose. "Indeed?"

There was a note in her voice which successfully halted all conversation; the three gentlemen, suddenly wary, glanced sidelong at each other.

"I think," Patience declared, "that I have rested long enough." Tossing aside the rug that had lain across her lap, she pushed herself to the edge of the daybed, and carefully let down her good leg, then the damaged one. "If you would be so good as to give me your arm . . . ?"

They all rushed to help. In the end, it wasn't as easy as she'd thought—her knee was still tender, and very stiff. Taking her full weight on that leg was out of the question.

Which made the stairs impossible. Edmond and Henry made a chair of their arms; Patience sat and held their shoulders for balance. Puffed with importance, Penwick led the way down, talking all the while. Henry and Edmond couldn't talk—they were concentrating too much on balancing her weight down the steep stairs.

They made it to the front hall without mishap, and set her carefully on her feet on the tiles. By then Patience was having second thoughts—or rather, she *would* have entertained second thoughts, if she hadn't been so exercised by the news that Vane had taken Angela to Northampton.

That Angela had enjoyed the drive—would even now be enjoying the drive—she herself had fantasized over, but had, for the greater good, not sought to claim.

She was not in a very good mood.

"The back parlor," she declared. Leaning on both Henry's and Edmond's arms, she hobbled along between them, trying not to wince. Penwick rattled on, recounting the number of bushels "their little patch" had produced, his matrimonial assumptions waving like flags in his words. Patience gritted her teeth. Once they gained the back parlor, she would dismiss them all—and then, very carefully, massage her knee.

No one would look for her in the back parlor.

"You're not supposed to be on your feet."

The statement, uttered in a flat tone, filled the sudden gap where Penwick's babble had been.

Patience looked up, then had to tip her chin higher—Vane was standing directly in front of her. He was wearing his caped greatcoat; the wind had ruffled his hair. Behind him, the side door stood open. Light streamed into the dim corridor, but didn't reach her. He blocked it—a very large, very male figure, made even larger by the capes of his greatcoat, spread wide by his broad shoulders. She couldn't see the expression on his face, in his eyes—she didn't need to. She knew his face was hard, his eyes steel grey, his lips thin.

Irritation poured from him in waves; in the confines of the corridor, it was a tangible force. "I did warn you," he said, his tones clipped, "what would happen."

Patience opened her lips; all she uttered was a gasp.

She was no longer on her feet, she was in his arms.

"Just a minute!"

"I say—!"

"Wait—!"

The ineffectual exclamations died behind them. Vane's swift strides had them back in the front hall before Penwick, Edmond, and Henry could do more than collectively blink.

Catching her breath, Patience glared. "Put me down!"

Vane glanced, very briefly, into her face. "No." He started up the stairs.

Patience drew in a breath—two maids were coming down the stairs. She smiled as they passed. And then they were in the gallery. It had taken the others ten full minutes to get her downstairs; Vane had accomplished the reverse in under a minute. "The other *gentlemen*," she acidly informed him, "were helping me to the back parlor."

"Sapskulls."

Patience's breasts swelled. "I *wanted* to be in the back parlor!"

"Why?"

Why? Because then, if he came looking for her after his fine day out at Northampton with Angela, he wouldn't have known where she was and might have been worried? "Because," Patience tartly replied, folding her arms defensively across her breasts, "I've grown sick of the upstairs parlor." The parlor he'd arranged for her. "I'm bored there."

Vane glanced at her as he juggled her to open the door. "Bored?"

Patience looked into his eyes and wished she'd used some other word. Bored was, apparently, a red rag to a rake. "It's not long to dinner, perhaps you should just take me to my room."

The door swung wide. Vane stepped through, then kicked it shut behind them. And smiled. "There's more than an hour before you need change. I'll carry you to your room—later."

His eyes had narrowed, silvery with intent. His voice had changed to his dangerous purr. Patience wondered if any of the other three would have the courage to follow—she couldn't believe they would. Ever since Vane had so coldly annihilated their senseless accusations of Gerrard, both Edmond and Henry treated him with respect—the sort of respect accorded dangerous carnivores. And Penwick knew Vane disliked him—intensely.

Vane advanced on the daybed. Patience eyed it with increasing misgiving. "What do you think you're doing?"

"Tying you to the daybed."

She tried to humph, tried to ignore the premonition tickling her spine. "Don't be silly—you just said that as a threat." Would it be wise to wind her arms about his neck?

He reached the back of the bed, and stopped. "I never issue threats." His words floated down to her as she stared at the cushions. "Only warnings."

With that, he swung her over the wrought-iron back and set her down with her spine against it. Patience immediately squirmed, trying to twist around. One large palm, splayed across her midriff, kept her firmly in place.

"And then," Vane continued, in the same, dangerous tone, "we'll have to see what we can do to . . . distract you."

"Distract me?" Patience stopped her futile wriggling.

"Hmm." His words feathered her ear. "To alleviate your boredom."

There was enough sensual weight in the words to temporarily freeze her wits—capture them and hold them in fascinated speculation—just long enough for him to grab a scarf from the pile of mending left in the basket by the daybed, thread it through the holes in the swirls of the ornate back and cinch it tight about her waist.

"What . . . ?" Patience looked down as his hand disappeared and the scarf drew tight. Then she glared. "This is ridiculous." She tugged at the scarf and tried to shift forward, but he'd already secured the knot. The silk gave just so far, then held. Vane strolled around to face her; Patience shot him a dagger glance—she didn't want to know about the smile on his lips. Compressing her own, she lifted her arms and reached over the back of the bed. The ornately worked railing reached halfway up her back—while she could lift her arms over it, she couldn't reach very far down. She couldn't touch his knot, let alone untie it.

Eyes narrowed, Patience looked up; Vane was watching her, a cool smile of ineffable male superiority etched on

his too-fascinating lips. She narrowed her eyes to slits.
"You will never live this down."

The curve of his lips deepened. "You're not uncomfortable. Just sit still for the next hour." His gaze sharpened.
"It'll do your knee good."

Patience gritted her teeth. "I'm not some infant who
needs to be restrained!"

"On the contrary it's clear you need someone to exercise
some control over you. You heard Mrs. Henderson—four
full days. Your four days is up tomorrow."

Astounded, Patience stared at him. "And just who appointed you my keeper?"

She caught his gaze, held the contact defiantly—and
waited. His eyes narrowed. "I feel guilty. I should have
sent you back to the house as soon as I found you in the
ruins."

All expression drained from Patience's face. "You wish
you'd sent me back to the house?"

Vane frowned. "I feel guilty because you were following
me when you got hurt."

Patience humphed and crossed her arms beneath her
breasts. "You told me it was *my* fault for not staying where
you'd told me to stay. Anyway, if Gerrard at seventeen is
old enough to be responsible for his own actions, why
would it be otherwise with me?"

Vane looked down at her; Patience felt sure she'd won
her point. Then he raised an arrogant brow. "*You're* the
one with the wrenched knee. *And* the twisted ankle."

Patience refused to surrender. "My ankle's fine." She
put her nose in the air. "And my knee's just a bit stiff. If
I could test it—"

"You can test it tomorrow. Who knows?" Vane's expression hardened. "You might need an extra day or two's
rest after today's excitement."

Patience narrowed her eyes. "Don't," she advised,
"even suggest it."

Vane raised both brows, then, turning away, prowled to
the window. Patience watched him, and tried to locate the
anger she felt sure she should feel. It simply wasn't to be
found. Stifling a disaffected humph, she settled more com-

fortably. "So what did you discover in Northampton?"

He glanced back, then fell to prowling back and forth between the windows. "Gerrard and I made the acquaintance of a very helpful individual—the Northampton Guildmaster, so to speak."

Patience frowned. "Of which guild?"

"The guild of moneylenders, thieves, and rogues—assuming there is one. He was intrigued with our investigations and amused enough to be helpful. His contacts are extensive. After two hours of consuming the best French brandy—at my expense, of course—he assured us no one had recently attempted to sell any items of the sort we're seeking."

"Do you think he's reliable?"

Vane nodded. "There was no reason for him to lie. The items, as he so succinctly put it, are of insufficient quality to attract his personal interest. He's also well-known as 'the man to contact.' "

Patience grimaced. "You'll check Kettering?"

Still pacing, Vane nodded.

Watching him, Patience conjured her most innocent expression. "And what did Mrs. Chadwick and Angela do while you and Gerrard met with this Guildmaster?"

Vane stopped pacing. He looked at Patience—studied her. His expression was unreadable. Eventually, he said, "I haven't the faintest idea."

His voice had altered, a subtle undercurrent of awakened interest sliding beneath the suave tones. Patience opened her eyes wide. "You mean Angela didn't tell you every last detail on the drive back?"

With long, languid strides, Vane came toward her. "She traveled—both ways—in the carriage."

Vane reached the edge of the daybed. His eyes gleamed with a predator's satisfaction. He leaned nearer—

"Patience? Are you awake?"

A peremptory knock was followed immediately by the sound of the latch lifting.

Patience swung around—as far as she could. Vane straightened; as the door opened, he reached the back of the daybed. Before he could tug the knotted scarf loose, Angela breezed in.

"Oh!" Angela stopped, eyes widening with delight. "Mr. Cynster! *Perfect*! You must give us your opinion of my purchases."

Eyeing the bandbox dangling from Angela's fingers with distinct disapprobation, Vane nodded a noncommittal greeting. As Angela eagerly made for the chairs facing the daybed, he stooped slightly, fingers reaching for the knot in the scarf, screened from view by his legs—only to have to straighten quickly as the door swung wider and Mrs. Chadwick entered.

Angela, settling in a chair, looked up. "See here, Mama—Mr. Cynster can tell us if the ribbons that I bought aren't just the right shade."

With a calm nod for Vane and a smile for Patience, Mrs. Chadwick headed for the second chair. "Now, Angela, I'm sure Mr. Cynster has other engagements . . ."

"No, how can he have? There's no one else here. Besides,"—Angela threw Vane a sweet, truly ingenuous smile—"that's how *ton*nish gentlemen pass their time— commenting on ladies' fashions."

The sigh of relief Patience had heard behind her was abruptly cut off. For one fractured instant, she was sorely tempted to twist about, look up—and inquire if Angela's foppish notion of his character found greater favor with him than her earlier, overly rakish one. Then again, both notions were partly right. Vane, she felt sure, when he commented on ladies' fashions, would do so while divesting the subject of his interest of them.

Mrs. Chadwick heaved a motherly sigh. "Actually, my dear, that's not quite right." She sent Vane an apologetic glance. "Not all gentlemen . . ." For Angela's edification, Mrs. Chadwick embarked on a careful explanation of the distinctions prevailing amongst *ton*nish males.

Leaning forward, ostensibly to straighten the wrap over Patience's legs, Vane murmured, "That's my cue to retreat."

Patience's gaze remained glued to Mrs. Chadwick. "I'm

still tied," she murmured back. "You can't leave me like this."

Fleetingly, her eyes met Vane's. He hesitated, then his face hardened. "I'll release you on condition that you wait here until I return to carry you to your room."

Reaching farther over her, he flicked out the edge of the wrap. Patience glared at his profile. "This is all your fault," she informed him in a whisper. "If I'd made it to the back parlor, I'd have been safe.

Straightening, Vane met her gaze. "Safe from what? There's a daybed there, too."

Her gaze trapped in his, Patience tried hard not to let the likely outcomes take shape in her mind. Determinedly, she blotted out all thought of what might have transpired had Angela not arrived as she had. If she thought too much of that, she'd very likely throttle Angela, too. The ranks of her potential victims were growing by the hour.

"Anyway . . ."—Vane's gaze flicked to Angela and Mrs. Chadwick. He stooped slightly; Patience felt the tug as he worked the knotted scarf free—"you said you were bored." The knot gave, and he straightened. Patience looked up and back—and met his eyes. His lips curved, too knowingly. One brown brow arched, subtlely wicked. "Isn't this what usually distracts ladies?"

He knew very well what ladies found most distracting— the look in his eyes, the sensual curve of his lips said as much, screamed as much. Patience narrowed her eyes at him, then, folding her arms, looked back at Mrs. Chadwick. "Coward," she taunted, just loudly enough for him to hear.

"When it comes to gushing schoolgirls, I freely admit it." The words fell softly, then he stepped away from the daybed's back. The movement caught both Angela's and Mrs. Chadwick's attention. Vane smiled, smoothly suave. "I'm afraid, ladies, that I'll have to leave you. I need to check on my horses." With a nod to Mrs. Chadwick, a vague smile for Angela, and a last, faintly challenging glance for Patience, he sketched an elegant bow and made his escape.

The door closed behind him. Angela's bright face darkened into a sulky pout. Patience inwardly groaned, and swore she'd extract suitable revenge. Meanwhile . . . Plastering an interested smile on her lips, she looked at the items spilling from Angela's bandox. "Is that a comb?"

Angela blinked, then brightened. "Yes, it is. Quite inexpensive, but so pretty." She held up a tortoiseshell comb dotted with paste "diamonds." "Don't you think it's just the thing for my hair?"

Patience resigned herself to perjury. Angela had bought cerise ribbon, too—by the yard. Patience silently added that to Vane's bill, and continued to smile sweetly.

Chapter 10

D anger.
    It should have been his middle name.
It should have been tatooed on his forehead.

"A warning would at least make it fairer." Patience waited for Myst to react; eventually, the cat blinked. "Humph!" Patience cut another branch of autumn color. Narrow-eyed, she bent and stuffed the branch into the pannier at her feet.

Three days had passed since she'd escaped the daybed; this morning, she'd eschewed Sir Humphrey's cane. Her first excursion had been a ramble about the old walled garden. In company with Vane.

That, in retrospect, had been a most peculiar outing—it had certainly left her in a most peculiar state. They'd been alone. Anticipation had soared, only to be frustrated—by Vane. By their location. Unfortunately, there had been no other private moments in the intervening days.

Which had left her in no very good mood—as if her emotions, raised by that one, intense, unfulfilled moment in the walled garden, were still swirling hotly, as yet unappeased. Her knee was weak, but no longer painful. She could walk freely, but could not yet go far.

She'd gone as far as the shrubbery, to collect a sheaf of bright leaves for the music room.

Picking up the full pannier, Patience balanced it against her hip. Waving Myst ahead, she started along the grassy path leading back to the house.

134

Life at the Hall, temporarily disrupted by Vane's arrival and her accident, was settling back into its usual routine. The only hitch in the smooth flow of mild household events was Vane's continuing presence. He was about somewhere—she had no idea where.

Emerging from the shrubbery, Patience scanned the lawns rolling away into the ruins. The General was striding up from the river, walking briskly and swinging his cane. In the ruins themselves, Gerrard sat on a stone, his easel before him. Patience studied the stones and archways nearby, then swept the ruins and lawns again.

Then realized what she was doing.

She headed for the side door. Edgar and Whitticombe would be buried in the library—not even sunshine would lure them out. Edmond's muse had turned demanding: He barely attended meals, and even then, was sunk in abstraction. Henry, of course, was as idle as ever. He had, however, developed a penchant for billiards and was frequently to be found practicing shots.

Opening the side door, Patience waited for Myst to trip daintily in, then followed and shut the door. Myst led the way up the corridor. Resetting her pannier, Patience heard voices in the back parlor. Angela's whine, followed by Mrs. Chadwick's patient reply. Grimacing, Patience walked on. Angela was town-bred, not used to the country, with its mild pursuits and slow seasons. Vane's arrival had transformed her into a typical, bright-eyed miss. Unfortunately, she'd now tired of that image and reverted to her usual, die-away airs.

Of the rest of the household, Edith continued with her tatting. And Alice had been so silent of late one could be forgiven for forgetting her existence.

From the front hall, Patience turned into a narrow corridor, and thus reached the garden hall. Setting the pannier on a side table, she selected a heavy vase. As she arranged her branches, she considered Minnie and Timms. Timms was happier, more relaxed now that Vane was here. The same and more could be said of Minnie. She was clearly sleeping better—her eyes were back to their sparkling best and her cheeks no longer sagged with worry.

Patience frowned, and concentrated on her twigs.

Gerrard was also more relaxed. The accusations and insinuations surrounding him had died, sunk without trace, dispersed like so much river mist. Just like the Spectre.

That was also Vane's doing—another benefit his presence had brought them. The Spectre hadn't been sighted again.

The thief, however, continued to strike: His latest trophy was nothing short of bizarre. Edith Swithin's pincushion—a beaded, pink-satin cushion four inches square, embroidered with a likeness of His Majesty George III, could hardly be considered valuable. That last disappearance had perplexed them all. Vane had shaken his head and given it as his opinion that they had a resident magpie roosting within the Hall.

"Resident raven more like." Patience looked at Myst. "Have you seen one?"

Settled on her brisket, Myst met her gaze, then yawned. Not delicately. Her fangs were quite impressive. "No raven either," Patience concluded.

Despite checking all inns and "dives" within reach, Vane, happily assisted by Gerrard, had not found any clue to suggest the thief was selling the stolen goods. It all remained an ongoing mystery.

Patience put away the pannier, then picked up the vase. Myst jumped from the table and, tail high, led the way. As she headed for the music room, Patience reflected that, with the exception of Vane's presence and the thief's eccentricities, the household had indeed sunk back into its previously untrammeled existence.

Before Vane's arrival, the music room had been her retreat—none of the others was musically inclined. She'd always played, every day for most of her life. Spending an hour with a pianoforte, or, as here, a harpsichord, always soothed her, eased the load that had always been hers.

Carrying the vase into the music room, she placed it on the central table. Returning to close the door, she surveyed her domain. And nodded. "Back to normal."

Myst was making herself comfortable on a chair. Patience headed for the harpsichord.

These days, she never decided what to play, but simply

let her fingers roam. She knew so many pieces, she just let her mind choose without conscious direction.

Five minutes of restless, disjointed playing—of drifting from one piece to another in search of her mood—was enough to bring home the truth. *Not* everything was back to normal.

Putting her hands in her lap, Patience frowned direfully at the keys. Things were back the way they were, the same as before Vane's arrival. The only changes were for the good; no need for her to fret. Less need to fret than before. Everything was proceeding smoothly. She had her usual round of small chores, lending order to her days—she'd found it satisfying before.

But far from sinking back into reassuring routine, she was . . . fretful. Dissatisfied.

Patience put her hands back on the keys. But no music came. Instead, her mind, entirely against her will, conjured up the source of her dissatisfaction. One elegant gentleman. Patience looked down at her fingers resting on the ivory keys. She was trying to fool herself and not doing a particularly good job of it.

Her mood was unsettled, her temper more so. As for her emotions, they'd taken up residence on a carousel. She didn't know what she wanted, she didn't know what she felt. For someone used to being in charge of her life, of directing that life, the situation was beyond irritating.

Patience narrowed her eyes. Her situation, in fact, was insupportable. Which meant it was past time she did something about it. The source of her condition was obvious— Vane. Just him—no one else was even peripherally involved. It was her interaction with him that was causing all her problems.

She could avoid him.

Patience considered that long and hard—and rejected it on the grounds that she couldn't do that without embarrassing herself and insulting Minnie. And Vane might not deign to be avoided.

And she might not be strong enough to avoid him.

Frowning, she shook her head. "Not a good idea." Her thoughts returned to their last moment alone, in the walled garden three days before. Her frown deepened. What was he about? His "not here" she'd later understood—the walled garden was overlooked by the house. But what had he meant by "not yet"?

"That," she informed Myst, "suggests a 'later.' A 'sometime.'" Patience set her teeth. "What I want to know is *when*?"

A scandalous, inadmissable want perhaps, but . . . "I'm twenty-six." Patience eyed Myst as if she'd argued. "I'm entitled to the knowledge." When Myst responded with an unblinking stare, Patience continued: "It's not as if I intend throwing my cap over the windmill. I'm not likely to forget who I am, let alone who and what he is. And neither is he. It should all be perfectly safe."

Myst tucked her nose into her paws.

Patience went back to frowning at the keyboard. "He won't seduce me under Minnie's roof." Of that, she was certain. Which raised a most pertinent question. What did he want—what did *he* expect to gain? What was his purpose in all this—did he even have one?

All questions for which she lacked answers. While, over the last days, Vane had not engineered any moment alone with her, she was always conscious of his gaze, always conscious of him, of his watchful presence.

"Perhaps this is dalliance? Or some part thereof?"

Yet more questions without answers.

Patience gritted her teeth, then forced herself to relax. She drew in a deep breath, exhaled and drew in another, then determinedly laid her fingers on the keys. She didn't understand Vane—the elegant gentleman with unpredictable reservations—indeed, he confused her at every turn. Worse, if this was dalliance, then it apparently proceeded at his whim, under his control, entirely outside hers—and, of that, she thoroughly disapproved.

She wasn't going to think about him anymore.

Patience closed her eyes, and let her fingers flow over the keys.

Delicate, hauntingly uncertain music floated out of the house. Vane heard it as he walked up from the stables. The lilting strains reached him, then wrapped about him, about his mind, sinking into his senses. They were a siren's song—and he knew precisely who was singing.

Halting on the graveled drive before the stable arch, he listened to the moody air. It drew him—he could feel the tug as if it was physical. The music spoke—of need, of restless frustration, of underlying rebellion.

The scrunch of gravel under his boots brought him to his senses. Frowning, he stopped again. The music room was on the ground floor, facing away from the ruins; its windows gave onto the terrace. At least one window had to be open, or he wouldn't hear the music so clearly.

For a long moment, he stared, unseeing, at the house. The music grew more eloquent, seeking to ensorcel him, insistently drawing him on. For one more minute, he resisted, then shook aside his hesitation. His face set, he strode for the terrace.

When the final notes died, Patience sighed and lifted her fingers from the keys. A measure of calm had returned to her, the music had released some of her restlessness, had soothed her soul. A catharsis.

She stood, more serene, more confident than when she'd sat. Pushing back the stool, she stepped about it and turned.

Toward the windows. Toward the man who stood beside the open French door. His expression was set, unreadable.

"I had thought," she said, her words deliberate, her eyes steady on his, "that you might be thinking of leaving."

Her challenge could not have been clearer.

"No." Vane answered without thinking; no thought was required. "Aside from unmasking the Spectre and discovering the thief, I haven't yet got that something I want."

Contained, commanding, Patience's chin rose another notch. Vane studied her, his words echoing in his head. When he'd first coined the phrase, he hadn't appreciated exactly what it was that he wanted. Now he knew. His goal, this time, was different from the prizes he habitually lusted after. This time, he wanted a great deal more.

He wanted her—all of her. Not just the physical her, but her devotion, her love, her heart—all the essential her, the tangible intangible of her being, her self. He wanted it all—and he wasn't going to be satisfied with anything less.

He knew why he wanted her, too. Why she was different. But he wasn't going to think about that.

She was his. He'd known it the instant he'd held her in his arms, that first evening with the storm lowering about them. She'd fitted—and he'd known, instinctively, immediately, at some level deeper than his bones. He hadn't come by his name by accident: he had a gift for recognizing what scent was on the breeze. An instinctive hunter, he responded to shifts in the mood, the atmosphere, taking advantage of whatever current was flowing without conscious thought.

He'd known from the first just what was in the wind—known from the instant he'd held Patience Debbington in his arms.

Now she stood before him, challenge lighting gold sparks in her eyes. That she was tired of their present hiatus was clear; what she envisioned replacing it was not so obvious. The only virtuous, willful women he'd interacted with were related to him; he'd never dallied with such ladies. He had no clue what Patience was thinking, how much she'd accepted. Taking a death grip on the reins of his own clamorous needs, he deliberately took the first steps to find out.

With slow, prowling strides, he approached her.

She didn't say a word. Instead, her eyes steady on his, she lifted one hand, one finger, and, slowly, giving him ample time to react, to stop her if he would, reached to touch his lips.

Vane didn't move.

The first tentative touch inwardly rocked him; he tightened his hold on his passions. She sensed the momentary turbulence. Her eyes widened, her breath caught. Then he stilled and she relaxed, and continued her tracing.

She seemed fascinated by his lips. Her gaze dropped to them; as her finger passed over his lower lip and returned to one corner, Vane moved his head just enough to brush a kiss across her fingertip.

Her eyes lifted again to his. Emboldened, she quested further, lifting her fingers higher to trace his cheek.

Vane returned the caress, slowly raising one hand to run the back of his fingers along the smooth curve of her jaw, then sliding them back until his palm cupped her chin. His fingers firmed; moving to the slow, steady drumbeat only he and she could hear, he tilted her face up.

Their gazes locked. Then he let his lids fall, knowing she did the same. In time with the slow beat, he lowered his lips to hers.

She hesitated for one instant, then kissed him back. He waited one beat more before demanding her mouth; she yielded it instantly. Sliding his fingers further, beneath the silken coil of hair at her nape, he raised his other hand and framed her jaw.

He held her face steady—and slowly, systematically, moving to the compelling rhythm that held them, drove them, plundered her mouth.

That kiss was a revelation—Patience had never imagined a simple kiss could be so bold, so heavily invested with meaning. His lips were hard; they moved over hers, parting them further, confidently managing her, ruthlessly teaching her all she was so eager to learn.

His tongue invaded her mouth with the arrogance of a conqueror claiming victory's spoils. Unhurriedly, he visited every corner of his domain, claiming each inch, branding it as his—knowing it. After a lengthy, devastatingly thorough inspection, he settled to sample her in a different way. The slow, languid thrusting seduced her willing senses.

She'd yielded, yet her passive surrender satisfied neither of them. Patience found herself drawn into the game—the slide of lips against lips, the sensual glide of hot tongue against tongue. She was more than willing. The promise in the heat rising, steadily building between them, and even more the tension—excitement and something more—that surged like a slow tide behind the warm glow, drew her on. The kiss stretched and time slowed—the drugging effect of shared breaths sent her wits into a slow spin.

He drew back, breaking the kiss, letting her catch her breath. But he didn't straighten; his lips, relentlessly hard, remained mere inches from hers.

Aware only of compulsion, of the steady driving beat in

her blood, she stretched upward and touched her lips to his.

He took her lips, her mouth, briefly, then again broke the contact.

Patience snatched a breath and, stretching up, followed his lips with hers. She needn't have worried—he wasn't going anywhere. His fingers firmed about her jaw; his lips returned, harder, more demanding as he angled his head over hers.

The kiss deepened. Patience hadn't dreamed there could be more, yet there was. Heat and hunger poured through her. She felt each caress, each bold, knowing stroke—she reveled in the hot pleasure, drank it in, and gave it back—and wanted more.

When next their lips parted, they were both breathing rapidly. Patience opened her eyes and met his watchful gaze. Subtle invitation, and even subtler challenge, melded in the grey; she considered the sight—and considered how much more he could teach her.

She paused. Then she stepped closer, sliding one hand, then the other, up over his broad shoulders. Her bodice touched his jacket; she moved closer still. Boldly holding his gaze, she pressed her hips to his thighs.

The locking of his control was palpable, like the sudden clenching of a fist. The reaction reassured her, allowed her to continue to meet his grey gaze. To meet the challenge in his eyes.

His hands had softened about her face; now they drifted away, resting briefly on her shoulders before, his gaze steady on hers, he swept them down, down her back, over her hips, drawing her fully against him.

Patience's breath caught. Her lids fell. Wordlessly, she lifted her face, offering her lips.

He took them, took her—as their lips fused, Patience felt his hands slide lower, deliberately tracing the ripe hemispheres of her bottom. He filled his hands, then kneaded—heat spread, prickling over her skin, leaving it fevered. Cupping her firm flesh, he molded her to him, easing her deeper into the V of his braced thighs.

She felt the evidence of his desire, felt the hard, heavy, throbbing reality pressed against her soft belly. He held her there, senses fully awake, fully aware, for one achingly intense instant, then his tongue slowly surged, thrusting deep into the softness of her mouth.

Patience would have gasped, but she couldn't. The evocative caress, his unhurried possession of her mouth, sent heat rolling through her. It pooled, hot and heavy, in her loins. As the kiss drew her in, drew her deeper, a heady langor spread, weighting her limbs, slowing her senses.

But not muting them.

She was achingly aware. Aware of the hardness that surrounded her, of the steely flex of hard muscle about her. Of her tightly furled nipples pressed hard to the wall of his chest; of the softness of her thighs held intimately against him. Of the relentless, driving passion he ruthlessly held back.

That last was a temptation, but one so potently, preeminently dangerous not even she dared prod it.

Not yet. There were other things she'd yet to learn.

Like the feel of his hand on her breast—different now he was kissing her so deeply, now she was so much in contact with him. Her breast swelled, warm and tight as his fingers closed about it; the nipple was already a ruched bud, excruciatingly sensitive to his knowing squeeze.

And their kiss went on, anchoring her to her own heartbeat, to the repetitive ebb and surge of a rhythm that played at the very edge of her consciousness. The pattern swirled and deepened, but still the beat was there, a crescendo of slow-burning desire, conducted, orchestrated, so that she never lost touch, was never overwhelmed by sensation.

He was teaching her.

Quite when that became clear, Patience couldn't have said, but she'd accepted it as truth when the gong for lunch sounded. Distantly.

She ignored it; so did Vane. At first. Then, with obvious reluctance, he drew back from their kiss.

"They'll notice if we miss lunch." He murmured the words against her lips—then resumed kissing them.

"Hmm," was all Patience cared to say.

Three minutes later, he lifted his head. And looked down at her.

Patience studied his eyes, his face. Not the smallest hint

of apology, of triumph, even of satisfaction, showed in the grey, in the hard, angular planes. Hunger was the dominant emotion—in him and in her. She could feel it deep within her, a primal craving stirred to life by their kiss but as yet unappeased. His hunger showed in the tension holding him, the control he'd never once eased.

His lips twisted wryly. "We'll have to go." Reluctantly, he released her.

Equally reluctant, Patience drew back, instantly regretting the loss of his heat and the sense of intimacy that, for the last uncounted moments, they'd shared.

There was, she discovered, nothing she wished to say. Vane offered his arm and she took it, and allowed him to lead her to the door.

Chapter 11

After his afternoon gallop with Gerrard, Vane strode determinedly back to the house.

He couldn't get Patience out of his mind. The taste of her, the feel of her, the evocatively heady scent of her wreathed his senses and preyed on his attention. He hadn't been this obsessed since he'd first lifted a woman's skirts, yet he recognized the symptoms. He wasn't going to be able to concentrate on anything else until he'd succeeded in putting Patience Debbington in her rightful place—on her back beneath him.

And he couldn't do *that* until he'd said the words, asked the question he'd known had been inevitable since she'd first landed in his arms.

In the front hall, he encountered Masters. Purposefully, Vane stripped off his gloves. "Where's Miss Debbington, Masters?"

"In the mistress's parlor, sir. She usually sits with the mistress and Mrs. Timms most afternoons."

One boot on the lowest stair, Vane considered the various excuses he could use to extract Patience from under Minnie's wing. Not one was sufficient to escape attracting Minnie's instant attention. Let alone Timms's. "Hmm." Lips setting, he swung about. "I'll be in the billiard room."

"Indeed, sir."

Contrary to Masters's belief, Patience wasn't in Minnie's parlor. Excusing herself from their usual sewing session, she'd taken refuge in the parlor on the floor below, where the daybed, now no longer needed, sat swathed in Holland covers.

So she could pace unrestricted, frowning, muttering distractedly, while she attempted to understand, to accurately comprehend, to justify and reconcile all that had happened in the music room that morning.

Her world had tilted. Abruptly. Without warning.

"That much," she waspishly informed an imperturbable Myst, curled comfortably on a chair, "is impossible to deny." That heated yet masterfully controlled kiss she and Vane had shared had been a revelation on more than one front.

Swinging about, Patience halted before the window. Folding her arms, she stared out, unseeing. The physical revelations, while unnerving enough, had been no real shock—they were, indeed, no more than her curiosity demanded. She wanted to know—he'd consented to teach her. That kiss had been her first lesson; that much was clear.

As for the rest—therein lay her problem.

"There was something else there." An emotion she'd never thought to feel, never expected to feel. "At least"—grimacing, she resumed her restless pacing—"I *think* there was."

The acute sense of loss she'd felt when they'd moved apart had not been simply a physical reaction—the separation had affected her on some other plane. And the compulsion to intimacy—to satisfy the hunger she sensed in him—*that* did not stem from curiosity.

"This is getting complicated." Rubbing a finger across her forehead in a vain attempt to erase her frown, Patience struggled to come to grips with her emotions, to clarify what she truly felt. If her feelings for Vane went beyond the physical, did that mean what she thought it meant?

"How on earth can I tell?" Spreading her hands, she appealed to Myst. "I've never felt this way before."

The thought suggested another possibility. Halting, Patience lifted her head, then, with returning confidence, drew herself up and glanced hopefully at Myst. "Perhaps I'm just imagining it?"

Myst stared, unblinking, through big blue eyes, then yawned, stretched, jumped down, and led the way to the door.

Patience sighed. And followed.

The telltale tension between them—there from the first—had intensified. Vane felt it as he held Patience's chair while she settled her skirts at the dinner table that evening. Consciousness slid under his guard, like the brush of raw silk across his body, raising hairs, leaving every pore tingling.

Inwardly cursing, he took his seat—and forced his attention to Edith Swithins. Beside him, Patience chatted easily with Henry Chadwick, with no detectable sign of confusion. As the courses came and went, Vane struggled not to resent that fact. She appeared breezily unconscious of any change in the temperature between them, while he was fighting to keep the lid on a boiling pot.

Dessert was finally over, and the ladies withdrew. Vane kept the conversation over the port to a minimum, then led the gentlemen back to the drawing room. As usual, Patience was standing with Angela and Mrs. Chadwick halfway down the long room.

She saw him coming; the fleeting flare of awareness in her eyes as he drew near was a momentary sop to his male pride. Very momentary—the instant he stopped by her side, her perfume reached him, the warmth of her soft curves tugged at his senses. Decidedly stiff, Vane inclined his head fractionally to all three ladies.

"I was just telling Patience," Angela blurted out, pouting sulkily, "that it's beyond anything paltry. The thief has stolen my new comb!"

"Your comb?" Vane flicked a glance at Patience.

"The one I bought in Northampton," Anglea wailed. "I didn't even get to wear it!"

"It may still turn up." Mrs. Chadwick tried to sound encouraging, but with her own, much more serious loss clearly in mind, she failed to soothe her daughter.

"It's *unfair*!" Flags of color flew in Angela's cheeks. She stamped her foot. "I want the thief caught!"

"Indeed." The single word, uttered in Vane's coolest, most bored drawl, succeeded in dousing Angela's imminent hysterics. "We would all, I fancy, like to lay our hands on this elusive, light-fingered felon."

"Light-fingered felon?" Edmond strolled up. "Has the thief struck again?"

Instantly, Angela reverted to her histrionic best; she poured out her tale to the rather more appreciative audience of Edmond, Gerrard, and Henry, all of whom joined the circle. Under cover of their exclamations, Vane glanced at Patience; she felt his gaze and looked up, meeting his eyes, a question forming in hers. Vane opened his lips, the details of an assignation on his tongue—he swallowed them as, to everyone's surprise, Whitticombe joined the group.

The garrulous recitation of the thief's latest exploit was instantly muted, but Whitticombe paid little heed. After a general nod to all, he leaned closer and murmured to Mrs. Chadwick. She immediately raised her head, looking across the room. "Thank you." Reaching out, she took Angela's arm. "Come, my dear."

Angela's face fell. "Oh, but . . ."

For once entirely deaf to her daughter's remonstrances, Mrs. Chadwick towed Angela to the *chaise* where Minnie sat.

Both Vane and Patience followed Mrs. Chadwick's progress, as did the others. Whitticombe's quiet question had them turning back to him.

"Am I to understand that something else has gone missing?"

Entirely by chance, he was now facing the others, all arrayed in a semicircle, as if joined in league against him. It was not a felicitous social grouping, yet none of them—Vane, Patience, Gerrard, Edmond, or Henry—made any move to shift position, to include Whitticombe more definitely in their circle.

"Angela's new comb." Henry briefly recited Angela's description.

"Diamonds?" Whitticombe's brows rose.

"Paste," Patience corrected. "It was a . . . *showy* piece."

"Hmm." Whitticombe frowned. "It really brings us

back to our earlier question—what on earth would anyone want with a garish pincushion and a cheap, somewhat tawdry, comb?''

Henry's jaw locked; Edmond shifted. Gerrard stared pugnaciously—directly at Whitticombe, who'd fixed his cold, transparently assessing gaze on him.

Beside Vane, Patience stiffened.

''Actually,'' Whitticombe drawled, the instant before at least three others spoke, ''I was wondering if it isn't time we instituted a search?'' He lifted a brow at Vane. ''What do you think, Cynster?''

''I think,'' Vane said, and paused, his chilly gaze fixed on Whitticombe's face, until there wasn't one of the company who did not know precisely what he truly thought, ''that a search will prove fruitless. Aside from the fact that the thief will certainly hear of the search before it begins, and have time aplenty to secrete or remove his cache, there's the not inconsiderable problem of our present location. The house is nothing short of a magpie's paradise, let alone the grounds. Things hidden in the ruins might never be found.''

Whitticombe's gaze momentarily blanked, then he blinked. ''Ah . . . yes.'' He nodded. ''I daresay you're right. Things might never be found. Quite true. Of course, a search would never do. If you'll excuse me?'' With a fleeting smile, he bowed and headed back across the room.

Puzzled to varying degrees, they all watched him go. And saw the small crowd gathered about the *chaise*. Timms waved. ''Patience!''

''Excuse me.'' With a fleeting touch on Vane's arm, Patience crossed to the *chaise*, to join Mrs. Chadwick and Timms, gathered about Minnie. Then Mrs. Chadwick stood back; Patience stepped closer and helped Timms assist Minnie to her feet.

Vane watched as, her arm about Minnie, Patience helped her to the door.

Intending to follow, Mrs. Chadwick shooed Angela ahead of her, then detoured to inform the deserted group of males: ''Minnie's not well—Patience and Timms will put her to bed. I'll go, too, in case they need help.''

So saying, she herded a reluctant Angela out of the room and closed the door behind them.

Vane stared at the closed door—and inwardly cursed. Fluently.

"Well." Henry shrugged. "Left to our own devices, what?" He glanced at Vane. "Fancy a return match in the billiard room, Cynster?"

Edmond looked up; so did Gerrard. The suggestion obviously met with their approval. His gaze on the closed door beyond them, Vane slowly raised his brows. "Why not?" Lips firming to an uncompromising line, his eyes unusually dark, he waved to the door. "There seems little else to do tonight."

The next morning, his expression tending grim, Vane descended the main stairs.

Henry Chadwick had beaten him at billiards.

If he'd needed any confirmation of how seriously the current impasse with Patience was affecting him, *that* had supplied it. Henry could barely sink a ball. Yet he'd been so distracted, he'd been even less able to sink anything, his mind totally engrossed with the where, the when, and the how—and the likely sensations—of sinking into Patience.

Striding across the front hall, his boots ringing on the tiles, he headed for the breakfast room. It was past time he and Patience talked.

And after that . . .

The table was half-full; the General, Whitticombe, and Edgar were all there, as was Henry, blithely gay with a wide grin on his face. Vane met it without expression. He helped himself to a large and varied breakfast, then took his seat to wait for Patience.

To his relief, Angela did not appear; Henry informed him that Gerrard and Edmond had already broken their fast and gone out to the ruins.

Vane nodded, and continued to eat—and wait.

Patience didn't appear.

When Masters and his minions appeared to clear the table, Vane rose. Every muscle felt locked, every sinew taut and tight. "Masters—where is Miss Debbington?"

His accents, while even, held more than a hint of cold steel.

Masters blinked. "Her Ladyship's unwell, sir—Miss Debbington is presently with Mrs. Henderson sorting menus and going over the household accounts, it being the day for those."

"I see." Vane stared unseeing at the empty doorway. "And just how long do menus and household accounts take?"

"I'm sure I couldn't say, sir—but they've only just begun, and Her Ladyship usually takes all morning."

Vane drew a deep breath—and held it. "Thank you, Masters."

Slowly, he moved out from behind the table and headed for the door.

He was past cursing. He paused in the hall, then, his face setting like stone, he turned on his heel and strode for the stables. In lieu of talking with Patience, and the likely aftermath, he'd have to settle for a long, hard ride—on a horse.

He caught her in the stillroom.

Pausing with his hand on the latch of the half-open door, Vane grinned, grimly satisfied. It was early afternoon; many of the household would be safely napping—the rest would at least be somnolent. Within the stillroom, he could hear Patience humming softly—other than the rustling of her gown, he could hear no other sound. He'd finally found her alone and in the perfect location. The stillroom, tucked away on the ground floor of one wing, was private, and contained no daybed, *chaise*, or similar piece of furniture.

In his present state, that was just as well. A gentleman should not, after all, go too far with the lady he intended making his wife before informing her of that fact. The absence of any of the customary aids to seduction should make coming to the point easy, after which they could retire to some place of greater comfort, so he could be comfortable again.

The thought—of how he would ease the discomfort that had dogged him for the past days—wound his spring a notch tighter. Jaw set, he drew a deep breath. Setting the door wide, he stepped over the threshold.

Patience whirled. Her face lit up. "Hello. Not riding?"

Scanning the dimly lit stillroom, Vane slowly closed the door. And slowly shook his head. "I went out this morning." The last time he'd been in here, he'd been nine years old—the room had appeared much more spacious. Now . . . Ducking a dangling sheaf of leaves, he edged around the table running down the center of the narrow room. "How's Minnie?"

Patience smiled, gloriously welcoming, and dusted her hands. "Just a sniffle—she'll be better soon, but we want to keep an eye on her. Timms is sitting with her at present."

"Ah." Dodging more branches of drying herbs, carefully avoiding a rack of large bottles, Vane eased down the aisle between the central table and the side counter at which Patience was working. He only just fitted. The fact registered, but dimly; his senses had focused on Patience. His eyes locked on hers as he closed the distance between them. "I've been chasing you for days."

Desire roughened his voice; he saw the same emotion flare in her eyes. He reached for her—in precisely the same moment she stepped toward him. She ended in his arms, her hands sliding up to frame his face, her face lifting to his.

Vane was kissing her before he knew what he—they— were about. It was the first time in his extensive career he'd misstepped, lost the thread of his predetermined plot. He'd intended *speaking* first, making the declaration he knew he should make; as Patience's lips parted invitingly under his, as her tongue boldly tangled with his, all thought of speech fled from his head. Her hands left his face to slide and lock over his shoulders, bringing her breasts against his chest, her thighs against his, the soft fullness of her belly caressing the aching ridge distorting the front of his breeches.

Need burst upon him—his, and, to his utter amazement, hers. His own lust he was used to controlling; hers was something else again. Vibrant, gloriously naive, eager in its innocence, it held a power far stronger than he'd expected. And it drew something from him—something deeper, stronger, a compulsion driven by something much more powerful than mere lust.

Heat rose between them; in desperation, Vane tried to lift his head. He only succeeded in altering the angle of their kiss. Deepening it. The failure—so totally unprecedented—jerked him to attention. Their reins had well and truly slipped from his grasp—Patience now held them—and she was driving far too fast.

He forced himself to draw back from their kiss. "Patience—"

She covered his lips with hers.

Vane closed his hands about her shoulders; he felt the wrench deep in his soul as he again pulled away. "Dammit woman—I want to *talk* to you!"

"Later." Eyes glinting from beneath heavy lids, Patience drew his head back to hers.

Vane fought to hold back. "Will you just—"

"Shut up." Stretching upward, pressing herself even more flagrantly against him, Patience brushed her lips against his. "I don't want to talk. Just kiss me—*show* me what comes next."

Which wasn't the wisest invitation to issue to a painfully aroused rake. Vane groaned as her tongue slid deep into his mouth, as he instinctively met it. The duel that followed was too heated for him to think; a haze of hot passion clouded his senses. The counter at his back made escape impossible, even if he could have summoned the strength.

She held him trapped in a net of desire—and with every kiss the strands grew stronger.

Patience gloried in their kiss, in the sudden revelation that she'd been waiting for just this—to experience again the heady thrill of desire sliding through her veins, to sense again the seductive lure of that elusive something—that emotion she had not yet named, as it wound about her—about them—and drew her deeper.

Deeper into his arms, deeper into passion. To where the desire to fulfill the craving she sensed beneath his expertise became a compulsion, a poignantly sweet urge swelling deep within her.

She could taste it on her tongue, in their kiss; she could

feel it—a slow throb—gradually building in her blood.

This was excitement. This was experience. *This* was precisely what her curious soul craved.

Above all, she needed to know.

Vane's hands on her hips urged her closer; hard, demanding, they slid down, grasping her firmly, fingers sinking deep as he lifted her against him. His rigid staff rode against her, impressing her softness with the hard evidence of his need. His evocative rocking motion sent heat pulsing through her; his staff was a brand—a brand with which he would claim her.

Their lips parted briefly, so they could haul in gasping breaths before need fused their lips again. An aching, spiraling urgency flowed through them, gaining in strength, flooding their senses. She sensed it in him—and knew it in her.

And together they strove, feeding the swelling compulsion, both driven by it. The wave rose and reared over them—then it broke. And they were caught in the rush, in the furious swirling urgency, tossed and tousled until they gasped and clung. Waves—of desire, passion, and need—beat upon them, forcing awareness of the emptiness within, of the burning need to fill it, to achieve completeness on the mortal plane.

"Miss?"

The tap on the door had them flying apart. The door opened; a maid looked in. She spied Patience, turning toward her in the dim light; to all appearances, Patience had been facing the counter, her hands in a pile of herbs. The maid held up a pannier full of lavender spikes. "What should I do with these now?"

Her pulse thundering in her ears, Patience struggled to focus on the question. She gave mute thanks for the lack of lighting—the maid hadn't yet seen Vane, leaning negligently on the counter four feet away. "Ah—" She coughed, then had to moisten her lips before she could speak. "You'll need to strip the leaves and snip off the heads. We'll use the leaves and heads for the scented bags, and the stalks we'll use to freshen rooms."

The maid nodded eagerly and moved to the central table.

Patience turned back to the counter. Her head was still whirling; her breasts rose and fell. She knew her lips were swollen—when she licked them again, they felt hot. Her pounding heartbeat suffused her entire body; she could feel it in her fingertips. She'd sent the maid to gather lavender; it needed to be processed immediately. A point on which she'd lectured the maid.

If she sent the maid away . . .

She glanced at Vane, silent and still in the shadows. Only she, close as she was, could see the way his chest rose and fell, could see the light that glowed like hot embers in his eyes. One burnished lock of hair had fallen across his forehead; as she watched, he straightened and brushed it back. And inclined his head. "I'll catch up with you later, my dear."

The maid started and looked up. Vane viewed her blandly. Reassured, the maid smiled and returned to the lavender.

From the corner of her eye, Patience watched Vane retreat, watched the door close slowly behind him. As the latch clicked shut, she closed her eyes. And fought, unsuccessfully, to quell the shudder that racked her—of anticipation. And need.

The tension between them had turned raw. Taut as a wire, heightened to excruciating sensitivity.

Vane felt it the instant Patience appeared in the drawing room that evening; the glance she threw him made it clear she felt it, too. But they had to play their parts, fill their expected roles, hiding the passion that shimmered, white-hot, between them.

And pray that no one else noticed.

Touching in any way, however innocuous, was out of the question; they artfully avoided it—until, in accepting a platter from Vane, Patience's fingers brushed his.

She nearly dropped the platter; Vane only just stifled his curse.

Jaw locked, he endured, as did she.

At last they were back in the drawing room. Tea had been drunk and Minnie, wreathed in shawls, was about to retire. Vane's mind was a blank; he had not a single clue as to what topics had been discussed over the past two hours. He did, however, recognize opportunity when he saw it.

Strolling to the *chaise*, he raised a brow at Minnie. "I'll carry you up."

"An excellent idea!" Timms declared.

"Humph!" Minnie sniffed, but, worn down by her cold, reluctantly acquiesced. "Very well." As Vane gathered her, shawls and all, into his arms, she grudgingly admitted: "Tonight, I *feel* old."

Vane chuckled and set himself to tease her into her usual, ebullient frame of mind. By the time they reached her room, he'd succeeded well enough to have her commenting on his arrogance.

"Far too sure of yourselves, you Cynsters."

Grinning, Vane lowered her into her usual chair by the hearth. Timms bustled up—she'd followed close on his heels.

So had Patience.

As Vane stood back, Minnie waved dismissively. "I don't need anyone but Timms—you two can go back to the drawing room."

Patience exchanged a fleeting glance with Vane, then looked at Minnie. "If you're sure . . . ?"

"I'm sure. Off you go."

They went—but not back to the drawing room. It was already late—neither felt any desire for aimless chat.

They did, however, feel desire. It flowed restlessly about them, between them, fell, an ensorcelling web, over them. As he strolled by Patience's side, by unspoken agreement escorting her to her chamber, Vane accepted that dealing with that desire, with what now shimmered between them, would fall to him, would be his responsiblity.

Patience, despite her propensity to grab the reins, was an innocent.

He reminded himself of that fact as they halted outside her door. She looked up at him—inwardly Vane sternly reiterated the conclusion he'd reached after the debacle of the stillroom. Until he'd said the words society dictated he should say, he and she should not meet alone except in the most formal of settings.

Outside her bedchamber door in the cool beginning of the night did not qualify; *inside* her bedchamber—where his baser self wished to be—was even less suitable.

Jaw setting, he reminded himself of that.

She searched his eyes, his face. Then, slowly but not hesitantly, she lifted a hand to his cheek, lightly tracing downward to his chin. Her gaze dropped to his lips.

Beyond his volition, Vane's gaze lowered to her lips, to the soft rose-tinted curves he now knew so well. Their shape was etched in his mind, their taste imprinted on his senses.

Patience's lids fluttered down. She stretched upward on her toes.

Vane couldn't have drawn back from the kiss—couldn't have avoided it—had his life depended on it.

Their lips touched, without the heat, without the driving compulsion that remained surging in their souls. Both held it back, denying it, content for one timeless moment simply to touch and be touched. To let the beauty of the fragile moment stretch, to let the magic of their heightened awareness wash over them.

It left them quivering. Yearning. Curiously breathless, as if they'd been running for hours, curiously weak, as if they'd been battling for too long and nearly lost.

It was an effort to lift his heavy lids. Having done so, Vane watched as Patience, even more slowly, opened her eyes.

Their gazes met; words were superfluous. Their eyes said all they needed to say; reading the message in hers, Vane forced himself to straighten from the doorframe which at some point he'd leaned against. Ruthlessly relocating his impassive mask, he raised one brow. "Tomorrow?" He needed to see her in a suitably formal setting.

Patience lightly grimaced. "That will depend on Minnie."

Vane's lips twisted, but he nodded. And forced himself to step away. "I'll see you at breakfast."

He swung on his heel and walked back up the corridor. Patience stood at her door and watched him leave.

Fifteen minutes later, a woolen shawl wrapped about her shoulders, Patience curled up in the old wing chair by her hearth and stared moodily into the flames. After a moment, she tucked her feet higher, beneath the hem of her night-gown, and, propping one elbow on the chair's arm, sank her chin into her palm.

Myst appeared, and, after surveying the possibilities, jumped up and took possession of her lap. Absentmindedly, Patience stroked her, gaze locked on the flames as her fingers slid over the pert grey ears and down the curving spine.

For long minutes, the only sounds in the room were the soft crackling of the flames and Myst's contented purr. Neither distracted Patience from her thoughts, from the realization she could not escape.

She was twenty-six. She might have lived in Derbyshire, but that wasn't quite the same as a nunnery. She'd met gentlemen aplenty, many of them of similar ilk to Vane Cynster. Many of those gentlemen had had some thoughts of her. She, however, had never had thoughts of them. Never before had she spent hours—not even minutes— thinking about any particular gentleman. One and all, they'd failed to fix her interest.

Vane commanded her attention at all times. When they were in the same room, he commanded her awareness, ef-fortlessly held her senses. Even when apart, he remained the focus of some part of her mind. His face was easy to conjure; he appeared regularly in her dreams.

Patience sighed, and stared at the flames.

She wasn't imagining it—imagining that her reaction to him was different, special, that he engaged her emotions at some deeper level. That wasn't imagination, it was fact.

And there was no point whatever in refusing to face facts—that trait was alien to her character. No point in pre-tense, in avoiding the thought of what would have occurred if he had not been so honorable and had asked, by word or deed, to enter this room tonight.

She would have welcomed him in, without fluster or hesitation. Her nerves might have turned skittish, but that would have been due to excitement, to anticipation, not uncertainty.

Country-bred, she was fully cognizant of the mechanism of mating; she was not ignorant on that front. But what caught her, held her—commanded her curiosity—was the emotions that, in this case, with Vane, had, in her mind, become entangled with the act. Or was it the act that had become entangled with the emotions?

Whatever, she'd been seduced—entirely and utterly, beyond recall—not by him, but by her *desire* for him. It was, she knew in her heart, in the depths of her soul, a most pertinent distinction.

This desire had to be what her mother had felt, what had driven her to accept Reginald Debbington in marriage and trapped her in a loveless union for all her days. She had every reason to distrust the emotion—to avoid it, reject it.

She couldn't. Patience knew that for fact, the emotion ran too strong, too compulsively within her, for her to ever be free of it.

But it, of itself, brought no pain, no sadness. Indeed, if she'd been given the choice, even now she would admit that she'd rather have the experience, the excitement, the knowledge, than live the rest of her life in ignorance.

There was, invested within that rogue emotion, power and joy and boundless excitement—all things she craved. She was already addicted; she wouldn't let it go. There was, after all, no need.

She had never truly thought of marriage; she could now face the fact that she had, indeed, been avoiding it. Finding excuse after excuse to put off even considering it. It was marriage—the trap—that had brought her mother undone. Simply loving, even if that love was unrequited, would be sweet—bittersweet maybe, but the experience was not one she would turn down.

Vane wanted her—he had not at any time tried to hide the effect she had on him, tried to screen the potent desire that glowed like hot coals in his eyes. The knowledge that she aroused him was like a grapple about her heart—a facet from some deep, heretofore unacknowledged dream.

He'd asked for tomorrow—that was in the lap of the gods, but when the time came, she would not, she knew, draw back.

She'd meet him—meet his passion, his desire, his need— and in fulfilling and satisfying him, fulfill and satisfy herself. That, she now knew, was the way it could be. It was the way she wanted it to be.

Their liaison would last for however long it might; while she would be sad when it ended, she wouldn't be caught, trapped in never-ending misery like her mother.

Smiling, wistfully wry, Patience looked down and stroked Myst's head. "He might want me, but he's still an elegant gentleman." She might wish that were not so, but it was. "Love is not something he has to give—and I'll never—hear me well—*never*—marry without that."

That was the crux of it—that was her true fate.

She had no intention of fighting it.

Chapter 12

V ane arrived early in the breakfast parlor the next morning. He served himself, then took his seat and waited for Patience to appear. The rest of the males wandered in, exchanging their usual greetings. Vane pushed back his plate and waved for Masters to pour him more coffee.

Coiled tension had him in its grip; how much longer would it be before he could release it? That, to his mind, was a point to which Patience should give her most urgent attention, yet he could hardly begrudge Minnie her aid.

When Patience failed to appear by the time they'd finished their meals, Vane inwardly sighed and fixed Gerrard with a severe glance. "I need a ride." He did, in more ways than one, but at least he could release some of his pent-up energy in a good gallop. "Interested?"

Gerrard squinted out of the window. "I was going to sketch, but the light looks flat. I'll come riding instead."

Vane raised a brow at Henry. "You game, Chadwick?"

"Actually"—Henry sat back in his chair—"I'd thought to practice my angle shots. Wouldn't do to get rusty."

Gerrard chuckled. "It was pure luck you beat Vane last time. Anyone could tell he was a trifle out of sorts."

A trifle out of sorts? Vane wondered if he should educate Patience's brother on precisely how "out of sorts" he was. A blue powder wouldn't cure his particular ache.

"Ah—but I did win." Henry clung to his moment of victory. "I've no intention of letting my advantage slip."

Vane merely smiled sardonically, inwardly grateful Henry would not be accompanying them. Gerrard rarely spoke when riding, which suited his mood far better than Henry's locquaciousness. "Edmond?"

They all looked down the table to where Edmond sat gazing at his empty plate, mumbling beneath his breath. His hair stuck out at odd angles where he'd clutched it.

Vane raised a brow at Gerrard, who shook his head. Edmond was clearly in the grip of his muse and deaf to all else. Vane and Gerrard pushed back their chairs and rose.

Patience hurried in. She paused just inside the room, and blinked at Vane, half-risen.

He immediately subsided into his chair. Gerrard turned, and saw him reseated; he also resumed his seat.

Reassured, Patience headed for the sideboard, picked up a plate, and went straight to the table. She was late; in the circumstances, she'd settle for tea and toast. "Minnie's better," she announced as she took her seat. Looking up the table, she met Vane's gaze. "She spent a sound night and has assured me she doesn't need me today."

She swept a brief smile over Henry and Edmond, thus rendering the information general.

Gerrard grinned at her. "I suppose you'll be off to the music room as usual. Vane and I are going for a ride."

Patience looked at Gerrard, then stared up the table at Vane. Who stared back. Patience blinked, then reached for the teapot. "Actually, if you'll wait a few minutes, I'll come with you. After being cooped up these last days, I could do with some air."

Gerrard looked at Vane, who was gazing at Patience, an unfathomable expression on his face. "We'll wait" was all he said.

By agreement, they met in the stable yard.

After scurrying into her habit, then rushing out of the house like a hoyden, Patience was mildly irritated to find Gerrard not yet there. Vane was already atop the grey hunter. Both rider and horse were restless.

Climbing into her sidesaddle, Patience took up her reins and glanced back toward the house. "Where is he?"

Lips compressed, Vane shrugged.

Three minutes later, just as she was about to dismount to go and search, Gerrard appeared. With his easel.

"I say, I'm sorry, but I've changed my mind." He grinned up at them. "There's clouds coming up and the light's turned grey—it's just the look I've been waiting to capture. I need to get it down before it changes again." He shifted his burden and continued to grin. "So go on without me—at least you've got each other for company."

Gerrard's disingenuity was transparently genuine; Vane swallowed a curse. He glanced swiftly at Patience; she met his gaze, questions in her eyes.

Vane understood the questions—but Gerrard was standing there, large as life, waiting to wave them away. Jaw firming, he gestured to the stable arch. "Shall we?"

After a fractional hesitation, Patience nodded and flicked her reins. With a perfunctory wave to Gerrard, she led the way out. Vane followed. As they thundered along the track past the ruins, he glanced back. So did Patience. Gerrard, slogging in their wake, waved gaily.

Vane cursed. Patience looked forward.

By unspoken accord, they put distance between themselves and the Hall, eventually drawing rein on the banks of the Nene. The river flowed steadily, a reflective grey ribbon smoothly rippling between thickly grassed banks. A well-beaten track followed the river; slowing the grey to a walk, Vane turned along it.

Patience brought her mare up beside him; Vane let his gaze roam her face, her figure.

Fingers tightening on the reins, he looked away. Over the lush riverbanks, insufficiently formal for the discussion he needed to have with her. The grassy banks would do nicely as a couch. Far too tempting. He wasn't sure he could trust himself in such a setting, and, after the stillroom, he knew he couldn't trust her. She, however, was an innocent; *he* had no excuse. Besides which, the area was too open, and Penwick often rode this way. Stopping by the river was untenable. And Patience deserved better than a few casual words and a question on horseback.

Thanks to Gerrard, it seemed he'd have to endure yet

another morning without progress. Meanwhile, he, and his demons, were champing at the bit.

Beside him, Patience, too, found the idea of wasting another morning less than appealing. Unlike Vane, she saw no reason not to use the time. Having surreptitiously filled her mind anew with the image of him on his hunter, she voiced the thought uppermost in her mind. "You mentioned having a brother—does he look like you?"

Vane glanced her way, brows rising. "Harry?" He considered. "Harry has curly blond-brown hair and blue eyes—but otherwise"—a slow smile transformed Vane's face—"yes, I suppose he does look a lot like me." He slanted Patience a rakish glance. "But then, all six of us are said to look similar—the stamp of our common ancestors, no doubt."

Patience ignored the subtle tenor of that comment. "All six? Which six?"

"The six eldest Cynster cousins—Devil, myself, Richard—he's Devil's brother—Harry, who's my only sibling, and Gabriel and Lucifer. We were all born within five or so years of each other."

Patience stared. The idea of six Vanes was . . . And two were called Gabriel and Lucifer? "Aren't there any females in the family?"

"In our generation, the females came later. The eldest are the twins—Amanda and Amelia. They're seventeen and have just weathered their first Season."

"And you all live in London?"

"For some part of the year. My parents' house is in Berkeley Square. My father, of course, grew up at Somersham Place, the ducal seat. To him, that's home. While he and my mother, indeed, the whole family, are always welcome there, my parents decided to make their primary home in London."

"So that's home to you."

Looking over the green meadows, Vane shook his head. "Not any more. I moved into lodgings years ago, and recently bought a town house. When Harry and I came of age, my father settled sizable sums on both of us and advised us to invest in property." His smile deepened.

"Cynsters always accumulate land. Land, after all, is power. Devil has the Place and all the ducal estates, which underpin the wealth of the family. While he looks after those, we're each expanding our own assests."

"You mentioned that your brother owns a stud."

"Close by Newmarket. That's Harry's enterprise of choice—he's a master when it comes to horses."

"And you?" Patience tilted her head, her eyes on his face. "What's your enterprise of choice?"

Vane grinned. "Hops."

Patience blinked. "Hops?"

"A vital ingredient used to flavor and clarify beers. I own Pembury Manor, an estate near Tunbridge in Kent."

"And you grow hops?"

Vane's smile teased. "As well as apples, pears, cherries, and cob nuts."

Drawing back in her saddle, Patience stared at him. "You're a farmer!"

One brown brow rose. "Among other things."

Recognizing the glint in his eyes, she swallowed a humph. "Describe this place—Pembury Manor."

Vane did, quite content to follow that tack. After a brief outline, bringing to life the orchards and fields spread over the Kentish Weald, he turned to the house itself—the house he would take her to. "Two stories in grey stone, with six bedrooms, five reception rooms, and the usual amenities. I haven't spent much time there—it needs redecorating."

He made the comment offhandedly, and was pleased to see a distant, considering expression on her face.

"Hmm" was all Patience said. "How far—"

She broke off and looked up; a second raindrop splattered her nose. As one, she and Vane looked up and behind them. With one voice, they cursed. Thunderheads had blown up, dark grey and menacing, swelling in the sky behind them. A leaden curtain of drenching rain steadily advanced, mere minutes away.

Looking about, they searched for shelter. It was Vane who spotted the slate roof of the old barn.

"There." He pointed. "Along the riverbank." He glanced behind again. "We might just make it."

Patience had already sprung her mare. Vane followed, holding the grey back, clear of the mare's heels. They thundered along the track. In the skies above, more thunder rumbled. The leading edge of the rain curtain reached them, flinging heavy drops on their backs. Doors closed, the barn nestled in a shallow depression set back from the track. Patience wrestled the now skittish mare to a halt before the doors. Vane hauled the grey to a slithering stop and flung himself from the saddle. Reins in one hand, he dragged open the barn door. Patience trotted the mare in and Vane followed, leading the grey.

Once in, he dropped the reins and strode back to the door. As he pulled it shut, thunder cracked, and the heavens opened. Rain came down in sheets. Standing catching his breath, Vane looked up at the rafters. Still perched on her mare, Patience did the same. The sound of the rain on the old roof was a steady, relentless roar.

Shaking his shoulders, Vane peered into the dimness. "This looks to be in use. The roof seems sound." His eyes growing accustomed to the gloom, he strolled forward. "There are stalls along that wall." He lifted Patience down. "We'd better settle the horses."

Eyes wide in the gloom, Patience nodded. They led the horses to the stalls; while Vane unsaddled them, Patience investigated further. She discovered a ladder leading up to the loft. She glanced back at Vane; he was still busy with the horses. Gathering her skirts, she climbed up, carefully checking each rung. But the ladder was sound. All in all, the barn was in good repair.

From the top of the ladder, Patience surveyed the loft. A wide chamber built over most of the barn, it housed a quantity of hay, some baled, some loose. The floor was sound timber. Stepping up, she dropped her skirts, brushed them down, then crossed to where the hay doors were fastened against the weather.

Lifting the latch, she peeked out. The hay doors faced south, away from the squall. Satisfied no rain would drive in, she opened the doors, admitting soft grey light into the loft. Despite the rain, perhaps because of the heavy clouds, the air was warm. The view revealed, of the river, whipped by wind, pocked with rain, and the gently sloping meadows, all seen through a grey screen, was soothing.

Glancing around, Patience lifted a brow. Her next lesson from Vane was long overdue; while the music room would have been preferable, the loft would do. With hay aplenty, there was no reason they couldn't be comfortable.

In the barn below, Vane took as long as he could tending the horses, but the rain showed no sign of abating. Not that he'd expected it to; having seen the extent of the clouds, he knew they'd be trapped for hours. When there was nothing left to do, he wiped his hands in clean straw and dusted them. Then, closing a mental fist firmly about his own reins, he set off after Patience. He'd caught a glimpse of her disappearing into the loft. His head cleared the loft floor; he looked about—and inwardly cursed.

He knew trouble when he saw it.

She turned her head and smiled, eliminating any possiblity of craven retreat. Washed by the soft light falling through the open hay doors, she sat in the midst of a huge pile of hay, her expression welcoming, her body radiating a sensual tug to which he was already too susceptible.

Drawing in a deep breath, Vane climbed the last rungs and stepped onto the loft floor. With every evidence of his customary cool command, he strolled toward Patience.

She shattered his calm—by smiling more deeply and holding out her hand. Instinctively, he took it, fingers closing firmly. Then he caught himself.

His expression rigidly impassive, he looked down at her face, into her eyes, all hazel-gold, warm and alluring, and struggled to find some way to tell her this was madness. That, after all that had passed between them, to sit together in the hay and look out at the rain was too dangerous. That he could no longer guarantee his behavior, his usual coolness under fire, his customary command. No words sprang to mind—he was not capable of making such an admission of weakness. Even though it was true.

Patience gave him no time to wrestle with his conscience—she tugged. With no excuse forthcoming, Vane inwardly sighed—sealed an iron fist about his demons' reins—and sank down to the straw beside her.

He had a trick or two up his sleeve. Before she could turn to him, he wrapped his arms about her and drew her back, settling the curve of her back against his side, so they could study the scenery together.

Theoretically a wise move. Patience relaxed against him, warm and trusting—only to impinge on his senses in a thousand different ways. Her very softness tensed his muscles; her curves, fitting against him, within his arms, invoked his demons. He drew a steadying breath—and her perfume washed through him, subtly evoking, enticing.

Her hands slid over his arms, wrapped about her waist, and came to rest on his hands, her warm palms curved over the backs of his. Outside, the rain continued; inside, heat rose. Jaw clenched, Vane fought to endure.

He might have succeeded if she hadn't, without warning, turned to him. Her head turned first—and her lips were mere inches from his. Her body followed, sliding sensuously around in his arms; he tightened his grip, sank his fingers into soft flesh, but it was already too late.

Her gaze had fixed on his lips.

Desperation could reduce even the strongest to pleading. Even him. "Patience—"

She cut him off, sealing his lips with hers.

Vane fought to hold her back, but there was no strength in his arms—not for that maneuver. Instead, his muscles strained to crush her to him. He managed to stop himself from doing that, only to feel the pair of them sinking back into the hay, the pile originally behind him increasingly beneath him as it compressed under their combined weights. Within seconds, they were close to horizontal, with her stretched against him, half-atop him. Vane inwardly groaned.

His lips had parted, and she was kissing him—and he was kissing her. Jettisoning his crusade against what had proved the inevitable, Vane focused on the kiss. Gradually, he wrested back control, distantly aware that she relinquished the reins too readily. But the small victory encouraged him; he reminded himself that he was stronger than she, infinitely more experienced than she—and that he'd successfully managed women far more knowledgeable than she in this arena for years.

He was in control.

The litany sang in his head as he rolled and pressed her into the hay. She accepted the change readily, clinging to their kiss. Vane deepened it, plundering her mouth, hoping thus to assuage the clamoring need swelling within him. He framed her face and drank deep; she met him, sliding her hands under his loose jacket, spreading them, sending them questing over his chest, around his sides and back.

His shirt was fine lawn. Through it, her hands burned.

The final battle was so short, Vane had lost it before he'd realized—and after that, he wasn't capable of realizing anything beyond the woman beneath him and the raging tide of his need.

Her hands, her lips, her body, arching lightly beneath him, urged him on. When he opened her velvet riding jacket and closed one hand about her blouse-covered breast, she only sighed and kissed him more urgently.

Under his hand, her breast swelled; between his fingers, her nipple was a tight bud. She gasped when he squeezed, arched when he stroked. And moaned when he kneaded.

The tiny buttons of her blouse slipped their moorings readily; the ribbons of her chemise needed no more than a tug to free them. And then her softness filled his hand, filled his senses. Skin like soft silk teased him; the heated weight of her inflamed him. And her.

When he broke their kiss to raise his head and survey the bounty he'd captured, she watched, eyes glinting goldly from under heavy lids. Watched as his head descended and he took her into his mouth. He suckled, and her eyes closed.

The next fractured gasp that filled the loft was the first note of a symphony, a symphony he orchestrated. She wanted more, and he gave it, pushing aside the soft blouse, drawing down her silk chemise, to bare her breasts fully to the soft grey light, the gentle coolness of the air, and his heated attentions.

Beneath them, she burned, as in his dreams he'd imagined her doing, until she was hot and aching—and frantic for more. Her small hands were everywhere, desperately searching, opening his shirt and greedily reaching, caressing, imploring.

That was when he finally realized that control was far beyond him. He didn't have a shred left—she'd stolen it from him and thrown it away. She certainly had none. That was abundantly clear as, panting, her lips gloriously swollen, she drew his face to hers and kissed him voraciously.

Half-beneath him, she lifted, her body caressing his in flagrant entreaty—the oldest method of beckoning known to woman. She wanted him—and heaven help him, he wanted her. Now.

His body was rigid with need, tense and heavy with it; he needed to claim her, to slide into her body and find release. The buttons fastening her velvet skirts were at her back; his fingers were already on them. He'd waited too long to speak, to formally offer for her hand. He couldn't focus enough to form a garbled sentence—but he had to try.

With a groan, Vane pulled back from their kiss. On his elbows above her, he waited for her to open her eyes. When her lashes flickered, he drew a huge breath—and lost it as her nipples brushed his expanding chest. He shuddered— she shivered, quivers rippling through her stomach to her thighs. His mind immediately focused—on the soft haven between her long limbs, experience supplying in gratifying detail just what her responses were achieving.

Vane shut his eyes—he tried to shut his mind and simply speak.

Instead, her voice reached him, clear, soft, sirenlike, a whisper of pure magic in the heavily laden air.

"Show me."

Entreaty silvered the words. In the same instant, Vane felt her fingers slide, glide, then gently close about him. Her tentative touch had him locking his jaw, locking every muscle against a raging impulse to ravish her. She seemed unaware of it; her gliding caress continued, cindering the last of his will.

"Teach me," she whispered, her breath feathering his cheek. And then she breathed against his lips, "All."

That last small word vanquished the last of his resistance,

the last remnant of caution, of cool command. Gone was any gentleman, any vestige of his facade—only the conqueror remained.

He wanted her—with every ounce of his body, every ounce of his blood. And she wanted him. Words were superfluous.

The only thing that still mattered was the manner of their joining. With ultimate victory assured, his demons—those spirits that moved him, drove him—were more than ready to lend their talents to achieving glory in the most satisfying way. Not control, but focused frenzy.

Patience felt it. And gloried in it—in the hardness of the hands that possessed her breasts, in the hardness of his lips as they returned to hers. She clung tight, hands clutching, then kneading the broad muscles of his back, a moment later sliding around to hungrily explore his chest.

She wanted to know—know it all—*now*. She couldn't bear to wait, to drag out the frustration. A yearning—for that knowledge—the fundamental experience all women craved—had bloomed, spread, and now consumed her. Drove her as she arched lightly, responding to the demand in his hands, in his lips, in the steady plundering of his tongue.

He was all heat and shockingly hot hardness. She wanted to draw him into her, to take his heat in and quench it, to release the fevered tension driving him—the same tension slowly suffusing her. She wanted to give herself to him— she wanted to take him into her body.

She knew it, and was long past denial. She knew who she was—she knew what was possible. She'd satisfied herself that she understood how things would be.

So there was nothing to cloud her enjoyment—of the moment, of him. She gave herself up to it gladly—to the shiver of excitement as he drew her velvet skirts down, then rolled her to spread them, a soft blanket, beneath her. Her full petticoats went the same route, becoming a wide sheet beneath her shoulders. She knew no shame as, his lips on hers, he drew her chemise from her, tossing it aside before gathering her to him.

Sharp delight was what she knew as his hands, hard and

knowing, possessed her, tracing every curve, every soft mound. One hand slid beneath her waist, then slid lower to cup her bottom. Strong fingers kneaded, caressed, and sweet fever spread, pooling in her belly, dewing her skin. The hand slid lower, tracing the long curve of the back of her thigh all the way to her knee, then slid to the front, reversing direction. To her hip, to that sensitive join where thigh met torso. One finger gently, insistently, stroked downward along the crease—she shuddered, suddenly desperate for breath.

And then he was parting her thighs, gently but firmly spreading them to lavish soothing caresses along the sensitive inner faces. His lips had gentled on hers, allowing her to focus on each touch, each searing response. On the excitement, the frantic, barely reined passion that had both of them in its grip.

Then his hand reached the end of his last caress and drifted higher, to stroke flesh that had never before been stroked, never before felt a man's touch.

The shudder that racked her was pure excitement—distilled sensual anticipation. Sinking into the soft hay, Patience gasped and spread her thighs wider—and felt the caresses grow firmer, more deliberate. More intimate, more evocative.

The soft folds seemed slick; he parted them. Knowing fingers found a point, a nub of flesh, and bolts of delight lanced through her. Fiery delight, hot and urgent, it struck deep inside her, caught hold and grew. Pressing her head back, she broke from their kiss. He let her go. He continued to play in the softness between her thighs; Patience hauled in a too-shallow breath and fought to lift her lids.

And saw him, his face a mask of concentration etched with passion, watching his fingers as they stroked and twirled. Then one probed.

The sound that escaped her was more gasp than moan, more scream than groan. He glanced at her face; his eyes locked on hers. She felt his hand press between her thighs—and felt the intrusion of his finger, gently but insistently penetrating.

She gasped again, and closed her eyes. He pressed farther, deeper.

Then he stroked her—inside—deep within, where she was all slick and hot and so full of desire. So full of molten passion. A passion he stirred, deliberately inciting, stoking that inner furnace.

On a shuddering moan, Patience felt herself melt, felt her senses soar.

Vane heard her, felt her surrender—and inwardly smiled, a touch grimly. She was trying his demons to the utmost; by now, most women new to the game would have gone over the edge, or, more likely, been so overcome by need that they would be begging him to take them. Not Patience. She'd let him bare her completely, without any maidenly confusion—she seemed to enjoy writhing naked beneath him as much as he enjoyed having her do so. And now, when even accomplished ladies might be expected to break, she was floating—taking all he lavished on her and waiting for more.

He gave her more, learning her intimately, filling his male senses with her feminine secrets. Slowly, he drove her upward, turning the wheel of the rack of sensual excitement with practiced ease.

Still, she didn't break. She gasped, moaned, and arched—and her eager body begged for yet more. Her needs were not those of the ladies he was accustomed to; as he took her further still, that was brought home beyond doubt. Patience was older, more mature, more sure of her own self. She was not, he realized, the innocent he had labeled her—strictly speaking, she didn't, in fact, have very much of that commodity. She knew enough to know what they were doing, and to have made her decision.

And it was that that was different. Her character and its consequences. She was straightforward, assured, used to taking what experiences life had to offer. To picking and choosing among the fruits of life's tree. And she'd chosen. Deliberately. This—and him.

That was what was different.

Vane looked at her—at her face lightly flushed with desire, at her eyes, glinting gold from beneath heavy lids. And couldn't breathe.

From sheer lust—from sheer need. The need to be inside her.

The need to claim her as his.

With a soft oath, he drew his hands from her and shrugged free of his jacket and shirt. His boots took an impatient minute, then he stood to strip off his breeches. He could feel her gaze on him, trailing down his back. He flung his breeches aside and glanced over his shoulder. She lay naked, asprawl in the hay, calmly waiting. Simmering.

Her breasts rose and fell rapidly; her skin was gently flushed.

Naked, fully aroused, he turned to her.

Not a single hint of shock showed in her face—the face of a Fragonard wanton. Her gaze slid down, over him, then slowly rose to his face.

She lifted her arms. To him.

Vane went to her—covered her—took her lips in a searing kiss and eased himself into her. She was hot and tight; she tensed as he tested her maidenhead. And cried out as, with one well-judged thrust, he breached it. He held still, for one long, achingly tense moment, then she eased about him. Instinct claimed him—he thrust powerfully, deep into her body—and claimed her.

His reins broke—his demons took charge. Driving him, driving her, in a frenzied mating.

Far beyond thought, beyond reason, beyond anything except feeling, Patience held tight and let their passion take her. Every sensation was new, battering in on her mind, her overloaded senses, yet she clung to each thrill, each new intimacy, determined to miss nothing, determined to feel all.

To know the sheer delight of his hard body heavy on hers, his chest hard, hair-roughened, rasping against her sensitive nipples and the soft swells of her breasts. To glory in the hardness that filled her, the steely velvet that pressed deep into her, stretching her, claiming her. To experience, with every gasp, with every desperate pant, the power with which he repeatedly drove into her, the flexing of his spine, the rhythmic fusing of their bodies. To sense her vulnerability, in her nakedness, in the weight that anchored her hips, in the blind wanting that drove her. To revel in the excitement, shamelessly hot, unquenchably erotic, that swelled, grew, built, then flooded them, a raging tide avidly seizing them.

And to feel, deep within her, the unfurling of an anchoring force, more powerful than desire, more deep, more enduring, than anything on earth. That force, all emotion, golden and silver, swelled and caught her. She gave herself up to it and bravely, eagerly, knowingly claimed it for her own.

Ecstasy filled her—eagerly, she shared it, through her lips and their hungry kisses, through the worship of her hands, her limbs, her body.

He did the same; she tasted it on his tongue, felt its heat in his body.

Whatever he needed she gave, whatever she craved, he delivered. Mouth to mouth, breasts to chest, urgent softness gripping his hardness.

On a groan, Vane straightened his arms, and managed to find support enough in the hay to lift from her. He drove himself into her, savoring every hot inch that closed about him, pausing for an instant to feel her throb about him, before withdrawing, only to thrust deeply again. And again.

Sating himself—and her.

She writhed, heated and urgent beneath him. He'd never seen anything so beautiful as her, locked in passion's snare. She lifted and twisted, her head turning blindly from side to side as, inside, she sought release. He sank deep and pushed her higher, but still held her back from the edge— she could go higher yet. So could he.

And he wanted to watch her—so splendidly wanton, so gloriously abandoned—as she took him in and held him, as she gave herself to him for the first time. The sight stole his breath—and more. He would have her again, many times, but none would be the same as this, as vested with emotion as this moment was.

He knew when the end was upon her, felt the keen edge of tension ready to explode—and felt the hot flowering within her. He drove into it, and let go—let his body do what came naturally and sent them both over the edge. And, at the last, he watched as the explosion took her, as desire coalesced and turned her womb molten, a hot, fertile pocket for his seed.

Gritting his teeth, he hung on for the last second, and saw her ease. Saw the lines of her face, drawn tight with passion, soften; felt, deep inside her, the strong ripples of her release. On a silent sigh, her body softened beneath him. The expression that washed over her face was that of an angel in the presence of the divine.

Vane felt the shudders rack him. Closing his eyes, he let them—let her—take him.

It had been more—much more—than he'd expected.

Lying on his back in the hay, Patience curled into his side, her skirts and petticoats flipped over her to keep her warm as she slept, Vane tried to come to grips with that reality. He couldn't begin to explain it, all he knew was that no other had ever been like this.

It therefore came as no surprise to discover, as his sated senses cleared, that he was once more possessed of an urgent desire.

Not the same urgent desire that had driven him for the past days, and which she'd so recently and so remarkably thoroughly sated, but a related desire—the compulsive need to secure her as his own.

As his wife.

The four-letter word had always made him flinch. In a reflexive manner, it still did. But he was not about to run counter to his fate—to what he knew, in his bones, was right.

She was the only one for him. If he was ever to marry, it had to be to her. And he wanted children—heirs. The thought of her, his son in her arms, had an instant effect on him. Uunder his breath, he swore.

He glanced sideways, at Patience's topmost curls, and willed her to wake. Gaining her formal agreement to their marriage had just become his top priority. His most urgent priority. In accepting him as her lover, she'd already agreed *in*formally. Once he'd made his offer and she'd said yes, they could indulge their senses as they willed. As often as they willed.

The thought intensified his growing discomfort. Gritting his teeth, he tried to think of something else.

Sometime later, Patience drifted back to consciousness. She came awake as she never had before, her body floating on a sea of golden pleasure, her mind hazed with a deep sense of golden peace. Her limbs were heavy, weighted with warm langor; her body felt buoyed, sated, replete. At peace. For long moments, no thought could pierce the glow, then, gradually, her surroundings impinged.

She was lying on her side, cocooned in warmth. Beside her, Vane lay stretched on his back, his body a hard rock to which she clung. Outside, the rain had ceased, but drips still fell from the eaves. Inside, the glow they'd created lingered, enclosing them within a heavenly world.

He had given her this—shown her the way to this state of grace. The delicious pleasure still lapped about her. Patience smiled. One hand rested on his chest; under her palm, beneath the curly brown hair, she could feel his heart beating, steady and sure. Her own heart swelled.

The emotion that poured through her was stronger than before, glowing golden and silver, so beautiful it made her heart ache, so piercingly sweet it brought tears to her eyes.

Patience closed her eyes tight. She'd been right—right to press for the knowledge, right to take this road. No matter what happened, she would treasure this moment—and all that had brought her here. No regrets. Not ever.

The intense emotion faded, sinking from her conscious mind. Lips gently curving, she shifted, and planted a warm kiss on Vane's chest.

He looked down. Looking up, Patience smiled more deeply and, eyes closing, sank against him. "Hmm—nice."

Nice? Looking down at her face, at the smile on her lips, Vane felt something in his chest shift. Then lock. The feeling, and the emotions that coursed, tumbled and jumbled, in its wake, were not nice at all. They shook him, and left him feeling vulnerable. Lifting one hand, he brushed back Patience's honey gold hair; the tangled mass caught in his fingers. He started releasing the strands, gathering her pins as he went. "Once we're married, you can feel nice every morning. And every night."

Concentrating on her hair, he didn't see the shock flare in Patience's eyes as, stunned, she looked up at him. Didn't see the shock fade into blankness. When he glanced down, she was staring at him, her expression closed, unreadable.

Vane frowned. "What is it?"

Patience drew a shuddering breath, and desperately tried to find her mental feet. She licked her lips, then focused on Vane's face. "Marriage." She had to pause before she could go on. "I don't recall discussing that." Her voice was flat, expressionless.

Vane's frown deepened. "We're discussing it now. I'd meant to speak earlier, but, as you well know, our attempts at rational discussion haven't met with any great success." He drew the last of her hair free and, raking it back with his fingers, laid it across the hay. "So." Finding her eyes once more, he raised a cool brow. "When's it to be?"

Patience simply stared. She was lying here, naked in his arms, her body so sated she couldn't move, and he, suddenly, entirely without warning, wanted to discuss marriage? No, not even discuss it, but simply decide when it was to be.

The golden glow had vanished, replaced with an arctic chill. A chill colder than the grey misery outside the hay doors, colder than the breeze that had sprung up. Icy panic sent gooseflesh rippling over her limbs, then sank to her marrow. She felt the touch of cold steel—the jaws of the trap that was slowly, steadily, closing on her.

"No." Summoning every ounce of her strength, she pressed against Vane's chest; closing her eyes to its bare state, she struggled to sit up. She would never have made it except that he deigned to help her.

He stared—as if he couldn't credit his hearing. "No?" He searched her face, then the shutters came down over his grey eyes. His expression leached. "No what?"

His steely accents made Patience shiver. Turning away from him, keeping her skirts over her lap, she reached for her chemise. She pulled it over her head. "I have never intended to marry. Not at all."

A white lie, perhaps, but a position more easily defended than the unvarnished truth. Marriage had never been high on her agenda—marriage to an elegant gentleman had never figured in her plans. Marriage to Vane was simply impossible—even more so after the last hour.

His voice, coolly precise, came from behind her. "Be that as it may, I would have thought the activities of the last hour would suggest that a rearrangement of your intentions was in order."

Tying the ribbons of her chemise, Patience pressed her lips together and shook her head. "I don't want to marry."

The sound he made as he sat up was derisive. "*All* young ladies want to marry."

"Not me. And I'm not that young." Patience finished pulling on her stockings. Swinging about, she grabbed her petticoats.

She heard Vane sigh. "Patience—"

"We'd better hurry—we've been out all morning." Standing, she hiked up her petticoats and cinched them at her waist. Behind her, she heard the hay rustle as he rose. "They'll worry if we don't return for lunch." Under cover of swiping up her skirt, she turned. Not daring to look directly at him—he was, after all, still naked—she could nevertheless see him from the corner of her eye, and prevent him from touching her. From catching hold of her.

If he did, her shaky, somewhat confused resolution might disintegrate—and the trap might slam shut on her. She could still feel his hands on her skin, sense the imprint of his body on hers. Feel the heat of him inside her.

She yanked her skirts up. "We can't afford to dally." In a state bordering on the frenzied, she scanned the floor for her jacket. It was lying beside his breeches. She hurried over.

Aware that he was standing, naked, hands on hips, frowning at her, she picked up her jacket, and flung his breeches at his head.

He caught them before they hit. His eyes narrowed even further.

"*Do* come on," she implored. "I'll get the horses." With that, she rushed to the ladder.

"*Patience!*"

That particular tone had been known to snap unruly, half-drunk soldiers to immediate attention; to Vane's disgust, it had no discernible affect on Patience. She disappeared down the ladder as if he hadn't spoken.

Leaving him disgusted—thoroughly and absolutely—with himself.

He'd muffed it. Completely and utterly. She was annoyed with him—piqued to her toes—and she had every right to feel so. His offer—well, he hadn't even made it; he'd tried instead to slide around it, to arrogantly push her into agreeing without having to ask.

He'd failed. And now she was in a royal snit.

Not for an instant did he believe that she didn't want to marry, that was merely the first excuse that had sprung to her mind—a weak excuse at that.

Swearing roundly—the only viable way he could relieve his temper—he hauled on his breeches, then reached for his shirt. He'd tried to avoid making the declaration he knew he had to make—and now it was going to be ten times worse.

Gritting his teeth, he stomped into his boots, swiped up his jacket, and stalked to the ladder.

Now he was going to have to beg.

Chapter 13

Begging did not come naturally.

That evening, Vane led the gentlemen back to the drawing room, feeling as if he was marching to his execution. He told himself proposing wouldn't really be that bad.

Keeping the lid on his temper all the way back to the Hall, and then through the long afternoon, had tried him sorely. But having accepted the inevitable—Patience's right to a formal, precisely correct proposal—he'd swallowed his ire and forced his conqueror's instincts, which she'd very effectively raised to his surface, into line.

How long they'd toe that line was a moot point, but he was determined it would be long enough for him to propose and for her to accept him.

Strolling through the drawing-room doors, he scanned the occupants, and inwardly smiled. Patience was not present. He'd grasped the moment as the ladies were rising from the table, when they'd been close as he'd drawn back her chair, to say, *sotto voce*: "We need to meet privately."

Her eyes, wide and golden, had flown to his.

"When and where?" he'd asked, struggling to keep all command from his tone.

She'd studied his eyes, his face, then looked down. She'd waited until the last minute, when she was about to turn and walk from him, to whisper, "The conservatory. I'll retire early."

Suppressing his impatience, he forced himself to stroll to

the *chaise*, where Minnie, as usual, sat in shawled splendor. She looked up as he neared. He raised a languid brow. "I take it you are, indeed, improved?"

"Pish!" Minnie waved dismissively. "It was no more than a cold—there's been far too much bother made over a mere sniffle."

She glanced pointedly at Timms, who humphed. "At least Patience had the sense to go up early, to make sure she took no lasting harm from getting so damp. I suppose you should go up early, too."

"I didn't get that wet." Affectionately brushing his fingers over Minnie's hand, Vane nodded to both women. "If you need help getting upstairs, call me."

He knew they wouldn't; only when she was truly ill would Minnie accept being carried. Turning from them, he strolled to where Gerrard and Edmond were teasing Henry.

Henry pounced the instant he joined them. "Just the one we need! These two have been bending my ear with their melodrama while I'd much rather take them on at billiards. What say you to that return match?"

"Not tonight, I fear." Vane stifled a fictitious yawn. "After spending half the day riding, I'm for bed as soon as possible." He made the comment unblushingly, but his body reacted to the veiled reference to his morning's activities, and his hopes for the night.

The others, of course, thought he was exhausted.

"Oh, come on. You can't be that tired." Edmond chided. "Must be used to being up to all hours in London."

"Indeed," Vane laconically agreed. "But being up is usually followed by a suitably long time prone." Not, of course, necessarily asleep; the conversation was doing nothing for his comfort.

"One game wouldn't take that long," Gerrard pleaded. "Just an hour or so."

Vane had no difficulty squashing a craven impulse to agree—to put off saying the inevitable words yet again. If he didn't get it right this time, present Patience with the speech he'd spent all afternoon rehearsing, God only knew what hideous punishment fate would concoct for him. Like having to go down on bended knee. "No." His determination made the answer definite. "You'll have to make do without me tonight."

The tea trolley saved him from further remonstrance. Once the cups were replaced and Minnie, steadfastly refusing his aid, had gone upstairs, Vane found himself forced to follow, to take refuge in his room until the others reached the billiard room and settled to their game. The conservatory lay beyond the billiard room, and could be reached only by passing the billiard-room door.

Fifteen minutes of pacing his bedchamber did nothing to improve his temper, but he had it well in hand when, having strolled silently past the billiard room, he opened the conservatory door. It opened and closed noiselessly, failing to alert Patience. Vane saw her instantly, peering out of one of the side windows through a bank of palms.

Puzzled, he drew closer. Only when he stood directly behind her did he see what she was so intently watching—the billiard game currently in progress.

Henry was leaning far over the table, his back to them, lining up one of his favorite shots. As they watched, he made his play, his elbow wobbling, the cue jerking.

Vane snorted. "How the devil did he beat me?"

With a gasp, Patience whirled. Eyes wider than wide, one hand pressed to her breast, she struggled to draw breath.

"Get *back*!" she hissed. She prodded him, then flapped her hands at him. "You're taller than the palms—they might see you!"

Vane obligingly backed, but stopped the instant they were beyond the line of the billiard room. And let Patience, fussing and fuming, run into him.

The impact, mild though it was, knocked what breath she'd managed to catch out of Patience. Mentally cursing, she fell back, flashing Vane a furious look as she fought to regain her composure. To calm her wretchedly leaping heart, to quell the impulse to step forward and let his arms steady her, to lift her face and let his kiss claim her.

He'd always affected her physically. Now that she'd lain naked in his arms, the effect was ten times worse.

Inwardly gritting her teeth, she infused impassivity into

her features and drew herself up. Defensively. Clasping her hands before her, she lifted her head, and tried to find the right level. Not challenge, but assurance.

Her nerves had been frazzled before he'd appeared—the jolt he'd just given her had scrambled them further. And worse was yet to come. She had to hear him out. There was no alternative. If he wished to offer for her, then it was only right she allow him to do so, so she could formally and definitively decline.

He stood directly before her, a large, lean, somewhat menacing figure. She'd held him silent with her eyes. Drawing a deep breath, she raised one brow. "You wished to speak with me?"

Vane's instincts had been screaming that all was not as he'd thought; the tone of her question confirmed it. He studied her eyes, shadowed in the dimness. The conservatory was lit only by moonlight pouring through the glassed roof; he wished, now, that he'd insisted on some more illuminated meeting place. His eyes narrowed. "I think you know what it is I wish to say to you." He waited for no acknowledgment, but went on, "I wish to ask for your hand in marriage. We're well suited, in all ways. I can offer you a home, a future, a station in keeping with your expectations. As my wife, you would have an assured place in the *ton*, should you wish to claim it. For my part, I would be content to live mostly in the country, but that would be as you wish."

He paused, increasingly tense. Not a glimmer of response had lit Patience's eyes or softened her features. Stepping closer, he took her hand, and found it cool. Raising it, he brushed a kiss across her cold fingers. Of its own accord, his voice lowered. "Should you agree to be my wife, I swear that your happiness and comfort would be my primary, and my most passionate, concern."

Her chin lifted slightly, but she made no answer.

Vane felt his face harden. "Will you marry me, Patience?" The question was soft, yet steely. "Will you be my wife?"

Patience drew a deep breath, and forced herself to hold his gaze. "I thank you for your offer. It does me more honor than I deserve. Please accept my heartfelt regrets.'' Despite her conviction, a last, small, desperate hope had clung to life in her heart, but his words had slain it. He'd said all the right things, the accepted things, but not the one important thing. He hadn't said he loved her; he'd made no promise to love her for all time. She drew a difficult breath and looked down, at his fingers lightly holding hers. ''I do not wish to marry.''

Silence—absolute and compelling—held them, then his fingers, very slowly, slid from hers.

Vane drew a not entirely steady breath, and forced himself to step back. The conqueror within him roared—and fought to reach for her, to haul her into his arms and take her, storm her castle and force her to acknowledge that she was his—only his. Fists tightly clenched, he forced himself to take a different tack. Slowly, as he had once before, he circled her.

''Why?'' He asked the question from directly behind her. She stiffened; her head rose. Eyes narrowed, he watched one golden curl quiver by her ear. ''I think, in the circumstances, I'm entitled to know that much.''

His voice was low, sibilantly soft, lethally restrained; Patience shivered. ''I've decided against marriage.''

''When did you make this decision?'' When she didn't immediately respond, he suggested, ''After we met?''

Patience wished she could lie. Instead, she lifted her head. ''Yes, but my decision was not solely an outcome of that. Meeting you simply clarified the matter for me.''

Tense silence again descended. He eventually broke it. ''Now how, precisely, am I to take that?''

Patience sucked in a desperate breath. She tensed, and would have whirled to face him, but his fingers on her nape, just the lightest touch, froze her.

''No. Just answer me.''

She could feel the heat of his body less than a foot away, sense the turbulence he held leashed. He could let the reins fall at any minute. Her wits whirled—giddiness threatened. It was so difficult to think.

Which, of course, was what he wanted—he wanted her to blurt out the truth.

Swallowing, she kept her head high. "I have never been particularly interested in marriage. I've grown used to my independence, to my freedom, to being my own mistress. There's nothing marriage can offer me that I value as highly that would compensate me for giving up all that."

"Not even what we shared in the barn this morning?"

She should, of course, have expected that, but she'd hoped to avoid it. Avoid facing it. Avoid discussing it. Avoid tarnishing the silver and the gold. She kept her chin high, and quietly, evenly, stated, "Not even that."

That, thank heaven, was true. Despite all she'd felt, all that he'd made her feel, all that her body now yearned for, having felt the power of that gold and silver emotion—love, what else could it be?—she was even more sure, even more certain, that her course was right.

She was in love with him, as her mother had loved her father. No other power was as great, no other power so fateful. If she made the mistake of marrying him, took the easy road and gave in, she would suffer the same fate her mother had, suffer the same lonely days and the same endless, aching, soul-destroying, lonely nights. "I do not, under any circumstances, wish to marry."

His fury escaped him; it vibrated around her. For one instant, she thought he would seize her. She only just stopped herself from whirling and stepping away.

"This is *insane!*" His anger scorched her. "You gave yourself to me this morning—or did I imagine it? Did I imagine you naked and panting beneath me? Tell me, did I imagine you writhing wantonly as I sank into you?"

Patience swallowed, and pressed her lips tightly together. She didn't want to discuss this morning—not any of it—but she listened. Listened as he used the golden moments to flay her, used the silvery delight like a lance to prick her to say yes.

But to agree would be stupid—after having been warned, having seen what would happen, to knowingly accept misery—she'd never been that witless.

And it would be misery.

That was borne out as she listened, listened carefully, as he reminded her, in graphic detail, of all that had passed between them in the barn. He was relentless, ruthless. He knew women too well not to know where to aim his barbs.

"Do you remember how you felt when I first slid inside you?"

He went on, and desire rose, flickering about her, within her. She recognized it for what it was; she heard it in his voice. Heard the passion rise, felt it, a tangible force as he appeared again beside her, looking down into her face, his features craved granite, his eyes burning darkly. When next he spoke, his voice was so deep, so low, it grated on her skin.

"You're a gentlewoman, born and bred—the position, the requirements, are in your blood. This morning you spread yourself for me—you wanted me, and I wanted you. You gave yourself to me. You took me in—and I took you. I took your maidenhead, I took your virginity—what innocence you had, I took that, too. But that was only the penultimate act in a script carved in stone. The final act is a wedding. *Ours*."

Patience met his gaze steadily, although it took all her will. Not once had he spoken of any softer emotion—not once had he alluded to even the existence of love, let alone suggested it might live in him. He was hard, ruthless—his nature was not soft. It was demanding, commanding, as unyielding as his body. Desire and passion were his forte; that he felt both for her was beyond doubt.

That was not enough. Not for her.

She wanted, needed, love.

She had long ago promised herself she would never marry without it. She'd spent the hour before dinner staring at a cameo portrait of her mother, remembering. The images she'd recalled were still vivid in her mind—of her mother alone, weeping, lonely, bereft of love, dying for want of it.

She lifted her chin, her eyes steady on his. "I do not wish to marry."

His eyes narrowed to grey shards. A long minute passed; he studied her face, her eyes. Then his chest swelled; he nodded once. "If you can tell me this morning meant nothing to you, I'll accept your dismissal."

Not for an instant did his eyes leave hers; Patience was forced to hold his gaze while inside, her heart ached. He'd left her no choice. Lifting her chin, she struggled to draw breath—and forced herself to shrug as she looked away. "This morning was very pleasant, quite eye-opening, but . . ." Shrugging again, she swung aside and stepped away. "Not enough to commit me to marriage."

"*Look at me, dammit!*" The command was issued through clenched teeth.

Swinging back to face him, Patience saw his fists clench—and sensed the battle he waged not to touch her. She immediately lifted her chin. "You're making too much of it—you, of all men, should know ladies do not marry all the men with whom they share their bodies." Her heart twisted; she forced her voice to lighten, forced her lips to curve lightly. "I have to admit this morning was very enjoyable, and I sincerely thank you for the experience. I'm quite looking forward to the next time—to the next gentleman who takes my fancy."

For one instant, she feared she'd gone too far. There was something—a flash in his eyes, an expression that flitted over his face—that locked her breath in her throat. But then he relaxed, not completely, but much of his frightening tension—battle-ready tension—seemed to flow out of him.

She saw his chest rise as he drew breath, then he was coming toward her, moving with his usual predatory grace. She wasn't sure which she found more unnerving—the warrior, or the predator.

"So you liked it?" His fingers, cool and steady, slid under her chin and tipped her face up to his. He smiled—but the gesture didn't reach his eyes. "Perhaps you should consider the fact that if you married me, you would have the pleasure you experienced this morning every day of your life?" His eyes locked on hers. "I'm perfectly prepared to swear that you'll never want for that particular pleasure if you become my wife."

Only desperation allowed her to keep her features still, to stop them from crumpling. Inside, she was weeping—for him, and for her. But she had to turn him from her. There were no words on earth to explain to him—proud descendant of a prideful warrior clan—that it was not in his power to give her the one thing she needed to become his wife.

The effort to lift one brow archly nearly felled her. "I suppose," she said, forcing herself to look into his eyes, to infuse consideration into her expression, "that it might be quite nice to try it again, but I can't see any need to marry you for that." His eyes blanked. She was at the end of her strength and she knew it. She put her last ounce into brightening her smile, her eyes, her expression. "I daresay it would be quite exciting to be your inamorata for a few weeks."

Nothing she could have said, nothing she could have done, would have hurt him, or shocked him, so much. Or been more certain to drive him from her. For a man like him, with his background, his honor, to refuse to be his wife but consent to be his mistress was the ultimate low blow. To his pride, to his ego, to his self-worth as a man.

Her fists clenched in her skirts so tightly, her nails cut into her palms. Patience forced herself to look inquiringly at him. Forced herself not to quail when she saw the disgust flare in his eyes the instant before the steel shutters came down. Forced herself to stand firm, head still high, when his lip curled.

"I ask you to be my wife . . . and you offer to be my whore."

The words were low, laced with contempt, bitter with an emotion she couldn't place.

He looked at her for one long minute, then, as if nothing of any great moment had transpired, swept her an elegant bow.

"Pray accept my apologies for any inconvenience my unwelcome proposition may have caused you." Only the ice in his tone hinted at his feelings. "As there's nothing more to be said, I'll bid you a good night."

With one of his usual graceful nods, he headed for the door. He opened it, and, without glancing back, left, pulling the door gently closed behind him.

Patience held her position; for a long while, she simply stood there, staring at the door, not daring to let herself think. Then the cold reached through her gown, and she shivered. Wrapping her arms about her, she forced herself to walk, to take a calming turn around the conservatory. She held the tears back. Why on earth was she crying? She'd done what had to be done. She reminded herself sternly that it was all for the best. That the numbness enveloping her would eventually pass.

That it didn't matter that she would never feel that golden and silver glow—or the joy of giving her love—again.

Vane was halfway across the neighboring county before he came to his senses. His greys were pacing steadily down the moonlit road, their easy action eating the last miles to Bedford, when, like Saint Paul, he was struck by a blinding revelation.

Miss Patience Debbington might not have lied, but she hadn't told the whole truth.

Cursing fluently, Vane slowed the greys. Eyes narrowing, he tried to think. Not an exercise he'd indulged in since leaving the conservatory.

On leaving Patience, he'd gone to the shrubbery, to pace and curse in private. Much good had it done him. Never in his life had he had to cope with such damage—he'd hurt in tender places he hadn't known he possessed. And she hadn't even touched him. Unable to quell the cauldron of emotions that, by then, had been seething inside him, he'd fastened on strategic retreat as his only viable option.

He'd gone to see Minnie. Knowing she slept lightly, he'd scratched on her door, and heard her bid him enter. The room had been in darkness, relieved only by a patch of moonlight. He'd stopped her lighting her candle; he hadn't wanted her, with her sharp old eyes, to see his face, read the turmoil and pain he was sure must be etched into his features. Let alone his eyes. She'd heard him out—he'd told her he'd remembered an urgent engagement in London. He would be back, he'd assured her, to deal with the Spectre and the thief in a few days. After he'd discovered how to deal with her niece, who wouldn't marry him—he'd managed to keep that confession from his lips.

Minnie, bless her huge heart, had bidden him go, of

course. And he'd gone, immediately, rousing only Masters to lock the house after him, and, of course, Duggan, presently perched behind him.

Now, however, with the moon wrapping him in her cool beams, with the night so dark about him, with his horses' hooves the only sound breaking the echoing stillness—now, sanity had deigned to return to him.

Things didn't add up. He was a firm believer in two and two making four. In Patience's case, as far as he could see, two and two made fifty-three.

How, he wondered, did a woman—a gently bred lady—who had, on first sight of him, deemed him likely to corrupt her brother simply by association, come to indulge in a far from quick roll in the hay with him?

Just what had impelled her to that?

For some women, witlessness might have been the answer, but this was a woman who'd had the courage, the unfaltering determination, to warn him off in an effort to protect her brother.

And had then had the courage to apologize.

This was also a woman who'd never before lain with a man, never before so much as shared a passionate kiss. Never given herself in any way—until she'd given herself to him.

At the age of twenty-six.

And she expected him to believe . . .

With a vitriolic curse, Vane hauled on the reins. He brought the greys to a halt, then proceeded to turn the curricle. He steeled himself for the inevitable comment from Duggan. His henchman's long-suffering silence was even more eloquent.

Muttering another curse—at his own temper and the woman who had, for some ungodly reason, provoked it—Vane set the greys pacing back to Bellamy Hall.

As the miles slid by, he went over everything Patience had said, in the conservatory and before. He still couldn't make head or tail of it. Replaying once again their words in the conservatory, he was conscious of a towering urge to lay hands on her, put her over his knee and beat her, then shake her, and then make violent love to her. How *dared* she paint herself in such a light?

Jaw clenched, he vowed to get to the bottom of it. That there was something behind her stance he had not a doubt. Patience was sensible, even logical for a woman; she wasn't the sort to play missish games. There'd be a reason, some point she saw as vitally important that he, as yet, couldn't see at all.

He'd have to convince her to tell him.

Considering the possibilities, he conceded, given her first nonsensical view of him, that she might have taken some odd, not to say fanciful, notion into her head. There was, however, from whichever angle one viewed the proposition, no reason whatever that they shouldn't wed—that she shouldn't become his wife. From his point of view, and from that of anyone with her best interests at heart, from the viewpoint of his family, and hers, and the *ton*'s, she was perfect for the position in every way.

All he had to do was convince her of that fact. Find out what hurdle was preventing her from marrying him and overcome it. Regardless of whether in order to do so he had to act in the teeth of her trenchant opposition.

As the roofs of Northampton rose before them, Vane smiled grimly. He'd always thrived on challenges.

Two hours later, as he stood on the lawn of Bellamy Hall and looked up at the dark window of Patience's bedchamber, he reminded himself of that fact.

It was after one o'clock; the house lay in darkness. Duggan had decided to sleep in the stables; Vane was damned if he'd do the same. But he'd personally checked all the locks throughout the Hall; there was no way inside other than by plying the front knocker—guaranteed to wake not only Masters, but the entire household.

Grimly, Vane studied Patience's third-floor window and the ancient ivy that grew past it. It was, after all, her fault that he was out here.

By the time he was halfway up, he'd run out of curses. He was too old for this. Thankfully, the thick central stem of the ivy passed close by Patience's window. As he neared the stone ledge, he suddenly realized he didn't know if she was a sound or a light sleeper. How hard could he knock on the pane while clinging to the ivy? And how much noise could he make without alerting Minnie or Timms, whose rooms lay farther along the wing?

To his relief, he didn't need to find out. He was almost up to the sill when he saw a grey shape behind the glass. The next instant, the shape shifted and stretched—Myst, he realized, reaching for the latch. He heard a scrape, then the window obligingly popped open.

Myst nudged it further with her head, and peered down. "*Meew*!"

Uttering a heartfelt prayer to the god of cats, Vane climbed up. Pushing the window wide, he hooked an arm over the top of it and managed to get one leg over the sill. The rest was easy.

Safe on solid timber, he bent down and ran his fingers along Myst's spine, then rubbed between her ears. She purred furiously, then, tail held high, the tip twitching, stalked off toward the fire. Vane straightened, and heard rustling from the direction of the huge four-poster bed. He was dusting leaves and twigs from his shoulders and the skirts of his greatcoat when Patience appeared out of the shadows. Her hair lay, a rippling bronze veil, over her shoulders; she clutched a shawl around her, over her fine lawn nightgown.

Her eyes were bigger than saucers. "What are you doing here?"

Vane raised his brows, and considered the way her nightgown clung to the long limbs beneath. Slowly, he let his gaze travel upward, until his eyes reached her face. "I've come to take you up on your offer."

If he'd had any doubt over his reading of her, the utter blankness that swamped her expression would have dispelled it.

"Ah—" Eyes still wide, she blinked at him. "Which offer is that?"

Vane decided it was wiser not to answer. He shrugged off his greatcoat and dropped it on the window seat. His coat followed. Patience watched with increasing agitation;

Vane pretended not to notice. He crossed to the hearth and crouched to tend the fire.

Hovering behind him, Patience literally wrung her hands—something she'd never done in her life before—and frantically wondered which tack to take now. Then she realized Vane was building up the fire. She frowned. "I don't need a roaring blaze now."

"You'll be glad of it soon enough."

She would? Patience stared at Vane's broad back, and tried not to notice the play of his muscles beneath the fine linen. Tried not to think of what he might mean, what he might be planning. Then she remembered his greatcoat. Frowning, she drifted back to the window seat, stepping lightly, her feet cold on the bare boards. She ran a hand over the capes of the greatcoat—they were damp. She looked out of the window; the river mist was rolling in.

"Where have you been?" Had he been searching for the Spectre?

"To Bedford and back."

"Bedford?" Patience noticed the open window. She swung around to face him. "How did you get in here?" When she'd woken and seen him, he'd been standing in the moonlight looking down at Myst.

Vane glanced back at her. "Through the window."

He turned back to the fire; Patience turned back to the window. "Through the . . . ?" She looked out—and down. "Good Lord—you might have been killed!"

"I wasn't."

"How did you get in? I'm sure I locked this window."

"Myst opened it."

Patience turned to stare at her cat, curled in her favorite position atop a small table to one side of the fire. Myst was observing Vane with feline approval—he was, after all, creating a nice blaze.

He was also creating utter confusion.

"What's going on?" Patience arrived back before the hearth just as Vane rose. He turned to her, and reached for her, helping her the last step into his arms.

Muted by nothing more than fine lawn, his touch seared her. Patience gasped. She looked up. "What—"

Vane sealed her lips with his, and drew her fully against him. Her lips parted instantly; inwardly Patience cursed. His tongue, his lips, his hands, all started to weave their magic. She made a wild mental grab—for shock, surprise, anger, even witless distraction—anything that would give her the strength to distance herself from . . . this.

From the drugging wonder of his kiss, the immediate yearning that swelled within her. She knew precisely what was happening, knew precisely where he was leading her. And was powerless to prevent it. Not while all of her body—and all of her heart—was madly in alt at the prospect.

When not even hauteur would come to her aid, she gave up all resistance and kissed him back. Hungrily. Had it only been this morning she'd had her last taste of him? If so, she was addicted. Beyond recall.

Her hands slid up, over his shoulders; her fingers found their way into his thick hair. Breasts swelling, nipples sensitive against the hard wall of his chest, Patience abruptly drew back, desperate for air.

She gasped as his lips slid down her throat, then fastened hotly over the spot where her pulse thundered. She shuddered and closed her eyes. "Why are you here?"

Her words were a thread of silver in the moonlight. His answer was deep as the deepest shadows.

"You offered to be my inamorata, remember?"

It was as she'd thought; he wasn't going to let her go yet. He hadn't finished with her, had not yet had his fill of her. Eyes closed tight, Patience knew she should fight. Instead, her willful heart sang. "Why did you go to Bedford?" Had he gone in search of information, or because . . .

"Because I lost my senses. I found them and came back."

Patience was very glad he, busy branding her throat with his lips, couldn't see the smile that curved hers—soft, gentle—utterly besotted. His words confirmed her reading of his character, his reactions; he had indeed been hurt and angry—furious enough to leave her. She would have thought a great deal less of him if, after all she'd said in the conservatory, he hadn't felt that way. As for the need that had brought him back to her—the desire and passion she sensed flowing so hotly in his veins—that, she could only be grateful for.

He raised his head, his lips returned to hers. One hand caressing his lean cheek, Patience welcomed him back. The kiss deepened; desire and passion blended and swelled. When next he lifted his head, they were both heated through—both very aware of what it was that shimmered hotly about them.

Their gazes locked. They were both breathing rapidly, both totally focused.

Feeling the touch of cooler air below her throat, Patience looked down. And saw Vane's fingers quickly, deliberately, slipping free the tiny buttons down the front of her night-gown. She studied the sight for an instant, aware of the throbbing in her blood, of the beat that seemed to vibrate about them. As his fingers passed the point between her breasts, and moved lower, she drew in a shuddering breath.

And closed her eyes. "I won't be your whore."

Vane heard the tremor in her voice. He regretted the word, but . . . He glanced at her face, then looked down, watching the small white buttons slide between his fingers, watching the halves of her nightgown slowly open, reveal-ing her soft, sumptuous body.

"I asked you to be my wife, you offered to be my lover. I still want you as my wife." Her eyes flew open. He met her gaze, his face set, etched with passion, hard with de-termination. "But if I can't have you as my wife, then I'll have you as my lover." Forever, if need be.

Her gown was open to her waist. He slid one hand inside, palm sliding possessively around her hip, fingers sinking into soft flesh as he drew her to him. He took her lips, her mouth—a second later, he felt the shudder that passed through her, her achingly sweet surrender.

He felt her fingers at his nape; they slid into his hair. Her lips were soft, pliant, eager to appease—he feasted, on them, on her mouth, on the warmth she so freely offered. She pressed herself to him. Inside her gown, he slid his hand down her back, to stroke, then cup the smooth swell of her bottom. The lower half of her gown was still fastened, restricting his reach; withdrawing his hand, Vane drew back from their kiss.

Patience blinked dazedly. He caught her hand and towed her the few steps to the chair. He sat, then caught her other hand, too, and drew her to stand between his knees. She watched, her breathing ragged, as he quickly unfastened the rest of her gown.

Then the two halves fell free. Slowly, almost reverently, Vane reached up and parted the gown fully, pushing it back to bare her rounded shoulders. To bare her entirely to his gaze. Chest tightening, groin aching, he looked his fill. Her body glowed ivory in the moonlight, her breasts proud mounds tipped with rose pink buds, her waist narrow, indented, the swell of her hips smooth as silk. Her belly was gently rounded, tapering to the fine thatch of bronzy curls at the apex of her thighs. Long, sleek thighs that had already clasped him once.

Vane drew a shuddering breath and reached for her.

His burning palms sliding over her back, urging her forward, broke the spell that had held Patience. On a gasp, she let him draw her near; she had to grasp his shoulders to steady herself. He looked up, the invitation in his eyes very clear. Patience bent her head and kissed him, longingly, openly, giving all she had to give.

She was his—she knew it. There was no reason she couldn't indulge him, and herself, in this way. No reason she couldn't let her body say what she would never say in words.

After a long, lengthy, satisfying kiss, his lips slid from hers to trace the curve of her throat, to heat the blood pulsing just under her skin. Patience tipped her head back to give him better access; her fingers sank into his shoulders, his tightened about her waist as he took full advantage. He held her steady as his lips drifted lower, over the ripening swells of her breasts. She drew a deep breath, murmuring appreciatively when the movement pressed her flesh more firmly to his lips.

Her murmur ended on a gasp as his teeth grazed one tightly furled nipple, then he took it into his mouth, and she felt her bones melt. One of her hands slid from shoulder to nape, then her fingers slid higher, to convulsively clutch his head as he laved her breasts, teasing the now aching peaks, soothing one moment, then tantalizing the next, easing her back one minute, then whipping her to an excruciating peak of feeling.

Her breathing was desperate long before his mouth moved on, lower, to explore the tender hollows of her waist, to feast on the sensitive cusp of her belly. His hands, palms hot and hard, fastened about her hips, supporting her. Then his tongue, hot and slick, probed her navel—the ragged hiss of her breathing fractured.

As his tongue delved, the rhythm evocatively familiar, she swayed and gasped his name. He didn't answer. Instead, he trailed lingering hot kisses down her quivering belly. And into the soft curls at its base.

"*Vane!*"

Her shocked protest carried little conviction; by the time it passed her lips, she was already arching, straining up on her toes, knees parting, limbs pliant, hips tilting as she instinctively offered herself for the next heated caress.

It came—a kiss so intimate she could barely cope with the shattering sensation. He followed it with more, not ruthless but relentless, not forceful but insistent. Then his tongue slid between his lips, and between hers.

For one, crystal moment, Patience was sure he'd pushed her too far and she would die—die of the glory sizzling down her nerves, of the distilled excitement searing every vein. It was too much—at the very least, she'd lose her wits.

His tongue slid lazily across her throbbing flesh—and high became higher, tight became tighter. Hot as a brand, it flicked and swirled, dipped and delved—and her limbs liquefied. Heat soared and roared through her.

She didn't die, and she didn't crumple to the ground in a witless heap. Instead, she clutched him to her, and lost any hope of pretending the truth was not real—that she wouldn't be his, be anything he wished.

He filled his palms with her, cupped her and supported her, held her steady as he tasted her. Explored her with his tongue, teased and tantalized her until she was sobbing.

Sobbing with urgency, moaning with need.

He was hungry—she let him feast; he was thirsty—she urged him to drink. Whatever he asked, she gave, even if he used no words, and she had only instinct to guide her. He took all she offered, and confidently opened further doors, walking in and claiming all as his unquestionable right. He kept her there, his, undeniably his, in a dizzying world of bright sensation, of nerve-tingling realization, of soul-stealing intimacy.

Fingers clenched in his hair, eyes closed, glory exploding, a golden haze on the inside of her lids, Patience shuddered and surrendered—to the welling heat, to the beckoning culmination.

With one last, lingering lick, savoring the tart taste of her, the indescribably erotic tang of her sinking to his bones, Vane drew back. One hand beneath the full swell of her bottom, and her convulsive grasp on his hair kept Patience upright. His gaze roaming her flushed face, he flicked the two buttons that closed his trousers undone.

She was already high, floating, pleasured to her toes; he had every intention of pleasuring her more.

It was the work of an experienced minute to ready himself, then he clasped her thighs and urged her knees onto the chair, sliding along on either side of his hips. The chair was an old one, low, deep and comfortable—made for just this.

Dazed, she followed his unspoken instructions, clearly unsure but eager to learn. He knew her body was ready—achingly empty, yearning for him to fill her. As her thighs slid past his hips, he grasped hers and drew her to him, then drew her down.

He sank into her—and saw her eyes close, lids falling as her breath expelled in a soft, long-drawn sigh. Her body stretched, her softness accommodating his hardness. Then she shifted, pressing deeper, to take more of him, to impale herself more completely.

For one fractured instant, he thought he'd lose his mind.

Certainly all control. He didn't, but it was a grim fight he waged with his demons, slavering to have her, to ravish her utterly. He beat them back, held them back—and set himself to giving her . . . everything he could.

He lifted her, then lowered her; she quickly caught the rhythm, quickly realized she could move herself. He eased his hold on her hips, let her have the illusion of setting the pace; in reality, he never let go, but counted every stroke, gauged the depth of every easy penetration.

It was a magical ride, timeless, without restraint. Using every ounce of his expertise, he created a sensual landscape for her, conjuring it out of her needs, her senses, so that all she felt, all she experienced was part of the staggering whole. His own needs he held back, his demons' cravings, allowing them only the sensations he felt as, rigid, engorged, giddy with passion, drunk on the lingering taste of her, he sank into her cloying heat, and felt her welcoming embrace.

He gave her that—unalloyed sensual joy, pleasured delight beyond description; under his subtle guidance, she gasped, swayed and panted as he filled her, thrilled her, pleasured her to oblivion. He gave her all, and more—he gave her himself.

Only when she started up the last stair, the last flight to heaven, did he loosen his reins and follow in her wake. He'd done everything he could to bind her to him with passion. At the end, as they gasped and clung and the beauty swept over them, through them, and between them, he let go and savored, in his marrow, in the deepest recesses of his heart, in the farthest corners of his being, the glory he intended to capture for all time.

Chapter 14

A deep, regular vibration woke Vane in the eerie hour before dawn. Blinking his eyes wide, struggling to make out shapes in the dim light, it was a full minute before he realized the vibration was emanating from the warm weight in the center of his chest.

Myst lay curled in the hollow just below his breastbone, looking at his face through unblinking blue eyes.

And purring fit to wake the dead.

Another source of warmth, the soft female body curled against his side, registered. Vane glanced sideways. Patience was clearly accustomed to Myst's roar of a purr—she remained dead to the world.

He couldn't stop the grin that curved his lips. Just as well she was asleep. Despite the ups and downs of yesterday, especially the downs, the ups, particularly the last up, dominated his mind.

Coming straight back and making passionate love to her had been the right tack to take. Masterful, yet not forceful. If he pushed too hard, she would dig in her heels and resist—and he'd never learn what it was that was holding her back from marriage.

This way, he could indulge his senses, slake his demons' urges, and wrap her in a sensual web that, regardless of what she might imagine, was quite as strong as the web she'd already woven, albeit unwittingly, about him. And in between tying knot after knot in the net that would bind her to him, he would, gently, carefully, win her confidence,

201

her trust, and she would, in the end, confide in him.

Then it would simply be a matter of slaying her particular dragon, and carrying her off. Simple.

Vane's grin turned wry. He struggled to subdue his cynical laugh. Myst did not appreciate his quaking chest; she dug in her claws, which abruptly cut off his laughter. He frowned at her, but, given her sterling assistance in the night, did not push her from her comfortable perch.

Aside from anything else, *he* was feeling decidedly comfortable—sunk in a warm bed with the lady he wanted as his wife softly sleeping beside him. At this precise moment, he couldn't think of anything else he wanted in the world; this haven was complete. Last night he'd confirmed, beyond all shadow of doubt, that Patience loved him. She might not know it—or she might, but be unwilling to admit it, even to herself. He didn't know which, but he knew the truth.

A lady like her could not give herself to him, take him into her body and love him as she had, if she didn't, truly, in her heart care for him. It needed more than curiosity, more than lust, or even trust, for a woman to give herself completely, utterly, as Patience did every time she gave herself to him.

That degree of selfless giving sprang from love and nothing else.

He'd had too many women not to know the difference, not to sense it and value it as a gift beyond price. How much Patience understood of it he didn't know, but the longer their association persisted, the more accustomed to it she would become.

Which seemed eminently desirable to him.

Vane smiled, devilishly, at Myst.

Who yawned and flexed her claws.

Vane hissed. Myst stood, stretched, then regally stepped off him and padded to the end of the bed. Pausing, she turned and stared back at him.

Frowning, Vane stared back—but the cat's action raised the question of "what next?" in his mind.

His body replied instantly, with an entirely predictable suggestion; he considered it, but rejected it. Henceforth, as far as he was concerned, Patience was his—his to care for, his to protect. At this juncture, protecting her meant preserving appearances. It would never do for some maid to stumble in and discover them, limbs entwined.

Grimacing, Vane edged to his side. Patience lay sunk in down, deeply asleep. He stared at her face, drank in her beauty, breathed in her warmth; he raised a hand to brush aside a curl—and stopped. If he touched her, she might wake—and he might not be able to leave. He stifled a sigh.

Silently, he slipped from her bed.

Before going down to breakfast, Vane detoured by Minnie's rooms. Her surprise at seeing him was written all over her face. Speculation filled her eyes. Before she could start in on him, he nonchalantly stated: "Halfway down, I realized that my London appointment was of far less moment than my obligations here. So I came back."

Minnie opened her old eyes wide. "*Indeed*?"

"Indeed." Vane saw Minnie exchange a laden glance with Timms—who'd clearly been informed of his departure. Knowing from experience the tortures they could put him to, he nodded curtly to them both. "So I'll leave you to your breakfasts, and go and find mine."

He got himself out of Minnie's room before they could recover and start to tease him.

He entered the breakfast parlor to the usual nods and greetings. The gentlemen of the household were all present; Patience was not. Suppressing a smug grin, Vane helped himself from the sideboard, then took his seat.

The glow that had suffused him since the early hours had yet to leave him; he responded to Edmond's variation on his latest scene with an easy smile and a few perfectly serious suggestions, which caused Edmond to depart in a rush, revived and eager to serve his demanding muse.

Vane turned to Gerrard. Who grinned.

"I'm determined to start a new sketch today. There's a particular view of the ruins, taking in the remains of the abbot's lodge, that I've always wanted to draw. The light's rarely good in that quarter, but it will be this morning." He drained his coffee cup. "I should get the essentials down by lunchtime. How about a ride this afternoon?''

''By all means.'' Vane returned Gerrard's grin. ''You shouldn't spend all your days squinting at rocks.''

''What I've always told him,'' humphed the General as he stumped out.

Gerrard pushed back his chair and followed the General. Which left Vane gazing at Edgar's mild profile.

''Which Bellamy are you currently researching?'' Vane inquired.

Whitticombe's contemptuous sniff was clearly audible. He pushed aside his plate and rose. Vane's smile deepened. He raised his brows encouragingly at Edgar.

Edgar slid a careful glance at Whitticombe. Only when his archrival had passed through the door did he turn back to Vane. ''Actually,'' Edgar confessed, ''I've started on the last bishop. He was one of the family, you know.''

''Indeed?''

Henry looked up. ''I say—was this place—the abbey, I mean—as important as Colby makes out?''

''Well . . .'' Edgar proceeded to give them a neat picture of Coldchurch Abbey in the years immediately preceding the Dissolution. His dissertation was refreshingly short and succinct; both Vane and Henry were sincerely impressed.

''And now I'd better get back to it.'' With a smile, Edgar left the table.

Leaving Vane and Henry. By the time Patience arrived, in a frantic froth of skirts, Vane's mellow mood had stretched to granting Henry his long-sought return match over the billiard table. Happy as a lark, Henry stood, and smiled at Patience. ''Best go look in on Mama.'' With a nod to Vane, he ambled off.

Thoroughly enamored—softened by his mood and this unexpected consequence—Vane subsided into his chair, angling it so he could gaze unimpeded at Patience as she helped herself from the sideboard, then came to the table. She took her usual seat, separated from his by Gerrard's vacant place. With a brief smile and a warning look, she applied herself to her breakfast. To the large mound she'd heaped on her plate.

Vane eyed it, straightfaced, then lifted his gaze to her

face. "Something must have agreed with you—your appetite's certainly improved."

Patience's fork froze in midair; she glanced down at her plate. Then she shrugged, ate the portion on her fork, then calmly looked at him. "I vaguely remember being excessively hot." She raised her brows, then looked back at her plate. "Quite feverish, in fact. I do hope it isn't catching." She forked up another mouthful, then slanted him a glance. "Did you pass a quiet night?"

Masters and his minions were hovering—well within earshot—waiting to clear the table.

"Actually, no." Vane met Patience's gaze. Memory had him shifting in his chair. "Whatever had you in its grip must have disturbed me, too—I suspect the malady might last for some time."

"How . . . distracting," Patience managed.

"Indeed," Vane returned, warming to his theme. "There were moments when I felt enclosed in damp hotness."

A blush spread over Patience's cheeks; Vane knew it extended to the tips of her breasts.

"How odd," she countered. She picked up her teacup and sipped. "To me, it felt like heat exploding inside."

Vane stiffened—further; he fought to avoid a telltale shuffle in his seat.

Setting down her cup, Patience pushed aside her plate. "Luckily, the affliction had vanished by morning."

They stood. Patience strolled to the door; Vane sauntered beside her. "Perhaps," he murmured as they passed into the front hall, his voice low, for her ears alone. "But I suspect you'll find your affliction will return tonight." She cast a half-wary, half-scandalized glance at his face; he smiled, all teeth. "Who knows? You might find yourself even more heated."

For one instant, she looked . . . intrigued. Then haughty dignity came to her aid. Coolly, she inclined her head. "If you'll excuse me, I think I'll go and practice my scales."

Pausing at the foot of the stairs, Vane watched as she glided across the hall—watched her hips sway with their usual unrestrained license; he couldn't quite stifle his wolfish grin. He was contemplating following—and trying his hand at disrupting her scales—when a footman came hurrying down the stairs.

"Mr. Cynster, sir. Her Ladyship's asking after you. Urgent, she says—quite in a tizz. She's in her parlor."

Vane shed his wolf's fur in the blink of an eye. With a curt nod for the footman, he started up the stairs. He took the second flight two at a time. Frowning, he strode rapidly for Minnie's rooms.

The instant he opened the door, he saw the footman hadn't lied; Minnie was huddled in her chair, shawls fluffed, looking like nothing so much as an ill owl—except for the tears streaming down her lined cheeks. Closing the door, Vane swiftly crossed the room and went down on one knee beside the chair. He clasped one of her frail hands in his. "What's happened?"

Minnie's eyes were swimming in tears. "My pearls," she whispered, her voice quavering. "They're gone."

Vane glanced at Timms, hovering protectively. Grimfaced, she nodded. "She wore them last night, as usual. I put them on the dresser myself, after we—Ada and I—helped Min to bed." She reached back, lifting a small brocade box from the side table behind her. "They were always kept in this, not locked away. Min wore them every night, so there never seemed much point. And with the thief delighting in tawdry glitter, there didn't seem much threat to the pearls."

Two long, matched strands, with matching drop earrings. Vane had seen them on Minnie for as long as he could remember.

"They were my bride gift from Humphrey." Minnie sniffed tearfully. "They were the one thing—the one piece of all he gave me—that was the most personal."

Vane swallowed the oath that sprang to this lips, swallowed the wave of anger that one of Minnie's charity cases should repay her in this way. He squeezed her hand, imparting sympathy and strength. "If they were here last night, when did they disappear?"

"It had to be this morning, when we went for our constitutional. Otherwise, there wasn't any time someone wasn't in the room." Timms looked angry enough to swear.

"We're in the habit of going for a short amble around the walled garden whenever the weather permits. These mornings, we usually go as soon as the fog lifts. Ada tidies in here while we're away, but she's always gone before we return."

"Today"—Minnie had to gulp before continuing—"as soon as we got through the door, I saw the box wasn't in its usual place. Ada always leaves everything just so, but the box was askew."

"It was empty." Timms's jaw locked. "This time, the thief has gone well and truly too far."

"Indeed." Grim-faced, Vane stood. He squeezed Minnie's hand, then released it. "We'll get back your pearls—I swear on my honor. Until then, try not to worry." He glanced at Timms. "Why not go down to the music room? You can tell Patience while I set a few matters in train."

Timms nodded. "An excellent idea."

Minnie frowned. "But it's Patience's practice time—I wouldn't want to intrude."

"I think you'll find," Vane said, helping Minnie to her feet, "that Patience won't forgive you if you *don't* intrude on her practice." Over Minnie's head, he exchanged a glance with Timms. "She won't want to be left out."

After seeing Minnie and Timms to the music room, and leaving his godmother in Patience's capable hands, Vane met with Masters, Mrs. Henderson, Ada, and Grisham, Minnie's senior servants.

Their shock, and their instant anger against whoever had dared hurt their generous mistress, was palpable. After assuring them that none of them was suspected, and receiving assurances that all the current staff was utterly reliable, Vane did what he could to bolt the stable door.

"The theft has only just occurred." He looked at Grisham. "Has anyone requested a horse or the gig?"

"No, sir." Grisham shook his head. "They're not much for getting out an' about, this lot."

"That should make our task easier. If anyone asks for transportation—or even for a groom to deliver something—put them off and get word to me immediately."

"Aye, sir." Grisham's face was grim. "I'll do that, right enough."

"As for indoors . . ." Vane swung to face Masters, Mrs. Henderson, and Ada. "I can't see any reason the staff can't be informed—the outdoor staff, too. We need everyone to keep their eyes peeled. I want to hear of anything that strikes anyone as odd, no matter how inconsequential."

Mrs. Henderson fleetingly grimaced. Vane raised his brows. "Has anything odd been reported recently?"

"Odd enough." Mrs. Henderson shrugged. "But I can't see as it could mean anything—not to do with the thief or the pearls."

"Nevertheless . . ." Vane gestured for her to speak.

"The maids have reported it again and again—it's making terrible scratches on the floor."

Vane frowned. "What's making terrible scratches?"

"Sand!" Mrs. Henderson heaved a put-upon sigh. "We can't make out where she gets it from, but we're constantly sweeping it up—just a trickle, every day—in Miss Colby's room. Scattered on and around the hearth rug, mostly." She wrinkled her nose. "She has this garish tin elephant—heathenish thing—she told one of the maids it was a memento left her by her father. He was a missionary in India, seemingly. The sand's usually not far from the elephant, but that doesn't seem to be the source. The maids have had a good go dusting it, but it seems perfectly clean. Yet still the sand is there—every day."

Vane's brows rose high, visions of Alice Colby sneaking out in the dead of night to bury pilfered items floating through his mind. "Perhaps she tracks the sand in from outside?"

Mrs. Henderson shook her head; her double chins wobbled vehemently. "Sea sand. I should have said—it's that that makes the whole so strange. Nice and silver-white, the grains are. And where, near here, could you find sand like that?"

Vane frowned, and let his fanciful images fade. He met Mrs. Henderson's eye. "I agree the matter's odd, but, like you, I can't see that it could mean anything. But that's precisely the sort of odd occurrence I want reported, whether it's obviously connected with the thief or not.''

''Indeed, sir.'' Masters drew himself up. ''We'll speak to the staff immediately. You may rely on us.''

Who else could he rely on?

That question revolved in Vane's brain as, leaving Mrs. Henderson's parlor, he wandered into the front hall. In his estimation, Patience, Minnie, and Timms—and Gerrard—had always been beyond suspicion. There was an element of openness, of candor, in both Patience and Gerrard that reminded Vane of Minnie herself; he knew, soul-deep, that neither they, nor Timms, were involved.

That left a host of others—others he felt far less sure of.

His first stop was the library. The door opened noiselessly, revealing a long room, paneled with floor-to-ceiling bookshelves down its entire length. Long windows punctuated the bookcases along one side, giving access to the terrace; one window was presently ajar, letting a light breeze, warmed by autumn sunshine, waft in.

Two desks faced each other down the length of the room. The larger, more imposing example, closer to the door, was weighed down with tomes, the remaining surface blanketed by papers covered in a cramped fist. The well-padded chair behind the desk was empty. In contrast, the desk at the far end of the room was almost bare. It played host to one book only, a heavy leather-covered volume with gilt-edged pages, presently open and supported by Edgar, who sat behind the desk. His head bent, his brow furrowed, he gave no indication he had heard Vane enter.

Vane advanced down the carpeted floor. He was abreast of the wing chair flanking the hearth, its back to the door, before he realized it was occupied. He halted.

Happily ensconced in the deep chair, Edith Swithins busily tatted. Her gaze fixed on the threads she was twining, she, too, gave no sign of noticing him. Vane suspected she was partially deaf, but hid it by reading people's lips.

Stepping more heavily, he approached her. She sensed his presence only when he was close. Starting, she glanced up.

Vane summoned a reassuring smile. ''I apologize for interrupting. Do you often spend your mornings here?''

Recognizing him, Edith smiled easily. "I'm here most mornings—I come down immediately after my breakfast and take my seat before the gentlemen get in. It's quiet and''—with her head she indicated the fire—"warm.''

Edgar lifted his head at the sound of voices; after one myopic glance, he retreated to his reading. Vane smiled at Edith. "Do you know where Colby is?''

Edith blinked. "Whitticombe?'' She peered around the edge of the wing chair. "Good heavens—fancy that! I thought he was there all the time.'' She smiled confidingly at Vane. "I sit here so I don't have to look at him. He's a very . . .''—she pursed her lips—''*cold* sort of man, don't you think?'' She shook her head, then shook out her tatting. "Not at all the sort of gentleman one needs dwell on.''

Vane's fleeting smile was genuine. Edith returned to her tatting. He resumed his progress down the room.

Edgar looked up as he neared and smiled ingenuously. "I don't know where Whitticombe is either.''

There was nothing wrong with Edgar's hearing. Vane halted by the desk.

Removing his pince-nez, Edgar polished them, staring up the long room at his archrival's desk. "I must confess I don't pay all that much attention to Whitticombe at the best of times. Like Edith, I thought he was there—behind his desk.'' Replacing the pince-nez, Edgar looked up at Vane through the thick lenses. "But then, I can't see that far, not with these on.''

Vane raised his brows. "You and Edith have worked out how to keep Whitticombe neatly at a distance.''

Edgar grinned. "Were you after something from the library? I'm sure I could help.''

"No, no.'' Vane deployed his rakish smile—the one designed to allay all suspicions. "I was just aimlessly wandering. I'll let you get back to your work.''

So saying, he retraced his steps. From the door of the library, he looked back. Edgar had retreated to his tome. Edith Swithins was not visible at all. Peace reigned in the library. Letting himself out, Vane frowned.

Without, he was the first to admit, any logical basis, he

had an instinctive feeling the thief was female. Edith Swith-ins's capacious tatting bag, which went everywhere with her, exerted an almost overpowering fascination. But to separate it from her long enough to search it was, he sus-pected, beyond his present powers. Besides, if she'd been in the library since before Whitticombe had left the break-fast parlor, it seemed unlikely she could have rifled Min-nie's room during the short time it had been empty.

Unlikely—but not impossible.

As he headed for the side door, Vane wrestled with an-other, even more complicating possiblity. Minnie's thief—the one who'd stolen the pearls—may not be the same person who'd perpetrated the earlier thefts. Someone might have seen the opportunity to use the "magpie" thief as scapegoat for a more serious crime.

Nearing the side door, Vane grimaced—and hoped that scenario, while not beyond him, was at least beyond the majority of the occupants of Bellamy Hall. Minnie's house-hold affairs were tangled enough as it was.

He'd intended to stroll to the ruins, to see if he could locate Edmond, Gerrard, Henry, and the General—accord-ing to Masters, they were all still outside. The voices em-anating from the back parlor halted him.

"I can't see *why* we can't drive into Northampton again." Angela's whine was pronounced. "There's nothing to do *here*."

"My dear, you really should cultivate some thankful-ness." Mrs. Chadwick sounded weary. "Minnie's been more than kind in taking us in."

"Oh, of course, I'm *grateful*." Angela's tone made it sound like a disease. "But it's just so *boring*, being stuck out here with nothing to look at but old stones."

Holding silent in the corridor, Vane could easily envisage Angela's pout.

"Mind you," she went on, "I did think that when Mr. Cynster came it would be different. You said he was a rake, after all."

"*Angela!* You're sixteen. Mr. Cynster is entirely out of your league!"

"Well, I know *that*—he's so old, for a start! And he's

far too serious. I did think Edmond might be my friend, but these days he's forever mumbling verses. Most times, they don't even make sense! And as for Gerrard—''

Comforted by the fact he wouldn't have to fend off any more of Angela's juvenile advances, Vane backtracked a few steps, and took a secondary stair upward.

From all he'd gleaned, Mrs. Chadwick kept Angela close, undoubtedly a wise decision. As Angela no longer attended the breakfast table, he suspected that meant she and Mrs. Chadwick had spent the whole morning together. Neither, to his mind, were good candidates for the role of thief, either of Minnie's pearls, or more generally.

Which left only one female member of the household as yet unaccounted for. Strolling down one of the Hall's endless corridors, Vane reflected that he had no idea how Alice Colby spent her days.

On the night he'd arrived, Alice had told him her room was on the floor below Agatha Chadwick's. Vane started at one end of the wing, and knocked on every door. If no answer came, he opened the door and looked in. Most rooms were empty, the furniture swathed in covers.

Halfway down the wing, however, just as he was about to push yet another door wide, the handle was hauled from his light grip—and he discovered himself the focus of Alice's black-eyed stare.

Malevolent black-eyed stare.

''Just what do you think you're doing, sir? Disturbing God-fearing people at their prayers! It's outrageous! Bad enough this mausoleum of a house doesn't have a chapel— not even a decent sanctuary—but I have to put up with interruptions from such as *you*.''

Letting the tirade drift past him, Vane scanned the room, conscious of a curiosity to rival Patience's. The curtains were drawn tight. There was no fire in the hearth, not even embers. There was a palpable coldness, as if the room was never warmed, never aired. What furniture he could see was plain and utilitarian, with none of the items of beauty generally found scattered throughout the Hall. As if Alice Colby had taken possession of the room and stamped her character on it.

The last items he noted were a prie-dieu with a well-worn cushion, a tattered Bible open on the shelf, and the elephant of Mrs. Henderson's tale. This last stood beside the fireplace, its gaudy metal flanks glinting in the light lancing through the open door.

"What do you have to say for yourself, that's what I'd like to know. What excuse do you have for interrupting my prayers?" Alice folded her arms across her scrawny chest and stared black daggers at him.

Vane brought his gaze back to her face. His expression hardened. "I apologize for disrupting your devotions, but it was necessary. Minnie's pearls have been stolen. I wanted to know if you'd heard anything or seen anyone strange about."

Alice blinked. Her expression changed not at all. "No, you stupid man. How could I see anyone? I was *praying*!"

With that, she stepped back and shut the door.

Vane stared at the panels—and fought down the urge to break them in. His temper—a true Cynster temper—was never a wise thing to prod. Right now, it was already prowling, a hungry beast seeking blood. Someone had harmed Minnie; to some, not exactly small, part of his mind, that equated to an act of aggression against him. He—the warrior concealed beneath the veneer of an elegant gentleman—reacted. Responded. Appropriately.

Drawing a deep breath, Vane forced himself to turn from Alice's door. There was no evidence to suggest she was involved, any more than anyone else.

He headed back to the side door. He might not stumble instantly over the culprit by checking people's whereabouts, but, at present, it was all he could do. Having located all the women, he went in search of the other males.

Warring with his instinctive conviction that the "magpie" thief was a woman had been a half-fledged hope the whole affair might prove a simple misdemeanor—like Edgar, Henry, or Edmond being strapped for cash and being foolish enough, and weak enough, to be tempted to the unthinkable. As he strode over the lawn, Vane let that idea die. Minnie's pearls were worth a small fortune.

Their simple thief, assuming it was one and the same, had just made the step up to grand larceny.

The ruins appeared deserted. From the wall of the cloisters, Vane saw Gerrard's easel, set up on the other side of the ruins, facing the abbot's lodge, a section of woods at Gerrard's back. The paper pinned to the easel riffled in the breeze. Gerrard's pencil box sat beneath the easel; his painter's stool sat behind it.

All that, Vane could see. Gerrard he couldn't see at all. Assuming he'd taken a moment to stretch his legs and wander, Vane turned away. No point asking Gerrard if he'd seen anything—he'd left the breakfast table with one goal in mind and had doubtless been blind to all else.

Turning back into the cloisters, Vane heard, faint on the breeze, an intense mumbling. He discovered Edmond in the nave, sitting by the ruined font, creating out aloud.

When the situation had been explained to him, Edmond blinked. "Didn't see anyone. But then, I wasn't looking. Whole troop of cavalry might have charged past, and I wouldn't have noticed." He frowned and looked down; Vane waited, hoping for some help, however slight.

Edmond looked up, his brows still knit. "I really can't decide whether this scene should be acted in the nave or the cloisters. What do you think?"

With remarkable restraint, Vane didn't tell him. After a pregnant pause, he shook his head, and headed back to the house.

He was skirting the tumbled stones when he heard his name called. Turning, he saw Henry and the General striding up from the woods. As they neared, he asked: "You went for a stroll together, I take it?"

"No, no," Henry assured him. "I stumbled across the General in the woods. I went for a ramble to the main road—there's a track that leads back through the woods."

Vane knew it. He nodded and looked at the General, huffing slightly as he leaned on his cane.

"Always go out by way of the ruins—a good, rousing walk over uneven terrain. Good for the heart, y'know." The General's eyes fastened on Vane's face. "But why'd you want to know, heh? Not into rambles yourself, I know.''

"Minnie's pearls have disappeared. I was going to ask if you'd seen anyone acting strangely on your walks?''

"Good God—Minnie's pearls!'' Henry looked shocked. "She must be terribly upset.''

Vane nodded; the General snorted. "Didn't see anyone until I ran into Henry here.''

Which, Vane noted, did not actually answer his question. He fell into step beside the General. Henry, on his other side, reverted to his garrulous best, filling the distance to the house with futile exclamations.

Shutting his ears to Henry's chatter, Vane mentally reviewed the household. He'd located everyone, excepting only Whitticombe, who was doubtless back in the library poring over his precious volumes. Vane supposed he'd better check, just to be sure.

He was saved the need by the gong for luncheon—Masters struck it as they reached the front hall. The General and Henry headed for the dining room. Vane hung back. In less than a minute, the library door opened. Whitticombe led the way, nose in the air, his aura of ineffable superiority billowing like a cloak about him. In his wake, Edgar helped Edith Swithins and her tatting bag from the library.

His expression impassive, Vane waited for Edgar and Edith to pass him, then followed in their wake.

Chapter 15

Minnie did not appear at the luncheon table; Patience and Timms were also absent. Gerrard did not show either, but, remembering Patience's comments on his ability to forget all while in pursuit of a particular view, Vane didn't fret about Gerrard.

Minnie was a different story.

Grim-faced, Vane ate the bare minimum, then climbed the stairs. He hated coping with feminine tears. They always left him feeling helpless—not an emotion his warrior self appreciated.

He reached Minnie's room; Timms let him in, her expression absentminded. They'd pulled Minnie's chair to the window. A lunch tray was balanced across the broad arms. Seated on the window seat before Minnie, Patience was coaxing her to eat.

Patience glanced up as Vane neared; their eyes touched briefly. Vane stopped beside Minnie's chair.

Minnie looked up, a heart-breakingly hopeful expression in her eyes.

Exuding impassivity, Vane hunkered down. His face level with Minnie's, he outlined what he'd done, what he'd learned—and a little of what he thought.

Timms nodded. Minnie tried to smile confidently. Vane put his arm around her and hugged her. "We'll find them, never fear."

Patience's gaze locked on his face. "Gerrard?"

Vane heard her full question in her tone. "He's been out

sketching since breakfast—apparently there's a difficult view rarely amenable to drawing.'' He held her gaze. ''Everyone saw him go—he hasn't returned yet.''

Relief flashed through her eyes; her swift smile was just for him. She immediately returned to her task of feeding Minnie. ''Come—you must keep up your strength.'' Deftly, she got Minnie to accept a morsel of chicken.

''Indeed,'' Timms put in from along the window seat. ''You heard your godson. We'll find your pearls. No sense fading to a cypher in the meantime.''

''I suppose not.'' Picking at the fringe of her outermost shawl, Minnie glanced, woe-stricken and frighteningly fragile, at Vane. ''I'd willed my pearls to Patience—I'd always intended them for her.''

''And I'll have them someday, to remind me of all this, and of how stubborn you can be about eating.'' Determinedly, Patience presented a piece of parsnip. ''You're worse than Gerrard ever was, and heaven knows, he was quite bad enough.''

Manufacturing a chuckle, Vane bent and kissed Minnie's paper-thin cheek. ''Stop worrying and do as you're told. We'll find the pearls—surely you don't doubt me? If so, I must be slipping.''

That last gained him a weak smile. Relieved to see even that, Vane bestowed a rakishly confident smile on them all and left.

He went in search of Duggan.

His henchman was out exercising the greys; Vane passed the time in the stables, chatting to Grisham and the grooms. Once Duggan returned and the greys had been stabled, Vane strolled out to take a look at a young colt in a nearby field—and took Duggan with him.

Duggan had been a young groom in his father's employ before being promoted to the position of personal groom to the eldest son of the house. He was an experienced and reliable servant. Vane trusted his abilities, and his opinions of other servants, implicitly. Duggan had visited Bellamy Hall many times over the years, both in his parents' entourage as well as with him.

And he knew Duggan well.

"Who is it this time?" Vane asked once they were clear of the stables.

Duggan tried an innocent expression. When Vane showed no sign of believing it, he grinned roguishly. "Pretty little parlormaid. Ellen."

"Parlormaid? That might be useful." Vane stopped by the fence of the colt's field and leaned on the top rail. "You've heard of the latest theft?"

Duggan nodded. "Masters told us all before lunch— even called in the gamekeeper and his lads."

"What's your reading of the servants. Any likely prospects there?"

Duggan considered, then slowly, definitely, shook his head. "A good bunch they are—none light-fingered, none hard-pressed. Her ladyship's generous and kind—none would want to hurt her."

Vane nodded, unsurprised to have Masters's confidence echoed. "Masters, Mrs. Henderson, and Ada will watch doings in the house; Grisham will handle the stables. I want you to spend as much time as you can keeping an eye on the grounds—from the perimeter of the house to as far as a man might walk."

Duggan's eyes narrowed. "You think someone might try to pass the pearls on?"

"That, or bury them. If you see any disturbance of the ground, investigate. The gardener's old—he won't be planting anywhere at this time of year."

"True enough."

"And I want you to listen to your parlormaid—encourage her to talk as much as she likes."

"Gawd." Duggan grimaced. "You don't know what you're asking."

"Nevertheless," Vane insisted. "While Masters and Mrs. Henderson will report anything odd, young maids, not wanting to appear silly, or to draw attention to something they've come across while doing something they shouldn't, might not mention an odd incident in the first place."

"Aye, well." Duggan tugged at his earlobe. "I suppose—seeing as it's the old lady and she's always been a good'un—I can make the sacrifice."

"Indeed," Vane replied dryly. "And if you hear anything, come straight to me."

Leaving Duggan musing on how to organize his searches, Vane strode back to the house. The sun was long past its zenith. Entering the front hall, he encountered Masters on his way to the dining room with the silverware. "Is Mr. Debbington about?"

"I haven't seen him since breakfast, sir. But he might have come in and be somewhere about."

Vane frowned. "He hasn't been into the kitchen after food?"

"No, sir."

Vane's frown deepened. "Where's his room?"

"Third floor, west wing—one but the last."

Vane took the stairs two at a time, then swung through the gallery and into the west wing. As he climbed the stairs to the third floor, he heard footsteps descending. He looked up, half-expecting to see Gerrard. Instead, he saw Whitticombe.

Whitticombe didn't see him until he swung onto the same flight; he hesitated fractionally, then continued his purposeful descent. He inclined his head. "Cynster."

Vane returned his nod. "Have you seen Gerrard?"

Whitticombe's brows rose superciliously. "Debbington's room is at the end of the wing, mine is by the stairhead. I didn't see him up there."

With another curt nod, Whitticombe passed on down the stairs. Frowning, Vane continued his climb.

He knew he had the right room the instant he opened the door; the combined smell of paper, ink, charcoal, and paint was confirmation enough. The room was surprisingly neat; Vane cynically suspected Patience's influence. A large wooden table had been pushed up to the wide windows; its surface, the only cluttered area in the room, was covered with piles of loose sketches, sketchbooks, and an array of pens, nibs, and pencils, nestling amidst a straw of pencil shavings.

Idly, Vane strolled to the desk and looked down.

The light streaming low through the window glanced off the surface of the table. Vane saw that the pencil shavings had recently been disturbed, then regathered. There were scraps of shavings between the edges of the loose sketches, and between the pages of the sketchbooks.

As if someone had leafed through the lot, then noticed the disturbed shavings and tidied them again.

Vane frowned, then he shook aside the idea. Probably just a curious—or smitten—maid.

He looked out of the windows. The west wing was on the opposite side of the house from the ruins. But the sun was steadily descending; Gerrard's rare morning light was long gone.

A tingle, an unnerving touch of premonition, slithered down Vane's spine. Vividly recalling the sight of Gerrard's easel and stool, but no Gerrard, Vane swore.

He descended the stairs much more rapidly than he'd climbed them.

His expression bleak, he strode through the hall, down the corridor, and out through the side door. And halted.

He was an instant too late in wiping the grim expression from his face. Patience, strolling in company with her harem, had instantly focused on him; alarm had already flared in her eyes. Inwardly, Vane cursed. Belatedly assuming his customary facade, he strolled to meet her.

And her harem.

Penwick was there. Vane gritted his teeth and returned Penwick's nod with distant arrogance.

"Minnie's resting," Patience informed him. Her eyes searched his. "I thought I'd get some air."

"A sound notion," Penwick pronounced. "Nothing like a turn about the gardens to blow away the megrims."

Everyone ignored him and looked at Vane.

"Thought you were going riding with young Gerrard," Henry said.

Vane resisted the urge to kick him. "I was," he replied. "I'm just going to haul him in."

Edmond frowned. "That's odd." He looked back at the ruins. "I can imagine he might miss lunch, but it's not that easy to put off the pangs this long. And the light's almost gone. He can't still be sketching."

"Perhaps we'd better mount a search," Henry suggested.

"He must have moved on from where he was this morning."

"He could be anywhere," Edmond put in.

Vane gritted his teeth. "I know where he was—I'll fetch him."

"I'll go with you." Patience's words were a statement. One look at her face told Vane arguing would be wasted effort. He nodded curtly.

"Allow me, my dear Miss Debbington." Unctuously, Penwick offered his arm. "Naturally, we'll all come, to make sure your mind is set at rest. I'll have a word or two to say to Debbington, never fear. We can't allow him to so heedlessly overset you."

The look Patience sent him was scathing. "You'll do no such thing. I have had quite enough of your attempted interference, sir!"

"Indeed." Seizing opportunity, Vane seized Patience's hand. Stepping forward, brushing Penwick aside, he drew her around. And set off for the ruins at a clipping pace.

Patience hurried beside him. Eyes scanning the ruins, she made no protest at having to half run to keep up.

Vane glanced down at her. "He was set up on the farside, beyond the cloister, facing the abbot's lodge."

Patience nodded. "He might have forgotten lunch, but he wouldn't have forgotten an engagement to ride with you."

Glancing back, Vane saw Edmond and Henry, throwing themselves into the excitement of a search, turn aside, Edmond heading for the old church, Henry for the opposite side of the cloisters. They, at least, were being helpful; Penwick, on the other hand, followed doggedly in their wake.

"Regardless," Vane said, as they reached the first crumbling wall, "he should have been back by now—the light's gone, and the angles would have changed by lunchtime."

He helped Patience over a patch of uneven stones, then they hurried along the west side of the cloister. Henry had just gained the east side. In the nave, they could hear Edmond, his poet's voice ringing, calling for Gerrard. No answer came.

Reaching the far wall, Vane helped Patience up onto the line of toppled stones from which she'd fallen so many nights before. Then he turned and looked toward the abbot's lodge.

The scene he beheld was as he'd seen it earlier. Precisely as he'd seen it earlier.

Vane swore. He didn't bother apologizing. Jumping down, he lifted Patience down to the old flags. Her hand tight in his, he headed for Gerrard's easel.

It took them ten minutes of scrambling—essentially crossing the entire abbey compound—to reach the grassed expanse on which Gerrard had stationed himself. The lawn rose gently as it led away from the abbot's lodge, then dipped into the scrubby edges of the wood. Gerrard had set up below the highest point of the rise, well in front of the dip, a few feet before a crumbling arched gateway, all that was left of the wall that had enclosed the abbot's garden.

Clasping Patience's hand, feeling her fingers clutch his, Vane strode straight to the easel. The page fluttering on it was blank.

Patience blanched. "He never started."

Vane's jaw set. "He started all right." He flicked the tattered remnants of paper caught under the pins. "It's been ripped away." Tightening his hold on Patience's hand, he looked toward the trees.

"Gerrard!"

His roar faded into silence.

A scuffling of boots heralded Henry's appearance. He clambered over a ruined wall, then, straightening, stared at the untended easel. Then he looked at Patience and Vane. "No sign of him the way I came."

Edmond appeared around the far edge of the ruins. Like Henry, he stared at the easel, then gestured behind him. "He's not anywhere around the church."

Stony-faced, Vane waved them to the trees. "You start from that end." They nodded and went. Vane looked down at Patience. "Would you rather wait here?"

She shook her head. "No, I'll come with you."

He'd expected nothing less. Her hand locked in his, they backtracked off the lawn and circled into the wood.

Penwick, huffing and puffing, caught up with them deep in the trees. Calling Gerrard's name, they were quartering the area; after pausing to catch his breath, Penwick tut-tutted censoriously. "If you'd allowed me to talk to Deb-bington earlier—bring him to a proper sense of his responsibilities—none of this nonsense, I flatter myself, would have occurred."

Pushing back a lock of hair from her forehead, Patience stared at him. "What nonsense?"

"It's obvious." Penwick had regained his breath and his customary attitude. "The boy's got an assignation with some flighty maid. Says he's busy drawing and slips away into the wood."

Patience's jaw dropped.

"Is that what you did at his age?" Vane inquired, forging ahead without pause.

"Well . . ." Penwick tugged his waistcoat into place, then he caught Patience's eye. "No! Of course not. Any-way, it's not me but young Debbington we're talking about here. Loose screw in the making, I've not the slightest doubt. Brought up by women. Pampered. Allowed to run wild without proper male guidance. What else can you ex-pect?"

Patience stiffened.

"Penwick." Vane caught Penwick's eye. "Either go home or shut up. Or I'll take great delight in knocking your teeth down your throat."

The inflexible steel in his voice made it clear he was speaking the truth.

Penwick paled, then flushed and drew himself up. "If my assistance isn't welcome, naturally, I'll take myself off."

Vane nodded. "Do."

Penwick looked at Patience; she stared stonily back. With the air of a rejected martyr, Penwick sniffed and turned on his heel.

When the crump of his retreating footsteps died, Patience sighed. "Thank you."

"It was entirely my pleasure," Vane growled. He flexed

his shoulders. "Actually, I was hoping he'd stay and keep talking."

Patience's giggle tangled in her throat.

After a further ten minutes of fruitless searching, they saw Edmond and Henry through the trees. Patience halted and heaved a troubled sigh. "You don't think," she said, turning to Vane as he stopped beside her, "that Gerrard actually might be off with some maid?"

Vane shook his head. "Trust me." He looked around—the belt of woodland was narrow; they hadn't missed any area. He looked down at Patience. "Gerrard's not that interested in females yet."

Henry and Edmond came up. Hands on hips, Vane glanced around one last time. "Let's get back to the ruins."

They stood on the lawn before Gerrard's easel and surveyed the gigantic pile of toppled stones and crumbling rock. The sun was painting the sky red; they would have only an hour before fading light made searching dangerous.

Henry put their thoughts into words. "It's really relatively open. It's not as if there's all *that* many places someone might lie concealed."

"There are holes, though," Patience said. "I fell into one, remember?"

Vane looked at her, then he looked back at the easel—at the rise of the lawn behind it. Swinging about, he strode to the lip, and looked down.

His jaw locked. "He's here."

Patience rushed to Vane's side; clutching his arm, teetering on the lip's edge, she looked down.

Gerrard lay sprawled on his back, arms flung out, his eyes closed. The dip, which appeared gentle enough from any other vantage point, was quite steep, dropping six feet vertically into a narrow cleft, concealed by the sloping banks on either side.

The blood drained from Patience's face. "Oh, no!"

Vane jumped down, landing by Gerrard's feet. Patience immediately sank onto the edge, gathering her skirts about her legs. Vane heard the rustling. He looked around. His eyes lit with warning; Patience tilted her chin stubbornly and wriggled closer to the edge.

Cursing softly, Vane swung back, gripped her waist, and lifted her down, setting her on her feet beside Gerrard.

Immediately Vane released her, Patience flung herself on her knees beside her brother. "Gerrard?" A cold fist clutched her heart. He was dreadfully pale, his lashes dark crescents against chalk white cheeks. With a shaking hand, she brushed back a lock of hair, then framed his face in her hands.

"Gently," Vane warned. "Don't try to shift him yet." He checked Gerrard's pulse. "His heartbeat's strong. He's probably not badly injured, but we should check for broken bones before we shift him."

Relieved on one score, she sat back and watched Vane check Gerrard's torso, arms, and legs. Reaching Gerrard's feet, he frowned. "Nothing seems broken."

Patience frowned back, then reached for Gerrard's head, spreading her hands, sliding her fingers through the thick hair to check his skull. Her searching fingers found a roughness, a deep abrasion, then her palm turned sticky. Patience froze—and looked up at Vane. She drew a shaky breath, then, gently laying Gerrard's head back down, she retrieved her hand and peered at the palm. At the red streaks upon it. Her expression blanking, she held up her hand for the others to see. "He's been . . ."

Her voice died.

Vane's expression turned granite-hard. "Hit."

Gerrard came to his senses with a painful groan.

Patience immediately flew to his side. Sitting on the edge of his bed, she squeezed out a cloth in a basin perched on the bedside table. Shoulders propped against the wall beyond the bed, Vane watched as she bathed Gerrard's forehead and face.

Gerrard groaned again, but surrendered to her ministrations. Grimly impassive, Vane waited. Once they'd established Gerrard had been knocked unconscious, he'd carried him back to the house. Edmond and Henry had packed up Gerrard's gear and followed. Patience, distraught and struggling to master it, had kept by his side.

She'd come into her own once they'd got Gerrard upstairs. She'd known just what to do, and had gone about doing it in her usual competent way. While she'd remained pale and drawn, she hadn't panicked. With silent approval, he'd left her issuing orders left and right, and gone to break the news to Minnie.

Crossing the gallery, he'd seen, in the hall below, Edmond and Henry holding court, informing the other household members of Gerrard's "accident." Before leaving the ruins, they'd found the rock that had hit him—part of the old gateway arch. To Edmond and Henry, that meant Gerrard had been standing beneath the arch at the wrong moment, been struck by the falling masonry, then stumbled back and fallen into the cleft. Vane's view was not so sanguine. Concealed in the shadows of the gallery, he'd studied each face, listened to each exclamation of horror. All had rung true—true to form, true to character; none gave any indication of prior knowledge, or of guilt. Grimacing, he'd continued to Minnie's rooms.

After informing Minnie and Timms, he'd returned to assist Patience in evicting all those who'd gathered—all of Minnie's odd household—from Gerrard's room. While he'd succeeded in that, he hadn't been able to evict Minnie and Timms.

Vane glanced to where Minnie sat huddled in the old chair by the fireplace, wherein a fire now roared. Timms stood beside her, one hand gripping Minnie's shoulder, imparting wordless comfort. Their attention was focused on the bed. Vane studied Minnie's face, and chalked up another entry in the Spectre's—or was it the thief's?—account. They'd pay—for every deepening line in Minnie's face, for the worry and fretful concern in her old eyes.

"*Oh*! My head!" Gerrard tried to sit up. Patience pushed him back down.

"You have a gash at the back, just lie quietly on your side."

Still dazed, Gerrard obeyed, blinking owlishly across the now dim room. His gaze fixed on the window. The sun had set; last banners of vermilion streaked the sky. "It's evening?"

" 'Fraid so." Pushing away from the wall, Vane strolled

forward to where Gerrard could see him. He smiled reassuringly. "You've missed the day."

Gerrard frowned. Patience rose to remove her basin; Gerrard raised a hand and gingerly felt the back of his head. His features contorted as he touched his wound. Lowering his hand, he looked at Vane. "What happened?"

Relieved, both by the clarity and directness of Gerrard's gaze, and his eminently sensible question, Vane grimaced. "I was hoping *you'd* be able to tell *us* that. You went out to sketch this morning, remember?"

Gerrard's frown returned. "The abbot's lodge from the west. I remember setting up."

He paused; Patience returned to sit beside him. She took one of his hands in hers. "Did you start sketching?"

"Yes." Gerrard went to nod, and winced. "I *did* sketch. I got the general lines down, then I got up and went to study the detail." He frowned in his effort to recall. "I went back to my stool, and kept sketching. Then. . . ." He grimaced, and glanced at Vane. "Nothing."

"You were hit on the back of the head with a rock," Vane informed him. "One that originally came from the gateway arch behind you. Try to think back—had you stood up, and stepped back? Or did you never leave your seat?"

Gerrard's frown deepened. "I didn't stand up," he eventually said. "I was sitting, sketching." He looked at Patience, then at Vane. "That's the last I remember."

"Did you see anything, sense anything? What's the very last thing you recall?"

Gerrard screwed up his face, then he shook his head— very slightly. "I didn't see or sense anything. I had my pencil in my hand and I was sketching—I'd started filling in the details around what's left of the abbot's front door." He looked at Patience. "You know what I'm like—I don't see anything, hear anything." He shifted his gaze to Vane. "I was well away."

Vane nodded. "How long were you sketching?"

Gerrard raised his brows in a facial shrug. "One hour? Two?" He lifted a shoulder. "Who knows. It could have been three, but I doubt it was that long. Give me a look at my sketch, and I'll have a better idea.''

He looked up expectantly; Vane exchanged a glance with Patience, then looked back at Gerrard. ''The sketch you were working on was torn from your easel.''

''*What*?''

Gerrard's incredulous exclamation was echoed by Timms. Gerrard carefully shook his head. ''That's ridiculous. My sketches aren't worth anything—why would the thief steal one? It wasn't even finished.''

Vane exchanged a long glance with Patience, then transferred his gaze back to Gerrard's face. ''It's possible that's why you were rendered unconscious—so you never did finish your latest view.''

''But why?'' The bewildered question came from Minnie.

Vane turned to face her. ''If we knew that, we'd know a great deal more.''

Later that night, by unanimous accord, they held a conference in Minnie's room. Minnie and Timms, Patience and Vane, gathered before Minnie's fire. Sinking onto the footstool beside Minnie's chair, one of Minnie's frail hands clasped in hers, Patience scanned the others' faces, lit by the flickering firelight.

Minnie was worried, but beneath her fragility ran a streak of pure stubbornness, and a determination to learn the truth. Timms seemed to consider the malefactors in their midst as a personal affront, if not to her dignity, then certainly to Minnie's. She was doggedly fixated on unmasking the villains.

As for Vane . . . Patience let her gaze roam his features, more austere than ever in the shifting golden light. All hard angles and planes, his face was set. He looked like . . . a warrior sworn. The fanciful notion popped into her head, but she didn't smile. The epithet fitted all too well—he looked set on eradicating, annihilating, whoever had dared disturb Minnie's peace.

And hers.

She knew that last was true—the knowledge had come

to her borne by the touch of his hands on her shoulders as he'd helped her with Gerrard, in the way his eyes had searched her face, watching for worry, for signs of distress.

The sensation of being within his protective circle was sweetly comforting. Even though she told herself it was only for now—for the present and not for the future—she couldn't stop herself drinking it in.

"How's Gerrard?" Timms asked, settling her skirts in the second chair.

"Safely sleeping," Patience replied. He'd turned fretful as the evening wore on, until she'd insisted on dosing him with laudanum. "He's snug in his bed, and Ada's watching over him."

Minnie looked down at her. "Is he truly all right?"

Vane, leaning against the mantelpiece, shifted. "There was no sign of concussion that I could see. I suspect that, other than a sore head, he'll be his usual self in the morning."

Timms snorted. "But who hit him? And why?"

"Are we sure he was hit?" Minnie looked at Vane.

Grimly, he nodded. "His recollections are clear and lucid, not hazy. If he was seated as he said, there's no way a falling stone could have struck him at that angle, with that sort of force."

"Which brings us back to my questions," Timms said. "Who? And why?"

"As to the who, it must be the Spectre or the thief." Patience glanced at Vane. "Presuming they're not one and the same."

Vane frowned. "There seems little reason to imagine they're the same person. The Spectre has lain low since I chased him, while the thief has continued his activities without pause. There's also been no hint that the thief has any interest in the ruins, while they've always been the Spectre's special haunt." He didn't mention his conviction that the thief was a female, and thus unlikely to have had the strength, or intestinal fortitude, to cosh Gerrard. "We can't rule out the thief as today's culprit, but the Spectre seems the more likely villain." Vane shifted his gaze to Timms's face. "As for the why, I suspect Gerrard saw something—something he may not even realize he's seen.''

"Or the villain *thought* he saw something," Timms replied.

"He's really very good with noting detail," Patience said.

"A fact the whole household knew. Anyone who's ever seen any of his sketches would be aware of the detail he includes.'' Vane stirred. "I think, given the disappearance of his last sketch, that we can safely conclude that he did indeed see something someone didn't want him to see.''

Patience grimaced. "He doesn't remember anything special about what he'd sketched."

Vane met her gaze. "There's no reason whatever it is would appear out of the ordinary to him."

They fell silent, then Minnie asked, "Do you think he's in any danger?"

Patience's gaze flew to Vane's face. He shook his head decisively. "Whoever it is knows Gerrard knows nothing to the point, and poses no real threat to Gerrard now." Reading a lack of conviction in all their eyes, he reluctantly elaborated, "He was lying out there for hours, unconscious. If he was a real threat to the villain, said villain had ample time to remove him permanently."

Patience shuddered, but nodded. Both Minnie's and Timm's faces grew bleak. "I want this villain caught," Minnie declared. "We can't go on like this."

"Indeed." Vane straightened. "Which is why I suggest we remove to London."

"London?"

"Why London?"

Resettling his shoulders against the mantelpiece, Vane looked at the three faces turned up to him. "We have two problems—the thief and the Spectre. If we consider the thief, then, while the thefts don't follow any rhyme or reason, the chances of the perpetrator being one of the household is high. Given the number of items stolen, there must be a cache somewhere—we've virtually eliminated any possiblity that the stolen goods have been sold. If we remove the entire household to London, then, as soon as we leave here, the staff, all of whom are above suspicion, can start a thorough search. Simultaneously, when we arrive in London, I'll arrange for all the luggage to be searched as well. In a house in London, further thefts and the hiding of items taken will be much more difficult."

Minnie nodded. "I can see that. But what about the Spectre?"

"The Spectre," Vane said, his expression growing grimmer, "is the most likely candidate for our villain of today. There's no evidence that the Spectre comes from outside—he's most likely one of the household. All that went before—the sounds and lights—could have been someone searching the ruins by night, when no one else was about. Today's events presumably arose because Gerrard unknowingly got too close to something the Spectre doesn't want seen. All that's happened suggests that the Spectre wants to hunt in the ruins without anyone else about. By removing to London, we give the Spectre precisely the situation he wants—the ruins, deserted."

Timms frowned. "But if he's one of the household, and the household's in London . . ." Her words faded as understanding lit her face. "He'll want to come back."

Vane grinned humorlessly. "Precisely. We'll just need to wait and see who makes the first move to return."

"But will he, do you think?" Minnie grimaced. "Will he persist, even after today? He must realize he needs to be more careful now—he must fear being caught."

"As for fearing being caught, I can't say. But"—Vane's jaw firmed—"I'm quite sure, if it's the empty ruins he wants, he won't be able to resist the opportunity of having them all to himself." He caught Minnie's eye. "Whoever the Spectre is, he's obsessed—whatever it is he's after, he's not going to give up."

And so it was decided: The whole household would remove to London as soon as Gerrard was fit enough to travel. As he did a final round of the silent, sleeping house, Vane made a mental list of preparations to be put in train tomorrow. The last leg of his watchman's round took him along the third floor of the west wing.

The door of Gerrard's room stood open; soft light spilled across the corridor floor.

Silently, Vane approached. He paused in the shadows of the doorway and studied Patience as, seated on a straight-backed chair set back from the bed, her hands clasped in her lap, she watched Gerrard sleep. Old Ada dozed, sunk in the armchair by the fireplace.

For long, uncounted moments, Vane simply looked—let his eyes drink their fill—of Patience's soft curves, of the sheening gloss of her hair, of her intrinsically feminine expression. The simple devotion in her pose, in her face, stirred him—thus would he want his children watched, cared for, protected. Not the sort of protection he provided, but protection, and support, of a different, equally important, sort. He would provide one, she would provide the other—two sides of the same, caring coin.

He felt the surge of emotion that gripped him; he was long past breaking free. The words he'd used to describe the Spectre rang in his head. The description applied equally well to him. He was obsessed, and was not going to give up.

Patience sensed his presence as he neared. She looked up and smiled fleetingly, then looked back at Gerrard. Vane curved his hands about her shoulders, then grasped and, gently but firmly, drew her to her feet. She frowned, but let him draw her into the circle of his arms.

Head bent, he spoke softly. "Come away. He's in no danger now."

She grimaced. "But—"

"He won't be happy if he wakes and finds you slumped asleep in that chair, watching over him as if he were six years old."

The look Patience bent on him stated very clearly that she knew precisely which string he was pulling. Vane met it with an arrogantly lifted brow. He tightened his arm about her. "No one's going to harm him, and Ada's here if he calls." He steered her to the door. "You'll be of more use to him tomorrow if you've had some sleep tonight."

Patience glanced over her shoulder. Gerrard remained sound asleep. "I suppose . . ."

"Precisely. I'm not about to leave you here, sitting through the night for no reason." Drawing her over the threshold, Vane pulled the door shut behind them.

Patience blinked her eyes wide; all she could see was darkness.

"Here."

Vane's arm slid around her waist, and tightened, locking her to his side. He turned her toward the main stairs, strolling slowly. Despite the lowering gloom, Patience found it easy to relax into his warmth, to sink into the comfort of his strength.

They walked in silence through the darkened house, and on into the opposite wing.

"You're sure Gerrard will be all right?" She asked the question as they reached the corridor leading to her room.

"Trust me." Vane's lips brushed her temple. "He'll be fine."

There was a note in his deep voice, rumbling softly through her, that reassured far more than mere words. The last of her edgy, perhaps irrational, sisterly trepidation slid away. Trust him?

Safely screened by the dark, Patience let her lips curve in a knowing, very womanly, smile.

Her door loomed before them. Vane set it wide and handed her through. A gentleman would have left at that point—he'd always known he wasn't a gentleman. He followed her in and shut the door behind him.

She needed to sleep; he wouldn't be able to rest until she was dreaming. Preferably curled in his arms.

Patience heard the latch fall home and knew he was in the room with her. She didn't look back but walked slowly to stand before the fire. It was blazing, stoked by some thoughtful servant. She stared into the flames.

And tried to clarify what she wanted. Now. This minute. From him.

He'd spoken truly—Gerrard was no longer six years old. Her time for watching over him was past. To cling would only be to hold him back. But he'd been the focus of her life for so long, she needed something to replace him. Someone to replace him.

At least for tonight.

She needed someone to take from her all she had to give. Giving was her outlet, her release—she needed to give in much the same way as she needed to breathe. She needed to be wanted—needed someone to take her as she was, for what she was. For what she could give them.

Her senses reached for Vane as he drew nearer. Drawing a deep breath, she turned.

And found him beside her.

She looked into his face, the angular planes burnished by the fire's glow. His eyes, cloudy grey, searched hers. Setting aside all thoughts of right and wrong, she raised her hands to his chest.

He stilled.

Sliding her arms upward, she stepped closer; locking her hands at his nape, she pressed herself to him and lifted her lips to his.

Their lips met. And fused. Hungrily. She felt his hands lock about her waist, then he shifted, and his arms closed, viselike, about her.

Her invitation, her acceptance, shook Vane to his soul; he only just managed not to crush her to him. His demons howled in triumph; he swiftly shackled them, leashed them, then turned his attention to her. Of her own volition, she pressed closer. Letting his hands glide down the delicate planes of her back, he molded her to him, urging her hips nearer, then, sliding his hands further, he cupped the firm curves of her derriere and drew her forcefully into the V of his braced thighs.

She gasped and offered him her mouth anew; rapaciously he claimed her. In the back of his mind rang a litany of warning, reminding him of his reined demons, of the concepts of civilized behavior, of sophisticated expertise—all the hallmarks of his rakish experience. Said experience, without conscious instruction, came up with a plan of action. It was warm before the fire—they could disrobe before it, then repair to the civilized comfort of her bed.

Having formulated a plan, he focused on its implementation. He kissed her deeply, searchingly, evocatively—and felt her flaring response. Her tongue boldly tangled with his; distracted, keen to experience the sweet response again, he tempted her, taunted her, to repeat the caress. She did, but slowly, so slowly his senses followed every flick, every sliding contact, with giddy intensity.

Not until he finally summoned his wits and eased back from their kiss did he feel her hands on his chest. Through his shirt, her palms branded him, her fingers kneading. She swept her hands up to his shoulders; his coat impeded the movement. She tried to push the coat off. Breaking their kiss, Vane released her and shrugged. Coat and waistcoat hit the floor.

She fell on his cravat, as eager as his demons. Brushing her hands aside, Vane rapidly flicked the knotted folds undone, then dragged the long strip free. Patience had already transferred her attentions to his shirt buttons; within seconds she had them undone. Hauling the tails free of his waistband, she flung the sides wide and greedily set her hands searching, fingers tangling in the crisp hair.

Looking into her face, Vane savored the look of sensual wonder in her features, the glow of anticipation in her eyes.

He reached for her laces.

Patience was enthralled. He'd explored her, but she hadn't, yet, had a chance to explore him. She spread her fingers, and her senses, drinking in the warm resilience of taut muscle stretched over hard bone. She investigated the hollows and broad planes of his chest, the wide ridges of his ribs. Crisp brown hair curled and caught at her slim digits; the flat discs of his nipples hardened at her touch.

It was all perfectly fascinating. Eager to extend her horizons, she seized the sides of his shirt.

Just as he seized the sleeves of her gown.

What followed had her giggling—foolishly, heatedly. Hands locked on each other, they rocked and swayed. Simultaneously, they both adjusted their grips. While she fought to wrestle his shirt from him, he—far more expertly—divested her of her gown.

He hauled her into his arms and ravished her mouth, plundering deeply, one arm locking her to him while his other hand dealt with the drawstring of her petticoat.

Patience answered the challenge and returned the kiss

avidly—while her busy fingers fought with the buttons of his breeches. Their lips met and melded, parting only to fuse heatedly again.

Her petticoats fell to the floor in the same instant she pushed his breeches over his hips. He broke from their kiss. Their eyes met, heated gazes colliding. With a soft curse, he stepped back and stripped off both boots and breeches.

Eyes wide, Patience drank in the sight of him, the brutally hard, sculpted planes of his body bathed in the fire's golden light.

He looked up and caught her watching. He straightened, but before he could reach for her, she grasped the lower edge of her chemise and, in one smooth movement, drew it up and over her head.

Her eyes locked on his, she let the soft silk fall, forgotten, from her fingers. Hands, arms, reaching for him, she deliberately stepped into his embrace.

The golden instant of meeting, the first touch of bare skin to bare skin, sent exquisite delight lancing through her. She sucked in a quick breath. Lids lowered, she draped her arms over his broad shoulders and pressed closer, settling her breasts against his chest, her thighs meeting his much harder ones, her soft belly a cradle for the rampant hardness of his staff.

Their bodies slid and shifted, then locked tight. His arms closed, a steel vise, about her.

And she felt the coiled tension that held him. The leashed tension he held back.

The power, the force, she sensed in his locked muscles, in the taut sinews that surrounded her, compelled her. Fascinated her. Emboldened and encouraged her. She wanted to know it—feel it, touch it, revel in it. Tightening her arms about his neck, she pressed even closer. Lifting her head, she brushed her lips across his. And whispered, "Let go."

Vane ignored her—she didn't know, couldn't know, what she was asking. Lowering his head, he captured her lips in a long, lengthy kiss designed to intensify the glorious sensation of her naked body sinking against his. She felt like cool silk, vibrant, delicate, and sensual; the slide of her against him was a potent caress, leaving him achingly aroused, achingly urgent.

He needed to get her to the bed. Soon.

She broke from their kiss to place hot, openmouthed kisses across his collarbone, across the sensitive skin just below his throat.

And to reach for him.

She touched him. Vane stilled. Delicately tentative, she curled her fingers about his rigid length. He stiffened—and hauled in a desperate breath.

Her bed. His demons roared.

Guided by unerring instinct, her fingers closing more confidently about him, she licked one flat nipple, her tongue scalding hot, and murmured, "Let the reins go."

Vane's head reeled.

Releasing him, she raised her head. Twining her arms about his neck, she stretched upward against him, and, bending one knee, lifted one firm, ivory thigh to his hip. "Take me."

She was out of her mind—but he was already out of his.

All thoughts of beds, and civilized sophistry, vanished from his head. Without conscious direction, his hands closed about the firm globes of her bottom and he lifted her. Instantly, she wrapped her long legs about his hips and drew herself tight against him.

It was she who made the necessary adjustment to capture the throbbing head of his staff in the slick flesh between her thighs, leaving him poised, aching and desperate, at her entrance.

And it was she who made the first move to sink down, to take him into her body, to impale herself on his rigid hardness.

Every muscle locked, Vane struggled to breathe, struggled to deny the impulse to ravish her. Sinking lower, she found his lips with hers, brushing them tantalizingly. "Let go."

He didn't, couldn't—to relinquish control completely was beyond him. But he loosened the reins, slackened them as much as he dared. Muscles bunching, flexing, he lifted her—and thrust upward as she sank down.

She learned quickly. The next time he lifted her, she relaxed, then tightened as he filled her, slowing her downward slide, extending it to take even more of him than before.

Vane set his teeth. His head whirled as, again and again, she closed, scalding hot, about him. When it was that the truth dawned and he realized she was loving him, knowingly pleasuring him, lavishing the most intimate of caresses upon him, he never knew. But it was suddenly crystal-clear.

He'd never been loved like this—had a woman set herself to lavish pleasure so determinedly upon him—to ravish him.

The slick caresses continued; he was sure he'd lose his mind. Fire rose, flame upon flame within him. He was burning, and she was the source of the heat.

He buried himself in the wet furnace she offered him, and felt her boldly embrace him. With a half-smothered groan, he sank to his knees on the rug before the hearth.

She adjusted instantly, eagerly using her new purchase on the floor to ride him more hungrily.

He couldn't take much more. Vane locked his hands about her hips and held her to him, trying to catch his breath, desperate to prolong the glorious congress. Patience squirmed, fighting to regain control. Vane set his teeth on an agonized hiss. Sliding both hands up, along her back, he tipped her back and away, arching her so her breasts, swollen and ripe, were his to feast on.

He feasted.

Patience heard her own gasp as his mouth fastened hungrily over one engorged nipple. A sobbing moan followed moments later. Hot and ravenous, he laved her breasts, then suckled the hypersensitized peaks until she was sure she would die. Within her, his heavy hardness filled her, completed her; pressed deeply into her, he rocked deeper still, claiming her—body, mind, and senses.

Trapped in his hold, she gasped and writhed; unable to rise on him, but refusing to be gainsaid, she changed direction, and rolled her hips against him.

It was Vane's turn to gasp. He felt the coiled tension

inside him tighten, then tighten again, invested with a force he had no hope of controlling. Of holding back.

Reaching between them, he slid his fingers through her damp curls, and found her. Just a touch was all it took, and she shattered, fragmented, her senses exploding in a fractured cry as she tumbled over that invisible precipice and into sated oblivion.

He followed a heartbeat later.

The fire had burned to embers before they stirred. Their bodies, locked together, felt too deeply enmeshed to part. Both roused, but neither shifted, both too content with their closeness, their intimacy.

Time stretched, and still they clung, their heartbeats slowing, their bodies cooling, their souls still locked in flight.

Eventually, Vane bent his head and brushed his lips across Patience's temple. She glanced up. He studied her eyes, then kissed her gently, lingeringly. As their lips parted, he asked, "Have you changed your mind yet?"

He sensed her confusion, then she understood. She didn't pull away, but shook her head. "No."

Vane didn't argue. He held her, and felt her warmth surround him, felt her heart beating in time with his. Uncounted minutes later, he lifted her from him and carried her to her bed.

Chapter 16

Why wouldn't she marry him?

What did she have against marriage?

Those questions revolved in Vane's brain as he headed his horses down the London road. It was the second morning after Gerrard's accident. Pronounced fit to travel, Gerrard sat on the box seat beside him, idly studying the scenery.

Vane didn't even see his leader's ears. He was too engrossed with thoughts of Patience, and the situation he now found himself in. The lady herself, with Minnie and Timms, was traveling in the carriage following his curricle; behind that, a pageant of hired coaches bore the rest of the Bellamy Hall household away from Bellamy Hall.

Sudden pressure on his left ankle made Vane glance down; he watched as Myst recurled herself against his left boot. Instead of joining Patience in the closed carriage, Myst had surprised her mistress and elected to ride with him. While he had nothing against cats, or youthful sprigs, Vane would readily have traded both his companions for Patience.

So he could interrogate her over her inexplicable stance.

She loved him, but refused to marry him. Given her circumstances, and his, that decision more than qualified as inexplicable. His jaw setting, Vane looked ahead, staring fixedly between his leader's ears.

His original plan—to break down Patience's barriers with passion, to so addict her to his loving that she would come to view marrying him as very much in her best interests, and so admit to him what was worrying her—had developed a major hitch. He hadn't reckoned with becoming addicted himself, possessed by a desire more powerful than any he'd known. Addicted to the extent that that desire—and his demons—were no longer subject to his will.

His demons—and that mindless need—had broken free that first time in the barn. He'd excused that as understandable, given the circumstances and his pent-up frustrations. On the night he'd invaded her bedchamber, he'd had all the reins firmly in his grasp; he'd coolly and successfully retained control, even under the full force of her fire. That success had left him complacent, confidently assured.

Their third interlude, two nights ago, had shattered his complacency.

He'd come within a whisker of losing control again.

Worse—she knew it. A golden-eyed siren, she'd deliberately tempted him—and very nearly lured him to the rocks.

That a woman could reduce his vaunted self-control to the merest vestige of its usual despotic strength was not a fact he liked to contemplate. He'd slept alone last night—not well. He'd spent half the night thinking, warily wondering. The truth was he was more deeply entangled than he'd thought. The truth was, he yearned to let go—to lose himself utterly—in loving her. Just formulating that thought was enough to unnerve him—he'd always equated losing control, especially in that arena, as a form of surrender.

To knowingly surrender—knowingly let go as she'd asked—was . . . too unnerving to imagine.

Their interaction had developed dangerous undercurrents—currents he'd failed to forsee when he'd set sail on this particular tack. What would happen if she held firm to her inexplicable refusal? Would he ever be able to give her up? Let her go? Marry some other woman?

Vane shifted on the hard seat and resettled the reins in his hands. He didn't even want to consider those questions. Indeed, he refused point-blank to consider them. If she could take a stance, so could he.

She was going to marry him—she was going to be his wife. He just had to convince her there was no sane alternative.

The first step was to discover the basis for her inexplicable stance, the reason she would not agree to marriage. As the curricle rolled on, the pace slow so the carriages could keep up, he wrestled with schemes to uncover Patience's problem, which had now become his.

They stopped briefly for lunch at Harpenden. Both Patience and Timms spent their time cosseting Minnie, still under the weather. Other than a low-voiced query as to Gerrard's strength, Patience had no time to spend with him. Laying her sisterly qualms to rest, he let her return to Minnie's side, squelching all thought of taking her up in his curricle. Minnie's need was greater than his.

Their cavalcade got under way again. Gerrard settled back, surveying all with a keen and curious eye. "I've never been this far south."

"Oh?" Vane kept his gaze on his horses. "Where, exactly, is your home?"

Gerrard told him, describing the valley outside Chesterfield using words like brushstrokes; Vane had no difficulty seeing it in his mind's eye. "We've always lived there," Gerrard concluded. "For the most part, Patience runs things, but she's been teaching me the ropes for the last year."

"It must have been hard when your father died so unexpectedly—difficult for your mother and Patience to take up the reins."

Gerrard shrugged. "Not really. They'd been managing the estate for years even then—first Mama, then Patience."

"But . . ." Vane frowned. He glanced at Gerrard. "Surely your father managed the estate?"

Gerrard shook his head. "He was never interested. Well, he was never there. He died when I was six, and I couldn't remember him even then. I can't recall him ever staying for more than a few nights. Mama said he preferred London and his London friends—he didn't come home very often. It used to make her sad."

His gaze grew distant as memory took hold. "She was

always trying to describe him to us, how handsome and gentlemanly he was, how he rode so well to hounds, how he carried the cloak of a gentleman so elegantly. Whenever he appeared, even if for only one day, she was always eager for us to see how impressive he was.'' He grimaced. ''But I can't recall what he looked like at all.''

A chill struck Vane's soul. For Gerrard, with his vivid visual memory, to have no recollection of his father spoke volumes. Yet for well-heeled gentlemen to behave toward their families as Reginald Debbington had was not unheard of and no crime. Vane knew it. But he'd never before been close to the children of such men, never before had cause to feel sorrow and anger on their behalf—sorrow and anger they themselves, the deprived, did not know they should feel—for what their father had not given them. All the things his own family, the Cynsters, held dear—all they stood for—family, home, and hearth. *To have and to hold* was the Cynster motto. The first necessitated the second— that was something all male Cynsters understood from their earliest years. You desired, you seized—then you accepted responsibility. Actively. When it came to family, Cynsters were nothing if not active.

As the curricle bowled along, Vane struggled to grasp the reality Gerrard had described—he could see Gerrard's home, but couldn't conceive of its atmosphere, how it had functioned. The entire concept—a family without its natural leader, its most stalwart defender—was alien to him.

He could, however, imagine how Patience—his determined, independent, practical wife-to-be—would have viewed her father's behavior. Vane frowned. ''Your father—was Patience very attached to him?''

Gerrard's puzzled look was answer enough. ''Attached to him?'' His brows rose. ''I don't think so. When he died, I remember her saying something about duty, and what was expected.'' After a moment, he added, ''It's difficult to become attached to someone who's not there.''

Someone who didn't value your attachment. Vane heard the words in his head—and wondered.

The shadows were lengthening when their cavalcade pulled up in Aldford Street, just west of South Audley

Street. Vane threw the reins to Duggan and jumped down. Minnie's traveling carriage rocked to a stop behind his curricle, directly before the steps of Number 22. A discreet, gentleman's residence, Number 22 had been hired at short notice by a certain Mr. Montague, man of business to many of the Cynsters.

Opening the door of Minnie's carriage, Vane handed Patience to the pavement. Timms followed, then Minnie. Vane knew better than to attempt to carry her. Instead, with Patience lending support on her other side, he helped Minnie climb the steep steps. The rest of Minnie's household began debouching from their carriages, attracting the attention of late strollers. An army of footmen swarmed out of the house to assist with the luggage.

At the top of the steps, the front door stood open. Patience, carefully guiding Minnie, looked up as they gained the narrow porch—and discovered a strange personage standing in the front hall, holding the door wide. Stoop-shouldered, wiry, with an expression that would have done credit to a drenched cat, he was the oddest butler she'd ever encountered.

Vane, however, appeared to find nothing odd about the man; he nodded briefly as he helped Minnie over the threshold. "Sligo."

Sligo bowed. "Sir."

Minnie looked up and beamed. "Why, Sligo, what a pleasant surprise."

Following in Minnie's wake, Patience could have sworn Sligo blushed. Looking uncomfortable, he bowed again. "Ma'am."

In the melee that followed, as Minnie and Timms, then all the others, were received and shown to their rooms, Patience had ample time to observe Sligo, and the absolute rule he wielded over the junior servants. Both Masters and Mrs. Henderson, who had traveled up with their mistress, clearly recognized Sligo and treated him as a respected equal.

To Patience's relief, Vane distracted Henry, Edmond, and Gerrard, keeping them out from under everyone's feet while the other members of the household were settled.

When those three at last took themselves off to explore their new accommodation in the hour left before dinner, Patience heaved a weary sigh and sank onto a *chaise* in the drawing room.

And looked up at Vane, standing in his usual pose, one shoulder propped against the mantelpiece. "Who," Patience asked, "is Sligo?"

Vane's lips curved slightly. "Devil's ex-batman."

Patience frowned. "Devil—the Duke of St. Ives?"

"One and the same. Sligo acts as Devil's caretaker when he's out of town. As it happens, Devil and his duchess, Honoria, returned to the fray yesterday, so I borrowed Sligo."

"Why?"

"Because we need someone trustworthy who knows a trick or two, here in the house. Sligo's presently coordinating the searches of all the arriving luggage. He's absolutely trustworthy and utterly reliable. If you want anything done—anything at all—ask him and he'll arrange it."

"But . . ." Patience's frown deepened. "You'll be here. Won't you?"

Vane met her gaze directly. "No." Dismay—or was it simply disappointment?—flitted through her golden eyes. Vane frowned. "I'm not deserting, but an instant's thought ought to show that Mr. Vane Cynster, known to have recently purchased a comfortable house just a stone's throw away in Curzon Street, cannot possibly have any acceptable need to reside under his godmother's roof."

Patience grimaced. "I hadn't thought of that. I suppose, now we're in London, we'll have to bow to society's dictates."

To whit, he couldn't spend the night in her bed. "Precisely." Vane suppressed his reaction. There were other options, but she didn't need to know about them yet. Once he'd manuevered their interaction onto a more manageable footing, he'd let her into the secret. Until then . . .

Straightening, he pushed away from the mantelpiece. "I'd better be on my way. I'll call tomorrow, to see how you've settled in."

Patience held his gaze, then coolly held out her hand. He

grasped it, then bent and brushed his lips over her knuckles. And felt the tiny jolt that went through her.

Satisfied for the moment, he left her.

"It's all *soooo* exciting!"

Hearing Angela's paean for the tenth time that morning, Patience ignored it. Ensconced in a corner of one of the two drawing-room *chaises*, she continued stitching yet another tray-cloth. The activity had palled, but she had to do something with her mind—her hands—while she waited for Vane to appear.

Presuming he would. It was already after eleven.

Beside her, Timms sat darning; Minnie, having survived the rigors of the journey surprisingly well, was sunk in the comfort of a large armchair before the hearth. The other *chaise* played host to Mrs. Chadwick and Edith Swithins. Angela—she of the senseless pronouncements—was standing beside the window, peeking through the lace curtains at the passersby.

"I can't wait to see it all—the theaters, the modistes, the milliners." Hands clasped to her breast, Angela whirled and twirled. "It'll be so *wondrously* exciting!" Ceasing her twirling, she looked at her mother. "Are you sure we can't go before luncheon?"

Mrs. Chadwick sighed. "As agreed, we'll go for a short excursion this afternoon to decide which modistes might be suitable."

"It will have to be one in Bruton Street," Angela declared. "But the best shops, Edmond says, are on Bond Street."

"Bond Street is just beyond Bruton Street." Patience had spent the journey down reading a guidebook. "Once we stroll the length of one, we'll have reached the other."

"Oh. Good." Her afternoon's prospects assured, Angela subsided back into her daydreams.

Patience resisted an urge to glance at the mantelpiece clock. She could hear its steady tick, counting away the minutes; it seemed like she'd been listening for hours.

She already knew town life would never suit her. Used to country hours, the routine of breakfasting at ten, of taking luncheon at two and dining at eight or later, would never find favor with her. Bad enough that she'd woken at her usual hour, and, finding the breakfast parlor empty, had had to make do with tea and toast in the back parlor. Bad enough that there was no piano with which she could distract herself. Much worse was the fact that it was, apparently, unacceptable for her to walk out unescorted. Worst of all was the fact that Number 22 Aldford Street was a great deal smaller than Bellamy Hall, which meant they were all thrown together, under each other's feet—each other's noses—all the time.

To have to bear with the others at such close quarters looked set to drive her demented.

And Vane had not yet arrived.

When he did, she would inform him in no uncertain terms what she thought of his idea of removing to London. They had better flush out the thief and the Spectre. Soon.

The clock ticked on. Patience gritted her teeth and persevered with her needle.

A knock on the street door had her looking up. Along with everyone else but Edith Swithins—she happily tatted on. The next instant, a deep rumbling voice reached all their straining ears. Patience inwardly sighed—with a relief she had no intention of examining too closely. Minnie's face lit up as familiar prowling footsteps neared. Timms grinned.

The door opened. Vane strolled in, to be greeted with a panoply of smiles. His gaze flicked to Patience. She met it coolly. She studied him as he nodded to them all, then greeted Minnie elegantly and affectionately, inquiring after her health and how she'd spent the night.

"I very likely got more sleep than you," Minnie replied, a roguish twinkle in her eye.

Vane smiled lazily down at her and made no move to deny it. "Are you ready to brave the park?"

Minnie grimaced. "Perhaps tomorrow I might let you persuade me to a stroll. For today, I'm content to sit quietly, gathering my failing strength."

Her color, better than it had been for days, showed she was in no danger of fading away. Reassured, Vane glanced at Patience, watching with a reserved coolness he didn't appreciate. "Perhaps," he said, looking back at Minnie, "if you're settled today, I might take Miss Debbington up in your stead."

"By all means." Minnie beamed at Patience and made shooing motions. "So trying for Patience to be cooped up inside."

Vane slanted a rakish glance at Patience. "Well, Miss Debbington? Are you game for a turn about the park?"

Her gaze locked with his, Patience hesitated.

Angela opened her mouth and stepped forward; Mrs. Chadwick motioned her back, mouthing a definite "No!" Angela subsided, sulking.

Unable to read anything in Vane's eyes to explain the challenge in his words, Patience raised a brow. "Indeed, sir. I would be glad of the chance of some fresh air."

Vane inwardly frowned at her temperate acceptance. He waited while she set aside her work and stood, then, with a nod to Minnie and the rest, offered Patience his arm from the room.

He halted in the hall.

Patience lifted her hand from his sleeve and turned to the stairs. "I won't keep you above a minute."

Vane reached out, grasped her elbow, and drew her back to him. All the way back until he looked down into her now wide eyes. After a moment, he softly asked, "The others. Where are they?"

Patience struggled to think. "Whitticombe has taken over the library—it's well stocked but unfortunately quite small. Edgar and the General had nowhere else to go, so they've braved the chill, but I don't know how long they'll remain there. Edgar said something about looking in at Tattersalls."

"Hmm." Vane frowned. "I'll make sure Sligo knows." He refocused on Patience. "The others?"

"Henry, Edmond, and Gerrard made straight for the billiard room." Vane's grip on her elbow slackened; twisting free, Patience straightened—and shot him a severe glance. "I won't tell you what I think of a house that has a billiard room but no music room."

Vane's lips twitched. "It is a *gentleman's* residence."

Patience humphed. "Regardless, I don't believe the allure of billiards will keep that trio satisfied. They were planning all manner of excursions." She gestured widely. "To Exeter Exchange, the Haymarket, Pall Mall. I even heard them mention some place called the Peerless Pool."

Vane blinked. "That's closed."

"Is it?" Patience raised her brows. "I'll tell them."

"Never mind. I'll tell them myself." Vane glanced at her again. "I'll have a chat with them while you fetch your pelisse and bonnet."

With a haughty nod, Patience acquiesced. Vane watched as she ascended the stairs, then, frowning more definitely, strode for the billiard room—to lay down a few ground rules.

He returned to the front hall as Patience regained the tiles. Minutes later, he handed her into his curricle and climbed up beside her. The park was close; as he headed his horses toward the trees, Vane checked over the list of Minnie's household. And frowned. "Alice Colby." He glanced at Patience. "Where's she?"

"She didn't come down to breakfast." Patience's brows rose. "I suppose she must be in her room. I haven't seen her about at all, now you mention it."

"She's probably praying. She seems to spend a good part of her time thus employed."

Patience shrugged and looked ahead. Vane glanced at her, letting his gaze slide appreciatively over her. Head high, face to the breeze, she scanned the avenue ahead. Beneath the poke of her bonnet, wispy tendrils of burnished brown fluttered against her cheeks. Her pelisse was the same powder blue as the simple morning gown she wore beneath it. His brain registered the fact that neither was new, much less in the latest style, but, to his eyes, the picture she presented as she sat on the box seat of his curricle was perfect. Even if her chin was tilted a touch too high, and her expression was a touch too reserved.

Inwardly, he frowned, and looked to his horses. "We'll need to ensure that none of Minnie's menagerie has a chance to get loose on their own. I think we can assume there's no conspiracy or partnership, at least between unrelated individuals. But we must ensure none of them has a chance to pass on any stolen valuables, like the pearls, to an accomplice. Which means we—you, me, Gerrard, Minnie, and Timms, with Sligo's help—will have to accompany them whenever they leave the house."

"Angela and Mrs. Chadwick plan to visit Bruton and Bond Streets this afternoon." Patience wrinkled her nose. "I suppose I could go with them."

Vane suppressed his grin. "Do." Most ladies of his acquaintance would hie off to Bruton and Bond Streets at the drop of a hat. Patience's lukewarm enthusiasms augered well for a peaceful life in Kent. "I've agreed, suitably reluctantly, to act as guide for Henry, Edmond, and Gerrard this afternoon, and I tipped Sligo the wink to keep his eye on Edgar and the General."

Patience frowned. "There are rather many to watch if they should decide to go out on their own."

"We'll have to curb their taste for town delights." Vane noted the carriages drawn up to the verge ahead. "Speaking of which . . . behold, the *grandes dames* of the *ton*."

Even without the warning, Patience would have recognized them. They sat delicately draped over velvet or leather seats, elegant turbans nodding, sharp eyes bright, gloved hands artfully waving as they dissected and discussed every snippet of potential gossip. From youthful but elegant matrons to eagle-eyed dowagers, they were assured, secure in their social positions. Their carriages lined the fashionable route as they exchanged information and invitations.

Many heads turned their way as they bowled steadily along. Turbans were graciously inclined; Vane returned the nods easily but did not stop. Patience noted that many of the eyes beneath the turbans came to rest on her. The expressions she detected were either arrested, haughtily disapproving, or both. Chin rising, she ignored them. She knew her pelisse and bonnet were unfashionable. Dowdy. Possibly even frumpish.

But she would only be in London for a few weeks—to catch a thief—so her wardrobe hardly mattered.

At least, not to her.

She glanced sidelong at Vane, but could detect no glimmer of consciousness in his expression. She couldn't read anything in it at all. He gave no sign of registering, let along responding, to the more artful of the looks directed his way. Patience cleared her throat. "There seem to be a lot of ladies present—I didn't think so many would have returned to town."

Vane shrugged. "Not everyone does, but Parliament's back in session, so the political hostesses are in residence, exerting their influence with the usual balls and dinners. That's what draws many of the *ton* back. The few weeks of social whirl nicely fill the time between the summer and the start of the shooting season."

"I see." Scanning the carriages ahead, Patience noted one lady who, rather than reclining languidly and watching them go by, had sat bolt upright. A second later, she waved—imperiously.

Patience glanced at Vane; from the direction of his gaze and his set lips, he'd already seen the lady. His hesitation was palpable, then, gathering tension as if girding his loins, he slowed his horses. The curricle rocked to a stop beside the elegant brougham.

Occupied by the lady, of similar age to Patience, with bright chestnut hair and a pair of exceedingly shrewd, blue-grey eyes. Said eyes instantly locked on Patience's face. Their owner smiled delightedly.

Grimly, Vane nodded. "Honoria."

The lady switched her bright smile to him. It deepened fractionally. "Vane. And who is this?"

"Allow me to present Miss Patience Debbington. Minnie's niece."

"Indeed?" Without waiting for more, the lady held out her hand to Patience. "Honoria, my dear Miss Debbington."

"Duchess of St. Ives," Vane grimly announced.

Honoria ignored him. "It's a pleasure to meet you, my dear. Is Minnie well?"

"She's much better than she was." Patience forgot about her shabby clothes and responded easily to the duchess's openness. "She took a chill a few weeks back, but she survived the journey down surprisingly well.''

Honoria nodded. "How long does she plan to stay in town?''

Until they caught their thief—unmasked their Spectre. Patience held the duchess's clear gaze. "Ah . . .''

"We're not certain,'' Vane drawled. "It's just one of Minnie's usual bolts to town, but this time she's brought her entire menagerie with her.'' He raised his brows in patent boredom. "Presumably for distraction.''

Honoria's gaze remained steady on his face long enough to make Patience wonder how much of Vane's glib explanation she believed. Then Honoria switched her gaze to her—and smiled warmly, welcomingly—far more personally than Patience had expected. "I'm sure we'll meet again shortly, Miss Debbington.'' Honoria pressed Patience's fingers. "I'll let you get on—you doubtless have a busy morning ahead of you. Indeed''—she shifted her gaze to Vane—"I've some calls to make, too.''

Vane, tight-lipped, nodded curtly—and gave his horses the office.

As they bowled down the avenue, Patience glanced at his set face. "The duchess seems very nice.''

"She is. Very nice.'' Also very nosy, and definitely too perceptive. Vane inwardly gritted his teeth. He'd known the family would find out sometime, but he hadn't expected it to be quite so soon. "Honoria's effectively the matriarch of the family.'' He struggled to find words to explain precisely what that meant—but gave up. Acknowledging the power Honoria—or any of the Cynster women—wielded within the family was something he, and all his male relatives, always found exceedingly difficult.

Vane narrowed his eyes and headed his team toward the park gates. "I'll call for you tomorrow, at much the same time. A drive or a walk seems the best way for us to exchange information on what the others have done, and where they're intending to go.''

Patience stiffened. He'd taken her for this drive so they could coordinate their plans—he viewed the outing as a campaign meeting. "Indeed,'' she replied, somewhat tartly. An instant later, she said, "Perhaps we should get Sligo to accompany us?'' When Vane, frowning, glanced her way, she added, "So we can get his views firsthand.''

Vane frowned harder—his horses distracted him.

As they negotiated the park gates and turned into the crowded thoroughfare, Patience sat, stiffly erect; inside, her emotions churned. As the horses' hooves struck the cobbles of Aldford Street, she lifted her chin. "I realize that you feel committed to identifying the thief and the Spectre, but, now you've returned to London, I daresay you have other engagements—other distractions—on which you'd much rather spend your time.'' She drew a tight breath; a cold vise had fastened about her chest. She felt Vane's quick glance. Head high, eyes forward, she continued, "I'm sure, now Sligo has joined us, we could find some way to get the relevant information to you without having to waste your time on unnecessary walks or drives.''

She would not cling. Now they were in town, and he could see that she didn't fit within his elegant world, couldn't hold a candle to the exquisitely arrayed beauties he was accustomed to consorting with, she would not try to hold on to him. Like her mother had clung to her father. Theirs was a temporary relationship; in her mind, she could already see its end. By taking the first step and acknowledging the inevitable, she might, just possibly, prepare her heart for the blow.

"I have no intention of not seeing you at least once a day.''

The words were bitten off, infused with a steely rage Patience could not possibly mistake. Taken aback, she glanced at Vane. The carriage rocked to a halt, he tied off the reins and jumped down.

Then swung around. He grasped her waist and lifted her bodily from the seat—and placed her, with quiveringly rigid control, on the pavement before him.

Steel shards, his eyes held hers. Breathless, Patience blinked up at him. His face was hard, a warrior's mask. Waves of anger and aggression lapped about her.

"When it comes to distraction,'' he informed her through clenched teeth, "nothing in this world could top you.''

His words were invested with meaning—a meaning she

didn't understand. Mentally at sea, Patience struggled to catch her breath. Before she succeeded, Vane had marched her up the steps and deposited her in the front hall.

Narrow-eyed, he looked down at her. "Don't expect to see the last of me anytime soon."

With that, he swung on his heel and stalked out.

Chapter 17

Two days later, Vane stalked up the steps of Number 22 Aldford Street, on his way to see Patience. If she wasn't ready to drive out with him this morning, there'd be trouble.

He was not in a good mood.

He hadn't been for the past two days.

After last leaving Patience in Aldford Street, his temper gnashing at the bit, he'd gone off to seek refuge at White's to calm down and think. He'd assumed, given their closeness, how much of himself he'd already revealed to her, that she wouldn't—couldn't possibly—confuse him with her father. He'd obviously assumed wrong. Her attitude, her comments, made it plain she was judging him against Reginald Debbington's standard—and was failing to perceive any significant difference.

His initial reaction had been a violent hurt he had not, even now, entirely suppressed. After her earlier efforts that had sent him fleeing from Bellamy Hall, he'd thought he'd surmounted "hurt." He'd been wrong on that score, too.

Sunk in a quiet corner of White's, he'd spent fruitless hours composing terse, pithy speeches designed to elucidate precisely how and in what manner he differed from her sire—a man to whom family had meant little. His periods had grown increasingly forceful; in the end, he'd jettisoned phrases in favor of action. That, as all Cynsters well knew, spoke far louder than words.

Judging that, by that time, the damage within the family

had already been done, he'd swallowed his pride and gone to call on Honoria—to ask, innocently, if she might consider giving one of her impromptu balls. Just for family and friends. Such a ball would be a useful tool in his avowed endeavor—to convince Patience that, to him as for all the Cynsters, the word "family" meant a great deal.

Honoria's wide eyes, and thoughtful consideration, had set his teeth on edge. But her agreement that an impromptu ball might, perhaps, be a good idea had gone some way to easing his temper. Leaving Devil's duchess to her plans, he'd retired to formulate his own. And to brood, darkly.

By the time yesterday morning had dawned, and he'd again set his horses' heads for Aldford Street, he'd come to the conclusion that there had to be more—more than just a simple misconception holding Patience back from marriage. He was absolutely certain what style of woman he'd chosen; he knew, soul-deep, that his reading of her was not wrong. Only a powerful reason would force a woman such as she, with so much affection and devotion to give, to view marriage as an unacceptable risk.

There was something more—something he had not yet learned about her parents' marriage.

He'd climbed the steps of Number 22 determined to learn what that something was—only to be informed Miss Debbington was not available to go driving with him. She had, it seemed, been seduced by the Bruton Street modistes. His temper had taken a downhill turn.

Luckily for Patience, Minnie had been watching for him. Unexpectedly spry, she'd claimed his escort for her promised stroll along the graveled walks of Green Park. On the way, she'd gaily informed him that, by some stroke of benign fate, Honoria had happened on Patience in Bruton Street the afternoon before, and had insisted on introducing her to her favored modiste, Celestine, the result being the fitting Patience was then attending for a series of gowns including, Minnie had taken great delight in assuring him, a positively *dashing* golden evening gown.

Arguing with benign fate was impossible. Even if, by virtue of Edith Swithins who had joined them for the stroll, said fate had ensured he had no chance to question Minnie about Patience's father, and the depths of his ignominy.

An hour later, reassured that Minnie's constitution was fully restored, he'd returned her to Number 22, only to discover Patience still absent. Leaving a tersely worded message with Minnie, he'd departed to find distraction elsewhere.

Today, he wanted Patience. If he had his way, he'd have Patience, but that was unlikely. Privacy of that sort, in the present circumstances, was unlikely to be on offer—and he had a wary premonition he'd be unwise to embark on any further seductive manuevers until he had their relationship on a steady, even keel.

With *his* hand firmly on the tiller.

Sligo opened the door to his peremptory knock. With a curt nod, Vane strode in. And stopped dead.

Patience was in the hall, waiting—the sight literally stole his breath. As his gaze, helplessly, slid over her, over the soft green merino pelisse, severely cut and snugly fitted, its upstanding collar framing her face, over the tan gloves and half boots, over the pale green skirts peeking beneath the pelisse's hem, Vane felt something inside him tighten, click, and lock.

Breathing was suddenly more difficult than if someone had buried a fist in his gut.

Her hair, glinting in the light streaming in through the door, was coiffed differently, to more artfully draw attention to her wide golden eyes, to the creaminess of her forehead and cheeks, and the delicate yet determined line of her jaw. And the soft vulnerability of her lips.

In some far corner of his thoroughly distracted brain, Vane uttered a thank-you to Honoria, then followed it with a curse. Before had been bad enough. How the hell was he supposed to cope with this?

Chest swelling, he forced his mind to draw back. He focused on Patience's face—and read her expression. It was calm, untinged by any emotion. She was dutifully waiting—as required by their plans—there was nothing more, so her expression declared, behind her drive with him.

It was her ''dutiful'' stance that did it—pricked his temper anew. Fighting to keep a scowl from his face, he nodded curtly and held out his arm. "Ready?"

Something flickered in her large eyes, but the hall was too dim for him to identify the emotion. Lightly, she inclined her head and glided forward to take his arm.

Patience sat, stiffly erect, on the box seat of Vane's curricle, and struggled to breathe through the iron cage locked about her chest. At least he couldn't disapprove of her appearance; she'd been assured, both by Celestine and Honoria, that her new pelisse and bonnet were all the crack. And her new gown, beneath it, was a definite improvement over her old one. Yet from his reaction, it seemed her appearance was of little consequence. She hadn't, she reminded herself sternly, really expected it would be. She'd bought the gowns because she hadn't refurbished her wardrobe for years and now seemed the perfect opportunity. After they caught the thief—and the Spectre—and Gerrard had acquired sufficient town bronze, she and he would retire once more to Derbyshire. She would probably never come to London again.

She'd bought a new wardrobe because it was the sensible thing to do, and because it wasn't reasonable to force Vane Cynster, elegant gentleman, to appear in public with a dowd.

Not that he seemed to care either way. Patience suppressed a sniff and tilted her chin. "As I told you, Mrs. Chadwick and Angela visited Bruton Street on our first afternoon. Angela dragged us into every modiste's establishment, even those designing for the dowagers. And asked the price of everything in sight. It was really most embarrassing. Luckily, the answers she received eventually took their toll. She seems to have accepted that it might be more practical to have a seamstress in to make up some gowns for her."

Eyes on his horses, Vane humphed. "Where were Angela and Mrs. Chadwick while you were in Celestine's?"

Patience colored. "Honoria came upon us in Bruton Street. She insisted on introducing me to Celestine—and things"—she gestured—"went on from there."

"*Things* have a habit of going that way once Honoria's involved."

"She was very kind," Patience retorted. "She even engaged Mrs. Chadwick and Angela in conversation all the while I was with Celestine."

Vane wondered how much Honoria was going to make him pay for that. And in what coin.

"Luckily, being able to haunt Celestine's salon and talk to a duchess quite buoyed Angela's spirits. We went on to Bond Street without further dramas. Neither Mrs. Chadwick nor Angela showed any hint of wanting to speak to any of the jewelers whose establishments we passed, nor in meeting anyone else along the way."

Vane grimaced. "I really don't think it's either of them. Mrs. Chadwick's bone-honest, and Angela's too witless."

"Indeed." Patience's tone turned ascerbic. "So witless nothing would do but she must cap the afternoon with a visit to Gunter's. Nothing would dissuade her. It was full to bursting with young sprigs, too many of whom spent the time ogling her. She wanted to go again yesterday afternoon—Mrs. Chadwick and I took her to Hatchards instead."

Vane's lips twitched. "She must have enjoyed that."

"She moaned the whole time." Patience shot him a glance. "That's all I have to report. What have the gentlemen been up to?"

"Sight-seeing." Vane uttered the word with loathing. "Henry and Edmond have been possessed by some demon which compels them to set eyes on every monument within the metropolis. Luckily, Gerrard is happy enough to go along and keep a watchful eye on them. So far, he's had nothing to report. The General and Edgar have settled on Tattersalls as the focus of their daily interest. Sligo or one of his minions follows and keeps watch, so far to no avail. I've been arranging their afternoons and evenings. The only ones who've not yet stirred from the house are the Colbys." Vane glanced at Patience. "Has Alice emerged from her room?"

"Not for long." Patience frowned. "She may actually have been the same at Bellamy Hall. I'd imagined her in the gardens, or in one of the parlors, but she might have stayed in her room the whole time. It's really rather unhealthy.''

Vane shrugged.

Patience glanced sideways, studying his face. He'd headed his horses down a less-frequented drive, away from the fashionable avenue. While there were carriages about, they didn't need to exchange greetings. "I haven't had a chance to speak to Sligo, but I presume he found nothing?''

Vane's expression turned grim. "Not a thing. There was no clue in the luggage. Sligo's surreptitiously searching all the rooms in case the stolen items were somehow smuggled in.''

"Smuggled? How?''

"Edith Swithins's tatting bag springs to mind.''

Patience stared. "You don't think *she* . . . ?''

"No. But it's possible someone else has noticed how deep that bag is, and is using it for the pearls, if nothing else. How often do you think Edith empties the bag out?''

Patience grimaced. "Probably never.''

Vane came to an intersection and turned smartly to the right. "Where is Edith now?''

"In the drawing room—tatting, of course.''

"Does her chair face the door?''

"Yes.'' Patience frowned. "Why?''

Vane shot her a glance. "Because she's deaf.''

Patience continued to frown, then understanding dawned. "Ah.''

"Precisely. So . . .''

"Hmm.'' Patience's expression turned considering. "I suppose . . .''

Half an hour later, the drawing-room door at Number 22 opened; Patience looked in. Edith Swithins sat on the *chaise* facing the door, tatting furiously. Her large knitted bag sat on the rug beside the *chaise*. There was no one else present.

Smiling brightly, Patience entered, and set the door to, ensuring the latch did not fall home. Just *how* deaf Edith was they didn't know. With determined cheerfulness, she swept down on Edith.

Who looked up—and returned her smile.

"I'm so glad I caught you," Patience began. "I've always wanted to learn how to tat. I wonder if you could show me the basics?"

Edith positively beamed. "Why of course, dear. It's really quite simple." She held up her work.

Patience squinted. "Actually"—she looked around—"perhaps we should move over by the window. The light's much better there."

Edith chuckled. "I must confess I really don't need to *see* the stitches, I've been doing it for so long." She eased off the *chaise*. "I'll just get my bag . . ."

"I'll get it." Patience reached for the bag—and inwardly conceded Vane was right. It was deep, full, and surprisingly heavy. It definitely needed to be searched. Hefting the bag, she whirled. "I'll pull that chair into place for you."

By the time Edith, cradling her work in progress, had crossed the room, Patience had a deep armchair positioned facing the window, its back to the door. Placing the tatting bag beside it, hidden from the occupant by the overhang of the arm, she helped Edith into the chair. "Now if I sit here, on the window seat, there'll be plenty of light for us both to see."

Obligingly, Edith settled back. "Now." She held up her work. "The first thing to note . . ."

Patience gazed at the fine threads. At the edge of her vision, the door slowly opened. Vane entered, and carefully shut the door. On silent feet, he drew closer. A board creaked under his weight. He froze. Patience tensed. Edith blithely chatted on.

Patience breathed again. Vane glided forward, then sank out of sight behind Edith's chair. From the corner of her eye, Patience saw Edith's tatting bag slide away.

She forced herself to listen to Edith's lecture, forced herself to follow enough to ask sensible questions. Beaming with pride, Edith imparted her knowledge; Patience encouraged and admired, and hoped the Almighty would forgive her her perjury, given it was committed in the pursuit of justice.

Hunkered down behind the chair, Vane poked about in the bag, then, realizing the futility of that, gingerly upended it on the rug. The contents, a welter of odds and ends, many unidentifiable, at least, to him, rolled out on the soft pile. He spread them, frowning, trying to recall the list of items pilfered over the past months. Whatever, Minnie's pearls were not in the tatting bag.

"And now," Edith said, "we just need a crochet hook . . ." She looked to where her tatting bag had been placed.

"I'll get it." Patience crouched, eyes down, hands reaching as if the bag was actually there. "A crochet hook," she repeated.

"A fine one," Edith added.

Crochet hook. A fine one. Behind the chair, Vane stared at the array of unnameable implements. What the hell was a crochet hook? What did it look like—fine or otherwise? Frantically examining and discarding various items in tortoiseshell, his fingers finally closed about a thin wand sprouting a fine steel prong, hooked at the end—a miniature fisherman's net hook.

"I know it's there somewhere." Edith's voice, slightly querulous, jolted Vane to action. Reaching around the chair back, he slid the implement into Patience's outstretched palm.

She clutched it. "Here it is!"

"Oh, good. Now, we just put it in here, like this . . ."

While Edith continued her lesson, and Patience dutifully learned, Vane stuffed the contents of the tatting bag back into the gaping maw. Giving the bag a shake to settle it, he eased it back into position beside the chair. Moving with intense care, he stood and crept to the door.

Hand on the knob, he glanced back; Patience did not look up. Only when he'd regained the front hall, with the drawing room door securely closed, did he breathe freely again.

* * *

Patience joined him in the billiard room half an hour later.

Blowing aside the fine errant curls tangling with her lashes, she met his gaze. "I now know more about tatting than I could possibly need to know, even should I live to be a hundred."

Vane grinned. And leaned over the table.

Patience grimaced. "I take it there was nothing there?"

"Nothing." Vane lined up his next shot. "No one's using Edith's tatting bag as a store, presumably because, once something goes in, it might never be found again."

Patience stifled a giggle. She watched as Vane shifted, lining up the ball. As at Bellamy Hall, when she'd watched from the conservatory, he'd taken off his coat. Under his tight waistcoat, muscles rippled, then tensed. He clipped the ball neatly, sending it rolling into the pocket opposite.

Vane straightened. He looked at Patience, and noted her fixed gaze. Lifting his cue from the table, he sauntered closer. And stopped directly in front of her.

She blinked, then drew in a quick breath and dragged her gaze up to his face.

Vane captured her gaze. After a moment, he murmured, "I foresee certain complications."

"Oh?" Patience's gaze had already drifted from his, fastening instead on his lips.

Leaning more heavily on the cue, Vane let his gaze roam her face. "Henry and Edmond." The curves of her lips caught and held his attention. "They're getting restless."

"Ah." The tip of Patience's tongue appeared between her lips, then delicately traced them.

Vane hauled in a desperate breath. And leaned closer. "I can hold their reins during the day, but the evenings . . ." He angled his head. "Could be a problem."

His words died away as Patience stretched upward.

Their lips touched, brushed, then locked. Both stopped breathing. Vane's hands closed tight about the billiard cue; Patience shivered. And sank into the kiss.

"He must be in the billard room."

Vane's head jerked up; he swore and shifted, screening Patience from the door. She scooted farther into the shadows beyond the table, where her blush would be less visible. Along with the heat in her eyes. The door swung open and Vane was potting a ball with nonchalant ease.

"There you are!" Henry ambled into the room.

Followed by Gerrard and Edmond.

"Seen enough sights for one day." Henry rubbed his hands together. "Perfect time for a quick game."

"Not for me, I fear." Coolly, Vane handed his cue to Gerrard, and resisted the urge to throttle them all. He reached for his coat. "I only dallied to tell you I'll come by at three. I'm expected elsewhere for lunch."

"Oh. All right." Henry cocked a brow at Edmond. "You game?"

Edmond, having exchanged a smile with Patience, shrugged. "Why not?"

Gerrard, with a nod for his sister, joined them. Her pulse thundering, still breathless, Patience preceded Vane as he left the room.

She heard the door shut behind them, but didn't stop. She didn't dare. She led the way into the front hall; only then did she turn and, with what calm she could muster, face Vane.

He looked down at her. His lips twisted wryly. "I meant what I said about Henry and Edmond. I've agreed to take Gerrard, Edgar, and the General to White's this evening. Henry and Edmond don't want to go, and we couldn't keep them in sight if they did. Any chance you could call them to heel?"

The look Patience cast him spoke volumes. "I'll see what I can do."

"If you can keep them on their leashes, I'll be forever grateful."

Patience studied the glint in his grey eyes and wondered how to best use such indebtedness. Just what she might have him do. Then she realized her gaze had refastened on his lips. She blinked and nodded curtly. "I'll try."

"Do." Capturing her gaze, Vane raised one finger and traced the line of her cheek. Then lightly tapped. "Later." With a nod, he strode for the door.

*	*	*

For Patience, Lady Hendricks's musicale that evening proved to be an eminently forgettable experience. As well as herself, Minnie and Timms, all three Chadwicks, and Edmond, attended.

Inducing Henry and Edmond to join the party had been simplicity itself; over luncheon, she'd blithely asked Gerrard to escort their otherwise all-female party that evening. Put on the spot, Gerrard had blushed and stumbled into an apology; from the corner of her eye, Patience had seen Henry and Edmond glance surreptitiously at each other. Before Gerrard got to the end of his explanation, Henry interrupted to offer his services. Edmond, recalling the connection between music and drama, declared he would come, too.

As they crossed the threshold of Lady Hendricks's music room, Patience congratulated herself on her masterful success.

They made their bows to their hostess, then passed on, into the already crowded room. In Minnie's wake, Patience walked on Edmond's arm. Henry's had been claimed by his mother. Minnie and Timms were well-known; those greeting them nodded and smiled at Patience, too. Garbed in a new gown, she returned the greetings serenely, inwardly amazed at the confidence imparted by a sheath of moss green silk.

Timms steered Minnie to a half-vacant *chaise*. They took possession of the free space, striking up a conversation with the lady already ensconced in the other corner. Leaving the rest of the party milling aimlessly.

With an inward sigh, Patience took charge. "There's a chair over there, Henry. Perhaps you might fetch it for your mama."

"Oh. Right." Henry strode to where a chair remained unclaimed by the wall. At the exhortation of their hostess, all the guests were settling; seating was suddenly in short supply.

They sat Mrs. Chadwick beside Minnie's *chaise*.

"What about me?" Angela, gowned in a white dress overendowed with pink rosettes and cerise ribbon, stood twisting her fingers in said ribbon.

"There're some chairs over there." Edmond indicated a few empty seats in the ranks of straight-backed chairs lined up before the pianoforte and harp.

Patience nodded. "We'll sit there."

They headed for the chairs. They'd almost gained their objective when Angela balked. "I think the other side might be better."

Patience was not deceived. The few youthful sprigs forced by their mamas to attend had clumped in a petulant group on the other side of the room. "Your mama would expect you to sit with your brother." Deftly twining arms, she anchored Angela to her side. "Young ladies who venture about on their own rapidly gain a reputation for being fast."

Angela pouted. And cast longing looks across the room. "It's only a few yards away."

"A few yards too many." Reaching the vacant chairs, Patience sat, dragging Angela down beside her. Edmond slid into the chair on Patience's left; rather than sit beside his sister, Henry opted to sit behind Patience. As the performers appeared to polite applause, Henry shuffled his chair forward, hissing *sotto voce* to Angela to move aside.

Disapproving glances were cast their way. Patience turned her head and glared. Henry desisted.

With an inward sigh of relief, Patience settled in her chair and prepared to give her attention to the music.

Henry leaned forward and hissed in her ear: "Quite a smart gathering, isn't it? Daresay this is how *ton*nish ladies spend most of their evenings."

Before Patience could react, the pianist laid her fingers on the keys and commenced a prelude, one of Patience's favorites. Inwardly sighing, she prepared to sink into the comfort of the familiar strains.

"Bach." Edmond leaned closer, head nodding with the beat. "A neat little piece. Designed to convey the joys of spring. Odd choice for this time of year."

Patience closed her eyes and clamped her lips shut. And heard Henry shift behind her shoulder.

"The harp sounds like spring rains, don't you think?"

Patience gritted her teeth.

Edmond's voice reached her. "My dear Miss Debbington, are you feeling quite the thing? You look rather pale."

Her hands tightly clasped in her lap against the urge to box a few ears, Patience opened her eyes. "I fear," she murmured, "that I might be developing a headache."

"Oh."

"Ah."

Blessed silence reigned—for all of half a minute.

"Perhaps if . . ."

Hands clenched tight, Patience closed her eyes, closed her lips, and wished she could close her ears. The next second, she felt a definite pang behind her temples.

Denied the music, denied all natural justice, she fell back on imagining the reward she would claim in recompense for the destruction of her evening. When next she saw Vane. Later. Whenever that proved to be.

At least Edith Swithins and the Colbys had had the good sense to stay home.

At precisely that moment, in the hallowed half gloom of the cardroom of White's, Vane, his gaze on the General and Edgar, both seated at a table playing whist, took a slow sip of the club's excellent claret and reflected that Patience's evening would not be—could not be—more boring than his.

Hanging back in the shadows, cloaked in the quiet, restrained ambience, redolent with the masculine scents of fine leather, cigar smoke, and sandalwood, he'd been forced to decline numerous invitations, forced to explain, with a languidly raised brow, that he was bear-leading his godmother's nephew. That, in itself, had raised no eyebrows. The fact that he apparently believed bear-leading precluded sitting down to a game of cards had.

He could hardly explain his real aim.

Stifling a yawn, he scanned the room, easily picking out Gerrard, watching the play at the hazard table. The interest Gerrard showed was academic—he seemed to harbor no deep wish to join in the play.

Making a mental note to inform Patience that her brother showed little susceptibility to the lure that brought too many men low, Vane straightened, eased his shoulders, then returned to propping the wall.

Five totally uneventful minutes later, Gerrard joined him.

"Any action yet?" Gerrard nodded to the table at which Edgar and the General sat.

"Not unless you count the General getting clubs confused with spades."

Gerrard grinned, and glanced over the room. "This doesn't seem a likely place for someone to pass on stolen goods."

"It is, however, a very good venue in which to unexpectedly bump into an old friend. Neither of our two pigeons, however, is showing any signs of wanting to curtail their scintillating activity."

Gerrard's grin broadened. "At least it makes watching them easy enough." He glanced at Vane. "I can manage here if you'd like to join your friends. I'll fetch you if they move."

Vane shook his head. "I'm not in the mood." He gestured to the tables. "Seeing we're here, you may as well widen your horizons. Just don't accept any challenges."

Gerrard laughed. "Not my style." He moved off again to stroll between the tables, many surrounded by gentlemen vicariously enjoying the play.

Vane sank back into the shadows. He hadn't been tempted, even vaguely, to take Gerrard up on his offer. At present, he was in no good mood to join in the usual camaraderie over a pack of cards. At present, his mind was entirely consumed by one unanswered question, by one conundrum, by one glaring anomaly.

By Patience.

He desperately needed to talk to Minnie, alone. Patience's home life, her father, held the key—the key to his future.

This evening had been wasted: no headway had been made. On any level.

Tomorrow would be different. He'd see to it.

The next morning dawned bright and clear. Vane strode up the steps of Number 22 as early as he dared. In the far distance, a bell tolled—eleven deep bongs. Face set, Vane grasped the knocker. Today, he was determined to see progress.

Two minutes later, he strode back down the steps. Leaping into his curricle, he flicked the reins free, barely waiting for Duggan to scramble up behind before setting the greys clattering toward the park.

Minnie had hired a brougham.

He knew the instant he spotted them that something momentous had occurred. They were—there was no other word for it—aflutter. They were all there, packed into the brougham—Patience, Minnie, Timms, Agatha Chadwick, Angela, Edith Swithins and, amazing though it seemed, Alice Colby. She was dressed in something so dark and drab it might have been widow's weeds; the others looked much more inviting. Patience, gowned in a stylish walking dress of fresh green, looked good enough to eat.

Drawing his curricle up behind the brougham, Vane reined in his appetites along with his horses, and languidly descended to the verge.

"You've just missed Honoria," Minnie informed him before he'd even reached the carriage. "She's holding one of her impromptu balls and has invited us all."

"Indeed?" Vane summoned his most innocent look.

"A real ball!" Angela jigged up and down on the seat. "It'll be simply *wonderful*! I'll have to get a new ball gown."

Agatha Chadwick nodded in greeting. "It was very kind of your cousin to invite us all."

"I haven't been to a ball since I don't know when." Edith Swithins beamed at Vane. "It'll almost be an *adventure*."

Vane couldn't help returning her smile. "When's it to be?"

"Hasn't Honoria told you?" Minnie frowned. "I thought she said you knew—it's next Tuesday."

"Tuesday." Vane nodded, as if committing the fact to memory. He looked at Patience.

"Giddy nonsense, balls." Alice Colby very nearly sniffed. "But as the lady's a duchess, I daresay Whitticombe will say we must go. At least it's sure to be a suitably refined and dignified affair.'' Alice made the comment to the world at large. Concluding, she shut her pinched lips and stared straight ahead.

Vane stared, po-faced, at her. So did Minnie and Timms. All of them had attended impromptu balls Honoria had given. With all the Cynsters gathered in one room, refined and dignified tended to be overwhelmed by robust and vigorous. Deciding it was time Alice learned how the other half lived, Vane merely raised a brow and returned his attention to Patience.

At precisely the same moment she looked at him. Their gazes met and held; inwardly, Vane cursed. He needed to talk to Minnie; he wanted to talk to Patience. With her sitting there, waiting for him to invite her for a stroll, he couldn't ask Minnie instead. Not without adding to his problems, without leaving Patience feeling that he had, after all, started to ease back in his affections.

His affections, which were currently ravenous. Starved. Slavering for attention. And her.

He raised a languid brow. ''Would you care for a stroll, Miss Debbington?''

Patience saw the hunger in his eyes, briefly, fleetingly, but quite clearly enough to recognize. The vise already locked about her chest tightened. Inclining her head graciously, she held out one gloved hand—and struggled to suppress the thrill that raced through her when his fingers closed strongly about hers.

He opened the door and handed her down. She turned to the carriage. Mrs. Chadwick smiled; Angela pouted. Edith Swithins positively grinned. Minnie, however, fluffed up her shawls and exchanged a quick glance with Timms.

''Actually,'' Timms said, ''I rather think we should be getting back. The breeze is a mite chilly.''

It was an Indian summer's day. The sun shone brightly, the breeze was almost balmy.

''Humph! Perhaps you're right,'' Minnie grumbled gruffly. She shot a glance at Patience. ''No reason you can't go for your stroll—Vane can bring you home in his curricule. I know how much you miss your rambles.''

"Indeed. We'll see you back at the house later." Timms poked the coachman with the tip of her parasol. "Home, Cedric!"

Left on the verge staring bemusedly after the carriage, Patience shook her head. Vane's arm appeared beside her. Placing her fingers on his sleeve, she glanced up into his face. "What was all that about?"

His eyes met hers. His brows rose. "Minnie and Timms are inveterate matchmakers. Didn't you know?"

Patience shook her head again. "They've never behaved like that with me before."

They'd never had him in their sights before either. Vane kept that thought to himself and guided Patience across the lawn. There were many couples strolling close to the carriageway. As they nodded and smiled, returning greetings as they headed for less-crowded terrain, Vane let his senses revel in the experience of having Patience once more by his side. He'd drawn her as close as propriety allowed; her green skirts swished against his boots. She was all woman, soft and curvaceous, mere inches away; he grew harder simply at the thought. The breeze, wafting past, lifted her perfume to his face—honeysuckle, roses, and that indefinable scent that evoked every hunter's instinct he possessed.

Abruptly, he cleared his throat. "Nothing happened last evening?" It was an effort to lift his voice from the gravelly depths to which it had sunk.

"Nothing." Patience slanted him a sharp, slightly curious glance. "Distressingly, Edmond and Henry have reverted to their competitive worst. Stolen items, or the disposal of same, seemed exceedingly far from their minds. If either of them are the thief or the Spectre, I'll eat my new bonnet."

Vane grimaced. "I don't think your new bonnet's in any danger." He studied the stylish creation perched atop her curls. "Is this it?"

"Yes," Patience returned, somewhat waspishly. He could at least have noticed.

"I thought it looked different." Vane flicked the cockade perched over her eyebrow—and met her gaze with a far-too-innocent look.

Patience humphed. "I take it the General and Edgar made no suspicious moves last night?"

"Suspicious moves aplenty, but more along the line of being suspiciously foxed. More to the point, however, Masters has heard from the Hall."

Patience's eyes widened. "And?"

Vane grimaced. "Nothing." Looking forward, he shook his head. "I can't understand it. We know the items haven't been sold. We haven't found them in the luggage brought up to town. But they aren't at the Hall. Grisham and the staff have been very thorough—they even checked the wainscot for hidden panels. There are a few. I didn't tell Grisham where they were, but he found them all. Empty, of course—I'd checked before we left. They searched every room, every nook and cranny. They checked under loose floorboards. They also searched the grounds and the ruins. Thoroughly. Incidentally, they did find some disturbance just beyond the door of the abbot's lodge."

"Oh?"

"Someone had cleared off a section of the flags. There's an iron ring set in a stone—an old hatch. But the hatch *hasn't* been opened recently." Vane caught Patience's gaze. "Devil and I lifted it years ago—the cellar beneath was filled in. There's nothing beneath that stone, not even a hole in which something might be hidden. So it doesn't explain anything, least of all why Gerrard was struck down."

"Hmm." Patience frowned. "I'll ask him if he's remembered anything more about what he saw before he was hit."

Vane nodded absently. "Unfortunately, none of that sheds any light on our mystery. The puzzle of where the stolen goods, including Minnie's pearls, have gone darkens with every passing day."

Patience grimaced and briefly tightened her hold on his arm—simply because it seemed the right thing to do, to comfort and sympathize. "We'll just have to remain vigilant. On our guard. Something will happen." She looked up and met Vane's eyes. "It has to."

There was no arguing with that. Vane slid his free hand over her fingers, anchoring her hand on his sleeve.

They walked for some minutes in silence, then Vane glanced at Patience's face. "Are you excited by the prospect of Honoria's ball?"

"Indeed." Patience glanced fleetingly up at him. "I understand it's an honor to be invited. As you saw, Mrs. Chadwick and Angela are in alt. I can only hope awe is sufficient to overcome Henry. Edmond, however, will remain unimpressed. I'm sure he'll come, but I doubt even a ducal ball has sufficient weight to puncture his self-assurance."

Vane made a mental note to mention that to Honoria.

Patience glanced up at him, a frown in her eyes. "Will you be there?"

Vane raised his brows. "When Honoria issues a summons, we all fall in."

"You do?"

"She's Devil's duchess." When Patience's puzzled frown persisted; Vane elaborated: "He's the head of the family."

Looking ahead, Patience mouthed an "Oh." She was clearly still puzzled.

Vane's lips twisted wryly.

"There were two other ladies in the carriage with Honoria when she stopped to invite us." Patience looked at Vane. "I think they were Cynsters, too."

Vane kept his expression impassive. "What did they look like?"

"They were older. One was dark and spoke with a French accent. She was introduced as the Dowager."

"Helena, Dowager Duchess of St. Ives—Devil's mother." His other godmother.

Patience nodded. "The other was brown-haired, tall, and stately—a Lady Horatia Cynster."

Vane's expression turned grim. "My mother."

"Oh." Patience glanced his way. "Both your mother and the Dowager were . . . very kind." She looked ahead. "I didn't realize. All three—Honoria and the other two ladies—seemed very close."

"They are." Resignation rang in Vane's tone. "Very close. The whole family's very close."

Mouthing another "Oh," Patience looked ahead again.

Glancing sidelong, Vane studied her profile, and wondered what she'd made of his mother—and what his mother had made of her. Not that he anticipated any resistance on that front. His mother would welcome his chosen bride with open arms. And a great deal of otherwise classified information and far-too-insightful advice. Within the Cynster clan, that was the way things were done.

A deep requirement, a need, for commitment to family, formed, he was now sure, part of Patience's bulwark, one part of the hurdle that stood between her and marriage. That was one element of her problem he barely needed to take aim at—all he needed to do was introduce her to *his* family to blow that part of her problem away.

Despite the sacrifices it demanded of him, St. Ives House next Tuesday night was definitely the right address to send her to. After she saw the Cynsters all together, in their natural setting, she would rest easy on that score.

She would see, and believe, that he cared about family. And then . . .

Unconsciously, his fingers tightened about hers; Patience looked up inquiringly.

Vane smiled—wolfishly. "Just dreaming."

Chapter 18

For Patience, the next three days passed in a whirl of brief meetings, of whispered conferences, of desperate endeavors to locate Minnie's pearls, punctuated by last-minute fittings for her new ball gown, all squeezed between the social excursions necessary to keep all Minnie's household under observation. Beneath the frenetic rush ran a sense of gathering excitement, a swelling thrill of anticipation.

Highlighted whenever she met Vane, whenever they exchanged glances, whenever she sensed the weight of his personal, highly passionate, regard.

There was no hiding it, no sidestepping it; the desire between them grew stronger, more charged, with every passing day. She didn't know whether to blame him, or herself.

By the time she climbed the imposing steps of St. Ives House and passed into the brilliantly lit hall, her nerves had wound taut, coiled tight in her stomach. She told herself it was nonsense to allow the moment to so affect her, to imagine anything great would come of the evening. This was merely a private family ball, an impromptu affair, as Honoria had been at great pains to assure her.

There was no reason—no sense—to her reaction.

"There you are!" Honoria, magnificently gowned in mulberry silk, informally greeting her guests by the door, all but pounced on Patience as she crossed the music room's threshold. Nodding to Minnie, Timms, and the rest

275

of their entourage, Honoria graciously waved them on, but kept hold of Patience. "I must introduce you to Devil."

Deftly linking arms with Patience, she swept up to where a tall, dramatically dark gentleman clothed in black stood talking to two matrons. Honoria jabbed his arm. "Devil— my husband. Duke of St. Ives."

The man turned, took in Patience, then slanted Honoria a mildly inquiring glance.

"Patience Debbington," his spouse supplied. "Minnie's niece."

Devil smiled, first at his wife, then at Patience. "It's a pleasure to meet you, Miss Debbington." He bowed gracefully. "You've just come up from Bellamy Hall, I hear. Vane seems to have found his stay there unexpectedly distracting."

The smooth tones of his deep voice, distinctly familiar, rolled over, and through, Patience. She resisted the urge to blink. Vane and Devil could have been brothers—the resemblance, the autocratic cast of their features, the aggressive line of nose and jaw, was impossible to mistake. The primary difference lay in their coloring—while Vane's hair was burnished brown, his eyes cool grey, Devil's hair was midnight black, his large eyes a pale green. There were other differences, too, but the similarities outweighed them. From their build, their distinctive height, and, most striking of all, the wicked glint in their eyes and the totally untrustworthy lilt to their lips, they were clearly as one beneath the skin. Wolves in human form.

Very masculine, distinctly distracting form.

"How do you do, Your Grace." Patience held out her hand, and would have sunk into the regulation deep curtsy, but Devil grasped her fingers and prevented it.

"*Not* 'Your Grace.'" He smiled, and Patience felt the mesmerizing power of his gaze as he raised her gloved fingers to his lips. "Call me Devil—everyone does."

For good reason, Patience decided. Despite that, she couldn't help but return his smile.

"There's Louise—I must speak with her." Honoria glanced at Patience. "I'll catch up with you later." Skirts swishing imperiously, she headed back to the door.

Devil grinned. He turned back to Patience—his gaze slid past her.

"Minnie's asking after you." Vane nodded to Patience as he halted beside her, then he returned his gaze to Devil. "She wants to relive some of our more embarrassing exploits—rather you than me."

Devil sighed feelingly. He raised his head, looking over the swelling throng to where Minnie was holding court, enthroned on a *chaise* by the wall. "Perhaps I could impress her with the weight of my ducal demeanor?" He raised his brows at Vane, who grinned.

"You could try."

Devil smiled. With a nod to Patience, he left them.

Patience met Vane's gaze; instantly, she was aware of the tension that held him. A peculiar shyness gripped her. "Good evening."

Something hot flashed through his eyes; his face hardened. He reached for her hand. She yielded it readily. He raised it, but instead of touching his lips to the backs of her gloved fingers, he reversed her hand. His eyes steady on hers, he pressed his lips to her inner wrist. Her pulse leapt beneath his caress.

"There's someone you should meet." His voice was low, gravelly. Placing her hand on his sleeve, he turned her.

"Hello, coz. Who's this?"

The gentleman who blocked their way was obviously another Cynster—one with light brown hair and blue eyes. Vane sighed, and made the introductions—and kept making them as more of them appeared. They were all similar—similarly dangerous—all large, all suavely assured—all elegant. The first went by the name of Gabriel; he was followed by Lucifer, Demon, and Scandal. Patience found it impossible not to soften under their practiced smiles. She grasped the moment to regain her breath, regain her poise. The pack—she instantly labeled them as such—chatted and sparred with effortless facility. She responded easily, but remained alert. How could one claim not to have been forewarned with names like that? She kept her hand firmly anchored to Vane's sleeve.

For his part, Vane showed no inclination to drift from her side. She told herself not to read too much into that fact. There simply might not be many ladies of the type to attract his interest in a crowd composed of family and friends.

A squeaky screech, followed by a plunk, heralded the start of the dancing. Four of the large men surrounding her hesitated; Vane did not. "Would you care to dance, my dear?"

Patience smiled her acceptance. With a gracious nod to the others, she consented to be led to the floor.

Stepping into the space rapidly clearing at the room's center, Vane confidently drew her into his arms. When her eyes widened, he raised a brow. "You do waltz in the wilds of Derbyshire, don't you?"

Patience lifted her chin. "Of course. I quite enjoy a good waltz."

"*Quite enjoy*?" The first strains of a waltz swelled. Vane's lips lifted wickedly. "Ah—but you've yet to waltz with a Cynster."

With that, he drew her closer, and whirled her into the dance.

Patience had parted her lips to haughtily ask just why Cynsters were thought such exponents of the art—by the time they'd revolved thrice, she had her answer. It took her three more revolutions before she managed to suck in a breath and close her mouth. She felt like she was airborne—swooping, sweeping. Effortlessly twirling, all in strict time.

Her startled gaze fell on the mulberry gown of the lady in the couple ahead of them, who was revolving every bit as vigorously as she. Honoria—their hostess. In the arms of her husband.

A quick glance revealed that all the Cynsters who'd been politely conversing with her earlier, had claimed ladies and taken to the floor. It was easy to pick them out among the crowd; they didn't revolve any faster than anyone else, but with greater enthusiasm, immensely greater power. Harnessed, controlled, power.

Feet flying, her skirts aswirl, compelled by the steely

arms that held her, the powerful body that so effortlessly steered her, checked her, reversed her and turned her, Patience clung tight—to her wits, and to Vane.

Not that she felt in any danger of being released.

The thought brought his nearness, his strength, into sharper focus. They neared the end of the room; his hand burning like a brand through the fine silk of her gown, he drew her closer, deeper into his protective embrace. They swung into the turn; Patience dragged in a desperate breath—and felt her bodice, her breasts, shift against his coat. Her nipples constricted, excruciatingly tight.

On a muted gasp, she looked up, and her gaze collided with his, silvery grey, mesmerically intent. She couldn't look away, could barely breathe, as the room revolved about them. Her senses narrowed, until the world she knew was encompassed within the circle of his arms.

Time stopped. All that was left was the sway of their bodies, caught in the compelling, powerful rhythm only they could hear. The violins played a minor theme; the music that played between them came from a different source.

It swelled and grew. Hips and thighs met, caressed, and parted as they shifted through the turns. The rhythm called, their bodies answered, flowing effortlessly with the dance, pulsing with the beat, heating slowly. Touching tantalizingly. Teasing and promising. When the violins ceased and their feet slowed, their music still played on.

Vane hauled in a deep breath; the moment shivered about them. He forced his arms from about Patience, caught her hand, and placed it on his sleeve, unable, even though he knew too many were watching avidly, to forgo placing his free hand over her fingers.

He felt her slight shudder, took her weight as, for an instant, she leaned more heavily on him, blinking rapidly as she struggled to pull free of the magic.

She lifted her eyes and studied his face. Coolly, a great deal more coolly than he felt, he raised a brow.

Patience straightened. Looking ahead, she put her nose in the air. "You waltz quite creditably."

Vane chuckled through his teeth. His jaw was set against

the urge to whisk her away, through one of the doors that led from the music room. He knew this house like the back of his hand. While she might not know their options, he did. But too many were watching them, and Honoria, for one, would never forgive him. Not so early in the evening, when sudden absences were too obvious.

Later. He'd already given up all thought that he could weather tonight without sating his demons. Not while she was wearing that dress.

Dashing, Minnie had termed it.

Dashed impossible, from his point of view.

He'd had every intention of toeing the line, at least until she'd accepted his offer. Now . . . There was such a thing as tempting a wolf too far.

He glanced down. Patience strolled serenely on his arm. The bronze-silk gown fitted snugly about her breasts, with only the tiniest wisps of sleeves, set off her shoulders, to distract from the glorious expanse of creamy skin, the ripe swells of her upper breasts, the delicate molding of her shoulders. The long straight skirts draped gently over her curvy hips, sleekly concealing her derriere; they fluttered elegantly about her legs, the hems ruffled to tantalizingly reveal her ankles as she walked.

While the neckline was low, there was nothing specifically outrageous about the gown. It was the combination of the woman wearing it and Celestine's faultlessly draped fabric that was causing his problems.

Only from his vantage point was it possible to see how deeply Patience's breasts rose and fell.

A second later, he forced himself to lift his head and look ahead.

Later.

He drew a deep breath, and held it.

"Evening, Cynster." An elegant gentleman stepped forward from the crowd, his gaze on Patience. "Miss . . . ?" Smoothly, he looked at Vane.

Who sighed. Audibly. And nodded. "Chillingworth." Vane glanced at Patience. "Allow me to present the earl of Chillingworth." He looked at Chillingworth. "Miss Debbington, Lady Bellamy's niece."

Patience curtsied. Chillingworth smiled charmingly, and bowed, as gracefully as any Cynster.

"I take it you've come up to town with Lady Bellamy, Miss Debbington. Are you finding the capital to your liking?"

"Actually, no." Patience saw no reason to prevaricate. "I fear I'm addicted to early mornings, my lord, a time the *ton* seems to eschew."

Chillingworth blinked. He glanced swiftly at Vane, then his gaze dropped fleetingly to where Vane's hand covered Patience's fingers, resting on his sleeve. He raised his brows and smiled suavely at Patience. "I'm almost tempted to explain, my dear, that our apparent dismissal of the morning hours is, in fact, a natural consequence of our activities in the *later* hours. Then again . . ." He slanted a glance at Vane. "Perhaps I had better leave such explanations to Cynster, here."

"Perhaps you had." There was no mistaking the steel in Vane's tone.

Fleetingly, Chillingworth grinned, but when he looked back at Patience, he was calmly serious once more. "You know, it's really quite odd." He smiled. "While I rarely find myself in agreement with Cynsters, one has to admit their taste in one respect resonates remarkably with mine."

"Indeed?" Patience acknowledged the veiled compliment with an assured smile. Having dealt with Vane for three weeks, the earl, charming and undeniably handsome though he was, had no chance of ruffling her feathers.

"Indeed." Chillingworth turned to quiz Vane. "Don't you find that remarkable, Cynster?"

"Not at all," Vane replied. "Some things are so blatantly obvious even you should appreciate them." Chillingworth's eyes sparked. Vane smoothly continued, "However, given your admittedly similar tastes, you might reflect on where following such tastes might land you." He nodded across the room.

Both Chillingworth and Patience followed his direction, and saw Devil and Honoria by the side of the ballroom, clearly engaged in some pointed discussion. As they watched, Honoria clasped her hands about Devil's arm and pushed to turn him down the room. The look Devil cast the ceiling, the long-suffering look he cast his wife as he acquiesced, made it clear who had won the round.

Chillingworth shook his head sadly. "Ah, how the mighty have fallen."

"You'd best be on your guard," Vane advised, "given that your tastes so parallel the Cynsters', that you don't find yourself in a situation you're constitutionally unprepared to handle."

Chillingworth grinned. "Ah, but I don't suffer from the Achilles' heel with which fate has hobbled the Cynsters." Still grinning, he bowed to Patience. "Your servant, Miss Debbington. Cynster." With a last nod, he went on his way, ignoring Vane's narrow-eyed glare.

Patience looked up into Vane's face. "What Achilles' heel?"

Vane stirred. "Nothing. It's just his notion of a joke."

If it was a joke, it had had an odd effect. "Who is he?" Patience asked. "Is he a Cynster connection of sorts?"

"He's not related—at least not by blood." After a moment, Vane added, "I suppose, these days, he's an honorary Cynster." He glanced at Patience. "We elected him for services rendered to the dukedom."

"Oh?" Patience let her eyes ask her question.

"He and Devil have a history. Ask Honoria about it sometime."

The musicians started up again. Before Patience could blink, Lucifer was bowing before her. Vane let her go, somewhat reluctantly, she thought. But as she whirled down the floor, she saw him whirling, too, a striking brunette in his arms.

Abruptly, Patience looked away, and gave her attention to the dance, and to dealing with Lucifer's glib tongue. And ignoring her sinking heart.

The end of the measure saw them well down the room. Lucifer introduced her to a group of ladies and gentlemen, all chatting easily. Patience tried to concentrate, tried to follow the conversation.

She literally jumped when hard fingers closed about hers,

lifted her hand from Lucifer's sleeve and placed it, firmly, on a familiar arm.

"Upstart," Vane growled. And deftly insinuated himself between Lucifer and Patience.

Lucifer grinned engagingly. "You need to work for it, coz. You know none of us appreciates that which comes too readily."

Vane slayed him with a look, then turned to Patience. "Come, let's stroll. Before he puts misguided notions into your head."

Intrigued, Patience allowed herself to be escorted on an amble up the room. "What misguided notions?"

"Never mind. *Good God*—there's Lady Osbaldestone! She's hated me ever since I stuck a marble up the end of her cane. She couldn't understand why it kept sliding away from her. Let's go the other way."

They tacked back and forth through the crowd, chatting here, exchanging introductions there. Yet when the music resumed, another Cynster appeared before her like magic.

Demon Harry, Vane's brother, stole her away; Vane stole her back the instant the music ceased. The voluptuous blonde he'd whirled around the room was nowhere in sight.

The next waltz brought Devil to bow, ineffably elegant before her. As he swung her into the first turn, he read the question in her eyes and grinned. "We always share."

His grin deepened as her eyes, beyond her control, widened. Only the wicked laughter in his eyes assured Patience he was teasing.

And so it went on, through waltz after waltz. After every one, Vane reappeared by her side. Patience tried to tell herself it meant nothing, that it could simply be that he'd found nothing more scintillating, no lady more enticing, with whom to spend his time.

She shouldn't make too much of it—yet her heart leapt one notch, one giddy rung higher on the ladder of irrational hope, every time he reclaimed her hand, and his position by her side.

"These balls of Honoria's are such a good idea." Louise Cynster, one of Vane's aunts, leaned on her husband, Lord Arthur Cynster's arm, and smiled at Patience. "Despite the fact we all move in the same circles, the family's so large, we can often go for weeks without meeting each other, at least not long enough to exchange our news.''

''What my dearest wife means,'' Lord Arthur smoothly said, ''is that, although the ladies of the family meet often, they miss the opportunity of seeing how the other half of the family's comporting itself, and these little gatherings of Honoria's guarantee we'll all turn out on parade.'' His eyes twinkled. ''To be inspected, as it were.''

''Bosh!'' Louise tapped him smartly on the arm with her fan. ''As if you men ever need any excuse to turn out on parade. And as for being inspected! There's not a lady in the *ton* who won't tell you that Cynsters are past masters at 'inspecting' themselves.''

The comment brought chuckles and grins all around. The group dissolved as the music resumed. Gabriel materialized to bow before Patience. ''My turn, I believe?''

Patience wondered if Cynsters had a monopoly on wolfish smiles. They also all had quick and ready tongues: During every dance, she'd found her attention firmly held by the brisk repartee that seemed their hallmark.

A minor ruckus ensued as they started to whirl. Passing close by its epicenter, Patience discovered Honoria grappling with Devil.

''We've already danced once. You should dance with one of our guests.''

''But I want to dance with *you*.''

The look that went with that was uncompromising. Despite her status, Honoria was clearly not immune. ''Oh, very well.'' The next instant, she was whirling, masterfully captured, then Devil bent his head to hers.

As she and Gabriel swirled past, Patience heard Honoria's ripple of laughter, saw the glow in her face as she looked up at her husband, then closed her eyes and let him whirl her away.

The sight caught at Patience's heart.

This time, when the music finally slowed and died, she'd lost sight of Vane. Assuming he'd soon reappear, she chatted easily with Gabriel. Demon joined them, as did a Mr. Aubrey-Wells, a dapper, very precise gentleman. His interest was the theater. Not having seen any of the current productions, Patience listened attentively.

Then, through a gap in the crowd, she saw Vane, talking to a young beauty. The girl was exquisite, with a wealth of blond hair. Her understated gown of pale blue silk positively screamed "outrageously expensive."

"I think you'll find the production at the Theatre Royal worth a visit," Mr. Aubrey-Wells intoned.

Patience, her gaze locked on the tableau on the other side of the room, nodded absently.

The beauty glanced about, then put her hand on Vane's arm. He looked behind them, then took her hand in his. Swiftly, he conducted her to a double door in the wall. Opening it, he handed her through and followed her in.

And shut the door.

Patience stiffened; the blood drained from her face. Abruptly, she looked back at Mr. Aubrey-Wells. "The Theatre Royal?"

Mr. Aubrey-Wells nodded—and continued his lecture.

"Hmm." Beside Patience, Gabriel nodded to Demon, then inclined his head toward the fateful door. "Looks serious."

Patience's heart plummeted.

Demon shrugged. "Daresay we'll hear later."

With that, they both turned attentively to Patience. Who kept her gaze fixed on Mr. Aubrey-Wells, parroting his remarks as if the theater filled her mind. In reality, her mind was full of the Cynsters, several and singular.

Elegant gentlemen, one and all. All and one.

She should never have forgotten it, should never have let her senses shut her eyes to the reality.

But she hadn't lost anything, given anything she hadn't wanted to give. She'd expected this from the first. With an effort, she suppressed a racking shiver. She'd felt surrounded by warmth and laughter; now bleak disappointment pierced her bones and froze her marrow. As for her heart, that was so cold she was sure that, at any moment, it would fracture. Shatter into frozen shards.

Her face felt the same way.

She let Mr. Aubrey-Wells's discourse flow past her, and

wondered what she should do. As if in answer, Gerrard's face swam into her restricted vision.

He smiled at her, then, more tentatively, at her escort.

Metaphorically, Patience grabbed him. "Mr. Cynster, Mr. Cynster and Mr. Aubrey-Wells—my brother, Gerrard Debbington."

She gave the men the minimum of time to exchange greetings, then, smiling too brightly, beamed at them all. "I really should check on Minnie." Mr. Aubrey-Wells looked confused; she beamed even more brightly. "My aunt, Lady Bellamy." Taking Gerrard's arm, she flung them another brilliant smile. "If you'll excuse us?"

They all bowed with ready grace, Gabriel and Demon easily outperforming Mr. Aubrey-Wells. Inwardly gritting her teeth, Patience steered Gerrard away. "Don't you ever dare bow like that."

Gerrard sent her a startled look. "Whyever not?"

"Never mind."

They had to tack through the crowd. The throng was at its height. Supper had yet to be served. All had arrived but few had yet departed.

In order to get to Minnie's *chaise*, they had perforce to pass by the double doors through which Vane and the beauty had disappeared. Patience had intended to sweep past, nose in the air. Instead, as they neared the innocent-looking panels, she slowed.

When she halted a few steps from the doors, Gerrard threw her an inquiring look. Patience saw it; she took a moment before she met it.

"You go on." Drawing a deep breath, she straightened. Lips setting, she lifted her hand from his sleeve. "I want to check on something. Can you see Minnie into supper?"

Gerrard shrugged. "Of course." Smiling, he ambled on.

Patience watched him go—then turned on her heel and marched straight to the double doors. She knew perfectly well what she was doing—even if she couldn't formulate a single coherent thought through the haze of fury clouding her brain. How *dare* Vane treat her like this? He hadn't even said good-bye. He might be an elegant gentleman to his toes, but he was going to have to learn some manners!

Besides, the beauty was too young for him, she could barely be more than seventeen. A chit out of the schoolroom—it was scandalous.

Her hand on the doorknob, Patience paused—and tried to think of an opening line—one suitable for the scene she might very likely stumble in upon. Nothing leapt to her tongue. Grimly, she shook aside her hesitation. If, in the heat of the moment, nothing occurred to her, she could always scream.

Eyes narrow, she grasped the handle and turned.

The door flew inward, pulled open from within. Yanked off her feet, Patience tripped on the raised threshold and fetched up against Vane's chest.

The impact knocked the air from her lungs; Vane's arm, locking about her, kept her breathless. Wide-eyed and gasping, Patience looked up into his face.

His eyes met hers. "Hel-*lo*."

His intent expression made Patience stiffen, only to realize the arm around her, steadying her, was also trapping her.

Hard against him.

Dazed, she glanced around; the dark shapes of huge leaves reared above the denser dark of heavy pots, grouped upon a tiled floor. Moonlight streamed through walls of long windows and panes in the ceiling, silvering paths wending between stands of palms and exotic blooms. The rich scents of earth and the warm humidity of growing things hung on the heavy air.

She and Vane stood within the shadows, just beyond the shaft of light lancing through the open door. A yard away, enveloped in soft gloom, stood the beauty, regarding her with open curiosity.

The beauty smiled and bobbed a curtsy. "How do you do? Miss Debbington, isn't it?"

"Ah—yes." Patience looked, but could see no signs of disarray—the girl appeared neat as a pin.

Into her total bewilderment Vane's voice fell, like a bell tolling. "Allow me to present Miss Amanda Cynster."

Stunned, Patience looked up; he captured her gaze and smiled. "My cousin."

Patience mouthed an innocent, "Oh."

"First cousin," he added.

Amanda cleared her throat. "If you'll excuse me?" With a quick nod, she slipped past, out of the door.

Abruptly, Vane raised his head. "Remember what I said."

"Of *course* I will." Amanda threw him a disgusted frown. "I'm going to tie him in knots, and then hoist him from his . . ." She gestured, then, with a swish of her skirts, stalked into the crowd.

Patience reflected that Amanda Cynster sounded like a beauty who would never need rescuing.

She, however, might.

Vane returned his attention to her. "What are you doing here?"

She blinked, and glanced around again—then hauled in a breath, difficult with her breasts pressed to his chest. She gestured to the room. "Someone mentioned it was a conservatory. I've been thinking of suggesting that Gerrard install one at the Grange. I thought I'd look in." She peered into the leafy gloom. "Study the amenities."

"Indeed?" Vane smiled, the merest lifting of his long lips, and released her. "By all means." With one hand, he pushed the door shut; with the other, he gestured to the room. "I'll be only too pleased to demonstrate some of the benefits of a conservatory."

Patience cast him a swift glance and quickly stepped forward, out of his reach. She gazed at the arches forming the ceiling. "Was this room always part of the house, or was it added on?"

Behind her, Vane slid the bolt on the doors; it engaged noiselessly. "It was, I believe, originally a loggia." Strolling unhurriedly, he followed Patience down the main pathway, into the palm-shrouded depths.

"Hmm, interesting." Patience eyed a palm towering above the path, handlike leaves poised as if to seize the unwary. "Where does Honoria get such plants?" Passing beneath the palm, she trailed her fingers through delicate fern fronds surrounding the palm's base—and threw a quick glance behind her. "Do the gardeners propagate them?"

Pacing steadily in her wake, Vane caught her gaze. His brows rose fractionally. "I've no idea."

Patience looked ahead—and quickened her pace. "I wonder what other plants do well in such a setting. Palms like these might be a bit hard to come by in Derbyshire."

"Indeed."

"Ivies, I daresay, would do well. And cacti, of course."

"Of course."

Flitting along the path, absentmindedly touching this plant or that, Patience stared ahead—and tried to spot the way out. The path wound randomly about; she was no longer entirely sure of her bearings. "Perhaps, for the Grange, an orangery might be more sensible."

"My mother has one."

The words came from just behind her. "She has?" A swift glance behind revealed Vane almost at her shoulder. Gulping in a quick breath, Patience mentally acknowledged the skittering excitement that had cinched tight about her lungs, that had started, very effectively, to draw her nerves taut. Expectation, anticipation, shivered in the moonlit dark. Breathless, wide-eyed, she lengthened her stride. "I must remember to ask Lady Horatia—oh!"

She broke off. For one moment, she stood stock-still, drinking in the simple beauty of the marble fountain, the base of its pedestal wreathed in delicate fronds, that stood, glowing lambently in the soft white light, in the center of a small, secluded, fern-shrouded clearing. Water poured steadily from the pitcher of the partially clad maiden frozen forever in her task of filling the wide, scroll-lipped basin.

The area had clearly been designed to provide the lady of the house with a private, refreshing, calming retreat in which to embroider, or simply rest and gather her thoughts. In the moonlit night, surrounded by mysterious shadow and steeped in a silence rendered only more intense by the distant sighing of music and the silvery tinkle of the water, it was a hauntingly magical place.

For three heartbeats, the magic held Patience immobile. Then, through the fine silk of her gown, she felt the heat of Vane's body. He did not touch her, but that heat, and the flaring awareness that raced through her, had her quickly stepping forward. Hauling in a desperate breath, she gestured to the fountain. "It's lovely."

"Hmm," came from close behind.

Too close behind. Patience found herself heading for a stone bench, shaded by a canopy of palms. Stifling a gasp, she veered away, toward the fountain.

The fountain's pedestal was set on a stone disc; she stepped onto the single, foot-wide step. Beneath her soles, she felt the change from tiles to marble. One hand on the rim of the basin, she glanced down, then, nerves flickering wildly, forced herself to bend and study the plants nestling at the pedestal's base. "These look rather exotic."

Behind her, Vane studied the way her gown had pulled tight over the curves of her bottom—and didn't argue. Lips lifting in anticipation, he moved in—to spring his trap.

Her heart racing, tripping in double time, Patience straightened, and went to slide around the fountain, to place it between herself and the wolf she was trapped in the conservatory with. Instead, she ran into an arm.

She blinked at it. One faultless grey sleeve enclosing solid bone well covered with steely muscle, large fist locked over the scrolled rim of the basin, it stated very clearly that she wasn't going anywhere.

Patience whirled—and found her retreat similarly blocked. Swinging farther, she met Vane's gaze; standing on the tiled floor, one step below her, arms braced on the rim, his eyes were nearly level with hers. She studied them, read his intent in the silvered grey, in the hardening lines of his face, the brutally sensual line of those uncompromising lips.

She couldn't believe her eyes.

"*Here*?" The word, weak though it was, accurately reflected her disbelief.

"Right here. Right now."

Her heart thudded wildly. Prickling awareness raced over her skin. The certainty in his voice, in the deepening tones, riveted her. The thought of what he was suggesting made her mind seize.

She swallowed, and moistened her lips, not daring to take her eyes from his. "But . . . someone might come in."

His gaze dropped from hers, his lids veiling his eyes. "I locked the door."

"You did?" Wildly, Patience glanced back toward the door; a tug at her bodice hauled her back, refocused her scattered wits. On the top button of her bodice, now undone. She stared at the gold-and-tortoiseshell whorl. "I thought they were just for show."

"So did I." Vane popped the second of the big buttons free. His fingers moved to the third and final button, below her breasts. "I must remember to commend Celestine on her farsighted design."

The final button slid free—his long fingers slid beneath the silk. Patience sucked in a desperate breath; he had very quick fingers—with locks, and other things. On the thought, she felt the ribbons of her chemise give; the fine silk slid down.

His hand, hot and hard, closed over her breast.

Patience gasped. She swayed—and grabbed his shoulders to keep herself upright. The next second, his lips were on hers; they shifted, then settled, hard and demanding. For one instant, she stood firm, savoring the heady taste of his desire—his need of her—then she yielded, opening to him, inviting him in, brazenly delighting in his conquest.

The kiss deepened, not by degrees, but in leaps and bounds, in a blind, breathless downhill rush, a giddy pursuit of sensual delights, carnal pleasures.

Parched for air, Patience drew back on a gasp. Head back, she breathed deeply. Her breasts rose dramatically; Vane bent his head to pay homage.

She felt his hand at her waist, burning through her thin gown as he held her steady before him; she felt his lips, hot as brands, tease and tug at her nipples. Then he took the engorged flesh into the wet heat of his mouth. She tensed. He suckled—her strangled cry shivered in the moonlight.

"Ah." His eyes glinted wickedly as he lifted his head and transferred his attention to her other breast. "You'll have to remember. This time, no screaming."

No screaming? Patience clung to him, clung desperately to her wits as he feasted. His mouth, his touch, drew and fragmented her attention, stoked and fed the desire already flaring hotly within her.

But it was impossible—it had to be.

There was the bench—but it was cold and narrow and surely too hard. Then she remembered how he'd once lifted her and loved her.

"My dress—it'll crush horribly. Everyone will guess."

His only response was to tuck the sides of her bodice back, completely baring her breasts.

Through her next gasp, Patience managed, "I meant my skirts. We'll never be able to . . ."

The rumbling chuckle that rolled through him left her shuddering.

"Not a single crease." His lips brushed the crests of her breasts, now tight and aching; his teeth grazed the furled tips, and daggers pierced her flesh. "Trust me."

His voice was deep, dark, heavy with passion. He lifted his head. His hands closed about her waist. Deliberately, he drew her to him, so her tingling breasts pressed against his coat. She gasped, and he bent his head and kissed her, kissed her until she had softened through and through, until her weakening limbs could barely support her.

"Where there's a will there's a way." He breathed the words against her lips. "And I *will* have you."

For one fractured instant, their gazes met—no pretense, no amount of guile could conceal the emotions driving them. Simple, uncomplicated. Urgent.

He turned her; Patience blinked at the fountain, pearly white in the moonlight, blinked at the barely robed maiden steadily filling the bowl. She felt Vane behind her, hot, solid—aroused. He bent his head; his lips grazed the side of her throat. Patience sank back against him, angling her head back, encouraging his caresses. She let her hands drop to her sides, to his thighs, hard as oak behind her. Spreading her fingers, she gripped the long, tensed muscles—and felt them harden even more.

He reached around her; she waited to feel his hands close about her breasts, to feel him fill his hands with her bounty.

Instead, with just the very tips of his fingers, he traced the swollen curves, circled the aching peaks. Patience shuddered—and sank deeper against him. His hands left her; she felt him reach out. She forced her eyes open. From under weighted lids, she watched as, with one hand, he traced the bare breast of the maiden, lovingly caressing the cool stone.

Leaving the maiden, his fingers trailed lightly in the clear water in the marble bowl. Then he raised the same fingers to her heated flesh—and touched her as he'd touched the maiden—delicately, evocatively. Enticingly.

Patience closed her eyes—and shivered. His fingers, cool, wet, trailed and traced—exquisite sensation lanced through her. Pressing her head back against his shoulder, she bit her lip against a moan, and flexed her fingers on his thighs.

And managed to gasp: "This is . . ."

"Meant to be."

After a moment, she licked her parched lips. "How?"

She sensed the change in him, the surge of passion he immediately leashed. Her flaring response, the urgent need to have him take her, completely and utterly, and give himself in the same way, stole her breath.

"Trust me." He reached around her again, moving closer; his strength flowed around her, surrounded her. His hands closed about her breasts, no longer delicately teasing but hungry. He filled his hands and kneaded; Patience felt the flames rise—in him, in her.

"Just do what I tell you. And don't think."

Patience mentally groaned. How? What . . . ? "Just remember my dress."

"I'm an expert, remember? Grasp the rim of the bowl with both hands."

Bemused, Patience did. Vane shifted behind her; the next instant, her skirts, then her petticoats, were flipped up, over her waist. Cool air washed over the backs of her thighs, over her bottom, exposed to the moonlight.

She blushed hotly—and opened her mouth on a protest.

The next second, she forgot about protest, forgot about

everything, as long, knowing fingers slid between her thighs.

Unerringly, he found her, already slick and swollen. He traced, and tantalized, teased and caressed, then evocatively probed her.

Eyes closed, Patience bit her lip against a moan. He reached deep, stroking into her softness; she gasped, and gripped the marble bowl more tightly.

Then he reached around her, one large palm sliding under her dress and petticoats, gliding over her hip to splay possessively over her naked stomach. The hand shifted, fingers searching boldly through her curls. Until one found and settled against her most sensitive spot.

She couldn't find enough breath to gasp—let alone moan or scream. Patience desperately drew air into her lungs, and felt him behind her. Felt the hot hard length of him press between her thighs. Felt the wide head nudge into her softness and find her entrance.

Slowly, he sank into her, easing her hips back, then holding her steady, bracing her as he slid fully home. And filled her.

Slowly, deliberately, he withdrew—and returned, pressing so deeply she rose on her toes.

Her gasp hung like shimmering silver in the moonlight, eloquent testimony to her state.

Again and again, with the same relentlessly restrained force, he filled her. Thrilled her. Loved her.

The hand at her belly didn't shift, but simply held her steady so she could receive him, could feel, again and again, his possession, the slow repetitive penetration impinging on her mind as well as her body, on her emotions as well as her senses.

She was his and she knew it. She gave herself gladly, received him joyfully, obediently struggled to hold back her moans as he shifted and sank deeper.

Tucking her bottom firmly against his hips, he moved more forcefully within her, thrusting more deeply, more powerfully.

The tension—within him, within her, holding them so tightly—grew, swelled, coiled. Patience swallowed a gasp—

and clung to sanity. And prayed for release while dazedly wondering if this time she really would lose her mind.

Again and again he filled her. The golden glimmer she now knew and desired glowed on her horizon. She tried to reach for it—to draw it nearer—tried to tighten about him and urge him on.

And suddenly realized that, in this position, her options were limited.

She was at his mercy and could do nothing to change it.

With a gasp, she lowered her head, her fingers tightening on the bowl's rim. Pleasure, relentless, passionate, rolled through her in waves, rearing every time he sank into her and stretched her. Completed her.

Patience felt a scream building—and bit her lip—hard.

Vane sank into her again and felt her quiver. He remained sunk in her heat for a fraction longer, then smoothly withdrew. And sank into her again.

He was in no hurry. Savoring the slick, scalding softness that welcomed him, the velvet glove that fitted him so well, glorying in all the heady signs of her body's acceptance of him—the natural, abandoned way the hemispheres of her bottom, glowing ivory in the moonlight, met his body, the slick wetness that made his staff gleam, the total absence of all restraint, the completeness of her surrender—he took time to appreciate it all.

Before him, she tightened, and tensed, and helplessly squirmed.

He held her steady. And slowly filled her again. She was close to frantic. He withdrew from her, nudged her legs wider, and filled her even more deeply.

A muted squeal escaped her.

Vane narrowed his eyes, and took firm hold of his reins. "What brought you here? To the conservatory?"

After a fractured minute, Patience gasped, "I told you—the amenities."

"Not because you saw me come in here with a lovely young lady?"

"No!" The answer came back too quickly. "Well," Patience breathlessly temporized, "she was your cousin."

With his free hand, Vane reached around her, filling his

palm with the swollen fullness of her breast. He searched and found the tight bud of her nipple—and rolled it gently between thumb and finger, before squeezing firmly. "You didn't know that until I told you."

Patience valiantly swallowed her scream. "The music's stopped—they must all be at supper." She was so breathless, she could barely speak. "We'll miss it all if you don't hurry."

She'd die if he didn't hurry.

Hard lips caressed her nape. "The lobster patties can wait. I'd rather have you."

To Patience's relief, he tightened his grip on her, held her even more rigidly, as he stroked more powerfully. The flames within her roared, then fused and coalesced; the bright sun of release drew steadily nearer. Grew steadily brighter. Then he paused.

"You seem to be missing something here."

Patience knew what she was missing. The bright sun stopped, three heartbeats away. She gritted her teeth—a scream welled in her throat—

"I told you—you're mine. I want you—and you alone."

The words, uttered softly, with rocklike conviction, drove all other thoughts from Patience's head. Opening her eyes, she stared unseeing at the marble maiden, shimmering softly in the moonlight.

"There's no other woman I want to be inside—no other woman I crave." She felt his body tense, gather—then he thrust deep. "Only you."

The sun crashed down on her.

Hot pleasure washed through her like a tidal wave, sweeping all before it. Her vision clouded; she was unaware that she screamed.

Shifting his hand to her lips, Vane muffled the worst of her ecstatic cry—the sound still shredded his control. His chest swelled; grimly, he struggled to contain the desire raging through him, pounding his senses, liquid fire in his loins.

He succeeded—until the ripples of her release caressed him. He felt the power gather, felt it swell, grow and build within him. And in that final moment, as the cosmos crashed about him, he surrendered.

And did as she'd once asked, let go—and poured himself into her.

The instant Minnie's carriage door closed, cloaking her in the safe dark, Patience slumped against the squabs. And prayed she'd be able to master her limbs sufficiently to leave the carriage and walk to her bed when they arrived in Aldford Street.

Her body no longer felt like hers. Vane had taken possession and left her limp. Wrung out. The half hour between their return to the ballroom and Minnie's departure had been a near-run thing. Only his surreptitious support, his careful maneuvering, had concealed her state. Her deeply sated state.

At least she'd been able to speak. Reasonably coherently. And think. In some ways, that had made things worse. Because all she could think about was what he'd said, whispered against her temple, when she'd finally stirred in his arms.

"Have you changed your mind yet?"

She'd had to search for the strength to say "No."

"Stubborn woman," in the tone of a soft curse, had been his reply.

He hadn't pressed her further, but he hadn't given up.

His question replayed in her mind. His tone—one of understated but unswerving determination—bothered her. His strength ran deep, not just a physical characteristic; overcoming it—convincing him she wouldn't acquiesce and be his wife—was proving a far harder battle than she'd foreseen. The unwelcome possibility that, unintentionally, she'd pricked his pride, taunted his conqueror's soul, and would now have to contend with the full force of that side of his character, too, wasn't a cheering thought.

Worst of all was the fact that she'd hesitated before saying "No."

Temptation, unheralded, had slunk in and slipped under her guard. After all she'd seen, all she'd observed, of the Cynsters, their wives, and their firmly stated and rigidly applied attitudes on the subject of family, it was impossible to escape the fact that Vane's offer was the best she'd ever get. Family—the one thing that was most important to her—was critically important to him.

Given all his other attributes—his wealth, his status, his handsomeness—what more could she possibly want?

The problem was, she knew the answer to that question.

That was why she had said "No." Why she would keep saying "No."

The Cynster attitude to family was possessive and protective. They were a warrior clan—the open commitment she'd initially found so surprising was, viewed in that light, perfectly understandable. Warriors defended what was theirs. Cynsters, it seemed, regarded their family as a possession, to be defended at all costs and in all arenas. Their feelings sprang from their conquerors' instincts—the instinct to hold on to whatever they'd won.

Perfectly understandable.

But it wasn't enough.

Not for her.

Her answer still remained—had to remain—"No."

Chapter 19

S ligo opened the front door of Number 22 at nine the next morning.

Vane nodded curtly and strode in. ''Where's Her Ladyship?'' He cast a quick glance about the hall; it was mercifully untenanted. Bar Sligo, who was gaping.

Vane frowned.

Sligo blinked.''Should think Her Ladyship would still be abed, sir. Should I send up—''

''No.'' Vane looked up the stairs. ''Which room is hers?''

''Last on the right.''

Vane started up. ''You haven't seen me. I'm not here.''

''Aye, sir.'' Sligo watched Vane ascend, then shook his head. And headed back to his porridge.

Locating what he fervently prayed was Minnie's door, Vane rapped lightly on the panels. An instant later, Minnie bade him enter. He did—quickly—silently shutting the door behind him.

Propped against her pillows, a steaming cup of cocoa in her hands, Minnie stared at him. ''Great heavens! It's been years since I've seen you up at cockcrow.''

Vane advanced on the bed. ''I need some sage advice, and you're the only one who can help me.''

Minnie beamed. ''Well then—what's afoot?''

''Nothing.'' Incapable of sitting, Vane paced beside the bed. ''That's the problem. What should be afoot is a wedding.'' He glanced sharply at Minnie. ''Mine.''

"Ah-hah!" Triumph glowed in Minnie's eyes. "Sits the wind in that quarter, heh?"

"As you well know," Vane stated, his accents clipped, "the wind's been in that quarter since I first set eyes on your niece."

"Perfectly proper—as it should be. So what's the rub?"

"She won't have me."

Minnie blinked. Her smug expression faded. "*Won't have you*?"

Total bewilderment rang in her tone; Vane struggled not to gnash his teeth. "Precisely. For some ungodly reason, I'm not suitable."

Minnie said nothing; her expression said it all.

Vane grimaced. "It's not me, specifically, but men, or marriage in general, she's set her mind against." He sent a saber-edged glance Minnie's way. "You know what that means. She's inherited your stubborness with interest."

Minnie sniffed, and set aside her cocoa. "A very clear-headed girl, Patience. But if she harbors reservations about marriage, I would have thought *you*, of all men, would have been up to the challenge of changing her mind."

"Don't think I haven't tried." Exasperation rang in Vane's words.

"You must have made a muddle of it. When did you offer for her? In the conservatory last night?"

Vane tried not to remember the conservatory last night. Vivid memories had kept him awake until dawn. "I first offered for her—twice—at Bellamy Hall. And I've repeated the offer several times since." He swung on his heel and stalked down the rug. "With increasing persuasiveness."

"Hmm." Minnie frowned. "This sounds serious."

"I think—" Vane halted; hands on hips, he looked up at the ceiling. "No—I *know* she initially confused me with her father. Expected me to behave as he had." He swung about and stalked back. "She first expected me to have no interest in marriage, and when I proved to think otherwise, she assumed I had no real interest in family. She thought I was offering for purely superficial reasons—because she might suit, in effect."

"A Cynster not caring about *family*?" Minnie humphed. "Now she's met so many of you, she can't still be blind."

"No, she can't. Which is precisely my point." Vane stopped beside the bed. "Even after the family's attitudes were paraded before her, she *still* wouldn't change her mind. Which means there's something more—something deeper. I felt there was from the first. Some fundamental reason she'd set her mind against marriage." He met Minnie's eyes. "And I think it derives from her parents' marriage, which is why I'm here, asking you."

Minnie held his gaze, then her expression grew distant. Slowly, she nodded. "You could be right." She refocused on Vane. "You want to know about Constance and Reggie?"

Vane nodded. Minnie sighed. "It was not a happy story."

"Meaning?"

"Constance loved Reggie. By that, I do *not* mean the usual affection found in many marriages, nor yet some warmer degree of affection. I mean love—selfless, complete and unswerving. For Constance, the world revolved about Reggie. Oh, she loved her children, but they were Reggie's and so within her purlieu. To give Reggie his due, he tried to cope, but, of course, from his point of view, the discovery that his wife loved him to distraction was more an embarrassment than a joy." Minnie snorted. "He was a true gentleman of his time. He hadn't married for any notion as outrageous as love. It was considered a good match on all sides—not his fault, really, that matters developed in such an unlooked-for direction."

Minnie shook her head. "He tried to let Constance down lightly, but her feelings were cast in stone, never to be rewritten. In the end, Reggie did the gentlemanly thing and kept away. He lost all touch with his children. He couldn't visit them without seeing Constance, which led to situations he couldn't countenance."

His frown deepening, Vane resumed his pacing. "What, for want of a better word, *lesson*, would Patience have drawn from that?"

Minnie watched him pace, then her gaze sharpened.

"You say it's this deep reason that's keeping her from accepting your offer—I presume you're therefore *certain* she would otherwise agree to your suit?"

Vane shot her a glance. "*Perfectly* certain."

"Humph!" Minnie narrowed her eyes at his back. "If that's the case," she declared, her tone tending censorious, "then, as far as I can see, the matter's perfectly obvious."

"*Obvious*?" Vane bit the word off as he rounded on the bed. "Would you care to share your insight with me?"

"Well"—Minnie gestured—"it stands to reason. If Patience is willing to accept you at *that* level, then the odds are that she's in love with you."

Vane didn't blink. "So?"

"So she watched her mother endure a life of misery through marrying a man she loved but who didn't love her, a man who cared nothing for her love."

Vane frowned and looked down. He continued to pace.

Eyes widening, Minnie raised her brows. "If you want to change Patience's mind, you'll have to convince her her love is safe with you—that you value it, rather than see it as a millstone 'round your neck." She caught Vane's eye. "You'll have to convince her to trust you with her love."

Vane scowled. "There's no reason she can't trust me with her love. I wouldn't behave like her father."

"I know that and you know that. But how does Patience know that?"

Vane's scowl turned black. He paced more aggressively.

After a moment, Minnie shrugged and folded her hands. "Funny thing, trust. People with reasons not to trust can be very defensive. The best way to encourage them to give their trust is if the same trust—the *complementary* trust— is freely given to them."

Vane shot her a far from complimentary glance; Minnie raised her brows back. "If you trust her, then she'll trust you. That's what it comes down to."

Vane glowered—mutinously.

Minnie nodded. Decisively. "You'll have to trust her as you want her to trust you, if you're going to win her to wife." She eyed him measuringly. "Think you're up to it?"

*   *   *

He honestly didn't know.

While he struggled with the answer to Minnie's question, Vane hadn't forgotten his other obligations. Half an hour after leaving Minnie, he was shown into the snug parlor of the house in Ryder Street shared by his uncle Martin's sons. Gabriel, so Vane had been informed, was still abed. Lucifer, seated at the table, engaged in devouring a plate of roast beef, looked up as he entered.

"Well!" Lucifer looked impressed. He glanced at the mantelpiece clock. "To what do we owe this unlooked-for—nothing less than startling—visit?" He waggled his brows. "News of an impending fixture?"

"Contain your transports." With an acid glance, Vane dropped into a chair and reached for the coffeepot. "The answer to your question is Minnie's pearls."

Like shedding a skin, Lucifer dropped his inanity. "Minnie's pearls?" His gaze grew distant. "Double strand, thirty inches if not more, exceptionally well-matched." His frown deepened. "Drop earrings, too, weren't there?"

"There were." Vane met his arrested gaze. "They're all gone."

Lucifer blinked. "Gone—as in stolen?"

"So we believe."

"When? And how?"

Briefly, Vane explained. Lucifer listened intently. Each member of the Bar Cynster had some special area of interest; Lucifer's specialty was gems and jewelry. "I came to ask," Vane concluded, "if you could sound out the cognescenti. If the pearls have slipped through our net and been passed on, I assume they'll pass through London?"

Lucifer nodded. "I'd say so. Any fence worth his salt would try to interest the denizens of Hatton Garden."

"All of whom you know."

Lucifer smiled; the gesture was not humorous. "As you say. Leave it with me. I'll report back as soon as I hear anything to the point."

Vane drained his coffee mug, then pushed back his chair. "Let me know the instant you hear."

*   *   *

An hour later, Vane was back in Aldford Street. Collecting a still sleepy Patience, he installed her in his curricle and made straight for the park.

"Any developments?" he asked as he headed his greys down one of the quieter avenues.

Yawning, Patience shook her head. "The only change, if change it be, is that Alice has turned even more prudishly odd." She glanced at Vane. "Alice declined Honoria's invitation. When Minnie asked why, Alice glared, and declared you were all devils."

Vane's lips twitched. "Strange to tell, she isn't the first to have labeled us that."

Patience grinned. "But to answer your *next* question, I spoke with Sligo—despite being left all alone, Alice did nothing more exciting than repair early to her chamber, where she remained for the whole evening."

"Praying for deliverance from devils, no doubt. Did Whitticombe attend the ball?"

"Indeed, yes. Whitticombe's not affected by any puritanical streak. While not jovial, he was at least willing to be entertained. According to Gerrard, Whitticombe spent most of his time chatting with various senior Cynsters. Gerrard thought he was sounding out possible patrons, although for what project remained unclear. Of course, Gerrard's not the most unbiased observer, not when it comes to Whitticombe."

"I wouldn't sell young Gerrard short. His artist's eye is remarkably keen." Vane slanted a glance at Patience. "And he still has the ears of a child."

Patience grinned. "He does love to listen." Then she sobered. "Unfortunately, he heard nothing to the point." She caught Vane's eye. "Minnie's starting to fret again."

"I've set Lucifer on the trail of the pearls. If they've made their way to London's jewelers, he'll hear of it."

"He will?"

Vane explained. Patience frowned. "I really don't understand how they can have so thoroughly disappeared."

"Along with everything else. Just consider—" Vane checked, then wheeled his team for the turn. "If there's only one thief, and, given none of the other stolen items have been found either, that seems a reasonable bet, then all the items are probably hidden in one place. But where?''

''Where indeed? We've hunted all over, yet they must be somewhere.'' Patience glanced at Vane. ''Is there anything more I can do?''

The question hung in the air between them; Vane kept his gaze on his horses until he could keep the words ''*Agree to marry me*'' from his lips. Now was not the time—pressing her was the wrong tack to take. He knew it, but swallowing the words took real effort.

''Check Minnie's inmates one more time.'' At a spanking pace, he set the curricle for the park gates. ''Don't look for anything specific, anything suspicious. Don't prejudge what you see—just study each one.'' He breathed deeply, and flicked Patience a hard glance. ''You're the one closest and yet most detached—look again, and tell me what you see. I'll call for you tomorrow.''

Patience nodded. ''Same time?''

Curtly, Vane acquiesced. And wondered how much longer he could refrain from doing something—saying something—rash.

''Miss Patience!''

Hurrying along the gallery on her way to join Vane, impatiently waiting downstairs, Patience paused, and waited for Mrs. Henderson, deserting her post supervising the maids down one corridor, to join her.

With a conspiratorial look, Mrs. Henderson came close and lowered her voice. ''If you'd be so good, miss, as to tell Mr. Cynster that the sand's back.''

''Sand?''

One hand to her ample bosom, Mrs. Henderson nodded. ''He'll know. Same as before, just a trickle here and there about that heathenish elephant. I can see it sparkling between the floorboards. Not that it comes from the gaudy beast—I took a cloth to it myself, but it was perfectly clean. Other than that, even with these London maids—and Sligo's hired ones with the sharpest eyes in Christendom—we've not spotted anything awry.''

Patience would have requested an explanation, if the expression on Vane's face when he'd called and found her in the drawing room, rather than ready, waiting for their drive, had not been indelibly imprinted on her mind.

He was impatient, champing at some invisible bit.

She smiled at Mrs. Henderson. ''I'll tell him.''

With that, she whirled, and, clutching her muff, hurried down the stairs.

''Sand?'' Her gaze fixed on Vane's face, Patience waited for clarification. They were in the park, taking their usual route far from the fashionable throng. She'd delivered Mrs. Henderson's message; it had been received with a frown.

''Where the devil is she getting it from?''

''Who?''

''Alice Colby.'' Grim-faced, Vane told her of the earlier report of sand in Alice's room. He shook his head. ''Heaven only knows what it means.'' He glanced at Patience. ''Did you check out the others?''

Patience nodded. ''There was nothing remotely odd about any of them, or their activities. The only thing I learned that I didn't know before was that Whitticombe brought books up from the Hall. I imagined, when he took such immediate possession of the library, that he'd found some tomes there and had settled to a new interest.''

''And he hasn't?''

''Far from it. He lugged at least six huge volumes along as luggage; no wonder their coach was straggling behind.''

Vane frowned. ''What's he studying at the moment— still Coldchurch Abbey?''

''Yes. He goes for a constitutional every afternoon—I slipped into the library and checked. All six books focus on the Dissolution—either just before or just after. The only exception was a ledger, dated nearly a century before.''

''Hmm.''

When Vane said nothing more, Patience jogged his elbow. ''Hmm what?''

He flicked her a glance, then looked back at his leader. ''Just that Whitticombe seems obsessed with the abbey. One would have thought he'd know everything there was

to know of it by now—at least enough to write his thesis.''
After a moment, he asked, ''Nothing suspicious to report
about any of the others?''

Patience shook her head. ''Did Lucifer learn anything?''

''In a way, yes.'' Vane threw her a frustrated glance.
''The pearls have *not* been cleared through London. In fact,
Lucifer's sources, which are second to none, are very sure
the pearls have not, in their idiom, 'become available.' ''

''Available?''

''Meaning that whoever stole them still has them. No
one's attempted to sell them.''

Patience grimaced. ''We seem to meet blank walls at
every turn.'' After a moment, she added, ''I calculated how
big a space would be needed to store everything that's been
stolen.'' She caught Vane's eye. ''Edith Swithin's tatting
bag, emptied of everything else, would barely hold it all.''

Vane's frown turned grim. ''It's all *got* to be somewhere.
I had Sligo search everyone's room again, but he turned up
empty-handed.''

''But it *is* somewhere.''

''Indeed. But where?''

Vane was back in Aldford Street at one o'clock the next
morning, assisting a weak-kneed Edmond up the front
steps. Gerrard was steering Henry, chortling at his own lo-
quaciousness. Edgar, a wide, distinctly silly grin on his
face, brought up the rear.

The General, thank heavens, had stayed home.

Sligo opened the door to them, and instantly took charge.
Nevertheless, it took another half hour and the concerted
efforts of the sober members of the group, to install Edmond, Henry, and Edgar in their respective beds.

Heaving a sigh of relief, Gerrard slumped against the
corridor wall. ''If we don't find the pearls soon, and get
this lot back to the Hall, they'll run amok—and run us into
the ground.''

The comment accurately reflected Vane's thoughts. He
grunted and resettled his coat.

Gerrard yawned, and nodded sleepily. ''I'm off to bed.
I'll see you tomorrow.''

Vane nodded. "Good night."

Gerrard headed down the corridor. His expression sober, Vane crossed the gallery to the stairs. At their head, he paused, looking down into the darkened front hall. About him, the house lay slumberous, the cloak of night, temporarily disturbed, settling back, a muffling shroud.

Vane felt the night drag at him, draining his strength. He was tired.

Tired of getting nowhere. Frustrated at every turn.

Tired of not winning, not succeeding.

Too tired to fight the compulsion that drove him. The compulsion to seek succor, support, surcease from his endeavors, in his love's arms.

He drew in a deep breath and felt his chest swell. He kept his gaze locked on the stairs, denying the impulse to look right, down the corridor that led to Patience's room.

It was time to go home, time to walk down the stairs, out through the front door, stroll the few blocks to his own house in Curzon Street, let himself into the silence of an empty house, walk up the elegant stairs and into the master bedroom. To sleep alone in his bed, between silken sheets, cold, unwarmed, unwelcoming.

A whisper of sound, and Sligo materialized beside him. Vane glanced sideways. "I'll let myself out."

If Sligo was surprised, he didn't show it. With a nod, he descended the stairs. Vane waited, watched as Sligo moved through the hall, checking the front door. He heard the bolt slide home, then the bobbing candle crossed the hall and disappeared through the green-baize door.

Leaving him in the silent darkness.

Still as a statue, Vane stood at the top of the stairs. In the present circumstances, inviting himself into Patience's bed was unacceptable, even reprehensible.

It was also inevitable.

His eyes fully adjusted to the dark, he turned right. Silently, he walked down the corridor, to the room at its end. Facing the door, he raised his hand—and hesitated. Then the planes of his face shifted, and set.

He knocked. Softly.

A silent minute passed, then he heard the soft patter of

bare feet on the boards. A heartbeat later, the door opened.

Flushed with sleep, her hair a tousled crown, Patience blinked at him. Her long white gown clung to her figure, outlined by the glow from the hearth. Lips parted, her breasts rising and falling, she radiated warmth and the promise of paradise.

Her eyes found his; for a long minute, she simply looked, then she stepped back and gestured him in.

Vane crossed the threshold and knew it to be his Rubicon. Patience shut the door behind him, then turned—into his arms.

He drew her close and kissed her; he needed no words for what he wanted to say. She opened to him instantly, offering all he wanted, all he needed. She sank against him, all soft womanly curves enticing, encouraging.

Vane caught his breath, caught the reins of his demons, and knew, this time, he wouldn't hold them for long. She set his blood afire too easily; she was the very essence of need to him.

The sole and dominant object of his desire.

Lifting his lids, he glanced at her bed. Reassuringly large, it was shrouded in shadow. The only light in the room came from the embers glowing in the hearth.

He wanted her in his bed, but tonight, he'd make do with hers. He also wanted to see her, to let his eyes, all his senses feast. His demons needed feeding. He also had to find a way to tell her the truth, to tell her what was in his heart. To utter the words he knew he had to say.

Minnie, damn her ancient shrewdness, had pointed unerringly to the truth. And, as much as one part of him wished to, he was powerless to duck, powerless to escape.

He had to do it.

Lifting his head, he drew in a breath so huge, his chest strained against his coat. "Come to the fire."

Sliding one arm around her, registering the glide of fine lawn over bare skin, he guided her toward the hearth. Pressing close, her head in the hollow of his shoulder, her hip against his, she acquiesced readily.

As one, they stopped before the hearth. With a naturalness he found enthralling, she turned into his arms. Sliding her hands over his shoulders, she lifted her face, her lips. He was kissing her before he thought of it.

With an inward sigh, Vane caught hold of his impulses, locked a mental fist about them, then, easing his arms from her, he closed his hands about her waist. And tried not to register the warmth beneath his palms, the softness under his fingers.

He lifted his head, breaking their kiss. "Patience—"

"Sssh." She stretched up on her toes and set her lips to his. Hers clung, softly teased; his firmed. Instinctively, he took charge again, effortlessly sliding into the next kiss.

Inwardly, Vane cursed. His reins were steadily fraying. His demons were grinning. In devilish anticipation. He tried again, this time whispering the words against her lips. "I need to t—"

She silenced him again, just as effectively.

Even more effectively, she reached for him, slim fingers closing possessively about his already rigid length.

Vane caught his breath—and gave up. There was no point battling on—he'd forgotten what it was he had to say. He slid his hands down and around; cupping her bottom, he drew her hips hard against his thighs. Her lips parted, her tongue flicked temptingly; he accepted her invitation and plundered. Ravenously.

Patience sighed with satisfaction and sank into his hard embrace. She wasn't interested in words. She was prepared to listen to pants, moans, even groans—but no words.

She didn't need to hear him explain why he was here; she didn't need to hear any excuses for why he needed her—his reasons had been there, shining silver in his eyes, when he'd stood in the dark on her threshold, his gaze locked, so hungrily, on her. The strength of that silvery force was etched in the driven planes of his face, there for her to see. She didn't want to hear him explain—and risk tarnishing the silver with mere words. Words could never do it justice—they'd only detract from the glory.

The glory of being needed. Needed like that. It had never happened to her before; it would likely never happen again.

Only with him. His was a need she could fill; she knew, to her bones, she was made for the task. The unalloyed pleasure she received from giving to him—giving herself to him and assuaging his need—was beyond all words, beyond all earthly measures.

This was what it meant to be a woman. A wife. A lover. This, of all things, was what her soul craved.

She wanted no words to get in her way.

Patience opened her singing heart and welcomed him in. She kissed him as ravenously as he kissed her, hands greedily searching through his clothes.

With a hissed curse, he drew back. "Wait."

Dragging the long pin from his cravat, he laid it on the mantelpiece; swiftly, he unknotted and unwound the long folds. Patience smiled and reached for him; his expression granite hard, he stepped aside and around—linen folds blocked her sight.

"What . . . ?" Patience raised her hands to her face.

"Trust me." Now behind her, Vane brushed her hands aside and deftly wound the linen twice about her head, then knotted it tight at the back. Then, closing his hands about her shoulders, he bent his head and trailed his lips, feather-light, up the curve of her throat. "It'll be better this way."

Better for him—he might retain some degree of control. He felt the responsiblity of being her love keenly; taking without giving was not in his nature. He needed to tell her what was in his heart. If he couldn't manage the words, at least he could demonstrate his feelings. For now, with desire rampant, pounding through his veins, that was the best he could do.

He knew very well what being "blind" would do to her. Without sight, her remaining senses would heighten—her sexual sensitivity, physical and emotional, would reach new peaks.

Slowly, he turned her to face him, and lifted his hands from her.

Senses flickering wildly, Patience waited. Her breathing was shallow, tight with anticipation; her skin prickled. Hands lax at her sides, she listened to her heartbeat, listened to desire thrum in her veins.

The first tug was so gentle she wasn't sure it was real, then another button on her nightgown slid free. Her senses told her Vane was near, close, but precisely where she couldn't tell. Tentatively, she reached out—

"No. Just stand still."

Obedient to his deep voice, to its compelling tone, she let her arms fall.

Her gown was buttoned down the front, all the way to the floor. Only the waft of air on her skin and the slightest of tugs told her when the last button fell free. Before she could imagine what might come next, quick tugs at her wrists had the lacings undone.

Blind, helpless, she shivered.

And felt her gown part and lift away, then it was sliding down her arms, down her back, slithering free of her hands to fall to the floor behind her.

She sucked in a tight breath—and felt Vane's gaze upon her. He stood before her; his gaze roved—her nipples puckered; heat spread beneath her skin. A warm flush followed his gaze, over her breasts, her belly, her thighs. She felt herself soften, felt anticipation surge.

He shifted—to the side. Tilting her head slightly, she strained to track his movements. Then he stepped closer. He stood to her left, bare inches away; she could sense him with every pore of her skin.

A hard fingertip slid beneath her chin and tipped her face up. Her lips throbbed; he covered them with his.

The kiss was long and deep, ardent, brutally candid. He surged deep and claimed her softness, then tasted her, languidly but thoroughly, a demonstration of what was to come. Then he drew back—and the fingertip slid away.

Naked, unable to see, with nothing beyond the soft glow from the fire and the heat of desire to warm her, Patience simmered. And waited.

One fingertip touched her right shoulder, then lazily meandered down, over the swell of her breast to circle her nipple. At the last, it flicked the achingly tight bud, then disappeared.

His second caress mirrored the first, teasing her left nipple, sending a long quivering shiver through her. She sucked in a fractured breath.

He leaned closer, reaching behind her to trace the long

muscles framing her spine, one, then the other, stopping where they trailed into the hollow below her waist.

Again his touch was withdrawn; again Patience waited. Then his palm, hard, hot, slightly rough on her smooth skin, settled low on her back, in the curve below her waist, then boldly traced down. And around. Proprietorially claiming the full curves, knowingly, appreciatively assessing. Patience felt desire flare, hot and urgent inside her, felt its dew dampen her skin.

She gasped softly; the sound echoed in the stillness. Vane bent his head; she sensed it and lifted her lips. They met his in a kiss so full of aching wanting she swayed. She lifted a hand to grasp his shoulder—

"No. Stand still." He breathed the words against her lips, then kissed her again. Then his lips trailed to her temple. "Don't move. Just feel. Don't do anything. Just let me love you."

Patience shivered—and mutely acquiesced.

The hand fondling her bottom remained, distractingly intimate. It dropped to briefly trace the backs of her thighs, then, long fingers trailing up the line between, returned to caressing her tensed curves.

Then a rogue fingertip found the hollow at the base of her throat. Involuntarily, Patience straightened. The finger slowly tracked down, sliding smoothly over her skin. It passed between her swollen breasts, continued down her sensitive midriff, over the line of her waist, to her navel. There, it circled, slowly, then trailed diagonally, to one hip, then down the midline of her thigh, stopping and disappearing just above her knee.

The fingertip returned to her throat. The long journey was followed again, this time diverting to her other hip and ending above her other knee.

Patience was not deceived. When the fingertip again came to rest below her throat, she dragged in a desperate breath. And held it.

The fingertip slid down, with the same lazy, langorous touch. Again, it circled her navel, then, deliberately, it slid into the small hollow. And probed. Gently. Evocatively. Repetitively.

Patience's breath escaped in a rush. The shiver that racked her was more like a shudder; breathing became even more difficult. She licked her parched lips, and the finger eased back.

And drifted lower.

She tensed.

The finger continued its leisurely descent, over the gentle swell of her belly, on, into the soft curls at its base.

She would have moved, but the hand behind her gripped and held her steady. With unhurried deliberation, the finger parted her curls, then parted her, and slid further.

Into the hot slickness between her thighs.

Every nerve in her body clenched tight; every square inch of her skin glowed hot. Every last fragment of her awareness was centered on the touch of that lazily questing fingertip.

It swirled, and she gasped; she thought her knees would buckle. For all she knew, they did, but the hand at her bottom supported her. Held her there, so she could feel every movement of that bold finger. It swirled again, and again, until her bones melted.

Within her, fire raged; Vane certainly knew it. But he was in no hurry—his finger pressed deeper, reached farther, and circled her, much as it had circled her above.

Breath bated, Patience waited. Waited. Knowing the moment would come when he would probe, when his finger would slide deep into her empty heat. Her breathing was so shallow she could hear the soft hiss; her lips were dry, parched, yet throbbing. Again and again, he hesitated at her entrance, only to slide away, to caress her swollen flesh, slick and throbbing with her heartbeat.

Finally, the moment came. He circled her one last time, then paused, his finger centered on her entrance. Patience shuddered and let her head fall back.

And he speared her, so slowly she thought she'd lose her mind. She gasped, then cried out as he reached deep.

His answer was to close his lips about one aching nipple.

Patience heard her responsive cry as if from a distance. Raising her hands, she clutched—and found his shoulders.

Vane shifted so she was fully before him, so he could

lave first one breast, then the other, while he sank one, then two long fingers into her scalding heat. With his other hand, he gripped the firm mounds of her bottom, knowing he'd leave bruises. If he didn't, she'd be on the floor—and so would he. Which would result in even more bruises.

He'd already depleted his stock of control; it had run out when he'd touched the wet heat between her thighs. He'd reckoned correctly on blind nakedness arousing her deeply—he hadn't foreseen her blind nakedness so arousing him. But he was determined to lavish every attention on her—every ounce he was capable of giving.

Mentally gritting his teeth, mentally girding his loins—in cast iron—he hung on. And lavished more loving on her.

All he had to give, given as only he could.

Patience hadn't known her body could feel so much, so intensely. Fire seared her veins; awareness invested her skin. She was sensitive to each shifting current of air, each and every bold touch, every nuance of every caress.

Every knowing stroke of Vane's hard fingers drove pleasure into her and through her; every tug of his lips, every wet sweep of his tongue caught the pleasure and drove it to shattering heights.

The pleasure grew, welled, swept and beat through her, then flared and coalesced into a familiar inner sun. Eyes closed beneath her blindfold, she gasped and waited for the sunburst to break over her, then fade. Instead, it swelled brighter, wider—and engulfed her.

And she was part of the sun, part of the pleasure, felt it wash through her and about her, buoy her up and lift her. She drifted, afloat on a sea of sensual bliss, pleasured to her very toes.

The sea stretched on and on; waves lapped at her senses, fed them, sated them. But still left them hungry.

Dimly, she was aware of Vane's hands shifting, aware of losing his intimate touch. Then he lifted her, cradling her against his chest, and carried her. To her bed. Gently, with soothing kisses that eased her parched lips, he laid her on top of her sheets. Patience waited for the blindfold to disappear. It didn't. Instead, she felt the cool slide of her satin coverlet over her sensitized skin.

She listened—ears straining, she heard a soft thud—one boot hitting the floor. In the dark, she smiled. Sinking into the feathers beneath her, she relaxed. And waited.

She expected him to join her beneath the coverlet; instead, a few minutes later, the coverlet was whisked away. He came onto the bed, and stopped. It took her a moment to realize where he was.

On his knees, straddling her thighs.

Anticipation struck her like lightning; in an instant, her body heated anew. Tensed, tightened—quivering with expectation.

Above her, she heard a hoarse chuckle. His hands clamped about her hips. The next instant, she felt his lips.

On her navel.

From there, things only got more heated.

When, endless panting, gasping, shatteringly intimate minutes later, he finally joined with her, she was hoarse, too. Hoarse from her muted cries, from her desperate attempts to breathe. He'd driven her into a state of endless delight, her body awash with exquisite sensation, sensitive to every touch, every unerringly intimate caress.

Now he drove into her, and drove her still further, into the heart of the sun, into the realm of glory. Patience blindly urged him on, let her body speak for her, caress him and hold him and love him as he was loving her.

Wholeheartedly. Unreservedly. Unrestrainedly.

The truth broke on her in the instant their sun imploded and shattered into a million shards. Glory rained about her—about them. Locked together, she felt his ecstasy as deeply as she felt hers.

Together they rose, buoyed on the final rapturous wave; together they fell, into deeply sated release. Wrapped in each other's arms, they floated in the realm reserved for lovers, where no mind was allowed to go.

"Hmm-hmm." Patience burrowed deeper into her warm bed and ignored the hand shaking her shoulder. She was in heaven, a heaven she couldn't remember being in before, and she wasn't interested in cutting short her stay. Even for him—he who had brought her here. There was a time for everything, especially for talking, and this was definitely not it. A warm glow lapped about her. Gratefully, she sank into it.

Vane tried again. Fully dressed, he leaned over, and shook Patience as hard as he dared. "Patience."

A disgruntled noise that sounded like "glumph" was all he got out of her. Exasperated, Vane sat back, and stared at the golden brown curls showing above the coverlet, all he could see of his wife-to-be.

As soon as he'd woken, and realized he'd have to leave, he'd tried to wake her—to tell her, simply and clearly, what he'd failed to tell her earlier. Before her passions had run away with them.

Unfortunately, he'd come to her late, and had stretched the time out as far as he'd been able. The result was that, only two hours later, she was still deeply sunk in bliss and highly resistant to being roused.

Vane sighed. He knew from experience that insisting on rousing her would result in an atmosphere totally inimical to the declaration he wanted to make. Which meant waking her was useless—worse than useless.

He'd have to wait. Until . . .

Muttering a curse, he stood, and headed for the door. He had to leave now or he'd trip over the maids. He would call and see Patience later—he'd have to do what he'd sworn he never would. Never expected he ever would.

Lay his heart on a platter—and calmly hand it to a woman.

Whether he was up to it no longer mattered. Securing Patience as his wife was the only thing that did.

Chapter 20

Was she imagining it?

Seated at the breakfast table the next morning, Patience carefully buttered a slice of toast. About her, the household chattered and clattered. Since breakfast was served later, in keeping with town hours, all the household attended, even Minnie and Timms. Even Edith. Even Alice.

Patience glanced about—and ignored the conversations wafting up and down the board. She was too distracted by her inner musings to waste time on less-urgent affairs.

She picked up her knife and reached for the butter.

And started to spread butter. On butter. She focused on the toast—then, very precisely, laid the knife aside and picked up her teacup. And sipped.

Langorous lassitude dragged at her limbs. Sweetly salacious thoughts dragged at her mind. Pleasured exhaustion had her in its grip; it was difficult to concentrate, but, again and again, she drew her mind back to the unexpected revelation of the night before. It required supreme effort to focus on the undercurrents that had run beneath their lovemaking, rather than on the lovemaking itself, but she was certain she wasn't inventing, that the underlying intensity she'd sensed had been real. The intensity of Vane's need, the intensity he'd brought to the act of loving her.

Loving her.

He'd used the words in the physical sense. For herself, she thought first in terms of the emotion, with the act the physical outpouring. Until last night, she'd assumed Vane's meaning was strictly physical—after last night, she wasn't so sure.

Last night, the physical had reached new heights, intensified by some force too powerful to be confined within limbs and flesh. She'd felt it, tasted it, gloried in it—she'd come to know it in herself. Last night, she'd recognized it in him.

Drawing a slow breath, she stared at the cruet set.

She was certain of what she'd sensed but—and here was the rub—he was such an accomplished lover, could he conjure that, too, without it being real? Was what she'd sensed simply a facade created by his undoubted expertise?

Setting down her teacup, she straightened. It was tempting to imagine that she might, perhaps, have misjudged, and his "love" was deeper than she'd supposed. She distrusted that conclusion. It was too neat—too self-serving. One part of her mind was trying to talk the rest into it. Into entertaining the notion that he might love her in the same way she loved him.

As distractions went, that won the crown.

Lips tightening, she picked up her well-buttered toast and crunched. After arriving on her threshold unheralded, he'd taken himself off the same way—before she'd had time to wake up, let alone think. But if what she thought was even half-true, she wanted to know. Now.

She glanced at the clock; it would be hours before he called.

"I say, can you pass the butter?"

Setting aside her impatience, Patience handed Edmond the butter dish. Beside him, Angela smiled brightly. Idly scanning the faces opposite, Patience encountered Alice Colby's black-eyed stare. Intensely cold, black-eyed stare.

Alice kept staring. Patience wondered if her topknot was askew. She was about to turn to Gerrard to ask—

Alice's features contorted. "*Scandalous!*" Uttered in a voice hoarse with righteous fury, the exclamation cut across the conversations. All heads turned; all eyes, startled, fixed on Alice. Who clapped her knife down on the table. "I don't know *how* you can, miss! Sitting there like a lady, taking breakfast with decent folk." Face mottling, Alice pushed back her chair. "I, for one, do not intend to put up with it a moment longer."

"Alice?" From the bottom of the table, Minnie stared. "What is this nonsense?"

"Nonsense? *Hah*!" Alice nodded at Patience. "Your niece is a fallen woman—do you call that nonsense?"

Stunned silence gripped the table.

"Fallen woman?" Whitticombe leaned forward to follow Alice's gaze.

The others looked, too. Patience kept her gaze steady on Alice's; her face had frozen, luckily in a relaxed expression. She was leaning on her elbows, her hands, steady, gripping her teacup. Outwardly, she consciously exuded calm; inside, her wits whirled. How to respond? Coolly, she raised one brow, faintly incredulous.

"*Really*, Alice!" Minnie frowned disapprovingly. "The things you do imagine!"

"*Imagine*?" Alice sat bolt upright. "I didn't imagine a large gentleman in the corridor in the middle of the night!"

Gerrard shifted. "That was Vane." He glanced at Henry and Edmond, then looked at Minnie. "He came upstairs with us when we got in."

"Yes. Indeed." Distinctly pale, Edmond cleared his throat. "He . . . ah . . ." He glanced at Minnie.

Who nodded, and looked at Alice. "See, there's a perfectly logical explanation."

Alice glowered. "That doesn't explain why he walked down the corridor to your niece's room."

Timms sighed. Dramatically. "Alice, Minnie doesn't have to explain all she does to everyone. After the disappearance of her pearls, naturally, Vane has been keeping an eye on the house. When he returned to the house late, he simply did a last watchman's round."

"Naturally." Minnie nodded, chins in unison. "Just the sort of thing he would do." She glanced, challengingly, at Alice. "He's very considerate in such ways. As for these aspersions you're casting on both Patience's and Vane's characters, you should really be careful of making outrageous accusations without foundation."

Flags flew in Alice cheeks. "I *know* what I saw—"

"Alice! That's enough." Whitticombe rose; his gaze locked with his sister's. "You mustn't distress people with your fantasies."

There was an emphasis in his words Patience didn't understand. Alice gaped. Then her color surged. Hands clenched, she glared at her brother. "I am *not*—"

"Enough!" Leaving his seat, Whitticombe quickly rounded the table. "I'm sure everyone will excuse us. You're clearly overwrought."

He manhandled Alice, incoherent with rage, from her chair and locked an arm about her scrawny shoulders. With a strained smile for the rest of the company, he turned her and marched her, stiff-legged, from the room.

Slightly dazed, Patience watched them go. And wondered how she'd weathered potential calamity without uttering a single word.

The answer was obvious, but she didn't understand it.

Somewhat subdued, the rest of the household dispersed. All made a point of smiling at Patience, to show they hadn't believed Alice's slander.

Retreating to her room, Patience paced. Then she heard the tap of Minnie's cane in the corridor. An instant later, Minnie's door opened, then shut.

An instant after that, Patience tapped on the panels, then entered. Minnie was easing into an armchair by the windows. She beamed at Patience.

"Well! That was a bit of unexpected excitement."

Patience fought not to narrow her eyes. Indeed, she fought to retain a proper degree of calm in the face of Minnie's twinkling eyes. Timms's smug smile.

They knew. And *that* was even more scandalous, to her thinking, than the fact Vane had spent the night—a number of nights—in her bed.

Lips thinning, Patience swept to the windows, and fell to pacing alongside Minnie. "I need to explain—"

"No." Minnie held up a commanding hand. "Actually, you need to keep your lips shut and concentrate on not saying anything I don't wish to hear."

Patience stared at her; Minnie grinned.

"You don't understand—"

"On the contrary, I understand very well." Minnie's impish smile surfaced. "Better than you, I'll warrant."

"It's obvious," Timms chimed in. "But these things take time to sort themselves out."

They thought she and Vane would marry. Patience opened her mouth to set them right. Minnie caught her eye. Reading the stubborness behind Minnie's faded blue gaze, Patience snapped her lips shut. And muttered through them, "It's not that simple."

"Simple? Bah!" Minnie fluffed up her shawls. "You should be relieved. Simple and easy is never worthwhile."

Pacing again, Patience recalled similar words—after a moment, she placed them as Lucifer's—to Vane. Arms folded, pacing slowly, she wrestled with her thoughts, her feelings. She should, she supposed, feel some measure of guilt, of shame. She felt neither. She was twenty-six; she'd made a rational decision to take what life offered her— she'd embarked on an affair with an elegant gentleman with her eyes fully open. And she'd found happiness—perhaps not forever, but happiness nonetheless. Bright moments of glory infused with heady joy.

She felt no guilt, and not the slightest regret. Not even for Minnie would she deny the fulfillment she'd found in Vane's arms.

But honesty insisted she set the record straight—she couldn't leave Minnie imagining wedding bells on the breeze. Drawing a deep breath, she halted by Minnie's chair. "I haven't accepted Vane's proposal."

"Very wise." Timms bent over her stitching. "The last thing you want is a Cynster taking you for granted."

"What I'm *trying* to say—"

"Is that you're far too wise to accept without being convinced. Without gaining a few meaningful assurances." Minnie looked up at her. "My dear, you're going about this in precisely the right way. Cynsters never give ground easily—their version of the matter is that, once seized, things, even wives, become theirs. The fact that in the instance of a wife, they might need to negotiate a trifle won't at first enter their heads. And even when it does, they'll try to ignore the issue as far as you'll allow them. I'm really very proud of you, standing firm like this. Until you gain sufficient promises, sufficient concessions, you most certainly shouldn't agree.''

Patience stood, stock-still, for a full minute, staring into Minnie's face. Then she blinked. "You *do* understand.''

Minnie raised her brows. "Of course.''

Timms snorted. "Just make sure he gets it right.''

Minnie grinned. Reaching out, she squeezed Patience's hand. "It's up to you to judge what will finally tip the scales. However, I have a few sage words, if you'll accept advice from an old woman who knows both you and Vane better than either of you seem to realize?''

Patience blushed. She waited, suitably penitent.

Minnie's grin turned wry. "There are three things you should remember. One, Vane is not your father. Two, you are not your mother. And, three, don't imagine—not for a moment—that you won't be marrying Vane Cynster.''

Patience looked long into Minnie's wise eyes, then turned aside and sank onto the window seat.

Minnie, of course, was right. She'd hit all three proverbial nails soundly on the head.

She had from the first visited her father's character on Vane. Now, holding one up against the other, that was patently a false image, a superficial glamor. Vane was an "elegant gentleman'' in appearance only, not in character. Not in any of the ways that were important to her.

As for her not being her mother, that was unquestionably true. Her mother had possessed a quite different nature—if her mother had sighted her father going into a conservatory with a youthful beauty, she would have put on her most brittle smile and clung to the pretense of not knowing. Not for her such meekness.

She knew what would have transpired if the beauty Vane had retired with had not been so innocent—so related. It would not have been a pleasant scene. While her mother had accepted infidelity as her lot, she would accept no such thing.

If she married Vane . . . The thought drew her into a daydream—of ifs, buts, and possibilities. Of how they'd interact, adjust to each other, if she took the risk, grabbed fate by the throat, and accepted him. It was a full five minutes before her mind moved on and the implication of Minnie's third statement dawned.

Minnie had known Vane from childhood. She also understood her own dilemma, that she would insist on love as her talisman for the future. That she would not accept Vane without his love declared. And Minnie was sure, convinced beyond all possibility, that she and Vane would marry.

Patience blinked. Abruptly, she looked at Minnie and discovered her aunt waiting, watching, a deep smile in her old eyes.

"Oh." Lips lifting, her heart leaping, Patience could think of nothing more to say.

Minnie nodded. "Precisely."

The incident at breakfast cast a long shadow. When the household sat down to lunch, the conversation was subdued. Patience noted it, but, her heart light, paid it little heed. She was waiting, as patiently as she could, to see Vane. To look deep into his eyes, to search for what Minnie was so certain must be there, concealed behind his elegant gentleman's mask.

He hadn't appeared for their usual midmorning drive. As she settled her skirts, Patience wryly reflected that, even a few days ago, she would have interpreted his absence as evidence of waning desire. Now, buoyed by an inner confidence, she was convinced that only some urgent matter to do with Minnie's pearls would have kept him from her side. The inner glow that went with that confidence was very pleasant indeed.

Alice did not join the table. As if in apology for her morning's outburst, Whitticombe set himself to be more pleasant than usual. Edith Swithins, beside him, was the main beneficiary of his careful erudition. At the end of one particularly tedious explanation, she beamed.

"How fascinating." Her gaze alighted on Edgar, sitting opposite. "But dear Edgar has studied that period, too. As I recall, his conclusions were different?" Her tone made the words a question. Everyone at the table held their breath.

Except Edgar, who launched into his own perspective.

To everyone's amazement, even, Patience suspected, Edith's and Edgar's, Whitticombe listened. His attitude had about it the air of gritted teeth, but he heard Edgar out, then nodded curtly. "Quite possibly."

Patience caught Gerrard's eye and fought to suppress a giggle.

Edmond, still pale and limply disheveled, chased a pea around his plate. "Actually, I was wondering when we might be heading back to the Hall."

Patience stiffened. Beside her, Gerrard straightened. They both looked at Minnie.

So did Edmond. "I really should get on with my drama, and there's precious little inspiration, and a great deal of distraction, here in town."

Minnie smiled. "Bear with the foibles of an old lady, my dear. I've no immediate plans to return to the Hall. Besides, there's only a skeleton staff left—we gave the maids leave, and Cook has gone to visit her mother."

"Oh." Edmond blinked. "No cook. Ah." He subsided into silence.

Surreptitiously, Patience grimaced at Gerrard. He shook his head, then turned to speak to Henry.

Patience glanced—for the fiftieth time—at the clock.

The door opened; Masters entered, his expression stiff. Approaching Minnie's chair, he bent and spoke quietly. Minnie blanched. Her face grew instantly old.

From the end of the table, Patience looked her concern and her question. Minnie saw; sinking back in her chair, she gestured to Masters to speak.

He cleared his throat, gathering all attention. "Some . . . gentlemen from Bow Street have arrived. It seems a report was lodged. They've come with a warrant to search the house."

An instant of stunned silence ensued, then cacophony erupted. Exclamations of shock and surprise came from all sides. Henry and Edmond competed for prominence.

Patience stared helplessly up the table at Minnie. Timms

was patting Minnie's hand. The cacophony continued un-abated. Lips setting, Patience grasped a soup ladle and wielded it against a dish cover.

The clangs cut through the din—and silenced the din makers. Patience raked the offenders with an irate glance. "Who? Who notified Bow Street?"

"I did." Pushing back his chair, the General stood. "Had to be done, don't y'know."

"Why?" Timms asked. "If Minnie'd wanted those dreadful Runners in her house, she'd have requested it."

The General flushed a choleric red. "Seemed that was the problem. Women—ladies. Too softhearted for your own good." He slid a glance Gerrard's way. "Had to be done—no sense in ducking it any longer. Not with the pearls missing, too." Regimentally stiff, the General drew himself upright. "I took it upon myself to notify the authorities. Acting on information received, don't y'know. Plain as a pikestaff it's young Debbington at fault. Search his room, and it'll all come to light."

Premonition seized Patience; she shook it off as irrational. She opened her mouth to defend Gerrard—he kicked her ankle. Hard. Sucking in a breath, she turned—and met a very straight stare.

"Let be," Gerrard whispered. "There's nothing there—let them play out their hand. Vane warned me something like this might happen. He said best to shrug and grin cynically and see what transpires."

To Patience's utter amazement, he proceeded to do just that, managing to convey an impression of patent boredom.

"By all means—search all you like." He grinned cynically again.

Pushing back from the table, Patience bustled to Minnie's side. Minnie clasped her hand tightly, then nodded to Masters. "Show the gentlemen in."

There were three of them, subtly unsavory to a man. Standing at Minnie's shoulder, firmly clasping her hand, Patience watched as, sharp eyes darting about the room, the Runners edged in and formed up in a row. Sligo slipped through the door after them.

The tallest Runner, in the center, bobbed a bow at Minnie. "Ma'am. As I hope yer man told you, we've a-come to search the premises. Seems there's some valuable pearls gone missing and a villain about."

"Indeed." Minnie studied them, then nodded. "Very well. You have my permission to search the house."

"We'll start with the bedchambers, if you don't mind, ma'am."

"If you must. Masters will accompany you." Minnie nodded a dismissal. Sligo held the door open, and Masters ushered the men out.

"I think," Minnie said, "that we should all remain here until the search is concluded."

Gerrard slouched, relaxed, in his chair. The others shifted and looked uncomfortable.

Patience turned on Sligo.

"I know, I know." He held up a placating hand as he reached for the door. "I'll find him and get him here." He slipped out. The door closed softly behind him.

Patience sighed and turned back to Minnie.

Half an hour had passed, and Patience was certain the face of the ormolu clock on the mantel was indelibly imprinted on her mind, before the door opened again.

Everyone straightened. Breaths caught.

Vane strode in.

Patience knew an instant of giddy relief. His gaze touched her, then passed on to Minnie. He went straight to her, pulling up a vacant chair.

"Tell me."

Minnie did, her voice lowered so the others, now gathered in groups about the room, could not hear. Aside from Minnie with Timms beside her, and Patience hovering, only Gerrard remained at the table, alone at the other end. As Minnie whispered her news, Vane's face hardened. He exchanged a charged glance with Gerrard.

Glancing up, Vane met Patience's eyes, then he looked back at Minnie. "It's all right—a good sign, in fact." He, too, spoke softly; his words reached no further than Patience. "We know there's nothing in Gerrard's room. Sligo searched only yesterday. And Sligo's very thorough. But this means something, at long last, is afoot.''

Minnie's look was tremulous.

Somewhat grimly, Vane smiled. "Trust me." Minnie drew in a breath, then smiled, weakly. He squeezed her hands, then stood.

He turned to Patience. Something shifted in his face, in his eyes.

Patience lost her breath.

"I apologize for not arriving this morning, but something came up."

He took her hand, raised it to his lips, then changed his grip and grasped firmly; Patience felt warm strength flow into her, around her. "Anything helpful?" she asked.

Vane grimaced. "Another blank wall. Gabriel heard of our problem—he has some surprising contacts. While we learned nothing about where the pearls are, we did learn where they haven't been. To wit, pawned." Patience opened her eyes wide. Vane nodded. "It was another possibility, but we've exhausted that avenue, too. For my money, the pearls have never left Minnie's household."

Patience nodded. She opened her mouth—

The door swung open and the Runners returned.

One glance at their triumphant expression, and Patience's premonition returned with a vengeance. Her heart stopped, chilled, then sank. Vane's grip on her fingers tightened; she curled her fingers and clung.

Carrying a small sack, the senior Runner advanced portentously on Minnie—then spilled the contents of the sack onto the table before her. "Can you identify these baubles, ma'am?"

The baubles included Minnie's pearls. They also included everything else that had gone missing.

"My comb!" Gleefully, Angela swooped down and plucked the gaudy trinket free.

"Dear me—there's my pincushion." Edith Swithins poked it aside.

The items were nudged apart—Timms's bracelet, the pearls and their matching earrings, Patience's bud vase. Everything was there—except—

"Only one." Agatha Chadwick looked down at the garnet drop earring she'd separated from the pile.

Everyone looked again. The Runner upended the sack, then peered into it. He shook his head. "Nothing here. And there wasn't any goods left lying in the drawer."

"Which drawer?" Patience asked.

The Runner glanced over his shoulder—to where his comrades had taken up position one on either side of Gerrard's chair. "The drawer of the bureau in what I 'ave been told is Mister Gerrard Debbington's bedchamber. Which bedchamber he has on his own, not sharing with anyone else."

The Runner made that last sound like a crime in itself. Her heart constricted, sunk to her slippers, Patience looked at Gerrard. And she saw he was struggling not to laugh.

Patience stiffened; Vane pinched her fingers.

"You'll a-have to come along of us, young gent." The Runner advanced on Gerrard. "There's some serious questions the magistrate'll have for you. You come along nice and quiet, and we won't have no fuss."

"Oh, indeed. No fuss."

Patience heard the suppressed laughter in Gerrard's voice as he obligingly stood—how *could* he be so flippant? She wanted to shake him.

Vane shook her—her hand, at any rate. She glanced at him; he frowned at her and shook his head fractionally.

"Trust me."

The words reached her on a whisper, a mere thread of sound.

Patience looked into his eyes, calmly grey—then she looked at Gerrard, her young brother, light of her life. Drawing in a steadying breath, she glanced back at Vane and almost imperceptibly nodded. If Gerrard could trust Vane, and play out his alloted role, how much more reason had she to place her trust in him.

"What's the charge?" Vane asked, as the Runners formed up around Gerrard.

"No charge as yet," the senior Runner replied. "That's up to the magistrate, that is. We just lay the evidence before him and see what he thinks."

Vane nodded. Patience saw the glance he exchanged with Gerrard.

"Right then." Gerrard grinned. "Which round house is it to be? Or do we go directly to Bow Street?"

Bow Street it was. Patience had to bite her lip to stop herself from intervening, or begging to go, too. Sligo, she noticed, at a nod from Vane, slid out in the Runners' wake. All the rest of the household remained in the dining room until the front door clanged shut behind the Runners and their charge.

For one instant, the tension held, then a sigh ran through the room.

Patience stiffened. Vane turned to her.

"I said it again and again, but you would pay no heed, Miss Debbington." Righteously patronizing, Whitticombe shook his head. "And now it's come to this. Perhaps, in future, you will take more note of those with more years in their cup than yourself."

"Hear, hear," came from the General. "Said it from the first. Boys' tricks." He frowned at Patience.

Emboldened, Whitticombe gestured at Minnie. "And just think of the sore distress you and your brother have so heedlessly caused our dear hostess."

Color high, Minnie thumped her cane. "I'll thank you not to get your causes muddled. I'm certainly distressed, but my distress, as far as I can see, has been occasioned by whoever called the Runners down on our heads." She glared at Whitticombe, then at the General.

Whitticombe sighed. "My dear cousin, you really must see the light."

"Actually." Vane's drawl, laced with an undercurrent of sharpened steel, sliced through Whitticombe's sugary tones. "Minnie *needs* do nothing. A charge is not a conviction— indeed, a charge has yet to be made." Vane held Whitticombe's gaze. "I rather think that, in this case, time will reveal who is at fault, and who needs adjust their thinking. It seems somewhat premature to make sweeping conclusions just yet."

Whitticombe tried to look down his nose contemptuously; as Vane was a half head taller, he didn't succeed.

Which irritated him even more. Face setting, he eyed Vane, then, deliberately, let his gaze slide to Patience. "I rather think you're in no position to act as defender of the righteous, Cynster."

Vane tensed; Patience locked her hand about his.

"Oh?"

At Vane's quiet prompt, Whitticombe's lips curled. Patience inwardly groaned and shifted her hold to Vane's arm. Everyone else in the room stilled, holding their collective breaths.

"Indeed," Whitticombe smiled spitefully. "My sister had some very interesting—quite riveting—insights to offer this morning. On you and Miss Debbington."

"Is that so?"

Deaf to anything but his own voice, Whitticombe failed to hear the warning in Vane's lethally flat tone. "Bad blood," he pronounced. "Must run in the family. One a bald-faced thief, the other—"

Belatedly, Whitticombe focused on Vane's face—and froze.

Patience felt the aggression lance through Vane; under her hands, the muscles of his arm locked, rock-hard. She clung, literally, and hissed a furious, "No!"

For one instant, she thought he might shake free and then Whitticome might just be dead. But she'd set her sights on living in Kent, not in exile on the Continent.

"Colby, I suggest you retire—now." Vane's tone promised instant retribution should he decline.

Stiffly, not daring to take his gaze from Vane's face, Whitticombe nodded to Minnie. "I'll be in the library." He backed to the door, then paused. "The righteous will be rewarded."

"Indeed," Vane replied. "I'm counting on it."

With a contemptuous glance, Whitticombe left. The tension gripping the room drained. Edmond slumped into a chair. "Gad, if I could only capture that on stage."

The comment sent a ripple of uneasy laughter through the others. Timms waved to Patience. "After that excitement, Minnie should rest."

"Indeed." Patience helped Timms gather Minnie's myriad shawls.

"Shall I carry you?" Vane asked.

"No!" Minnie waved him away. "You've other things on your plate just now—more urgent things. Why are you still here?"

"There's time."

Despite Minnie's shooing, Vane insisted on helping her up the stairs and seeing her installed in her room. Only then did he consent to leave. Patience followed him into the corridor, pulling the door shut behind her.

Vane pulled her to him and kissed her—hard and quick.

"Don't worry," he said the instant he raised his head. "We had a plan in case something like this happened. I'll go and make sure all's fallen into place."

"Do." Patience met his eyes, searched them briefly, then nodded and stepped back. "We'll hold the line here."

Swiftly, Vane raised her hands and kissed them, then stepped back. "I'll keep Gerrard safe."

"I know." Patience clutched his hand. "Come to me later."

The invitation was deliberate; she acknowledged it with her eyes.

Vane's chest swelled; his face was a conqueror's mask, hard and unyielding. His eyes held hers, then he nodded. "Later."

With that, he left her.

Chapter 21

C ome to me later, she'd said.

Vane returned to Aldford Street just after ten o'clock.

The house was quiet when Masters let him in. His expression implacable, Vane handed Masters his cane, hat, and gloves. "I'll go up to Her Ladyship and Miss Debbington. You needn't wait up—I'll show myself out."

"As you wish, sir."

As he climbed the stairs, Vane recalled Chillingworth's words: *How the mighty have fallen.* The steely determination that had taken possession of him wound a notch tighter. He wasn't sure how deep the changes within him had gone, but as of this afternoon, he'd sworn off all attempts to hide his connection with Patience Debbington. The lady who would be his wife.

There was no doubt of that fact, no possibility of error, no room for maneuver—and absolutely none for negotiation. He was finished with excuses, with playing the game according to society's rules. Conquerors wrote their own rules. That was something Patience would have to come to terms with—he intended shortly to inform her of the fact.

But first, he'd set Minnie's heart at rest.

He found her propped on her pillows, eyes expectantly wide. Timms was present; Patience was not. Quickly, concisely, he explained and reassured. Then he left Timms to tuck Minnie, at ease once again, up for the night.

He knew they were grinning behind his back, but was

333

not about to acknowledge it. Shutting Minnie's door with a definite click, he turned and strode down the corridor.

With a token, peremptory tap, he opened Patience's door and walked in, then shut it behind him. Rising from the chair by the hearth, she blinked, then resettled the shawl she'd draped over her shoulders, and calmly waited.

Beneath the soft shawl, she was wearing a fine silk nightgown, cinched with a drawstring under her breasts. And nothing else.

The blaze in the hearth roared.

One hand on the doorknob, Vane drank in the sight, luscious curves and sleek limbs outlined by the flames. The embers inside him ignited; a rush of fiery lust seared his veins. He straightened and slowly stalked toward her.

"Gerrard's with Devil and Honoria at St. Ives House." The words fell from his lips slowly, as, starting at her nightgown's hem, he let his gaze rise, noting the fascinating way the silk clung to each curve, to her long, sleek thighs, rounded hips, the soft swell of her belly, how it cradled the warm globes of her breasts. Her nipples peaked as his gaze feasted.

She tightened her hold on her shawl. "Was that part of your plan?"

Halting before her, Vane lifted his gaze to her face. "Yes. I hadn't imagined Bow Street, but something along those lines was in the cards. Someone had, from the first, tried to cast Gerrard as the thief."

"What happened?" Patience's words were breathless; her lungs had seized. She held Vane's gaze and tried not to shiver. Not with fear, but anticipation. The stark planes of his face, the silvery flames in his eyes, all screamed of reined passion.

He studied her eyes, then raised one brow. "By the time I reached Bow Street, Devil had descended and whisked Gerrard away. I followed them to St. Ives House. According to Gerrard, he didn't even have time to look around Bow Street before Devil arrived, courtesy of Sligo. He must have run all the way to Grosvenor Square."

Her eyes locked on his, Patience licked her lips. "He's really been a big help over this business."

"Indeed. As he could swear that the stolen goods were not in Gerrard's room yesterday, and nor was the sack in which they were found, the magistrate was understandably diffident over laying any charge." Vane's lips lifted. "Particularly with Devil leaning on the charge desk."

Bracing one hand on the mantelpiece, he leaned closer. Decidedly giddy, Patience tilted her chin. "I suspect your cousin enjoys intimidating people."

Vane's lips quirked. His gaze lowered to her lips. "Let's just say Devil's rarely backward in exercising his authority, especially in support of one of the family."

"I . . . see." Her gaze fixed on his long lips, Patience decided to let his description of Gerrard as "family" pass unchallenged. The tension investing his large frame, so close beside her, was fascinating—and deliciously unnerving.

"The magistrate decided something odd was going on. The report hadn't come from Minnie, and, of course, there was the matter of Sligo, Devil's servant, masquerading as Minnie's hired help. He couldn't understand it, so he elected to make no finding at present. He released Gerrard into Devil's care, pending any further developments."

"And Gerrard?"

"I left him happily ensconced with Devil and Honoria. Honoria told me to tell you they were grateful for the excuse to stay home. While they keep up appearances, they only came to town to catch up with the family. They'll be returning to Somersham any day."

Patience licked her lips again; under his gaze, they'd started to throb. "Will that—them leaving town—create problems if Gerrard's still in Devil's care?"

"No." Vane lifted his gaze to her eyes. "I'll assume the charge."

Patience mouthed a silent "Oh."

"But tell me." Vane pushed away from the mantelpiece and straightened. "Has anything happened here?" He started to unbutton his coat.

"No." Patience managed to find enough breath for a sigh. "Alice hasn't been sighted since this morning." She glanced at Vane. "She saw you in the corridor last night."

Vane frowned, and shrugged out of his coat. "What the devil was she doing up at that hour?"

Patience shrugged, and watched him toss his coat on the chair. "Whatever, she didn't come down for dinner. Everyone else did, but all were understandably subdued."

"Even Henry?"

"Even Henry. Whitticombe preserved a censorious silence. The General spent the entire time grumbling, and snapping at anyone who loomed in his path. Edgar and Edith kept their heads down, together for the most part, whispering. About what I know not." Vane's fingers closed about the buttons of his waistcoat. Patience drew a tight breath. "Edmond's succumbed to his muse again. Angela is quietly happy because she got her comb back. Henry, however, was idling about because he couldn't find anyone with whom to play billiards."

Patience shifted, giving Vane space to strip off his waistcoat. "Oh—there was one point of interest—Mrs. Chadwick quietly asked Minnie and me if she could search Gerrard's bureau for her missing earring. Poor dear, it seemed the least we could do. I went with her—we searched high and low, and through all the other drawers, too. There was no sign of it anywhere."

She turned to Vane—just as he freed his cravat and drew the long strip from his neck. His gaze on her, he held it between his hands. "So," he murmured, his tone deep, "nothing of any moment happened here."

Her gaze transfixed by the long strip of linen, Patience tried to speak and couldn't—she shook her head.

"Good." The word was a feral purr. With a negligent flick, Vane sent the cravat to join his coat. "So there's nothing to distract you."

Patience dragged her gaze up to his face. "Distract me?"

"From the subject we need to discuss."

"You want to discuss something?" She hauled in a breath and tried to steady her giddy head.

Vane trapped her gaze. "You. Me." His face hardened. "Us."

With a supreme effort, Patience raised her brows. "What about 'us'?"

A muscle in his jaw flickered. From the corner of her eye, she saw his fist clench. "I," he declared, "have reached the end of my tether."

He stepped toward her; she took a sliding step back.

"I do not approve of any situation that leaves you a target for the likes of such as the Colbys—regardless of whether said situation arises from my actions or otherwise." His lips a thin line, he stepped forward; Patience instinctively edged back. "I cannot, and will not, condone any scenario whereby your reputation is in any way sullied—even by me with the best of intentions."

He continued to stalk her; she continued to retreat. Patience longed to whirl around and scurry out of his reach, but she didn't dare take her eyes from his. "What are you doing here then?"

She was trapped, mesmerized—she knew he'd soon pounce. As if to confirm that, his eyes narrowed, and he tugged his shirt from his waistband. Without taking his eyes from her, he started undoing the buttons, still advancing, still forcing her to retreat. Toward the bed.

"I'm here"—he bit the words off—"because I can't see any sense in being anywhere else. You're *mine*—henceforth, you sleep with me. As you're sleeping here at the moment, *ergo*, so do I. If my bed is not yet yours, then yours will have to be mine."

"You just said you didn't want my reputation sullied."

His shirt fell fully open. He continued to advance. Patience didn't know where to look. Where she most wanted to look.

"Precisely. So you'll have to marry me. Soon. Which is what we need to discuss." With that, he looked down, and unlaced his cuffs.

Poised to seize the moment to dash to safety, Patience froze. "I don't *have* to marry you."

He looked up, and stripped off his shirt. "Not in that sense, no. But for you, marriage to me is inevitable. All we need to determine—what we are *going* to determine—tonight—is what it's going to take to make you agree."

His shirt hit the floor—he stepped forward.

Belatedly, Patience scurried three steps back—and

fetched up against the bedpost. Before she could whisk around it, Vane was there, reaching around her, hands locking about the post behind her. Trapping her within the circle of his arms, facing him, and his bare chest.

Dragging in a desperate breath, Patience locked her eyes on his. "I told you—I will *not* simply marry you."

"I think I can guarantee there'll be nothing simple about our marriage."

Patience opened her lips on an acid retort—he sealed them, with a kiss so potent by the time he raised his head, she was clinging for dear life to the bedpost.

"Just listen." He said the words against her lips, as if they were forced from him.

Patience stilled. Her heart thumping wildly, she waited. He didn't straighten, or draw away. Lids lowered, her gaze fixed on his lips, she watched the words form as he spoke.

"I'm renowned within the *ton* as being cool under fire— around you, I'm never cool. I'm heated—I seethe—I burn with desire. If I'm in the same room, all I can think about is heat—your heat—and how you'll feel around me."

Patience felt the heat rise, a real force between them.

"I've gained the reputation of being the soul of discretion—now look at me. I've seduced my godmother's niece—and been seduced by her. I share her bed openly, even under my godmother's roof." His lips twisted wryly. "So much for discretion."

He drew a deep breath; his chest brushed her breasts.

"And as for my vaunted, up-until-you *legendary* control—the instant I'm inside you that evaporates like water on hot steel."

What prompted her Patience never knew. His lips were so close—with her teeth, she nipped the lower. "I told you to let go—I won't break."

The tension, pouring off him in waves, eased, just a little. He sighed, and rested his forehead on hers. "It's not that." After a moment, he went on, "I don't like losing control— it's like losing myself—in you."

She felt him gather himself, felt the tension swell and coalesce about them.

"It's giving myself to you—so that I'm in your keeping."

The words, low and gravelly, rolled through her; closing her eyes, she drew in a shallow breath. "And you don't like doing that."

"I don't like it—but I crave it. I don't approve of it, yet I yearn for it." His words feathered her cheek, then his lips touched hers. "Do you understand? I haven't any choice."

Patience felt his chest swell as he drew a deep breath.

"I love you."

She shivered, eyes shut tight, and felt the world shift about her.

"Losing myself in you—giving my heart and soul into your keeping—is part of that."

His lips brushed hers in an inexpressibly tender caress.

"Trusting you is part of that. Telling you I love you is part of that."

His lips touched hers again; Patience didn't wait for more. She kissed him. Letting go of the post, she slid her hands up, framing his face, so she could let him know— let him feel—her response to all he'd said.

He felt it, sensed it—and reacted; his arms locked tight about her. She couldn't breathe, but she didn't care. All she cared about was the emotion that held them, that flowed so effortlessly between them.

Silver and gold, it wound about them, investing each touch with its magic. Silver and gold, it shimmered about them, and quivered in their fractured breaths. It was immediate compulsion and future promise, heavenly delight and earthly pleasure. It was here and now—and forever.

With a soft oath, Vane drew back and stripped off his trousers. Released, Patience lowered her arms and let her shawl fall, then tugged the tie of her nightgown free. A quick shift and a shrug sent the silk sliding to the floor.

Vane straightened—she stepped into his arms, setting her naked limbs to his.

He sucked in a breath, then let it out in a groan as she stretched sinuously against him. He wrapped her in his arms and bent his head to hers; their lips met, and desire ran free.

He lifted her and laid her on the sheets, and followed her down. She welcomed him to her, took him into her body with joyous abandon.

And this time, there was no holding back, no reticence, no control, no vestige of rational thought. Passion and desire bloomed, then ran riot. They were one—in mind, in thought, in deed. Pleasure for one was the other's delight. They gave themselves, again and again, and still found more to give.

And over and between ran the shimmering glory, stronger than steel and more precious than pearls.

When they crested the final wave, and clung to each other as the maelstrom took them, it intensified and filled them. Until all existence became that wondrous glow; as they drifted, deeply sated, into dreamless sleep, it settled over them.

A blessing—the most desired of benedictions.

What followed was entirely Myst's fault.

Vane woke, as he had once before, to discover the small cat once again curled on his chest, purring furiously. Sleepily sated, he scratched one grey ear while waiting for his senses to refocus. His limbs were heavy with deep satiation—a drugging glow still filled him. He glanced toward the window. The sky had started to lighten.

He and Patience needed to talk.

Vane lifted his hand from Myst's ear.

The cat promptly flexed her claws.

Vane hissed—and glared. "Your claws are more lethal than your mistress's."

"Hmm?" Heavy-eyed, Patience emerged from beneath the sheets.

Vane waved at Myst. "I was about to ask if you'd consider removing your resident predator."

Patience stared at him, then blinked, and looked down. "Oh. Myst." Fighting free of the tangled sheets, she leaned over and scooped Myst up. "Off, Myst. Come on." Wriggling, Patience slid fully across Vane—her hips slid over his—as Vane sucked in an agonized breath.

Patience grinned, and dropped Myst over the side of the

bed. "Off you go." She watched the cat stalk off, offended, then, entirely deliberately, wriggled back across Vane.

And stopped halfway.

"Hmm." Finding her lips level with one flat nipple, she stuck out her tongue and licked. The jolt that shook him made her smile. "Interesting."

She uttered the word as she wriggled some more, so her torso was more or less atop him, her legs sliding over his.

Vane frowned. "Patience . . ."

Warm flesh encased in smooth satin slithered over his hips, over the rigid length of his erection. Vane blinked, several times, and tried to recall what he'd been about to say.

"Hmm?"

Patience's tone suggested she had other things on her mind: She was busily trailing warm, openmouthed kisses down his increasingly tense torso.

Jaw setting, Vane gathered his resolve—and reached for her. "Patience, we need to—" A groan cut off his words— he was almost surprised to recognize it as his. Muscle after muscle tensed and locked. Lust roared through him—in response to her artless, inquisitive touch, to the husky chuckle she gave. Soft fingers trailed up his rigid length, then slid about him and tentatively closed. She traced and caressed, then explored further, squirming downward as she did— clearly delighted by his helpless reaction.

Rigid to his toes, Vane jerked as she circled his sensitive, swollen head. "*Good God, woman*! What . . . ?" His voice suspended as she reached further still, and closed her hand. Vane groaned, and closed his eyes. The inside of his lids burned with raging lust.

He dragged in a desperate breath, and reached down, fighting through the tangled sheets to try to capture her hand. She chuckled again and eluded him easily; he slumped back, breathing too fast. His limbs had turned heavy, weighted with lust, burning with desire.

"Don't you like it?" The teasing question, clearly rhetorical, floated up from under the sheets. Then she squirmed again. "Perhaps you'd like this better."

Vane did, but he wasn't about to say so. Gritting his

teeth, he suffered the hot, wet sweep of her tongue, the gentle caress of her lips. She didn't have the faintest idea what she was doing—thank God. What she was doing was bad enough. If expertise was added to the equation, he'd be dead.

He tried to remind himself that the experience was hardly new to him—the rationalization didn't work. He couldn't distance himself from Patience's touch, couldn't imagine she was some faceless lady with whom he was sharing a bed. No logic seemed strong enough to quench or control the fire she was igniting.

He heard himself gasp. He licked lips suddenly dry. "Where the devil did you get the idea . . . ?"

"I heard some maids talking."

Inwardly cursing all wanton maids, he summoned the last of his strength. She'd gone far enough. Jaw clenched so hard his teeth ached, he reached for her. Beneath the soft sheets, he found her head; he threaded his fingers through her hair, searching downward for her shoulders.

Beneath his hands, she shifted.

Hot wetness closed about him.

His fingers spasmed and clutched. The rest of his body reacted equally predictably. For one instant, Vane thought he'd die. Of heart failure. Then she released him. He groaned—and she took him into her mouth again. Eyes closed, he fell back on the pillows, and surrendered.

She had him at her mercy.

She knew it—she set about enjoying her newfound mastery. To the hilt. Extrapolating wantonly. Inventing with gay abandon.

Until, with a desperate groan, he was driven to expend his last ounce of strength and capture her, wrestle free, and find her waist and lift her. Over him. He lowered her, expertly nudging into the slick flesh between her thighs. Then he pulled her down, impaling her on the achingly urgent phallus she'd spent the last ten minutes inciting.

She gasped, then sank farther, her hands fastening tight about his forearms as she deliberately took him all. She rose on her knees immediately, pushing his hands from her, refusing to allow him to set the pace.

He acquiesced, filling his hands with her breasts instead, drawing the tight peaks to his mouth. She rode him with reckless abandon; he filled her and feasted, until, in a glorious, giddy rush, they fell over the edge of the world and, locked together, plunged into the selfless void.

They had no time to talk, no time to speak, no time to discuss anything at all. When, with the house waking about them, Vane, mildly irritated, left her, Patience was incapable of conscious thought.

Some four hours later, Patience sat at the breakfast table. Smiling. Glowingly. She'd seen the sight in her mirror, but hadn't been able to find any expression capable of disguising her joy.

She'd woken to find the tweeny quietly cleaning her grate, and Vane nowhere in sight. Which was undoubtedly just as well. The last sight she'd had of him would have driven the tweeny into hysterics. Lolling in her bed, which had looked like a whirlwind had struck it, she'd considered going and telling Minnie her news. But she'd decided against saying anything yet, not until she and Vane had discussed the details. From what she'd seen of the Cynsters, and what she knew of Minnie, once they made an announcement, *things* would simply happen.

So she'd lolled some more, replaying Vane's declaration, committing every word, every nuance, to memory. No doubt of the veracity, or the strength of his feelings, could ever assail her—not with memories like that. She had, indeed, started to wonder if her desire to hear that particular assurance stated, in words, might, in the end, be too much to ask, an unrealistic expectation from a man like him. Men like the Cynsters did not set their tongue to that four-letter word lightly. "Love" was not something they gave readily, and, as Minnie had warned her, even once given, they did not easily acknowledge it.

Vane had.

In simple words so laden with feeling she could not doubt, could not question. She'd wanted that, needed it, so he'd given it. No matter the cost.

Was it any wonder her heart was light, singing joyfully?

In contrast, the rest of the household remained subdued; Gerrard's empty place cast a pall over the conversation. Only Minnie and Timms, at the other end of the table, were unaffected; Patience beamed a happy smile up the board, and knew in her heart that Minnie understood.

But Minnie waggled her head at her and frowned. Recalling that she was supposed to be the anguished sister of a young sprig hauled off to face justice, Patience dutifully tried to mask her glow.

"Have you heard anything?" Henry's nod to Gerrard's empty chair clarified his question.

Patience hid her face behind her teacup. "I haven't heard of any charges."

"I fancy we'll hear by this afternoon." Whitticombe, his expression coldly severe, reached for the coffeepot. "I daresay the magistrate was not available yesterday. Theft, I fear, is a common enough crime."

Edgar shifted uneasily. Agatha Chadwick looked shocked. But no one said anything.

Henry cleared his throat, and looked at Edmond. "Where shall we go today, do you think?"

Edmond humphed. "Not really in the mood for more sights today. Think I'll dust off my script."

Henry nodded glumly.

Silence fell, then Whitticombe eased back his chair. He turned to Minnie. "By your leave, cousin, I believe Alice and I should return to Bellamy Hall." Patting his thin lips with his napkin, he laid it aside. "We are, as you know, somewhat rigid in our beliefs. Old-fashioned, some might call it. But neither my dear sister nor I can countenance close association with those we believe transgress acceptable moral codes." He paused long enough for his meaning to sink in, then smiled, unctuously patronizing, at Minnie. "Of course, we appreciate your position, even applaud your devotion, misguided though it sadly seems to be. However, Alice and I seek your permission to repair to the Hall, there to await your return."

He concluded with an obsequious nod.

Everyone looked at Minnie. There was, however, nothing to be read in her unusually closed expression. She studied

Whitticombe for a full minute, then solemnly nodded. "If that is what you wish, then certainly, you may return to the Hall. However, I warn you I do not have any immediate plans to return there myself."

Whitticombe raised his hand in a gracious gesture. "You need not concern yourself with us, cousin. Alice and I can entertain ourselves well enough." He glanced at Alice, all in black. At no time since she'd entered the room had she looked anywhere but at her plate. "With your permission," Whitticombe continued, "we'll leave immediately. The weather looks like turning, and we have no reason to dally." He glanced at Minnie, then looked up at Masters, standing behind her chair. "Our boxes could be sent on."

Minnie nodded. Tight-lipped, she glanced up at Masters, who bowed. "I'll arrange it, ma'am."

Bestowing a last unctuous, ingratiating smile on Minnie, Whitticombe rose. "Come, Alice. You'll need to pack."

Without a word, without a glance, Alice rose and preceded Whitticombe from the room.

The instant the door closed behind them, Patience looked at Minnie. Who waved her to silence. To some semblance of discretion.

Patience bit her lip, and munched her toast, and waited.

A few minutes later, Minnie heaved a sigh and pushed back her chair. "Ah, me. I'm going to rest for the morning. All these unexpected happenings." Shaking her head, she rose and looked down the table. "Patience?"

She didn't need to be summoned twice. Dropping her napkin on her plate, Patience hurried to assist Timms help Minnie from the room. They went straight to Minnie's bedchamber, summoning Sligo on the way.

He arrived as Minnie sank into her chair.

"Whitticombe's making a dash for the Hall." Minnie pointed her cane at Sligo. "Go fetch that godson of mine—fast!" She shot a glance at Patience. "I don't care if you have to drag him from his bed, just tell him our hare has finally bolted."

"Indeed, ma'am. Right away, ma'am." Sligo headed for the door. "Even in his nightshirt."

Minnie grinned grimly. "Right!" She thumped the floor

with her cane. "And not before time." She looked up at Patience. "If it does turn out to be that worm, Whitticombe, behind it all, I'll disown him utterly."

Patience gripped the hand Minnie held out to her. "Let's wait and see what Vane thinks."

There was one problem with that—Vane couldn't be found.

Sligo returned to Aldford Street an hour later, with the news Vane was not at any of his habitual haunts. Minnie sent Sligo back out with a flea in his ear and a dire warning not to return without Vane.

"Where could he be?" Minnie looked at Patience.

Mystified, Patience shook her head. "I'd assumed he'd gone home—to Curzon Street."

She frowned. He couldn't possibly be walking the streets with a creased, reused cravat. Not Vane Cynster.

"He gave you no hint as to any lead he might be following?" Timms asked.

Patience grimaced. "I was under the impression he'd run out of possiblities."

Minnie humphed. "So was I. So *where* is he?"

No one answered. And Sligo didn't return.

Not until late afternoon, by which time Minnie, Timms, and Patience had reached the end of their collective tether. Whitticombe and Alice had departed at noon in a hired carriage. Their boxes were piled in the front hall, awaiting the carter. Lunch had come and gone, the household marginally more relaxed. Edmond and Henry were playing billiards. The General and Edgar had taken their usual constitutional to Tattersalls. Edith was tatting with Mrs. Chadwick and Angela for company in the drawing room.

In Minnie's room, Patience and Timms took turns by the window; it was Patience who saw Vane's curricle bowl up and stop before the door. "He's here!"

"Well you can't run downstairs," Minnie admonished her. "Just contain your transports until he gets here. *I* want to hear where he's *been*."

Minutes later, Vane strolled in, smoothly elegant as ever.

His eyes went straight to Patience, then he bent and kissed Minnie's cheek.

"Where, by all that's holy, have you *been*?" she demanded.

Vane raised his brows. "Out. Sligo told me Whitticombe's left. What did you want to see me for?"

Minnie stared at him, then swiped at his leg with one hand. "To find out what comes *next*, of course!" She glared at him. "Don't try your high-handed Cynster ways with me."

Vane's brows rose higher. "I wouldn't dream of it. But there's no need for any panic. Whitticombe and Alice have gone—I'll follow, and see what they get up to. Simple."

"I'm coming, too," Minnie declared. "If Humphrey's nephew's a bad egg, I owe it to Humphrey to see the proof with my own eyes. After all, it's me who'll have to decide what to do."

"Of course, I'll go with Minnie," Timms added.

Patience caught Vane's eye. "If you think I'm staying behind, think again. Gerrard's my brother—if Whitticombe's the one who knocked him on the head . . ." She didn't finish her sentence—her expression said it all.

Vane sighed. "There's really no need—"

"Cynster! Have to show you—"

With a clatter of boots, the General, followed by Edgar, burst into the room. Seeing Minnie, the General flushed, and ducked his head. "Apologies, Minnie, and all that, but thought you'd all be interested. Best see this."

Crossing the room, he bent and awkwardly slid a small object from his large palm onto Minnie's lap.

"Great *heavens*!" Minnie picked the object up, and held it to the light. "Agatha's earring." She looked at the General. "The other one?"

"Must be," Edgar put in. He glanced at Vane. "We found it in the elephant sitting in the front hall."

"The *elephant*?" Vane looked from Edgar to the General.

"Indian contraption. Recognized it instantly. Seen ones like it in India, don't y'know." The General nodded. "Couldn't resist opening it—showed it to Edgar here. One of the tusks is the catch. Twist it, and the beast's back opens up. Indian wallahs used the things to store treasure.''

''It's full of sand,'' Edgar said. ''Fine, white stuff.''

''Used for weight,'' the General explained. ''The sand stabilizes the beast, then the treasure's settled in the sand. I grabbed up a handful to show Edgar—sharp eyes, he has—spotted the gleam of that trinket in the pile.''

''I'm afraid we made rather a mess unearthing it.'' Edgar looked at the earring in Minnie's fingers. ''But it is Agatha's, isn't it?''

''Isn't what?''

They all looked up; Mrs. Chadwick entered, followed by Angela, with Edith Swithins trailing vaguely behind. Agatha Chadwick grimaced apologetically at Minnie. ''We heard the commotion . . .''

''Just as well.'' Minnie held up the earring. ''This is yours, I believe.''

Agatha took it. The smile that broke across her face was all the answer anyone needed. ''Where was it?'' She looked at Minnie—who looked up at Vane.

Who shook his head in amazement. ''In Alice Colby's room, in the elephant she kept by her hearth.'' He glanced at Patience—

''There's sand all over the front hall!'' Mrs. Henderson swept in, a galleon in full sail; Henry, supported by Edmond and Masters, hobbled in in her wake. Mrs. Henderson gestured at him. ''Mister Chadwick slipped and nearly broke his head.'' She looked at Vane. ''It's from *inside* that evil elephant!''

''I say.'' Edmond had focused on the earring in Agatha Chadwick's hand. ''What's going on?''

The question drew a spate of garbled answers. Recognizing opportunity, Vane edged to the door.

''Stop right there!'' Minnie's order brought an abrupt end to the cacophony. She waved her cane at Vane. ''Don't you *dare* try to leave us behind.''

Patience swung about—and glared daggers at Vane.

''What's afoot?'' Edmond demanded.

Minnie folded her arms and snorted, then glared at Vane. Everyone turned and looked at Vane.

He sighed. "It's like this." His explanation—that who-ever attempted to return to the Hall without the rest of the household was odds on to be the Spectre, and said Spectre was almost certainly the villain who'd coshed Gerrard in the ruins—even stripped to the bare bones, still raised everyone's hackles.

"Colby! *Well*!" Henry straightened, and eased his full weight onto his wrenched ankle. "First, he coshes young Gerrard, then he makes out Gerrard's the thief, and *then* he gloats so . . . so . . . *superiorly*." He tugged his coat straight. "You may count me in—I certainly want to see Whitticombe get his just desserts."

"Blissful thought!" Edmond grinned. "I'll come, too."

"And me." The General glowered. "Colby must have known his sister was the thief—or perhaps it was him, and he used his sister's room as a store. Whatever, the bounder talked me into sending for the Runners—wouldn't have entered my head but for him. He should be strung up!"

Vane drew a deep breath. "There's really no need—"

"I'm coming, too." Agatha Chadwick lifted her head high. "Whoever was the thief, whoever has so grievously wronged Gerrard, I want to see justice done!"

"Indeed!" Edith Swithins nodded determinedly. "I even had my tatting bag searched, all because of this thief. I'll certainly want to hear his—or her—explanation."

It was at that point Vane gave up arguing. By the time he'd crossed the room to Minnie's side, the whole house-hold, bar only Masters and Mrs. Henderson, had resolved to follow Whitticombe and Alice back to the Hall.

Bending over Minnie, Vane spoke through his teeth. "I'm taking Patience—I'll pick Gerrard up on the way. As far as I'm concerned, the rest of you would do well to remain in London. If you want to hie across the counties with the weather closing in, you'll have to organize it your-selves. *However*!"—he let his exasperation show—"whatever you do, *for God's sake remember* to come up the back track, *not* the main drive, and *don't* come closer to the house than the second barn."

He glared at Minnie, who glared belligerently back. Then tipped her nose in the air. "We'll wait for you there."

Swallowing a curse, Vane grabbed Patience's hand and strode for the door. In the corridor, he glanced at Patience's gown. "You'll need your pelisse. There's snow on the way."

Patience nodded. "I'll meet you outside."

She hurried down the steps minutes later, rugged up against the deepening chill. Vane handed her into the curricle, then climbed up beside her. And sprang his horses for Grosvenor Square.

"Well, the drought's broken." Looking up as Vane walked through his library door, Devil grinned. "Who is it?"

"Colby." Vane nodded to Gerrard, perched on the arm of a chair beside Devil, who was sprawled on the rug before the hearth.

Following Vane in, Patience noted that last with surprise, until, moving closer, she saw the small being rolling on the soft rug, fists and feet waving madly, protected from any chance of a flying cinder by Devil's large body.

Following the direction of her gaze, Devil grinned. "Allow me to present Sebastian, Marquess of Earith." He looked down. "My heir."

The last words were infused with such deep and abiding love, Patience found herself smiling mistily. Devil scratched the baby's tummy; Sebastian cooed and gurgled and batted clumsily at his father's finger. Blinking rapidly, Patience glanced at Vane. He was smiling easily—he clearly found nothing odd in the sight of his powerful, domineering cousin playing nursemaid.

She looked at Gerrard; he laughed as Sebastian latched on to Devil's finger and wrestled.

"Vane?" All turned as Honoria swept into the room. "Ah—Patience." As if they were already related, Honoria enveloped Patience in a scented embrace and touched cheeks. "What's happened?"

Vane brought them up-to-date. Honoria sank onto the *chaise* beside Devil. Patience noted that, after a quick glance to check, Honoria left Sebastian in Devil's care. Until, recognizing her voice as she questioned Vane, Sebastian lost interest in Devil's finger and, with a cry, waved his arms for his mother. Devil passed his heir over, then glanced at Vane.

"Is Colby likely to prove dangerous?"

Vane shook his head. "Not in our terms."

Patience didn't need to ask what their terms were. Devil got to his feet, and the room shrank. It was clear that, if Vane had said there'd be danger, Devil would have accompanied them. Instead, he grinned at Vane. "We're going back to the Place tomorrow. Head our way once you've finished tidying up for Minnie."

"Indeed." Honoria seconded her husband's edict. "We'll need to discuss the arrangements."

Patience stared at her. Honoria smiled, openly affectionate. Both Devil and Vane shot Honoria, then Patience, identical, unreadable, masculine looks, then exchanged a long-suffering glance.

"I'll see you out." Devil gestured to the hall.

Honoria came, too, Sebastian at her shoulder. While they stood chatting, waiting for Gerrard to fetch his coat, the baby, bored, fell to tugging Honoria's earring. Noticing his wife's difficulty, without pausing in his discussion with Vane, Devil reached out, scooped his heir out of Honoria's arms, and settled Sebastian against his chest, so the diamond pin anchoring his cravat was level with the baby's eyes.

Sebastian cooed, and happily grasped the winking pin in a chubby fist—and proceeded to destroy what had been a perfectly tied *Trone d'Amour*. Patience blinked, but neither Devil, Vane, nor Honoria seemed to find anything remarkable in the sight.

An hour later, as London fell behind and Vane whipped up his horses, Patience was still mulling over Devil, his wife, and his son. And the atmosphere that hung, a warm, welcoming glow, throughout their elegant house. Family—family feeling, family affection—of the sort the Cynsters took for granted, was something she'd never known.

Having a family like that was her dearest, deepest, wildest dream.

She glanced at Vane, beside her, his eyes fixed on the

road, his face a mask of concentration as he drove his horses into the lowering night. Patience smiled softly. With him, her dream would come true; she'd made her decision—she knew it was right. To see him with their son, lounging by the fire like Devil, caring without even stopping to think—that was her new aim.

It was his aim, too—she knew without asking. He was a Cynster—that was their code. Family. The most important thing in their lives.

Vane glanced down. "Are you warm enough?"

Wedged between him and Gerrard, with, at his insistence, two rugs tucked firmly around her, she was in no danger of taking a chill. "I'm fine." She smiled, and snuggled closer. "Just drive."

He grunted, and did.

About them, an eerie twilight fell; thick, swirling clouds, pale grey, hung low. The air was bitter, the wind laced with ice.

Vane's powerful greys drew the curricle on, wheels rolling smoothly over the macadam. They raced through the evening, into the night.

On toward Bellamy Hall, to the last act in the long drama, to the final curtain call for the Spectre and their mysterious thief. So they could bring the curtain down, send the players on their way—and then get on with living their lives.

Creating their dream.

Chapter 22

I t was full dark when Vane eased his horses off the road onto the back track leading to the Bellamy Hall stables. The night had turned icy, crisply chill; the horses's breaths steamed in the still air.

"The fog will be heavy tonight," Vane whispered.

Beside him, pressed close, Patience nodded.

The back barn, second of two, loomed ahead; Vane uttered a silent prayer. It went unanswered. As he rolled the curricle to a halt just inside the barn, he saw Minnie's menagerie milling at the other entrance, peering toward the main barn, the stables, and the house beyond. They were all there, even, he noted, glimpsing a grey shadow darting about, Myst. He jumped to the ground, then lifted Patience down. The others came hurrying up, Myst in the lead.

Leaving Patience to deal with Minnie and the rest, Vane helped Duggan and Gerrard stable the greys. Then, grim-faced, he returned to the whispering group thronging the barn's center.

Minnie immediately stated, "If you're entertaining the notion of ordering us to wait in this drafty barn, you may save your breath."

Her belligerence was reflected in her stance and was echoed by the usually practical Timms, who nodded direfully. Every member of Minnie's ill-assorted ménage was likewise imbued with decisive determination.

The General summed up their mood. "Blighter's kinged it over us all—need to see him exposed, don't y'know."

353

Vane scanned their faces, his features set. "Very well." He spoke through clenched teeth. "But if any of you makes the *slightest* sound, or are so witless as to alert Colby or Alice to our presence *before* we've gained sufficient details to prove beyond doubt who the Spectre and the thief are . . ."—he let the moment stretch as he scanned their faces—"they'll answer to me. Is that understood?"

A flurry of nodding heads replied.

"You'll need to do exactly as I say." He looked pointedly at Edmond and Henry. "No bright ideas, no sudden elaborations to the plan."

Edmond nodded. "Right."

"Indubitably," Henry swore.

Vane glanced around again. They all looked back, meek and earnest. He gritted his teeth and grabbed Patience's hand. "Come on, then. And *no* talking."

He strode for the main barn. Halfway there, shielded from the house by the bulk of the stables, he halted, and, rigidly impatient, waited for the others to catch up.

"Don't walk on the gravel or on the paths," he instructed. "Keep to the grass. It's foggy; sound travels well in fog. We can't assume they're snug in the parlor—they might be in the kitchen, or even outside."

He turned and strode on, blocking out all thoughts of how Minnie was coping. She wouldn't thank him, and, at the moment, he needed to concentrate on other things.

Like where Grisham was.

Leading Patience, with Gerrard close behind, he reached the stables. Grisham's quarters gave off it. "Wait here," Vane whispered, his lips close by Patience's ear. "Stop the others here. I'll return in a moment."

With that, he slid into the shadows. The last thing he wanted was Grisham imagining they were intruders and sounding the alarm.

But Grisham's room was empty; Vane rejoined his ill-assorted hunting party at the rear of the dark stables. Duggan had checked the grooms' rooms. He shook his head and mouthed, "No one here." Vane nodded. Minnie had mentioned she'd given most of the staff leave.

"We'll try the side door." They could force the window

of the back parlor—that wing was farthest from the library, Whitticombe's favorite bolt-hole. "Follow me, not too close together. And remember—*no sound.*"

They all nodded mutely.

Swallowing a futile curse, Vane made for the shrubbery. The high hedges and grassed paths eased his mind of one worry, but as he and Patience, Duggan and Gerrard at their backs, neared the place where the hedges gave way to open lawn, a light flashed across their path.

They froze. The light disappeared.

"Wait here." On the whisper, Vane edged forward until he could look across the lawn. Beyond lay the house, the side door closed. But a light was bobbing up from the ruins—the Spectre was walking tonight.

The light rose again briefly; in its beam, Vane saw a large, dark figure lumbering along the side of the lawn, heading their way.

"Back!" he hissed, pushing Patience, who'd edged up to his shoulder, into the hedge behind him. In the lee of the hedge, he waited, counting the seconds, then the lumbering figure swung into the path—and was upon them.

Vane grabbed him in a headlock; Duggan clung to one muscled arm. The figure tensed to fight.

"Cynster!" Vane hissed, and the figure went limp.

"Thank Gawd!" Grisham blinked at them. Vane released him. Looking down the path, Vane was mollified to see that the rest of the party had frozen, strung out in the shadows. Now, however, they clustered closer.

"I didn't know what to do." Grisham rubbed his neck.

Vane checked; the carrier of the bobbing light was still some distance away, negotiating the tumbled stones. He turned back to Grisham. "What happened?"

"The Colbys arrived late afternoon. I figured it was the sign we was watching for. I told 'em straight off there was only me and two maids in the house—if anything, Colby seemed well pleased. He had me make up the fire in the library, then called for dinner early. After that, he told us we could retire, as if he was doing us a favor an'all." Grisham snorted softly. "I kept a close eye on 'em, of course.

They waited a while, then took one of the library lamps and headed for the ruins."

Grisham glanced back. Vane checked, then nodded for him to continue. They still had a few minutes before whispers became too dangerous.

"They went all the way across to the abbot's lodge." Grisham grinned. "I stayed close. Miss Colby grumbled all the way, but I wasn't near enough to make out what she said. Colby went straight for that stone I told you about." Grisham nodded at Vane. "Checked it over real careful-like, making sure no one had lifted it. He was right pleased with himself after that. They started back then—I came on ahead, so's I'd be here to see what's next."

Vane raised his brows. "What indeed?"

The light flashed again, much closer now—everyone froze. Vane clung to the edge of the hedge, aware of Patience pressed to his side. The others edged closer, wedged together so they could all see the section of lawn before the side door.

"It's not *fair*! I don't see *why* you had to give back my treasure." Alice Colby's disgruntled whine floated on the frosty air. "You're going to get *your* treasure, but *I* won't have anything!"

"I told you those things weren't yours!" Whitticombe's tone turned from aggravated to scathing. "I would have thought you'd have learned after last time. I won't have you caught with things that *aren't yours*. The very idea of being branded the brother of a thief!"

"Your treasure isn't yours *either*!"

"That's different." Whitticombe stumped into view before the side door; he looked around at Alice, trailing after him. And sniffed contemptuously. "At least, this time, I could put your little foible to some use. It was just what I needed to deflect Cynster's attention. While he's getting young Debbington cleared, I'll have the time I need to complete my work."

"*Work*?" Alice's contempt matched Whitticombe's. "You're obsessed with this foolish treasure hunt. Is it here, or is it there?" she parroted in a singsong voice.

Whitticombe threw open the door. "Just go inside."

Still singing her little ditty, Alice walked in.

Vane looked at Grisham. "Run like the devil—through the kitchen, into the old parlor behind the library. We'll come to the windows."

Grisham nodded and set off at a run.

Vane turned to the others; they all looked at him in mute expectation. He set his teeth. "We're going to backtrack, quickly and quietly, around the house to the terrace. On the terrace, we'll have to be especially quiet—Whitticombe will probably make for the library. We need to know more about this treasure of his, and whether he was, indeed, the one who struck Gerrard."

As one, they all nodded. Resisting a strong urge to groan, Vane, Patience's hand locked in his, led the way back through the shrubbery.

They picked their way along the verge bordering the carriage drive, then gingerly climbed to the terrace flags. Myst, a swift shadow, ran ahead; Vane silently cursed—and prayed the fiendish animal would behave.

Grisham was waiting, a wraith at the long parlor windows. He eased back the catch—Vane stepped in, then helped Patience over the raised sill.

"They're arguing in the hall," Grisham whispered, "over who owns some elephant or other."

Vane nodded. He looked back and saw Timms and Edmond help Minnie in. Turning, he strode to the wall—and opened a door concealed in the paneling—revealing the back of another door, set into the paneling of the next room, the library. His hand on the latch of the second door, Vane glanced, frowning, over his shoulder.

The assembled company obediently held their breaths.

Vane eased opened the door.

The library was empty, lit only by the flames dancing in the hearth.

Scanning the room, Vane saw two large, four-paneled screens, used during summer to protect the old tomes from sunlight. The screens hadn't been folded away; they stood open, parallel to the fireplace, effectively screening the area before the hearth from the terrace windows.

Stepping back, Vane drew Patience to him. Nodding to

the screens, he gently pushed her through the door. Quickly, her gaze on the library door, she scooted across the floor, blessedly covered in a long Turkish rug, and took refuge behind the farthest screen.

Before Vane could blink, Gerrard followed his sister.

Vane glanced back, nodded the others toward the room, then followed his brother-in-law-to-be.

When footsteps fell outside the library door, the entire company, barring only Grisham, who'd elected to remain in the parlor, were all crammed behind the two screens, eyes glued to the fine slits between the panels.

Vane prayed no one would sneeze.

The door handle turned; Whitticombe led the way in, his expression disdainful. "It matters not who *owned* the elephant. The fact is, the goods *inside it* weren't *yours!*"

"But *I* wanted them!" Face mottled, Alice clenched her fists. "The others lost them, and they became mine—but you took them away! You always take my things away!"

"That's because they're not yours to begin with!" Grinding his teeth, Whitticombe pushed Alice into the chair by the fire. "Just sit there and keep quiet!"

"I will *not* keep quiet!" Alice's eyes blazed. "You always tell me I can't have things I want—that it's wrong to take them—but you're going to take the abbey treasure. And *that* doesn't belong to *you!*"

"*It's not the same!*" Whitticombe thundered. He fixed Alice with a baleful eye. "I know the distinction is hard for you to grasp, but retrieving—resurrecting—lost church plate—restoring the magnificence of Coldchurch Abbey—is not the same as *stealing!*"

"But you want it all for *yourself!*"

"*No!*" Whitticombe forced himself to draw a calming breath, and lowered his voice. "*I* want to be the one to *find* it. I fully intend to hand it over to the proper authorities, *but . . .*" He lifted his head and straightened. "The *fame* of finding it, the glory of being the one who, through his tireless scholarship, traced and restored the lost plate of Coldchurch Abbey—*that*," he declared, "will be *mine.*"

Behind the screen, Patience caught Vane's eye. He smiled grimly.

"All very well," Alice grumped. "But you needn't make out you're such a saint. Nothing saintly about hitting that fool boy with a rock."

Whitticombe stilled. He stared down at Alice.

Who smirked. "Didn't think I knew, did you. But I was in dear Patience's room at the time and chanced to look out over the ruins." She smiled maliciously. "I saw you do it—saw you pick up the rock, then creep up close. Saw you strike him down."

She sat back, her gaze fixed on Whitticombe's face. "Oh, no, dear brother, *you're* no saint."

Whitticombe sniffed, and waved dismissively. "Just a concussion—I didn't hit him that hard. Just enough to make sure he never finished that sketch." He started to pace. "When I think of the shock I got when I saw him poking about the abbot's cellar door! It's a wonder I didn't hit him too hard. If he'd been more curious, and mentioned it to one of those other dunderheads—Chadwick, Edmond, or, heaven forbid, Edgar—Lord knows what might have happened. The fools might have stolen my discovery!"

"*Your* discovery?"

"*Mine*! The glory will be *mine*!" Whitticombe paced on. "As it is, everything's worked out perfectly. That tap on the head was enough to scare the old woman into taking her precious nephew off to London—mercifully, she took all the others as well. So now—tomorrow—I can hire some itinerants to help me lift that stone, and then—!"

Triumphant, Whitticombe whirled—and froze.

All those peeking through the screens saw him, hand upraised as if to exhort adulation, staring, goggle-eyed, into the shadows at the side of the room. Everyone tensed. No one could see, or imagine, what he was staring at.

His mouth started to work first, opening and closing to no effect. Then: "*Aaarrrrgh!!!*" His face a mask of abject horror, Whitticombe pointed. "*What's that cat doing here*?"

Alice looked, then frowned at him. "That's Myst. Patience's cat."

"I *know*." Whitticombe's voice shook; his gaze didn't shift.

Risking a glance around the screen, Vane sighted Myst, sitting neatly erect, her ancient, all-seeing blue gaze fixed, unwinking, on Whitticombe's face.

"But it was in *London*!" Whitticombe gasped. "How did it get here?"

Alice shrugged. "It didn't come down with us."

"*I know that*!"

Someone choked on a laugh; the second screen wobbled, then teetered. A hand appeared at the top and righted it, then disappeared.

Vane sighed, and stepped out, around the other screen. Whitticombe's eyes, which Vane would have sworn could not get any wider, did.

"Evening, Colby." Vane waved Minnie forward; the others followed.

As the company assembled in full sight, Alice chortled. "So much for your secrets, dear brother." She sank back in her chair, grinning maliciously, clearly unconcerned by her own misdemeanors.

Whitticombe threw her a swift glance and drew himself up. "I don't know how much you heard—"

"All of it," Vane replied.

Whitticombe blanched—and glanced at Minnie.

Who stared at him, disgust and disaffection clear in her face. "Why?" she demanded. "You had a roof over your head and a comfortable living. Was fame so important you would commit crimes—and for what? A foolish dream?"

Whitticombe stiffened. "It's *not* a foolish dream. The church plate and the abbey's treasure were buried before the Dissolution. There's clear reference made in the abbey records—but after the Dissolution there's no mention of it at all. It took me forever to track down where they'd hidden it—the crypt was the obvious place, but there's nothing but rubble there. And the records clearly state a cellar, but the old cellars were excavated long ago—and nothing was found." He drew himself up, inflated with self-importance. "Only *I* traced the abbot's cellar. It's there—I found the trapdoor." He looked at Minnie, avaricious hope lighting his eyes. "You'll see—tomorrow. Then you'll understand." Confidence renewed, he nodded.

Bleakly, Minnie shook her head. "I'll never understand, Whitticombe."

Edgar cleared his throat. "And I'm afraid you won't find anything, either. There's nothing to be found."

Whitticombe's lip curled. "Dilettante," he scoffed. "What would you know of research?"

Edgar shrugged. "I don't know about research, but I do know about the Bellamys. The last abbot was one—not in name—but he became the grandfather of the next generation. And he told his grandsons of the buried treasure—the tale was passed on until, at the Restoration, a Bellamy asked for and was granted the old abbey's lands."

Edgar smiled vaguely at Minnie. "The treasure is all around us." He gestured to the walls, the ceiling. "That first Bellamy of Bellamy Hall dug up the plate and treasure as soon as he set foot on his new lands—he sold them, and used the proceeds to build the Hall, and to provide the foundation for the future wealth of the family."

Meeting Whitticombe's stunned stare, Edgar smiled. "The treasure's been here, in plain sight, all along."

"No," Whitticombe said, but there was no strength in his denial.

"Oh, yes," Vane replied, his gaze hard. "If you'd asked, I—or Grisham—could have told you the abbot's cellar was filled in more than a hundred years ago. All you'll find under that trapdoor is solid earth."

Whitticombe continued to stare, then his eyes glazed.

"I rather think, Colby, that it's time for some apologies, what?" The General glared at Whitticombe.

Whitticombe blinked, then stiffened, and lifted his head arrogantly. "I don't see that I've done anything particularly reprehensible—not by the standards of *this* company." Features contorting, he scanned the others. And gestured disdainfully. "There's Mrs. Agatha Chadwick, struggling to bury a nincompoop of a husband and settle a daughter with not two wits to her name and a son not much better. And Edmond Montrose—a poet and dramatist with so much flair he never accomplishes anything. And we mustn't forget you, must we?" Whitticombe glared vituperatively at the General. "A General with no troops, who was nothing but a sergeant major in a dusty barracks, if truth be known. And we shouldn't forget Miss Edith Swithins, so sweet, so mild—oh, no. Don't forget her, and the fact she's consorting with Edgar, the rambling historian, and thinking no one knows. At her age!''

Whitticombe poured out his scorn. ''And last but not least,'' he pronounced with relish, ''we have Miss Patience Debbington, our esteemed hostess's niece—''

Crunnnch! Whitticombe sailed backward and landed on the floor, some yards away.

Patience, who'd been standing beside Vane, quickly stepped forward—to come up with Vane, who'd stepped forward as he delivered the blow that had lifted Whitticombe from his feet.

Clutching Vane's arm, Patience looked down—and prayed Whitticombe had the sense to stay down. She could feel the steel in the muscles beneath her fingers. If Whitticombe was foolish enough to fight back, Vane would demolish him.

Stunned, Whitticombe blinked back to full consciousness. As the others gathered about, he raised one hand to his jaw. And winced. ''Assault!'' he croaked.

''The battery might yet follow.'' The warning—entirely unneccessary from Patience's perspective—came from Vane. One look at his face, as hard as granite and equally unyielding, would have informed any sane person of that fact.

Whitticombe stared—then he scanned the circle about him. ''He hit me!''

''Did he?'' Edmond opened his eyes wide. ''Didn't see it myself.'' He looked at Vane. ''Would you care to do it again?''

''No!'' Whitticombe looked shocked.

''Why not?'' the General inquired. ''A sound thrashing—do you good. Might even knock some sense into you. Here—we'll all come and watch. Ensure fair play and all that. No blows below the belt, what?''

The horrified look on Whitticombe's face as he gazed around the circle of faces—and found not one showing the slightest glimmer of sympathy—would have been comic if any had been in the mood to be amused. When his gaze returned to Vane, he sucked in a breath, and sniveled: "Don't hit me."

Narrow-eyed, Vane looked down at him, and shook his head. His battle-ready tension eased; he stepped back. "A coward—through and through."

The verdict was greeted with nods and humphs of agreement. Duggan pushed forward and grasped Whitticombe by the collar. He hauled the miserable figure upright. Duggan looked at Vane. "I'll lock him in the cellar, shall I?"

Vane looked at Minnie. Tight-lipped, she nodded.

Alice, who had watched it all, face alight with vindictive glee, laughed and waved at Whitticombe. "Off you go, brother! You wanted to look at a cellar all these months— enjoy it while you can." Cackling, she slumped back in her chair.

Agatha Chadwick laid a hand on Minnie's arm. "Allow me." With considerable dignity, she descended on Alice. "Angela."

For once, Angela did not drag her heels. Joining her mother, her face a mask of determination, she grasped Alice's other arm; together, they hoisted Alice to her feet.

"Come along, now." Mrs. Chadwick turned to the door.

Alice glanced from one to the other. "Did you bring my elephant? It *is* mine, you know."

"It's on its way from London." Agatha Chadwick glanced at Minnie. "We'll lock her in her room."

Minnie nodded.

All watched the trio pass through the door. The instant it closed behind them, the iron that had kept Minnie's spine straight for the past hours dissolved. She slumped against Timms. Vane softly cursed—without requesting permission, he scooped Minnie up in his arms and gently eased her into the chair Alice had vacated.

Minnie smiled tremulously up at him. "I'm all right— just a bit rattled." She grinned. "But I enjoyed seeing Whitticombe fly through the air."

Relieved to see that grin, Vane stepped back, letting Patience get closer. Edith Swithins, likewise at the end of her resources, was being solicitously helped into the second armchair by Edgar.

As she sank down, she, too, smiled at Vane. "I've never seen any fisticuffs before—it was quite exciting." Rummaging in her bag, she retrieved two bottles of smelling salts. She handed Minnie one. "I thought I'd lost this one years ago, but lo and behold, it turned up at the top of my bag last week."

Edith sniffed from her bottle, eyes twinkling at Vane.

Who discovered he could still blush. He glanced around; the General and Gerrard had been conferring—the General looked up. "Just discussing the dispositions, what? No staff here—and we haven't dined yet."

The observation got them all moving, lighting fires, making up beds, and preparing and serving a hot, sustaining dinner. Grisham, Duggan, and the two maids assisted, but everyone, bar only Alice and Whitticombe, readily contributed their share.

As no fire had been lit in the drawing room, the ladies remained at the table while the port did the rounds. The glow of common experience, of camaraderie, was evident as they shared thoughts of the past weeks.

At the end, as yawns started to interrupt their reminiscences, Timms turned to Minnie. "What will you do with them?"

Everyone quieted. Minnie grimaced. "They really are pitiful. I'll speak to them tomorrow, but, in all Christian charity, I can't throw them out. At least not at the moment, not into the snow."

"Snow?" Edmond raised his head, then rose and pulled back one of the drapes. Fine flakes swirled across the beam of light shining out. "Well, fancy that."

Vane did not fancy that. He had plans—a heavy fall of snow was not part of them. He glanced at Patience, seated beside him. Then he smiled, and quaffed the last of his port.

Fate couldn't be that cruel.

He was the last to climb the stairs, after walking a last round about the huge house. All was silent, all was still. It seemed the only other life in the old house was Myst, darting up the stairs before him. The small cat had elected to follow him on his round, weaving about his boots, then dashing into the shadows. He'd walked out of the side door to study the sky. Myst had disappeared into the dark, only to return a few minutes later, sneezing snowflakes off her pink nose, shaking them disdainfully from her fur.

His thoughts in the future, Vane followed Myst up the stairs, through the gallery, down one flight, and along the corridor. He reached his room and opened the door; Myst darted through.

Vane grinned and followed—then remembered he'd meant to go to Patience's room. He looked around, to call Myst back—and saw Patience, dozing in the chair by the fire.

Lips curving, Vane closed the door. Myst woke Patience before he reached her—she looked up, then smiled, rose—and walked straight into his arms. He closed them about her.

Eyes shining, she looked into his. "I love you."

Vane's lips lifted as he bent to kiss her. "I know."

Patience returned the gentle caress. "Was I that obvious?"

"Yes." Vane kissed her again. "That part of the equation was never in doubt." Briefly, his lips brushed hers. "Nor was the rest of it. Not from the moment I first held you in my arms."

The rest of it—his part of the equation—his feelings for her.

Patience drew back so she could study his face. She lifted a hand to his cheek. "I needed to know."

The planes of his face shifted; desire flared in his eyes. "Now you do." He lowered his head and kissed her again. "Incidentally, don't ever forget it."

Already breathless, Patience chuckled. "You'll have to make sure you remind me."

"Oh, I will. Every morning and every night."

The words were a vow—a promise. Patience found his lips with hers and kissed him until she was witless. Chuckling, Vane lifted his head. Wrapping one arm around her, he steered her to the bed. "Theoretically, you shouldn't be here."

"Why? What's the difference—your bed or mine?"

"Quite a lot, by servants' standards. They'll accept the sight of gentlemen wandering the house in the early hours, but for some reason, the sight of ladies flitting through the dawn in their nightgowns incites rampant speculation."

"Ah," Patience said, as they halted by the bed. "But I'll be fully clothed." She gestured to her gown. "There'll be no reason for speculation."

Vane met her gaze. "What about your hair?"

"My hair?" Patience blinked. "You'll just have to help me put it up again. I assume 'elegant gentlemen,' such as you, learn such useful skills very early in life."

"Actually, no." Straight-faced, Vane reached for her pins. "Us rakes-of-the-first-order . . ." Dropping pins left and right, he set her hair cascading down. With a satisfied smile, he caught her about the waist and drew her hard against him. "We," he said, looking into her eyes, "spend our time concentrating on rather different skills—like letting ladies' hair down. And getting them out of their clothes. Getting them into bed. And other things."

He demonstrated—very effectively.

As he spread her thighs and sank deeply into her, Patience's breath fractured on a gasp.

He moved within her, claiming her, pressing deep, only to withdraw and fill her again. Arms braced, he reared above her, and loved her; beneath him, Patience writhed. When he bent his head and found her lips, she clung to the caress, clung to the moment. Clung to him.

Their lips parted, and she sighed. And felt his words against her lips as he moved deeply within her.

"With my body, I thee worship. With my heart, I thee adore. I love you. And if you want me to say it a thousand times, I will. Just as long as you'll be my wife."

"I will." Patience heard the words in her head, tasted them on her lips—she felt them resonate in her heart.

The next hour passed, and not a single coherent phrase passed their lips. The warm stillness within the room was broken only by the rustling of sheets, and soft, urgent murmurs. Then the silence gave way to soft moans, groans, breathless pants, desperate gasps. Culminating in a soft, piercingly sweet scream, dying, sobbing, into a deep guttural groan.

Outside, the moon rose; inside, the fire died.

Wrapped in each other's arms, limbs and hearts entwined, they slept.

"Bye!" Gerrard stood on the front steps and, smiling hugely, waved them away.

With a cheery wave, Patience faced forward, settling herself under the thick rug. The rug Vane had insisted she needed in order to go driving with him. She glanced at him. "You aren't going to fuss over me, are you?"

"Who? Me?" He threw her an uncomprehending glance. "Perish the thought."

"Good." Patience tipped her head back and looked at the sky, still threatening snow. "There's really no need— I'm perfectly accustomed to looking after myself."

Vane kept his eyes on his horses's ears.

Patience slanted him another glance. "Incidentally, I meant to mention . . ." When he merely raised an inquiring brow, and kept his gaze forward, she put her nose in the air and baldly stated, "If you dare, ever, to go into a conservatory with a beautiful woman, even if she's related— even a first cousin—I will not be held accountable for the outcome."

That got her a glance, a mildly curious one.

"Outcome?"

"The fracas that will inevitably ensue."

"Ah." Vane looked forward again, easing his horses down the lane to the main road. "What about you?" he eventually asked. Meekly mild, he raised his brows at her. "Don't you like conservatories?"

"You may take me to see any conservatory you please," Patience snapped. "My liking for pot plants is not, as you well know, the subject of this discussion."

Vane's lips quirked, then lifted—lightly. "Indeed. But you may put that particular subject from your head." The look in his eyes told Patience he was deadly serious. Then he smiled, his wolfish, Cynster smile. "What would I want with other beautiful women, if I can show you conservatories instead?''

Patience blushed, and humphed, and looked ahead.

A fine sprinkling of snow covered the landscape and sparkled in the weak sunshine. The breeze was chilly, the clouds leaden grey, but the day remained fine—fine enough for their drive. They reached the main road, and Vane turned north. He flicked the reins, and his greys stepped out. Lifting her face to the breeze, Patience thrilled to the steady rolling rhythm, to the sense of traveling quickly along a new road. In a new direction.

The roofs of Kettering lay ahead. Drawing a deep breath, she said, ''I suppose we should start making plans.''

''Probably,'' Vane conceded. He slowed the greys as they entered the town. ''I'd imagined we'd spend most of our time in Kent.'' He glanced at Patience. ''The house in Curzon Street is big enough for a family, but other than the obligatory appearances during the height of the Season, I can't imagine we'll be there all that much. Unless you've discovered a liking for town life?''

''No—of course not.'' Patience blinked. ''Kent sounds wonderful.''

''Good—did I mention there's a deal of redecorating to do?'' Vane grinned at her. ''Infinitely better you than me. Most of the house needs attention—especially the nurseries.''

Patience mouthed an ''Oh.''

''Of course,'' Vane continued, deftly steering his cattle through the main street, ''*before* we get to the nurseries, I suppose we should consider the main bedchamber.'' His expression impossibly innocent, he caught Patience's eye. ''I daresay you'll need to make changes there, too.''

Patience narrowed her eyes at him. ''*Before* we get to the main bedchamber, don't you think we should get to a church?''

Vane's lips twitched; he looked ahead. ''Ah, well. Now that poses some problems.''

''Problems?''

''Hmm—like which church.''

Patience frowned. "Is there some tradition in your family?"

"Not really. Nothing we need concern ourselves with. It really comes down to personal preference." With the town behind then, Vane set the greys pacing. And turned his attention to Patience. "Do you want a big wedding?"

She frowned. "I hadn't given it much thought."

"Well, do. And you might like to ponder the fact that there are approximately three hundred friends and connections who will have to be invited from the Cynster side alone, should you elect to go that route."

"Three *hundred*?"

"That's just the close ones."

It didn't take Patience long to shake her head. "I really don't think a big wedding is called for. It sounds like it'll take forever to organize."

"Very likely."

"So—what's the alternative?"

"There are a few," Vane admitted. "But the fastest method would be to marry by special license. That can be done at virtually anytime, and would take next to no time to organize."

"Beyond obtaining the license."

"Hmm." Vane looked ahead. "So, the question is, when would you like to marry?"

Patience considered. She looked at Vane, at his profile, puzzled when he kept his eyes forward and refused to meet her gaze. "I don't know," she said. "You pick a date."

He looked at her then. "You're sure? You won't mind what I decide?"

Patience shrugged. "Why should I? The sooner the better, if we're to go on as we are."

Vane let out a breath, and whipped up his horses. "This afternoon."

"This after . . ." Patience swiveled on the seat to stare at him. Then she snapped her mouth shut. "You've already got a license."

"In my pocket." Vane grinned—wolfishly. "That was where I was yesterday, while Sligo was hunting high and low."

Patience slumped back against the seat. Then their pace, Gerrard's wide grin, and the distance they'd already traveled, registered. "Where are we going?"

"To get married. In Somersham." Vane smiled. "There's a church in the village by the ducal estate, which you could say I've a connection with. Of all the churches in this land, I'd like to be married there. And the vicar, Mr. Postlethwaite, will fall over himself to do the honors."

Feeling slightly dizzy, Patience drew in a deep breath—then let it out. "Well, then—let's be married in Somersham village."

Vane glanced her way. "You're sure?"

Meeting his eyes, reading the uncertainty, the question, in the grey, Patience smiled, and slid closer. "I'm overwhelmed." She let her smile deepen, let her joy show. "But I'm sure."

Tucking one hand in Vane's arm, she gestured grandly. "Drive on!"

Vane grinned, and complied. Patience clung close, and listened to the wheels' steady clatter. Their journey together had already begun. Their dream was waiting—just beyond the next bend.

Epilogue

Their wedding was small, select, intensely personal; their wedding breakfast, held one month after the initiating event, was enormous.

Honoria and the other Cynster ladies organized it. It was held at Somersham Place.

"You took your time!" Lady Osbaldestone poked Vane with a skeletal finger, then wagged the same finger at Patience. "Make sure you keep him in line—there've been too many Cynsters loose for too long."

She stumped off to speak to Minnie. Vane breathed again—Patience caught his eye. "She's a terror," he said defensively. "Ask anyone."

Patience laughed. Gowned in silk the color of old gold, she tightened her hold on Vane's arm. "Come do the pretty."

Vane smiled, and let her lead him into the throng, to chat with the guests gathered to wish them well. She was all he could ask for, all he needed. And she was his.

He was perfectly willing to listen to congratulations on that fact until the sky fell.

Circulating through the guests, they eventually came up with Honoria and Devil, doing the same.

Patience hugged Honoria. "You've done us proud."

A pleased and proud matriarch, Honoria glowed. "I think the cake was the highlight—Mrs. Hull surpassed herself." The many-tiered marzipan-covered fruit cake had been topped by a weather vane, delicately executed in spun sugar.

"Very inventive," Vane commented dryly.

Honoria humphed. "You men never appreciate such things as you ought." She glanced at Patience. "At least there'll be no wagers for you to contend with."

"Wagers?" A great many cheers, and ribald and raucous suggestions, had flown when they'd cut the cake. But wagers? Then she remembered. Oh.

Honoria smiled tightly, and flicked Vane a darkling glance. "Hardly surprising your husband has a fondness for the church in Somersham. He, after all, helped pay for its roof."

Patience glanced at Vane—his expression all innocence, he looked at Devil.

"Where's Richard?"

"Gone north." Deftly snagging Honoria in one arm, Devil anchored her to his side, preventing her from embroiling them in further social conversations. "He got a letter from some Scottish clerk regarding an inheritance from his mother. For some reason, he had to be present in the flesh to collect."

Vane frowned. "But she's been dead for—how long? Nearly thirty years?"

"Almost." Devil looked down as Honoria tugged. "It was a ghostly whisper from the past—a past he'd thought long buried. He went, of course—out of curiosity if nothing else." Looking up, Devil shot Vane a pointed glance. "Town life, I fear, has begun to pall for our Scandal."

Vane met Devil's gaze. "Did you warn him?"

Devil grinned. "Of what? To beware storms and unattached ladies?"

Vane grinned. "Put like that, it does sound a mite farfetched."

"No doubt Scandal will return, hale and whole, safe and sound, with nothing more than a few battle scars and several new notches on his—"

"That's the duchess of Leicester to your right!" Honoria hissed. She glared at Devil. "Behave!"

The soul of injured innocence, he put his hand to his heart. "I thought I was."

Honoria made a distinctly rude sound. Winning free of his hold, she whirled and pushed him toward the duchess. She nodded over her shoulder at Patience. "Take him"— her nod indicated Vane—"the other way, or you'll never meet everyone."

Patience grinned, and obeyed. Vane went quietly. His gaze dwelling on Patience's face, on her figure, he found it no chore to play the proud and besotted groom.

From the other side of the ballroom, Vane's mother, Lady Horatia Cynster, watched him, and Patience, and sighed. "If only they hadn't married in such a rush. There was obviously no need for it."

Her second son, Harry, better known as Demon, to whom this was addressed, shot her a glance. "I suspect your notion of 'need' and Vane's differ in certain pertinent respects."

Horatia humphed. "Whatever." Deserting the sight of her firstborn, so well and appropriately settled, she turned her sights on Harry. "Just as long as you never try the same thing."

"Who? Me?" Harry was honestly shocked.

"Yes—*you.*" Horatia jabbed his chest. "I hereby give you fair warning, Harry Cynster, that if you *dare* marry by special license, I'll never, *ever*, forgive you."

Harry promptly held up his hand. "I swear by all that's holy that I will never marry by special license."

"Humph!" Horatia nodded. "Good."

Harry smiled—and completed his vow in silence. *Or any other way.*

He was determined to be the first Cynster in history to escape fate's decree. The notion of tying himself up to some chit—of restricting himself to one woman—was ludicrous. *He* wasn't getting married—ever.

"Think I'll go see how Gabriel's doing." With a sweeping, ineffably elegant bow, he escaped his mother's orbit, and went in search of less scarifying company. People who weren't fixated on weddings.

The afternoon passed; the shadows slowly lengthened. Guests started to take their leave, then the bulk left in a rush. The long day drew to a close with Vane and Patience on the front porch of the Place, waving the last of the guests away. Even the family had departed. Only Devil and Honoria remained at the Place—and they'd retired to their apartments to play with Sebastian, who'd spent much of the afternoon with his nurse.

As the last carriage rumbled away down the drive, Vane glanced at Patience, close by his side.

His wife.

The four-letter word no longer shook him, at least, not in the same way. Now, in his head, it rang with possessiveness, a possessiveness that satisfied, that sat well with his conqueror's soul. He'd found her, he'd seized her—now he could enjoy her.

He studied her face, then raised one brow. And turned her back into the house.

"Did I tell you this place has an extremely interesting conservatory?"

Turn the page for a preview of

Scandal's Bride

the next thrillingly romantic novel in the wonderful
Regency romance Bar Cynster series from
Stephanie Laurens

Coming soon from Piatkus Books!

Prologue

December 1, 1819
Casphairn Manor, the Vale of Casphairn
Galloway Hills, Scotland

She'd never had a vision like it before.

Eyes—blue, blue—blue as the skies over Merrick's high head, blue as the cornflowers dotting the vale's fields. They were the eyes of a thinker, far-sighted yet focused.

Or the eyes of a warrior.

Catriona awoke, almost surprised to find herself alone. From the depths of her big bed, she scanned her familiar surrounds, the thick velvet curtains half shrouding the bed, their mates drawn tight across the windows beyond which the wind murmured, telling tales of the coming winter to any still awake. In the grate, embers gleamed, shedding a glow over polished wood, the soft sheen of the floor, the lighter hues of chair and dresser. It was deep night, the hour between one day and the next. All was reassuringly normal; nothing had changed.

Yet it had.

Her heart slowing, Catriona tugged the covers about her and considered the vision that had visited her—the vision of a man's face. The details remained strongly etched in her mind. Along with the conviction that this man would mean something, impinge on her life in some vital way.

1

He might even be the one The Lady had chosen for her.

The thought was not unwelcome. She was, after all, twenty-two, long past the age when girls invited lovers to their beds, when she might have expected to play her part in that never-ending rite. Not that she regretted that her life had been otherwise, which was just as well, for her path had been set from the instant of her birth. *She* was "the lady of the vale."

The title, one of local custom, was hers and hers alone; none other could claim it. As the only child of her parents, on their deaths, she'd inherited Casphairn Manor, along with the vale and its attendant responsiblities. Her mother had been the same, inheriting manor, lands, and position from her mother before her. Each of her direct female ancestors had been "the lady of the vale."

Cocooned in warm down, Catriona smiled. Just what her title meant few outsiders understood. Some thought her a witch—she'd even used the fiction to scare away would-be suitors. Both church and state had little love of witches, but the vale's isolation kept her safe; there were few who knew of her existence, and none to question her authority or the doctrine from which it sprang.

All the inhabitants of the vale knew what she was, what her position entailed. With roots buried generations deep in the fertile soil, her tenants, all those who lived and worked in the vale, viewed "their lady" as the local representative of The Lady herself, older than time, spirit of the earth that supported them, guardian of their past and their future. They all, each in his own way, paid homage to The Lady and, with absolute and unquestioning confidence, relied on her earthly representative to watch over them and the vale.

To guard, to protect, to nurture, nourish, and heal—those were The Lady's tenets, the only directives Catriona followed and to which she'd unstintingly devoted her life. As had her mother, grandmother and great-grandmother before her. She lived life simply, in accordance with The Lady's dictates, which was usually an easy task.

Except in one arena.

Her gaze shifted to the parchment left unfolded on her dresser. A Perth solicitor had written to inform her of the death of her guardian, Seamus McEnery, and to bid her attend McEnery House for the reading of the will. McEnery House stood on a bleak hillside in The Trossachs, north and west of Perth; in her mind's eye, Catriona could see it clearly—it was the one place outside the vale in which she'd spent more than a day.

When, six years ago, her parents had died, Seamus, her father's cousin, had, by custom, become her legal guardian. A cold, hard man, he had insisted she take up residence at McEnery House, so he could better find a suitor for her hand—a man to take over her lands. With his rigid fist clamped on her purse strings, she'd been forced to obey; she'd left the vale and gone north to meet Seamus.

To do battle with Seamus—for her inheritance, her independence, her inalienable right to remain the lady of the vale, to reside at Casphairn Manor and care for her people. Three weeks of turmoil and drama later, she'd returned to the vale; Seamus had spoken no more of suitors, nor of her calling. And, Catriona was quite certain, he had never again taken The Lady's name in vain.

Now Seamus, the devil she'd conquered, was gone. His eldest son, Jamie, would succeed him. Catriona knew Jamie; like all Seamus's children, he was mild-mannered and weak-willed. Jamie was no Seamus. In considering how best to respond to the solicitor's request, she'd been much inclined to start as she meant to go on, and reply suggesting that, after the will was read and Jamie formally appointed as her guardian, Jamie should call on her here, at the manor. Although she foresaw no difficulty in handling Jamie, she preferred to deal from a position of strength. The vale was her home; within its arms, she reigned supreme. Yet . . .

She focused again on the parchment; after an instant, the outline blurred—once more the vision swam before her mind's eye. For a full minute, she studied it; she saw the face clearly—strong patriarchal nose, determinedly square chin, features chiselled from rock in their angularity and hardness. His brow was concealed by a lock of black hair; those piercing blue eyes were deep-set beneath arched black brows and framed by black lashes. His lips, held in a straight, uncompromising line, told her little—indeed, that was her summation of his face—one meant to conceal his thoughts, his emotions. From chance observers.

She wasn't a chance observer. Presentiment—nay, *certainty*—of future contact compelled her; she focused her mind and slid beneath his guard, behind his reserved facade, and tentatively opened her senses.

Hunger—hot, ravenous—a prowling, animalistic urge, swept over her. It caressed her with fingers of heat; its tug was even more physical. Beyond it, in the deeper shadows, lay . . . restlessness. A soul-deep sense of drifting, rudderless, upon life's sea.

Catriona blinked, and drew back, into her familiar chamber. And saw the letter still lying on her desk. She grimaced. She was adept at intepreting The Lady's messages—this one was crystal clear. She should go to Mc-Enery House and, at some point, she would meet the restless, hungry, reserved stranger with the granite face and warrior's eyes.

A lost warrior—a warrior without a cause.

Catriona frowned and wriggled deeper under the covers. When she'd first seen that face, she'd felt, instinctively, deep inside, that, at long last, The Lady was sending her a consort—the one who would stand by her side, who would share the burden of the vale's protection—the man she would take to her bed. At last. Now, however . . .

"His face is too strong. *Far* too strong."

As the lady of the vale, it was imperative that she be the dominant partner in her marriage, as her mother had been in hers. It was written in stone that no man could rule her. Not for her an arrogant, domineering husband—*that* would never do. Which was, in this case, a pity. A real disappointment.

She'd immediately recognized the source of his restlessness, the restlessness of those without purpose, but she'd never met anything like the hunger that prowled within him. Alive, a tangible force, it had reached out and touched her, and she'd felt a compulsion to sate it. A reactive urge to soothe him, to bring him surcease. To . . .

Her frown deepened; she couldn't find the words, but there'd been a sense of excitment, of daring, of challenge. Not elements she generally met in her daily round of duties. Then again, perhaps it was simply her healer's instincts prodding her? Catriona humphed. "Whatever, he *can't* be the one The Lady means for me—not with a face like *that.*"

Was The Lady sending her a wounded male, a lame duck for her to cure? His eyes, those hard-edged features, hadn't looked lame.

Not that it mattered; she had her instructions. She would go to the highlands, to McEnery House, and see what—or rather, who—came her way.

With another humph, Catriona slid deeper beneath the covers. Turning on her side, she closed her eyes—and willed her mind away from, once again, seeking the stranger's face.

Chapter 1

December 5, 1819
Keltyburn, The Trossachs
Scottish Highlands

"**W**ill there be anything else, sir?"

An artful arrangement of sleek, nubile, naked female limbs sprang to Richard Cynster's mind. The innkeeper had finished clearing the remnants of his dinner—the feminine limbs would satisfy that appetite still unappeased. But . . .

Richard shook his head. Not that he feared shocking his studiously correct gentleman's gentleman, Worboys, standing poker-straight at his elbow. Having been in his employ for eight years, Worboys was past being shocked. He was, however, no magician, and Richard was of the firm opinion that it would take magical powers to find a satisfying armful in Keltyburn.

They'd arrived in the hamlet as the last light left the leaden sky; night had fallen swiftly, a black shroud. The thick mist that had lowered over the mountains, hanging heavy across their path, obscuring the narrow, winding road leading up Keltyhead to their destination, had made passing the night in the dubious comfort of the Keltyburn Arms an attractive proposition.

Besides, he had a wish to have his first sight of his

6

mother's last home in daylight, and before he left Kelty-burn, there was one thing he wished to do.

Richard stirred. "I'll be retiring shortly. Go to bed—I won't need you further tonight." Worboys hesitated; Richard knew he was thinking of who would brush and hang his coat, who would take care of his boots. He sighed. "Go to bed, Worboys."

Worboys stiffened. "Very well, sir—but I do wish we'd pressed on to McEnery House. There, at least, I could have trusted the bootboys."

"Just be thankful we're here," Richard advised, "and not run off the road or stuck in a drift halfway up that damned mountain."

Worboys sniffed eloquently. His clear intimation was that being stuck in a snowdrift in weather cold enough to freeze the proverbial appendages off brass monkeys was preferable to bad blacking. But he obediently took his rotund self off, rolling away into the shadowy depths of the inn.

His lips twitching into a slight smile, Richard stretched his long legs to the fire roaring in the grate. Whatever the state of the inn's blacking, the landlord hadn't stinted in making them comfortable. Richard had seen no other guests, but in such a quiet backwater, that was unsurprising.

The flames flared; Richard fixed his gaze on them—and wondered, not for the first time, whether this expedition to the Highlands, precipitated by boredom and a very specific fear, hadn't been a trifle rash. But London's entertainments had grown stale; the perfumed bodies so readily—too readily—offered him no longer held any allure. While desire and lust were still there, he'd become finicky, choosy, even more so than he'd already been. He wanted more from a woman than her body and a few moments of earthly bliss.

He frowned and resettled his shoulders—and redirected his thoughts. It was a letter that had brought him here, one from the executor of his long-dead mother's husband, Seamus McEnery, who had recently departed this earth. The uninformative legal missive had summoned him to the reading of the will, to be held the day after tomorrow at McEnery House. If he wished to claim a bequest his mother had made to him, and which Seamus had apparently withheld for nearly thirty years, he had to attend in person.

From what little he'd learned of his late mother's husband, that sounded like Seamus McEnery. The man had been a hothead, brash and vigorous, a hard, determined, wily despot. Which was almost certainly why he'd been born. His mother had not enjoyed being married to such a man; his father, Sebastian Cynster, 5th Duke of St. Ives, sent to McEnery House to douse Seamus's political fire, had taken pity on her and given her what joy he could.

Which had resulted in Richard. The story was so old—thirty years old, to be precise—he no longer felt anything over it, bar a distant regret. For the mother he'd never known. She'd died of fever bare months after his birth; Seamus had sent him post-haste to the Cynsters, the most merciful thing he could have done. They'd claimed him and reared him as one of their own, which, in all ways that mattered, he was. Cynsters bred true, especially the males. He was a Cynster through and through.

And that was the other reason he'd left London. The only important social event he was missing was his cousin Vane's belated wedding breakfast, an occasion he'd viewed with misgiving. He wasn't blind—he'd seen the gleam steadily glowing in the eyes of the older Cynster ladies. Like Helena, the Dowager, his much-loved step-mother, not to mention his fleet of aunts. If he'd attended Vane and Patience's celebration, they'd have set their sights on him. He wasn't yet bored enough, restless enough, to offer himself up, fodder for their matrimonial machinations. Not yet.

He knew himself well, perhaps too well. He wasn't an impulsive man. He liked his life well ordered, predictable—he liked to be in control. He'd seen war in his time but he was a man of peace. Of passion. Of home and hearth.

The phrase raised images in his mind—of Vane and his

new bride, of his own half-brother, Devil, and his duchess, Honoria, and their son. Richard shifted and settled, conscious, too conscious, of what his brother and cousin now had. What he himself wanted. Yearned for. He was, after all, a Cynster; he was starting to suspect such plaguey thoughts were ingrained, an inherited susceptiblity. They got under a man's skin and made him . . . edgy. Dissatisfied.

Restless.

Vulnerable.

A board creaked; Richard lifted his gaze, looking through the archway into the hall beyond. A woman emerged from the shadows. Wrapped in a drab cloak, she met his gaze directly, an older woman, her face heavily lined. She measured him swiftly; her gaze turned frosty. Richard suppressed a grin. Spine stiff, her pace unfaltering, the woman turned and climbed the stairs.

Sinking back in his chair, Richard let his lips curve. He was safe from temptation at the Keltyburn Arms.

He looked back at the flames; gradually, his smile died. He shifted once more, easing his shoulders; a minute later, he fluidly rose and crossed to the fogged window.

Rubbing a clear space, he looked out. A starry, moonlit scene met his eyes, a light covering of snow crisping on the ground. Squinting sideways, he could see the church. The kirk. Richard hesitated, then straightened. Collecting his coat from the stand by the door, he went outside.

Abovestairs, Catriona sat at a small wooden table, its surface bare except for a silver bowl, filled with pure spring water, into which she steadily gazed. Distantly, she heard her companion, Algaria, pace along the corridor and enter the room next door, but she was deep in the water, her senses merging with its surface, locked upon it.

And the image formed—the same strong features, the same arrogant eyes. The same aura of restlessness. She didn't probe further—she didn't dare. The image was sharp—he was near.

Dragging in a swift breath, Catriona blinked and pulled back. A knock fell on the door; it opened—Algaria stepped inside. And instantly saw what she'd been up to. She swiftly shut the door. "What did you see?"

Catriona shook her head. "It's confusing." The face was even harder than she'd thought it; the essence of the man's strength was there, clearly delineated for anyone to read. He was a man with no reason to hide his character—he bore the signs openly, arrogantly, like a chieftain.

Like a warrior.

Catriona frowned. She kept stumbling across that word, but she didn't need a warrior—she needed a tame, complaisant, preferably readily besotted gentleman she could marry and so beget an heiress. This man fitted her prescription in only one respect—he was indisputably male. The Lady, She Who Knew All, couldn't possibly mean this man for her.

"But if not that, then what?" Pushing aside the silver bowl, she leaned on the table and cupped her chin in one hand. "I must be getting my messages crossed." But she hadn't done that since she was fourteen. "Perhaps there are two of them?"

"Two of whom?" Algaria hovered near. "What was the vision?"

Catriona shook her head. The matter was too personal—too sensitive—to divulge to anyone else, even Algaria, her mentor since her mother's death. Not until she'd got to the truth of the matter herself and understood it fully.

Whatever it was she was supposed to understand.

"It's no use." Determinedly, she stood. "I must consult The Lady directly."

"What? *Now*?" Algaria stared. "It's freezing outside."

"I'm only going to the circle at the end of the graveyard. I won't be out long." She hated uncertainty, not being sure of her road. And this time, uncertainty had brought an un-

usual tenseness, a sense of expectation, an unsettling presentiment of excitement. Not the sort of excitement she was
accustomed to, either, but something more scintillating,
more enticing. Swinging her cloak about her, she looped
the ribbons at her throat.

"There's a gentleman downstairs." Algaria's black eyes
flashed. "He's one you should avoid."

"Oh?" Catriona hesitated. Could her man be here, under
the same roof? The tension that gripped her hardened her
resolve; she tied off her ribbons. "I'll make sure he doesn't
see me. And everyone in the village knows me by sight—at
least, this sight." She released her knotted hair, letting it
swish about her shoulders. "There's no danger here."

Algaria sighed. "Very well—but don't dally. I suppose
you'll tell me what this is all about when you can."

From the door, Catriona flashed her a smile. "I promise.
Just as soon as I'm sure."

Halfway down the stairs, she saw the gentleman, short,
rotund, and fastidiously dressed, checking the discarded
news sheets in the inn's main parlor. His face was as circular as his form; he was definitely not her warrior. Catriona slipped silently down the hall. It was the work of a
minute to ease open the heavy door, not yet latched for the
night.

And then she was outside.

Pausing on the inn's stone step, she breathed in the crisp,
chilly air, and felt the cold reach her head. Invigorated, she
pulled her cloak close and stepped out, watching her feet,
careful not to slip on the icing snow.

In the graveyard, in the lee of one wall, Richard looked
down at his mother's grave. The inscription on the head-
stone was brief: *Lady Eleanor McEnery, wife of Seamus
McEnery, Laird of Keltyhead.* That, and nothing more. No
affectionate remembrance; no mention of the bastard son
she'd left behind.

Richard's expression didn't change; he'd come to terms

with his status long ago. When he'd been abandoned on his father's doorstep, Helena, Devil's mother, had stunned everyone by claiming him as her own. In doing so, she'd given him his place in the ton—no one, even now, would risk her displeasure, or that of the entire Cynster clan, by so much as hinting he was not who she claimed he was. His father's legitimate son. Instinctively shrewd, ebulliently generous, Helena had secured for him his position in society's elite, for which, in his heart, he had never ceased to thank her.

The woman whose bones lay beneath this cold stone had, however, given him life—and he could do nothing to thank her.

Except, perhaps, to live life fully.

His only knowledge of his mother had come from his father; when, in all innocence, he'd asked if his father had loved his mother, Sebastian had ruffled his hair and said: "She was very lovely and very lonely—she deserved more than she got from her marriage." He'd paused, then added: "I felt sorry for her." He'd looked at him, and his slow smile had creased his face. "But I love you. I regret her death, but I can't regret your birth."

He could understand how his father had felt—he was, after all, a Cynster to the bone. Family, children, home, and hearth—those were what mattered to Cynsters. Those were their quintessential warrior goals, for them the ultimate victories of life.

For long, silent minutes, he stood before the grave, until the cold finally penetrated his boots. With a sigh, he shifted, then straightened and, after one last, long look, turned and retraced his steps.

What was it his mother had left him? And why, having concealed her bequest all these years, had Seamus summoned him back now, after his own death? Richard rounded the kirk, his stride slow, the sound of his footfalls subsumed by the breeze softly whistling through snow-laden branches. He reached the main path and stepped onto it—and heard crisp, determined footsteps approaching from beyond the kirk. Halting, he turned and beheld . . .

A creature of magic and moonlight.

A woman, her dark cloak billowing about her, her head bare. Over her shoulders and down her back spread the most glorious mane of thick, rippling, silken hair, sheening copper-bright in the moonlight, a beacon against the wintering trees behind her. Her stride was definite, every footfall decisive; her eyes were cast down, but he would have sworn she wasn't watching her steps.

She came on without pause, heading directly for him. He couldn't see her face, or her figure beneath the full cloak, but well-honed instincts rarely lied. His senses stirred, stretched, then focused powerfully—a clear case of lust at first sight. Lips lifting in wolfish anticipation, Richard silently turned and prepared to make the lady's acquaintance.

Catriona strode briskly up the path, lips compressed, a frown knitting her brows. She'd been a disciple of The Lady too long not to know how to couch her requests for clarification; the question she'd asked had been succinct and to the point. She'd asked for the true significance of the man whose face haunted her. The Lady's reply, the words that had formed in her mind, had been brutally concise: *He will father your children.*

There were not, no matter how she twisted them, very many ways in which to interpret those words.

Which left her with a very large problem. Unprecedented though it might be, The Lady *must* have made a mistake. This man, whoever he was, was arrogant, ruthless—dominant. *She* needed a sweet, simple soul, one content to remain quietly supportive while she ruled their roost. She didn't need strength—she needed weakness. There was absolutely no point sending her a warrior without a cause.

Catriona humphed; her breath steamed before her face. Through the clearing wisps, she spied—the very last thing she expected to see—a pair of large, black, highly polished Hessians, directly in her path. She tried to stop; her soles found no grip on the icy path—her momentum sent her skidding on. She tried to flail her arms; they were trapped beneath her cloak. On a gasp, she looked up, just as she collided with the owner of the boots.

The impact knocked the air from her lungs; for one instant, she was sure she'd hit a tree. But her nose buried itself in a soft cravat, mid-chest, just above the V of a silk waistcoat. His chin passed above her head; her scalp prickled as long hairs were gently brushed. And arms like steel slowly closed about her.

Instinct awoke in a flustered rush; raising her hands, she pushed against his chest.

Her feet slipped, then slid.

She gasped again—and clutched wildly instead of pushing. The steely arms tightened, and suddenly only her toes touched the snow. Catriona dragged in a breath—one too shallow to steady her whirling head. Her lungs had seized; her senses skittered wildly, informing her, in breathless detail, that she was pressed, breast to thigh, against a man.

Not just any man—one with a body like warm, flexing steel. She had to lean back to look into his face.

Blue, blue eyes met hers.

Catriona stilled; she stared. Then she blinked. It took half a second to check—arrogant mien, decisive chin—it was he.

Narrowing her eyes, she fixed them on his; if The Lady had made no mistake, then it behooved her to begin as she meant to go on. "Put me down."

She'd learned the knack of commanding obedience at her mother's knee; her simple words held echoes of authority, undertones of compulsion.

He heard them; he angled his head, one black brow rising, then the ends of his long lips lifted. "In a minute."

It was her turn to listen and hear the intent in his deep purr. Her eyes flew wide.

"But first . . ."

If she'd been able to think, she'd have screamed, but the

shock of his touch, the intimate warmth of his palm as he framed her face, distracted her. His lips completed the conquest—they swooped, arrogantly confident, and settled over hers.

The first contact stunned her; she ceased to breathe. The very concept of breathing drifted from her mind as his lips moved lazily on hers. They were neither warm nor cool, yet heat lingered in their touch. They pressed close, then eased, sipped, supped, then returned. Firm and demanding, they impinged on her senses, reaching deep, stirring her.

She stirred in his encirling arm; it locked tight about her. Heat surrounded her—even through her thick cloak, it reached for her, enveloped her, then sank into her flesh. And grew, built, a crescendo of warmth seeking release. His hot hunger had infected her. Utterly distracted, she tried to hold it back, tried to deny its existence, tried vainly to dampen it down.

And couldn't. She was facing ignominious defeat—with not a clue of what followed—when the hard hand tilting her face shifted. He altered his grip; one thumb pressed insistently in the center of her chin.

Her jaw eased; her lips parted.

He entered.

The shock of the first touch of tongue against tongue literally curled her toes. She would have gasped, but that was impossible; all she could do was feel. Feel and follow, and sense the reality of that hot hunger, the surprisingly subtle, deeply evocative, seductively physical need. And hold hard against the temptation that streaked through her.

Even while he took arrogance to new heights.

She hadn't thought it possible, but he gathered her more closely, imprinting her soft flesh with the male hardness of his. Ruthlessly confident, he angled his head and tasted her—languorously, unhurriedly—as if he had all the time in the world.

Then he settled to play.

To advance and retreat, to artfully entice her into joining

the game. The very idea shocked her to her toes—and sent shards of excitement flying down her nerves. They stretched, tightened. His lips and tongue continued their tantalizing dance.

She responded—tentatively; instead of the aggressive response she expected, his lips softened fractionally, encouragingly. She dared more, returning the pressure of his lips, the sensuous caress of his tongue.

Without even knowing it, she sank into the kiss.